Julian Rathbone is the author of twenty-nine novels, two of which (*King Fisher Lives* and *Joseph*) were shortlisted for the Booker Prize; his other work includes several screen plays. He has been awarded short-story, crime fiction and poetry prizes and has been translated into fourteen languages. *Intimacy* and *Blame Hitler*, his two most recent contemporary novels are available in Indigo paperback. Julian Rathbone lives in Hampshire.

D1628148

Also by Julian Rathbone

KING FISHER LIVES

JOSEPH

A LAST RESORT

A SPY OF THE OLD SCHOOL

NASTY, VERY

LYING IN STATE

SAND BLIND

INTIMACY

BLAME HITLER

THE LAST ENGLISH KING

Trajectories

JULIAN RATHBONE

PHOENIX

A PHOENIX PAPERBACK

First published in Great Britain
by Victor Gollancz in 1998
This paperback edition published in 1999 by Phoenix,
an imprint of Orion Books Ltd,
Orion House, 5 Upper St Martin's Lane,
London WC2H 9EA

A CIP catalogue record for this book
is available from the British Library.

ISBN: 0 75380 845 5

Printed and bound in Great Britain by
The Guernsey Press Co. Ltd, Guernsey, C.I.

The rainbow comes and goes
And lovely is the rose;
The moon doth with delight
Look round her when the heavens are bare;
Waters on a starry night
Are beautiful and fair;
The sunshine is a glorious birth;
But yet I know, where'er I go,
That there hath pass'd away a glory from the earth.

For
Alayne,
Arthur and Nina
with love

Liz Knights
1955–1996

Prologue

On the sixteenth of March 1998, a bright spring day with daffodils and forsythia nodding outside his window and thanks,
perhaps, to global warming, even mimosa in luxuriant bloom
in the village at the bottom of the hill, Thomas Somers, retired
educationist, now a not very successful writer, typed out on
his Amstrad ALT 286 laptop the last section of what he hoped
would be his breakthrough work. The one that would pay
his pension and get his children through university without
thousands of pounds of debt round their necks. It might even
allow his wife Katherine to give up the translating agency she
ran from the spare bedroom.

> Two days later the Sea Spray passed through Spithead
> and then rounded the Foreland. Bembridge, Sandown,
> Shanklin to starboard, alternating cliffs and beaches. On
> the other side blue water, foam-flecked, a bit of a swell
> beneath white clouds and blue sky. Richard recalled
> wonderful paintings by Turner – *The Fleet Making Sail* and
> so forth. Gulls kept effortless station in the breeze, while
> on the landward side terns, sea-swallows, arrowed like
> missiles into the waves and came up with small-fry.

It had been a bit of rush job this last draft, but he'd printed out
the rest, checked it, even counted the words on each file and
added them up, written the covering letter. Then he
remembered that his editor had asked for a copy on diskette
as well. He hoped he had a spare blank in his stationery drawer
– if not, he would have to borrow one from his wife.

He typed on. Problem was, he was due to check into the
Royal Bournemouth at one o'clock for an endoscopy and a
possible injection into his varices – the aftermath, although he
hadn't touched a drop now for eighteen months, of four

decades of committed drinking, and he was determined to stop and get the package in the post on the way.

He glanced at his watch, nine-thirty-two, and typed on . . .

The morning sun made the sails almost incandescent. The little yacht rode the gentle swell with an easy motion, and under full sail now her beam dipped low enough for Kate to trail one hand in the foamy crests . . .

PART I

1

Richard Somers finished his espresso, a blend of Pyrenean arabicas, stacked the Teflon cup in the water-free dish-cleaner, walked down a long white curving corridor hung with framed platinum and gold discs, passed off-white doors with gold-plated door-handles shaped to fit his hand and let himself into his semicircular, windowless workroom. It had once been a cast-iron and glass conservatory, big and grand enough to attract the title 'orangery'. It was the remaining original feature of a neo-Georgian house he had rebuilt to make something he could call home.

It was still a place for growing citrus bushes in pots, but now they were small and kept up against the glass walls which formed a hexagonal skin. None were above waist-high and almost all bore tiny ornamental fruits, lemons and mandarins, and some were in blossom. The sharp scent freshened the air. The grooves cut in the marble floor to take off surplus water were dry; the light, filtered through plastic coatings on the domed ceiling, was dim. He lowered himself into a black kid-skin chair he had designed: electronically self-adjusting, it responded yieldingly to every move he made. He paused for a moment, then leant forward over a huge horseshoe-shaped central console of switches, rheostats, digital displays and graphs. His fingers played over them.

The huge room dimmed to darkness and a giant matt-black screen, constructed out of three curved but almost seamless panels, eight feet high and making a three-hundred degree arc which enclosed the console, began to glow, then brighten. Powered by hundreds of hard discs, DEEP CDs, the mother-boards and microprocessors and thousands of clever chips, images slowly formed on the screens. They deepened to an illusion of the third dimension which was not exactly holographic since they appeared to remain inside and behind the

11

surface of the screens, but real enough for you to feel you should be able to enter the spaces, and walk amongst them if you chose to.

A steeply perspectived catwalk came out of a crimson tunnel and went on for ever. A woman appeared wrapped in a black cloak. She walked steadily towards him out of nothing, from a distant dot, with the thrusting, swaying walk of a professional model. The reds of the squared tunnel she was in sharpened, the angles of the perspective grew more acute, until she filled the middle screen; indeed the top of her head and her feet were out of the frame. The focus sharpened, the cloak was now seen to be textured with rows of soft fur-like balls. Slowly she brought her hands, which had been clasped in front of her, out to the side and upwards, almost to shoulder height, taking the robe with them, so it still hung behind her, but revealing that beneath it she was entirely naked.

Her hair was reddish gold, her eyes heavy-lidded, blue or violet, her face well-boned, but tired and older than one expected, her lips wide, full but not thick, with just a hint of a smile. Her neck was strong, her upper chest and breasts white, the nipples small but erect. Her torso was long and lean but muscled and used – you felt she had had children. Her legs were long and lean, strong without suggesting the professional athlete, a woman's legs, not a girl's.

She was not real.

She was an image based on a famous photograph of a Versace model dating from the nineteen-nineties. Richard, Pygmalion-like, had brought her to virtual life. Through the aid of computerized animation using a program that could look at a two-dimensional still and, from that information alone, reconstruct a living, moving, walking doll, he had created . . . a goddess.

He froze her now, much as she had been in the original photograph, and waited for the words which he knew were there to come out from wherever they were hiding in the databases of his brain.

They came.

12

Her lips were red, her looks were free,
Her locks were yellow as gold:
Her skin was white as leprosy,
The night-mare LIFE-IN-DEATH was she,
Who thicks man's blood with cold.

Using a voice bank of his own voice he now put the words into sounds, and began to play with pitch, timbre, phrasing, until they sounded like the lyric of a rock anthem. With rising excitement he added drums, in a feathery beat, then rhythm, bass and finally a lead guitar which took off into a Jimi Hendrix lick as the lyric ended. He pasted it all in so the lick began just as she spread her arms.

He worked for three hours and was pleased with what he achieved: fifty-five seconds of sound and vision. Trouble was the lyric had now run out. Coleridge's lady had been playing dice with Death on a skeletal ship. None of what went before or came after would fit the concept for a pop-spec that had come to him in the night. Twenty years earlier he had pioneered the pop-spec concept, taking the old pop-video into virtual reality, just when film and TV were going the same way. Of course he could repeat phrases of the lyric for as long as he liked, until they became meaningless mantras, but then . . . what to do visually?

He sighed, quite certain he could do no more with it and that he had not produced anything commercially viable. Never mind, he'd enjoyed himself, had kidded himself it was work; and money? Money, he had enough.

He backed it all up and filed it on the national computer, as the law required, as well as in his own in-house storage and retrieval systems, checked and double-checked and finally pressed for close-down. He turned up the background light to a low glow, stretched and yawned.

He'd go for a walk, he thought. A hot August, very hot – they always were these days – but by three o'clock in the after-noon the bite of the heat would be fading. He slipped into a light-weight jacket, pushing his still heavy ponytail, a hank of coarse straw with some silver in it, out from under the collar and checked the pockets for receiver buttons. In his living room he paused in front of a mirror to smear white sun-block on his thickish lips, strong but not dominating cheekbones and the bridge of his nose.

Blue eyes looked out of a face still handsome and fair-skinned though coarsened a little by sun and age, with deep lines from the nostrils to the corners of his wide mouth, the edges of which drooped a little. Here, and occasionally in his eyes, his friends saw signs of a brooding dissatisfaction, a sense that for all his fame and wealth he had not done as well as he had wanted or, perhaps, had failed to direct his energy and talents to significant ends.

Powerful broad hands, whose short nails were painted in black metallic gloss, pulled on a wide-brimmed linen hat and he let himself out on to the wrought-iron and stucco portico. It was flanked by giant begonias and strelitzia, while the pale-blue starry flowers of plumbago climbed to the bays and protuberances, the fancifully wrought iron balconies, he had had grafted on to the façade of the house, in imitation of Spanish *modernismo* architecture.

The heat folded round him like a blanket. He paused at the top of the gravel drive that wound through sloping lawns. On either side of the drive stood two large metal sculptures made from shaped and bent girders, bolted and welded together, painted in primary reds, blues and yellows. Twelve feet high, they suggested a rock guitarist striking the final chord of a rock anthem: arms, legs and guitar represented four times each, as if caught in a multiple exposure photograph. The original had been a wooden maquette he had made in 1997 for his Art A-Level.

High gates, matching the balconies behind him, identified his presence and opened for him on to the road which climbed out of the Street and then on to the long spur that ran west from Castle Hill.

The Street was what the upper part of the Hurling Enclave was called. It was not a street at all, just a track with maybe twenty or so houses beneath the heath it climbed up to. At the top, a hot steady wind blew out of the south-east from across the Island, but not strongly enough to shift the heavy oily smog which hung almost permanently over the Sandbourne Bay oil-field to the west. Up here the sky remained cloudless and piercingly bright and he began to sweat.

Presently he left the track and his feet crunched through the friable black ash of what had, he rather thought, once been heather and gorse. Dad would have known. Dad knew plants, and birds. He had especially liked birds of prey and had always been on the look-out for them when they went on holidays in the Spanish or French Pyrenees. There were a couple now soaring on big wingspans above the hot bowl below. Kites? Vultures? Richard wished he knew.

He sighed, fished the receiver buttons out of his pocket and clipped them into the tiny but permanently grafted mounts on his ear lobes, so the speakers fitted up into his ears. He used the remote that was built into his wristwatch to make a random selection. Back in Small Acres the player flicked through his library of over fifteen thousand recordings and identified and activated what he had chosen.

But nothing we do is random. 'Living In A Prayer' remix. Jon Bon Jovi. Not random, for once he had seen and heard the man live, and Dad had been there too, and today his dad was padding around at the back of his head.

It had been in the big park down in Sandbourne on a hot August afternoon; not as hot as August was now, but pleasantly hot. He recalled an enormous crowd in front of a huge van whose sides had been folded out to form a sound stage with a giant TV screen above it. Radio One . . . Roadshow? A helicopter. He's landed. He came on, shooed away the DJ, saying, 'I don't share the stage with anyone.' Just another guitarist, that's all. Acoustic. Both acoustic. Good performer, better live than on record. And, yes, his dad had, after all, liked him. 'Lots of chutzpah,' he'd said. 'Charisma even.'

Dad must have been what at that time? Sixty-two? And in good nick – a touch overweight, but still very lively; crew-cut grey to white hair; wore clothes a thirty-year-old might wear and tacky jewellery as well, a chunky silver ring like an owl's head – he had a thing about owls. And Jon Bon Jovi? Richard had felt the charisma too, the charisma that comes with adulation, total confidence and lorry-loads of money. Already then Richard had known he would be a rock star in that class, and he sensed that day what it might mean.

Suddenly he felt a bitter anger, mild but penetrating, welling up like bile at the back of his throat. His material, 'product' was the word his mind sarcastically hit on, had never been in the least Bon Jovi-ish – but for all it had achieved it might just as well have been. He kicked at the ash so a puff of black dust floated round his canvas shoes and then settled.

He clicked for silence and became aware that he was not alone. Thirty yards away and striding towards him with a smile on her face, the ash swirling about her feet, her red dogs galumphing round her, Susie Cowper. His age, wearing a summer kaftan, orange printed with cadmium sunflowers, and sandals studded with silvery buttons, her long black hair – must be tinted – tied back under a scarf folded into a triangle. No block on her face or a sun hat because she had had the skin job done – something Richard had so far backed off from.

2

He fell in beside her and they walked together along the escarpment towards the fence. On their own like this he felt a touch awkward, shy even. He'd known Susie, Susannah, off and on, for most of his life, but they had never been close, just chummy. As a teenager perhaps she had fancied him for a time, especially during the period he had been lead guitarist with Bad Grama, a local rock group that had performed at parties and in pubs. Five years before he formed Evil Trend.

And when he came back to Hurling nearly forty years later, over five years ago, Susie was still there but married now to a commodity broker called Maurice Coen. She of course was still Cowper: from 2010 married women were required to keep their original surnames – it mucked up the National Register if they changed.

'What are you working on at the moment?' she asked. They always did, these Hurling people. Because of what he was, it was a subject of conversation that usually produced something to talk about, since month by month the answer could change.

'Rock-spec. Art-rock.'

She pursed her lips, gave her head a slight shake.

'I do wish you'd go back to those classic concert things you did for a bit. Oh, Archie! Don't do that! Now I'll have to bath him when we get back.'

One of her dogs was rolling in the black ash.

She went on, 'Every now and then Maurice still gets out that Beethoven thing you did.' She giggled. 'But he always messes up the woodwind entries quite near the beginning. It's a shame you couldn't do more of those.'

'Cost a bomb to do, and not enough punters bought them. Lost a lot of money on that.'

Interactive performances of classical music. The punter conducted and the players more or less responded to him. Or her.

One way of keeping symphony orchestras in being, he had thought at the time – a worthy use of his money, but it had not caught on. He decided to change the subject.

'Why,' he asked, 'do you bring your dogs up here if you don't want them to get dirty?'

'It's like an oven down in the forest. Not a breath of air. Anyway. I like it up here.'

They paused. They were on the edge of the escarpment now. The hillside tumbled away from them, still black from the fires, but deeply eroded, riven with deep crevices to a wide bowl which, Richard recalled, had once, in winter at any rate, been quite marshy. Now small cliffs of very white sand broke through the blackness. Then the fence. Fifteen feet of chainlink, topped with electrically charged razor and miniature cameras, no bigger than golf balls, set at ten-metre intervals.

A mile beyond the fence the ground was green again, the brilliant green of tree-crowns in serried ranks, peaches for the most part, and now, in August, hung with crimson and purple fruit, rolling across the hillsides to a visual ridge a further mile or so away. Under-workers, bused up from Linwood, were moving through them filling aluminium tubs, watched by a handful of protectors. Along the ridge of Daw Hill umbrella pines had replaced the larches and firs which had died out, not from the heat but the conifer moth, twenty? thirty? years earlier. And beyond Daw Hill, to the west, the haze deepened into the perma-smog, lit by flares where, for whatever reason, the capping of gushing wells had cracked or failed.

'It's not like it used to be,' he said.

She looked across at him. If anything she was by half an inch the taller of the two.

'I suppose not. But it all happened so gradually I hardly noticed the changes.'

'Ah well. That must be because you never moved away. It was quite a shock when I came back. You see everything change all around you, wherever you are, but you expect the places where you spent your childhood to remain untouched.'

They walked on.

'And do you remember?' she asked. 'Do you remember what it was like?'

He laughed self-consciously, almost guiltily.

'Not really. Not in detail. But you could see Sandbourne, and Poole Harbour beyond. And, on a clear day, the Isle of Purbeck. And closer it was all sort of wild really, heather was it? Which bloomed about now? Sheets of purple . . . ?' Another thing his dad used to go on about.

'I remember that.'

'Ponies, and, oh, I don't know, all a bit more friendly, and cleaner.'

'It wouldn't be so bad if it wasn't for the oilfield.'

'No.'

They had almost reached the point where the enclave fence came up the hill, crossed the track, closing it off with a gate, before curving round to the north and east behind them. A quarter of a mile beyond it the main road, dual-carriageway, still tarmacked but badly pot-holed, switchbacked across the burnt heath before dropping down the other side to Linwood. An old car, small and white but with rust showing, shaped like a soapdish on wheels, a late version of the revised Mini that came out round about the millennium, turned off the road and rumbled along the track towards them. Its loose exhaust clanged on the ridges. It came to within fifty yards of the fence, then turned south into what had been a lay-by overlooking the hills and plain down to Sandbourne and the sea. It parked and the engine was turned off. It had always been a favourite spot for people to pause, picnic maybe, and look at the panoramic view.

Richard and Susannah moved up to the gate. An old man, in his seventies at least, got out of the driver's seat, reached into the back and pulled out about ten feet of garden hose. Fidgeting because the end of the exhaust was still hot, he used a jubilee clip and a screwdriver to fix the hose on to it, then he ran the other end round to the driver's window and passed it through. A woman of about his age took the end, pulled it in a foot or so and wound up the window so the glass held it in place with a gap of only half an inch left at the top. Richard could see that the man's face was blotched a deep crimson and raw vermilion and that his eyes watered. One of the skin diseases, probably a cancer.

Richard shook the gate and a spark flashed above his head. He knew it was hopeless – it kept people in as well as out. He felt a sense of isolation, of being cut-off from the realities of life outside. Whenever he spoke of this to other enclavists they generally laughed: 'But,' they said, 'that's what living in an enclave is for, it's what it's all about.'

'Have you got your mobile with you?' he asked.

'There's no point in using it.' Susannah sighed. 'It'll be far too late before anyone gets here.'

'The engine's not running. We could call out. Talk to them.'

'Why?' Now she was impatient, disturbed but determined not to be involved. 'They know what they're doing. They've made up their minds. Why should we interfere? It happens all the time. Favourite spot. Nice view.'

She turned away and faced north. Sunlight flashed from windscreens, and the throaty but distant roar of maybe half a dozen large vehicles with faulty engines spread across the spaces between.

'Travellers?'

'I suppose so.' Richard still wanted to do something about the would-be suicides.

'Maurice says there are too many of them. The government ought not to allow so many.'

Did she mean travellers or suicides? Whichever, Maurice would, wouldn't he?

Sunlight flashed again.

'Goodness, the lead vehicle's a Volkie camper. Split windscreen. Must be all of sixty, even seventy, years old.'

'Really?' But she was bored. How could anyone sensible be interested in the sort of vehicles the travellers drove and lived in? 'Come here, Archie. Archie. Good dog. And you, Bess. Home time. Din-dins.'

The convoy of travellers rumbled on down the hill. As the noise faded Richard heard the engine of the small car cough, then take. The interior began to fill with fumes. He bit his lip, swallowed, looked up again at the fence and the gate. No point in trying to climb it: the voltage at the top was strong enough to kill.

'Are you coming to the audition tonight?'

'Is it tonight? Yes, I'll be there.'

'The Dame?'

'I expect so. Unless someone else wants to do it.'

Hurling Enclave pantomime. Every Christmas. Richard usually played the Dame. His dad had too. Indeed, now he thought about it, his dad had played Widow Twankey to Susannah's principal boy – Aladdin. And he, Richard, had had a walk-on part. 1994? Somewhere round then. The heaviness of nostalgia thickened inside his head. When so much had gone wrong you clung on to a past, probably make-believe, when things had seemed, well, nicer. And in between, chances missed, loved ones gone, betrayals and treachery, ah, treachery, peaked like an uncrossable mountain range. Was that why these shut-off, alienated, supposedly privileged enclavists kept up the old traditions – flower-arranging, a painting club, amateur dramatics? Even, for Christ's sake, church?

He kept pace with her as they retraced their footsteps down the hill. Behind them the engine of the small car faltered, coughed, and died. It did not start up again.

3

The convoy, two very big articulated lorries, a large, old-fashioned pantechnicon, a couple of Range Rovers and a Renault Espace, following the even more ancient VW camper, rattled on down the hill to Linwood. They were painted up in the old-fashioned lettering which a few, even in 2035, associated with travelling circuses and the like. This spelt out, on each vehicle, *Harem Dance Troupe – Tap, Adagio, Apaché and Spanish our Specialities. Strictly No Nudes or Sex Shows.*

The central span of the overpass had fallen in but the slipway into the town was still open. They cruised round the big car park and came to an untidy halt not far from a small brick blockhouse which had once been a public convenience. It made a good blockhouse. The only windows were vertical slits filled with thick, frosted, shatterproof glass; the doors to the outer world were doubled up, leaving a tiny vestibule which could now be used as a second line of defence. Much of the building of that time, the eighties of the previous century, had looked as if it had been designed to repel; even places like supermarkets which surely were intended to attract people in. There were a couple, now boarded up, on two sides of the car park. They had squat square towers in the middle, and walls shaped into bastions and redoubts.

A couple of protectors came out of the blockhouse as the last vehicle shuddered to a halt and a sort of silence settled over the area undercut by the stereophonic but distant racket from an interactive spec arcade in the High Street. It was a large car park, right in the centre of the small town, with shops on two sides, and beyond them the square-towered Norman church. All had been let go, though the top of the church tower was littered with cameras, aerials and dishes, some of which occasionally swivelled or shifted as the programs that controlled them identified, tracked and recorded an unusual movement or occurence on the ground or even in the sky. That sort of thing too had begun back in the eighties.

The protectors wore dun-coloured uniforms with desert boots and peaked caps. They were hung about with miniature radios, pistols, gas canisters and batons. One, with a sergeant's chevrons on her arm and her hair tied back, carried a clipboard with an electronic scanner, a light pen and a ballpoint attached. They hung back, waiting, knowing that the leader of the convoy would come to them. It was against regs as well as plain foolish for them to go more than ten paces from the blockhouse until they knew whom they were dealing with.

A tall lean woman, about fifty, climbed down from the driver's seat of the old VW camper. Her greying hair was tied back in a high bun. Her face was beautiful, tanned deeply, lined with crow's-feet but well-sculpted with good cheekbones, a neat chin, a fine mouth above a long neck. Only her nose was a little larger than conventional good looks would have dictated, with a high spreading bridge. She was wearing a white muslin cotton top, very full with open collar and sleeves rolled halfway up her lean, slightly mottled forearms, and jeans cropped at the calves above long sandalled feet with painted toenails. She wore a lot of gold bangles on her wrists and two or three on her ankles. Her fingers were also long and spun expressive patterns in the air around her when she spoke, making the bangles chime. She looked about, taking it all in, and a sort of half-smile, perhaps cut with a little sadness, glowed in her eyes.

Moving a little stiffly, as if her knees bothered her, she crossed the cracked tarmac and offered a fat black plastic wallet to the sergeant. Opened, it revealed several plastic cards printed with bar codes, striped with magnetic tape and slotted into a concertina folder.

'Hi,' she said, and let the concertina drop out so the cards dangled.

The sergeant grunted, ran her scanner over the cards. It was attached by a black sprung flex to a small black box with an LCD display. Occasionally it bleeped.

'I'll have to check those out.' She meant the bleeps. 'Hannah-Rosa Daytona?'

'That's me.'

'Staying long?'

'Through the weekend, leaving after the Sunday performance.'

'You reckon you can get audiences for that many performances?'

'Hope so. We do three different shows.'

'Your power allowance is a bit low. Might fail on you.'

'I don't think so. We use a lot of natural light. Torches, flares, that sort of thing.'

'You mean like naked flames?' Incredulous.

Ms Daytona indicated one of the lower cards the electronic pen had not yet scanned.

'You'll find we're licensed to,' she said.

'It says here you have fifteen females in the troupe and six gee-effs. And that four of you are of ethnic origin, two Asian, two Afro-Caribbean. Has there been any change from that?'

'No.'

'OK.' The sergeant returned the wallet, cards dangling. Hannah-Rosa folded them back into the wallet and snapped it shut.

'You can pitch where you've parked, next to that hedge.'

'We'd rather go on up to Carver's Field. That's where we want to perform.'

The sergeant frowned.

'You know this town then? You've performed here before? No record on your data says so.'

'Not performed. I was brought up not far from here. Long time ago.'

Business-like until then, her voice faded a little as she said this.

The sergeant chewed her nail, then stuck her thumbs in her belt.

'You stay here till we've checked you out.'

'How long will that take?'

'A day. Maybe two. If we clear you, then you can go to Carver's.'

The older woman was careful not to allow impatience or

even resignation to show. She flashed a less personal smile and turned to go.

The sergeant had one more thing to say.

'There isn't a lot of credit about. The maize harvest failed again. Flattened by gales. And now we have peach-tree fly – all the fruit's got worms.'

The protector behind her, who had said and done nothing throughout the meeting, spat a plum stone out on to the tarmac and grinned, hitched her loaded belt.

Ms Daytona went back to the VW. The woman who had been in the passenger seat climbed down and joined her on the blacktop. She was a little plumper than Hannah-Rosa, and, like Hannah, older than the rest, though her hair still had some blond in it. She wore a long cotton skirt with an Indian printed pattern, and beads rather than bangles.

'We're here for the night, Em. Maybe longer.'

'I've been in worse spots than this,' said Emma. She grinned. She grinned a lot.

'It's not changed much, has it?' she added.

HAnnah-Rosa and EMma. HAR-EM.

The whole troupe were now spilling out of the other vehicles, gossiping, stretching and, once the word had gone round that they were staying where they were, methodically following an established arrival routine. Most of them were dressed tattily but in bright colours, wore cheap jewellery, had long unkempt hair. A couple did cartwheels, a lean Afro-Caribbean juggled with clubs, three girls in leotards were already using the top rail of a car-park divider as a bar and doing bar exercises. A soul track, Marvin Gaye, 'Heard It On The Grape-vine', played in the background. One, a girl, stood out from the rest. She was about seventeen, her hair, a deep rich brown, was cut very short, her jeans were oatmeal, clean, and baggy at the waist, and her top, a plain blue cotton shirt with mother-of-pearl press-studs instead of buttons, was pressed and also clean.

A couple of men, gee-effs, gender-free, one of them very big, very strong and very black, erected a large frame tent, attaching the guys to the car-park rails since they could not use pegs in the hard-top, while two Asian girls, twins, were setting up a small cooking range fuelled with bottled gas. The girl with the short hair took the sections of a silver soprano saxophone from its black case and began to push them together. Presently she and a girl with a cornet killed Marvin Gaye and began practising unison riffs together. The sun touched the tops of poplars on the other side of the road. Yellow leaves that never fell rustled sibilantly in a breath of evening breeze that brought with it the acrid smell from the oilfield, although the perimeter fences were ten miles away.

Suddenly the soprano sax took off in a soaring lick. The cornet tried to stay with her, faltered and gave up.

Hannah-Rosa frowned. At her side Emma allowed herself a sympathetic grin.

'You've got to admit she's good.'

'No need to show off, though.'

'Just expressing herself.'

'She should be lending a hand with the meal. Get that out of the way, so there's time for a proper rehearsal.'

'Oh, we old ones can do that. Let the youngsters enjoy themselves,' and Emma bustled away towards the stove.

The girl with the short hair took the mouthpiece from her lips, wiped her mouth on the back of her hand, came over to the VW.

'What do you think, Mum? I don't often get the register break as neat as that.'

'Not bad, Kate, not bad at all.' Hannah-Rosa grinned back, but managed to qualify the praise by her tone of voice. Just as her own mother, whose first name had also been Kate, used to do, she'd have told her daughter to tidy her bedroom before practising – if she'd had a proper bedroom to tidy. As it was, she told her to help Emma and the twins with the meal.

4

'Did you see the news?' Self-importantly Damien Floyd took the pipe from his mouth and examined its bowl. 'Damn thing's out again.' He thought for a moment. With a cup of coffee in the other hand he had to give up one or the other. He stuffed his pipe in his blazer pocket. 'I mean, of course, the real news.'

He was a big man, in his fifties. He carried himself with a slight stoop and wore a navy blazer above lightweight cavalry twill trousers. Under his open shirt collar he wore a silk scarf, striped to suggest membership of a sporting club or maybe some academic establishment. In spite of the easy superiority of his manner, his face had a greyish tinge: he had peptic inflammation which occasionally, when he was stressed, flared into a potential ulcer – the occupational hazard of someone who has been promoted beyond their abilities. It was the reason he was allowed to smoke – a herbal mixture.

They were in the kitchen area at the back of Hurling Enclave Centre, ten or so of them, the core membership of Hurling Enclave Players. The Centre was a prefabricated barn of a place made out of building blocks and steel joists and roofed with felt. Richard remembered a small hall with a wooden plank floor, a tiny stage, almost no room backstage and black rafters supporting a gabled roof. It had been a homely, welcoming sort of place which an audience of a hundred and twenty packed. He and his dad had burnt it down in 2002 through overloading the wiring during their production of a closet *King Lear*. Dad had directed and played the lead, Richard had done the music, sound effects, lighting and scenery.

No one answered Floyd, but most got on with helping themselves to coffee and biscuits. He was not much liked. As a sub-regional sub-controller he was important as well as self-important and his position gave him access to the ministry newscasts and updates, something he liked to show off about.

'NATO want another hundred thousand from us for the Sicily bastion. Apparently the Libyans have patched up a pact with the Trans-Saharans after all.' He gave up on the coffee – you can't pontificate with a coffee cup. Out came the pipe and a flame-thrower of a gaslighter. 'The Out of Africa movement seems to be growing legs again after all.'

'Waterwings would be more use, I should have thought,' remarked Paul Digby. He was the pantomime director, a thin lawyer with a frivolous sense of humour and a raucous, horsy laugh.

'Shouldn't be any difficulty about that, the hundred thousand I mean. Most non-workers will jump at the opportunity,' some-one else chipped in.

'Under-workers too.'

'Bloody hot in Sicily.'

'It's not the men that are the problem.' Damien wreathed his heavy head in clouds of smoke. 'It's paying for them, that's the problem. Probably mean having to go cap in hand yet again to the Honkers and Shankers.'

In-talk for the Hong Kong and Shanghai bank.

'Nuke 'em, I say.' This from Frederick. Small man with specs, ex-army brigadier.

'What their rulers would like, I expect – with a hundred million more than they can feed.'

'Trouble is,' said Maurice, Susannah's husband, a small round dark man, 'in the long term it would suit the Rimmers if the African Nation did overrun Europe.'

'They'll not get their credits back if that happens.'

'No, but think of the investment possibilities. Africans rebuilding Europe from whatever's left and a huge new market waiting to replace everything that's been destroyed.'

'You mean the way the Americans did after the Second World War?'

'Something like that, I suppose,' said Maurice, rather vaguely. Long time ago, all that stuff, was the implication.

Susannah took her coffee and stood by the kitchen door, close to Richard. They looked down the wide bare hall. Danny Blake was banging away on the old Yamaha keyboard. His head was shaved or bald, his face smooth and plump, his body, beneath a soft leather jacket, T-shirt and jeans, red loafers, thickset but still tough for all he too was in his fifties. He had made a fortune arranging the music for a series of spec musicals in the twenties, when pastiches of 1920's music, Charlestons and the like, had been all the rage. He was playing one of his tunes now – a slinky, sleazy little number called 'That Black Tummy Of Mine'. Two nubile adolescents, midriffs bare between cropped bustiers and low-slung jeans, were on the stage undulating to the music, weaving snaky patterns in the air with their long bare arms. Both were competent and enjoying themselves. The one on the left, Susie's daughter Delice, followed Sophie Pribendum's lead. Sophie was the more talented of the two – as a dancer, at any rate.

'This must all seem dreadfully tacky to you,' Susannah suggested.

'Not at all. They make mistakes, they laugh, they're having a good time. It's spontaneous. That's a quality no spec program can capture.'

'I can remember your sister and the Biggs girl carrying on in much the same way, what, forty years ago?'

'Can you really? As long ago as that? Yes, I suppose they did.'

'That's what this is all about,' Paul Digby had joined them. 'It's not just that we are putting on live, real performances, it's the tradition that counts. Keeping a bit of the past alive. I don't just mean pantomime tradition but Hurling tradition too. It's wonderful the way so many of you go back to the last century, that you're carrying on what your parents and grandparents did.'

Pompous ass, Richard thought. What really matters is flesh, fresh skin, blood, nipples, tummy buttons and buttocks. The girl on the right. Some Indian in her, maybe Afro. Glossy black hair. High cheekbones. Ever such a sweet mouth, heavy-lidded almost oriental dark eyes, maybe a touch small, but a bit of a smile in them; she knows what she's doing, even though she's only fifteen. Or less. Those arms, wind them round me, and with luck, come the actual production, they'll have her bare-

29

legged in a long gauze skirt with a slit up the front. Not to say old Susie's daughter isn't almost as enticing, but she's leggy and jolly, gives off no whiff of funkiness.

'Who's Delice's friend, then?' Floyd's wife, Annette, was at his shoulder. He had in fact already been aware of her – her perfume, Obligation, was very familiar to him. Not just her perfume, either. She was tall, just forty, with a generous mouth, greenish eyes, her red hair softened by dyes to auburn. He knew the name of the new girl; there had been introductions at the start. He half-turned to Annette, who surreptitiously took his hand, gave it a brief squeeze and released it.

'Sophie. Sophie Pribendum,' he said. 'They're new in Hurling, not really into enclave life yet. They bought old Tom Rich's house up in Denny Close.'

'Ah yes. I remember someone telling me about them.'

'Must have a bob or two. What does Daddy do?'

'No Dad. Just Mum. No one's very sure. The whisper is IS reporting direct to the minister. She has a couple of protectors living in and a lot of IT hardware came with her. So Virginia says.'

'Someone taking my name in vain?' Virginia Burroughs had joined them. They moved away from the kitchen door into the main body of the hall. Virginia, short, not quite fifty, kept horses for other people; her husband, Don, was social secretary of the golf club. A banker, he'd taken early retirement when Barclays-Nat merged with Frank-Deutsche. She was secretary, unpaid of course, of the Hurling Enclave Players. By giving services the locals appreciated, the Burroughs, wife and husband, managed to hold on to their enclave lease.

'Miriam Pribendum?' she went on. 'It's not a whisper. She told me. Stops rumours if I come out with it, she said. Internal security, yes. But she wouldn't say what branch or how senior. But I can tell you a state security protector brought Sophie down in a government mobilette. Don reckons that puts her at a very senior level indeed.'

'One of the bosses, then. Let's hope she's not in art funding,' Paul remarked. 'She'll put the boot in if she is.'

'Why?' Richard asked.

'It's an old script. Jokes about New Labour.'

'That old? Cut them.'

'Give the princess part to her daughter,' Damien Floyd counselled, Polonius-like, through pipe smoke.

'I think that would be a pity,' said Richard. 'She dances very seductively.'

'Talking of seductive dancing—' Virginia injected a note of enthusiasm, even eagerness, into her voice.

'Wasn't sure we were,' Paul again with his horsy laugh. 'But I don't mind if we do, as my dad used to say.'

'Talking of seductive dancing,' Virginia very firm now, 'there's a troupe of travellers in Linwood called Harem. Basically dance to live music. They got a good write-up on the Local Live web-site. I thought we might get up a coach party, if enough are interested. They're there through the weekend, last performance on Sunday.'

The music had stopped and the girls joined them on the edge of the group. Richard turned to Sophie.

'Are you interested?' he asked. 'You should be.'

'In what and why?'

'Dance troupe in Linwood. You seem keen on dancing. Virginia is trying to get up a party to see them.'

'I'll ask Mum. Are you really Dick Somers? Of Evil Trend?'

'Really. But off-duty I prefer Richard.'

'Mum's a great fan. Was, anyway. I mean she still is, but like when she was a teeny she called herself a Trendy.'

'Didn't we all?' Virginia chortled. She swung away, her feet moving in a little dance.

'"And what would you say?"' she sang. '"Do psychedelic carpets bring you down? Would you go all the way?"'

Richard felt the heavy sourness an ageing rock star experiences when he realizes his most ardent fans are menopausal.

'You dance very well,' he said. But he said it to Sophie.

He waited. The dimples just outside the corners of her mouth deepened. The knowing look returned to her eyes. He had hoped it would.

'Thank you,' she said.

Paul returned.

'Richard,' he said, 'I'd like you to do the Dame again if you don't mind. Poor old Frederick just isn't up to it.'

'What about Damien?'

'Can't sing. You can. Known for it, actually. And Sophie, I think you'd make an excellent princess, with Delice as principal boy. And there, I think, we have a play fitted.'

As they left Annette squeezed Richard's hand again.

'Tomorrow?' she murmured.

5

With the sun setting over the shattered fly-over, Harem had parked their biggest trailer facing it and pulled out the fold-up stage to catch the last light. That way they could have a quick run-through of their new opening number without using valuable generator fuel.

'Step, step, touch, kick. Again. Step, step, touch, kick. *Strong* a-a-arms, back, connect, spin. Right, have you *got* it? From the top . . .'

Jacques, probably the oldest member of the troupe apart from Hannah-Rosa and Emma, was overseeing the routine with his harsh, penetrating voice, making his brown hands and fingers shape the movements in flowing but sharp gestures. Thin and dark, in a Mediterranean sort of way, he wore jeans and very distressed trainers beneath a floppy synthetic jumper. His shoulder-length curly black hair was dyed. He choreographed the modern and tap, supervised most of the rehearsals.

A nod from Jacques and the little band at the side of the stage – soprano sax, played by Kate, an alto and a tenor, a cornet, a trombone, a double bass and a small drum kit – paused, moistened their reeds or mouthpieces and glanced at the female drummer, a bulky lady with an open red face, wearing a Clash II T-shirt and denim jeans. She pushed a sweaty lock of hair off her forehead with the end of her drumstick and gave them a nod. On the small stage five female dancers and five apparently male, all in black leotards over scarlet body-stockings swung into it again.

'Turn, turn, right, left, up, down, up, down, look sexy AND step, step, touch, kick . . . Beryl, can we do that moderato, do you think, they are new to it, you know?'

Beryl, the drummer, grimaced slightly at the rest of the band, most of whom nodded back. 'After two, then,' she said, 'One . . . two—'

'Stop,' shouted Jacques. 'I didn't ask for a fucking funeral march, you know?'

'Tst, tst,' said Hannah-Rosa, from the shadows of a tolerably healthy-looking acacia twenty yards away. 'There's no need to go over the top.' But she said it to Emma, who was sitting beside her. 'You know what it is?'

'I do, but I can't place it.'

'*A Chorus Line*.'

'Of course!'

'We videoed the film when I was a kid. I must have watched it a hundred times.'

'Me too. It's a good curtain raiser.'

'If we had a curtain.' Hannah-Rosa called above the sound of the band. 'Jacques?'

'Hold it! Yes, Han?'

'If you get the front line spread out downstage during the second reprise, filling the space, then you can get the blokes coming through. It'll add a touch, know what I mean?'

'Yes, Han. We have just started, you know?'

'I know, I know. We'll come back in twenty minutes and stick our oars in properly, OK?'

The two older women walked off to the side, following a low myrtle hedge towards one of the boarded-up supermarkets. Some of the big letters still stuck to the facia above the windows – SAIN ROS. Saintroses. Hannah-Rosa's fingers were nimble and busy with a roll-up. She looked over her shoulder at the blockhouse, but the lights were out and the protectors seemed to have gone home. She slipped in a couple of pellets of hash, lit it, took a drag, handed the spliff to Emma. It was the tobacco of course that was illegal. They sat on a bench beneath more acacias next to a glassless bus shelter, its frame twisted.

'Han, why are we here?' Em leant back in the corner of the bench, one plump golden arm along the top, the other hand dangling in the narrow space between them with the spliff between her fingers.

'In Linwood?'

'Yes.'

'Six miles from where we were born and brought up?'

34

'I was born in a leafy suburb of London, but brought up in Hurling, yes.'

'Well, why not?'

'Why?' Emma persisted. 'There's no credits here. You heard what the protector said. Crop failures. Bugs in the peaches, the maize flattened by gales back in early July.'

'Bitch protector! Class traitor! Let's say . . .' Han reached forward and down, took the spliff back, inhaled, held it, let the smoke out slowly, 'unfinished business.'

Silence for a moment, or almost. The band had stopped playing. Beryl and Jacques were in a stand-off but their voices were not yet raised. Creative tension rather than artistic incompatibility. That could come later. Filling the space they had made, the silvery soprano sax curled the first subject of a Vivaldi oboe concerto into the still warm air around them. Kate had played the oboe before taking up the soprano sax, following exactly in her mother's footsteps by doing so. She'd kept up with the keyboard too. But whereas Hannah-Rosa finally specialized as a dancer, Kate had so far remained first and foremost a musician.

A cat clambered out of the open side door of their ancient VW camper, and ran towards them, tail up, in a brisk sort of hobble. Emma stroked her. Pinta was one rear leg short of a full set, which was why she was content to travel with them. They also had a hamster called Garth, named after the character in *Wayne's World*. Hamsters came and went but were always called Garth or Dream-Woman.

A Chorus Line started up again.

Emma had trained as a vet. By 2015 only agri-business, which she would have nothing to do with, could afford vets, and she'd dropped out to scratch a living as a dancer on the fringes of show biz. Later she became a traveller. Travellers were licensed itinerant entertainers allowed to move freely about the countryside – so long as they earned enough credits to keep them on the road. But she had continued to take the animal kingdom seriously, especially domestic pets, caring for any casualties they came across and maintaining a vegan life-style even though many of her customers were carnivores.

'You haven't been back for what? More than twenty years?'

They had been together for ten. As children and adolescents they had taken their ballet, modern and tap grades at the same school of dancing, had lost touch but finally met up again by chance in Barcelona in 2025.

'Much more. Not since I got my first real dancing job in Australia. I wanted to come back later, but after Dad died Mum stayed in Brussels.' Hannah-Rosa sighed, pinched out the end of the spliff. 'Sun's gone.'

They turned back towards their encampment. Emma carried the cat. The group on the stage was beginning to break up. Jacques walked across to meet them.

'It's not coming on too badly,' he said. 'Any chance of a bit more rehearsal time tomorrow morning?'

'All day if you like. We can't move to Carver's until the day after tomorrow.'

They exchanged good-nights and Emma and Hannah-Rosa climbed back into the front seats of the VW. Emma lit an oil lamp.

Outside giant moths banged against the windows. When they settled on the uncurtained windscreen their red eyes glowed like laser sources behind feathery antennae, their fat grub-like bodies pulsed with inner life. Emma claimed they were mutations or maybe genetically engineered escapes. Hannah-Rosa, however, was sure they were oleander hawk moths, migrants from the continent. At all events they didn't bother her.

Not a lot did. The only emotions she normally showed were pleasure, glee even, when the troupe got a routine going in much the way she wanted, and anger, anger with regulations, bureaucracy, anything that interfered. This she usually bottled up until the cause was out of earshot. The rest of what she felt she suppressed – or let out in her work, arranging dances, teaching dance, still dancing a bit herself, especially Spanish.

'Unfinished business?' Emma repeated. 'Why now?'

'I've always known I would come back one day. Had to. Have to. There are things at the house I have to get. If they're still there. Things of Dad's,' she added, pre-empting Emma's next question, and with a finality she hoped would shut her

friend up. 'Why now? I don't know – apart from the fact that
we were in this neck of the woods anyway. No knowing when
we'd be so close again.'

Actually they hadn't been that close – the last gig had been
at Basingstoke. Em had wanted to head west – Stonehenge
maybe; Glastonbury; Bristol even, now the plague quarantine
period there had expired; or south perhaps to Southampton
Common. Though they'd heard there had been civil distur-
bances in Southampton. Generally speaking, a rumour of that
sort concealed something more serious.

They needed the extra money, the credits, if they were to get
across the Channel and into Brittany or even as far as Gascony,
which is what they usually did in the winter. English winters
were mostly (but not predictably, nothing was predictable
about weather patterns now) very wet, too wet for people who
lived in campers or tents, plagued with storms and sometimes
cold; while winters in the south-west of France were usually
dry and sunny once the sub-tropical rainy season was over.

Emma smoothed down her long cheese-cloth skirt, then
pushed with her palms at pins in her hair which was threatening to drop. She thought about what Han had said.

'So, you're going to try to get up to Thorney Hill. It's not
part of the Hurling Enclave, is it?'

'Shouldn't think so. Not with two miles of forest and heath
between.'

'So what's there now?'

'Em, I have absolutely no idea at all. But I'd like to find out.'

'And since that protector we spoke to wants to get us checked
out, we've got a day or two to spare.'

'That's right.'

'We'll have to walk.'

'Yes. *We?*'

'I'm not letting you go on your own. Six miles there. And
back. Better get an early night.'

They climbed between the front seats and into the back of
the van, and, following a very well-established routine, converted the table, cushions and banquettes into a bed. Although
the spaces were cramped and awkward, they shrugged

themselves out of clothes and into the shirts they kept for nightwear. From a locker above, Emma pulled down a duvet and pillows.

'What about Kate?' she asked.

'What about Kate?'

'Is she coming too?'

Hannah-Rosa thought about that for a moment.

'I'd rather she didn't.'

They got under the duvet at opposite ends, head to tail, and Hannah-Rosa wound down the wick of the oil lamp. It was quite like 'stop-overs' when they were kids – except now it happened every night.

6

Light from outside continued to flicker through the thin curtains on the side windows or through the windscreen. The vans had been marshalled in an irregular circle, like corralled wagons in an old Western. In the middle of the circle a small fire burnt. Round it the rest of the troupe came and went; some, like Hannah-Rosa and Emma, prepared for bed. Two or three strummed guitars while Hannah-Rosa's daughter Kate improvised on her sax. In the distance, from the old High Street, the noise from the interactive spec arcade diminished step by step as each machine was turned off. There were a few raucous shouts from under-worker youths as they made their way back to their cabins, high on home-brew crystal-meth, and somewhere a girl screamed, but not, Protector Sergeant Marge Whitlock thought, in earnest.

She gave her heavy belt a hitch and moved out of the shadows from which she had been watching the Harem encampment and began to make her way home too. She had to cross a patch of wasteland where, amongst the brambles and dogwood, pools and oil-drums still held rain-water from the last storm. After a hot day it stank of rotting vegetation, sewage and worse. Huge nocturnal insects, most of them moths and giant crickets, circled her head like the biplanes in *King Kong* but some buzzed wickedly: mosquitoes an inch long carrying Malaria B. All were kept outside a twelve-inch seclusion zone by the repellent with which her cap and uniform were impregnated.

Picking her way through the edges of the rubble from the collapsed fly-over, she used the old pedestrian tunnel to get to the sub-enclave where she lived with her husband. Rats scuttled below the grating of the storm drain that ran down the middle and light from the far end partially illuminated the old murals and graffitti that dated from the turn of the millennium. 'New

Labour, Same Old Tory Shit.' 'Radiohead are Wankers.' 'Evil Trend are God.' She had to push her way through an ankle-deep litter of cans and plastic bottles, overflows from recycling bins that had not been emptied for years.

A hundred yards beyond the exit there was a high, tubular steel-framed gate which recognized her voice and opened into a time-warp. Here everything was neat and tidy, the verges green Astroturf, the flowerbeds a mass of mesembryanthemums, now closed in the darkness, genetically improved *impatiens* and petunias, cacti and other succulents bred to withstand long summer droughts interspersed with torrential downpours and gales. The virulent blue lights of insect killers glowed on the lamp-posts beneath the security cameras and occasionally flashed yellow and white as moths or bugs blundered into the high voltage mesh.

Her house was a detached three-bedroomed Barratts, built in the nineties, one of many in a cluster of closes and crescents. Mostly they were occupied by members of what was popularly categorized as the 'Social' – protectors, inspectors, low-grade public servants and the like – all making up a neat and desirable sub-enclave. 'Sub-enclave' because, unlike Hurling, a full enclave, it was not self-contained, and the people that lived there were in direct physical contact with the outside world as part of their duties and responsibilities.

Several of the houses had cars parked in their driveways – rarely used now, but lovingly kept up although the last fossil-fuel private car had gone out of production seventeen years earlier. A generator hummed and light glowed in a few downstairs rooms where residents were still experiencing their specs of choice: at that time a redigitalized version of the Athens Olympics in 2004 was topping the charts again. They were the first Games in which most leading competitors had carried miniaturized cameras. Computerized enhancements now gave you the opportunity to experience what it had been like to win the high jump or the marathon. The last full Olympics had been in 2016: since then catastrophes, environmental and political, had rendered them impossible. In their place, those countries that cared now ran off national competitions at home and entered recorded performances to a Virtual Games which was processed in one of the Rimmer capitals. Since the Rimmers always won all the medals, it was generally assumed they were fixed.

Having passed the sub-enclave security systems, Marge was able to let herself into her house with the original latchkey. Her husband, Jack, was sitting in the living room in front of a picture screen with a console, laboriously, but presumably with some satisfaction, electronically recreating brushstroke by brush-stroke Van Gogh's painting of crows above a windswept wheatfield. Since Jack had not seen a field of wheat for ten years and very few crows at all, the finished painting had a strangely abstract feel for him, though its broodingly depressive character was real enough. Marge had asked the therapist what sort of reasoning lay behind the choice and had been answered with what she considered to be a load of guff about externaliz-ing negatively impacted psychic circuits.

Jack had been in therapy for both his mind and his legs since being thrown through a second-floor window of Sandbourne Town Hall, where he had been part of the mayor's bodyguard during the Right to Work riots of 2029.

Marge undid her belt and slung it across the back of an armchair which rocked for a moment with the weight and then dropped her cap on to the seat. She ran her fingers through hair tightly but fashionably permed, then slumped on to the sofa next to her husband.

'Anything on the news?' she asked.

'Nothing unusual.' He added an angry 'brushstroke' to the curly clouds on the horizon and the programme bleeped at him. An artificial voice told him to add white. 'Chair Booth, accompanied by her grandchildren, returned to Birmingham from her holiday on the Island to defuse criticism of the way the protectors are handling the annual pilgrimage to Lady Di's tomb—'

'They set off earlier each year,' Marge commented.

'That's what Booth said. Rumours that more troops are to be sent to the Sicily Bastion have been denied—'

'So they must be true. They never bother to deny lies.'

41

'The opposition's request that in view of the African crisis ethnics should remain within ten miles of their official addresses is considered to be premature.' He dabbed again at his virtual painting. 'And the local said there are travellers in town, a dance troupe with live music. Did you see them?'

'I checked them in. In the car park.'

Jack attempted a squiggle for a crow and got bleeped again – not enough black.

'All right, were they?'

'I suppose so. Is there any home-brew in the larder?'

'Should be. Fetch me a glass if you're getting some.'

Three minutes and two crows later she was back.

'Cheers. So what was wrong with them?'

'Wrong with who?'

'The travellers. The dancing troupe.'

'Not a lot. Nothing really. Cheers. Tough, though, for them if ethnics are confined to their home areas. There were two, no four, in the troupe.' She drank, put the glass down on her arm-rest and went on. 'Another thing. Their leader seemed to know her way about, where Carver's Field is, that sort of thing, though their record said they'd never performed here before. And there are quite a lot of them, twenty or more, I forget just how many, and I don't see they stand any chance at all of getting enough credits from Linwood to make their run here pay.'

'So, why are they here?'

'Exactly. Anyway, I said there were one or two things needed checking out before they could move up to Carver's. That will give me a day or two to see what they're up to. Anything on the Protector Net?'

'Local or national?'

'Local.'

'Group of urbanites in the Broadlands area. Said to be armed. Officially they're Afro-Caribbeans who lost under-worker status in Eastleigh a month ago. In fact, I'm pretty sure they're refugees from Southampton. Even the Protector Net has gone blank on Southampton, so things must be pretty bad there.'

'Not our pigeon anyway. God, that picture's gloomy. I wish she'd given you sunflowers.'

'Sunflowers?'

7

They were up early, not long after daybreak, pushing open the rumbling side door of the camper, then pushing it shut before the cat could get out. Han carried a small leather bag over her shoulder with a bottle of drinking water and a handful of small cakes. Around them the usual dawn chorus of whooping-like coughs from the vans and campers broke out. Summer ozone weighed heavy, especially in the low, wide river valley on the edge of which Linwood was situated. No doubt the oilfield smog, which hung like a pall to the west, contributed too.

'Where are you going?'

Kate, standing in the doorway of the Espace, elbow on one stanchion, rubbed her eyes with the other hand.

'Damn,' Hannah-Rosa said under her breath. And out loud, 'Just for a walk.' Then, consciously referring to a family joke half a century old, 'We may be some time.'

'How long? When will you be back?'

'Afternoon.' She thought about it, twelve miles plus an hour or so once they were there. 'Late afternoon.'

'But where are you going?'

'Back to the house I grew up in. It's about six miles from here.'

'Why?'

Hannah-Rosa shrugged. This was a question whose answer remained complex and emotional. One she was not prepared to go into just then. Kate went on, coming down out of the Espace: 'Can I come too?'

'No.'

The one syllable was as conclusive as a firmly closed door. Kate looked at her mother for a moment, puzzled, then angry.

'Well, fuck off then.' And she climbed back into the van.

As Hannah-Rosa and Emma left the car park, Emma said, 'That was a bit rough, wasn't it?'

Hannah-Rosa's lips went thin. She never readily admitted to being in the wrong; never had.

'I didn't want to get into an argument about it, a discussion. We'd have been here all day.'

'Why were you so keen she shouldn't come?'

They walked on for a few yards, past the old Kwik-Save supermarket. It was boarded up, but a local baker was laying out bread on a trestle table and a small queue of women was forming in front of it.

'Because it would make ... the wrong sort of outing out of it. Oh, you know, I did this here and that there. This was my bedroom, this is where your gran used to work, all that sort of thing. It's not going to be like that.'

'She'll be upset you're taking me and not her.'

'But that's the point. You're part of all that, part of that past. I don't have to explain it to you. Kate belongs to after. After all that.'

Emma shrugged, and they walked on. Surveillance cameras tracked their progress as they turned into Old Christbourne road. It meandered for a mile between the ruins of terraced eighteenth- and nineteenth-century cottages, some of which Han remembered had, thirty or forty years earlier, been twee-ed up into antique shops, bistros and art galleries. Occasional faces, emaciated, scabbed with sores, grey or rubiginous with skin diseases, peered from unglazed windows or around doorways from which the doors had long since been taken for firewood. These were people, for the most part old or very young, who had slipped for one reason or another through the safety nets of Chair Booth's Caring Community: because of lost documentation, bureaucratic error, maybe sheer fecklessness, they could no longer qualify for the food handouts and basic health care to which non- and under-workers were still entitled.

Among the heaps of fly-infested garbage that filled the pavements, colonies of feral cats tore up and crunched, heads on one side the way they do, the carcasses of rats. The smells and insects were almost intolerable, but knowing they were going for a walk in the country Hannah-Rosa and Emma had pulled on long trousers tucked into wellingtons, wore gloves and wide-brimmed hats with nets like those bee-keepers used to wear. Beneath these their noses and mouths were also protected by the standard ministry-issue moulded face-masks.

Soon, however, they were able to push these down so they hung round their necks. The road widened and straightened between grass verges grazed by tethered goats (an inspired piece of legislation ten years earlier had outlawed the use of lawnmowers outside enclaves), front gardens as well as back were planted with tomatoes, maize and beans, and hens scratched everywhere. What rubbish there was was eaten by pigs. Here the occupants, many of them already tending their allotments or patches of garden, some on their way to workshops in the few units still functioning on the industrial estate, looked healthier, smiled at the two women or nodded abrupt but friendly greetings. In a rural market-town the under-worker system seemed to flourish reasonably well, though it had been more or less ignored in the urban areas Harem occasionally ventured into.

The legislation had been put into place following the Right to Work riots. Under it anyone who did a certain minimum of work in any year, fixed according to age, sex, number of dependants and so on, was given credits, vouchers really, which took their earnings beyond subsistence level. Just. Such people were labelled under-workers. Full workers were people who worked a thirty-hour week and received a take-home pay which enabled them to buy education vouchers for their children, care vouchers for their old age and insurance against illness, as well as the basics. Most full workers worked for the Social and lived in sub-enclaves. Under-workers lived where they could or where they liked. There had been no shortage of housing since the late twenties. Following the epidemics and catastrophes, both directly man-made like nuclear reactors melting down, or man-made at one or more removes like epidemics of plague, new strains of tuberculosis and the CFJ3 outbreak, the population of England was now officially down to thirty million, though many believed it was much lower than that.

After another mile the women took a left marked by a

deserted and vandalized filling station on the corner. A broken display announced 'Unleaded: £12.59 a gallon'. This dated it post 2019, the year when the EC finally ceased to function in any meaningful way and imperial measurements were brought back – to the dismay of the younger two-thirds of the population who had been taught the metric system from birth.

Climbing a slight incline, the two women now began to move away from habitation, or at any rate used habitation, into open countryside. They also left the surveillance cameras behind.

Thirty years earlier what they were on had been a country road, not much more than a lane: blacktop but already potholed and with its edges going, it had linked Linwood with Horney Hill. Now little of the Tarmac remained but what did was enough to prevent Hannah-Rosa and Emma from getting lost. To begin with it wound through small stands of shattered brown maize and European cane, with occasional orchards, carved out of fields that had been broken up when the larger farms were appropriated, and then it became a tunnel through the wild and luxurious undergrowth which marked where the hedges had been.

The plants themselves were a strange mix. There was still a fair amount of bramble, hazel and hawthorn. However, close to ancient brooks and rivulets, many of which had broken free from centuries-old ditches to wander back to their even more ancient water-courses, huge-leafed riparian monsters flourished in dark shade beneath hovering, jewelled dragonflies almost a foot long. There were creepers and vines too, some, like hops and even grape, escaped cultivars, others which had mutated from relatively benign plants like woodbine, eglantine and traveller's joy into luxurious tangles of tendrils and flowers. There were ferns too, much larger than those the two women had known when they were children, clusters of fan-palms, cacti, and Venus flytraps, carnivores adapted to take insects larger than midges and the smaller flies.

This was as well, for there were very few birds but very many insects, the latter often, through natural adaptation to insecticides and mutation caused by exposure to radioactive dust, or escapes from genetic engineering laboratories, large and vicious. Though birds were rare in this sort of habitat, some species were said to be recovering from near extinction and there was an abundance of insect-eating snakes, lizards and small rodents. An equilibrium was re-establishing itself, so the scientists said, much like that which had existed after the extinction which killed the dinosaurs sixty million years ago – an abundance of decaying organic matter, both vegetable and animal, had left a habitat in which insects thrived and their predators too.

There were few forest trees – English varieties of oak, beech, larch, fir and pine had all been wiped out by succeeding plagues of insect larvae and fungi, by forest fires following droughts, or swept away in flash floods ripping gashes out of the hillsides. Holly, however, had survived and wild apple, and both were now colonizing the old plantations.

After an hour or so the track began to climb and as it did the landscape and flora changed. The soil was no longer the chalky loam of the valley but the acid sand and gravel of the ancient forest. Huge banks of rhododendron, clustered with brittle seed cases where the violet blooms had been shed, over-arched the track for a time, then, higher up, with less vegetation, the views opened out – Sandbourne and the oilfield behind them, the heath, the abortive peach plantations and finally Castle Hill and Hurling to their left. On the other side the sea, sheened with oil, gleamed beyond Hengistbury Head. A mile away in front of them blue smoke spiralled up into the clear sky from the midst of what appeared to be a large copse or small wood of umbrella pines and cypresses.

'Thorney Hill?' asked Emma, panting slightly.

'Must be,' Hannah replied, biting her lip.

'How long since you left?'

'Thirty years. The year before Super Phénix.'

She was referring to the catastrophic meltdown of the fast-breeder reactor at Creys Malville, twenty-five miles from Lyons. Half a ton of plutonium had leaked as a fine, microscopic dust, a pin-head of which, eaten or breathed in, could kill; fires caused by exposure to the air of the coolant, liquid sodium, had raged for months; the Rhône and the Rhône basin in the north Mediterranean had been rendered lifeless; millions had died of cancer and other diseases related to radioactivity and, through countless knock-on effects, the acceleration of European society into economic and cultural decline had been increased exponentially.

'At least,' Emma went on, 'you can visit your old home.' She gestured to their left across the charred heath to the distant woods. 'Mine is locked away in Hurling Enclave.'

Beyond a hedge of brambles reduced by the fire to a blackened simulacrum of barbed wire, the broken hump of a bronze-age burial rose like a small whale from the ashes of the heath.

'Dad used to take us blackberrying here,' she said, 'and whenever we passed that barrow he'd recite a silly verse he'd made up.' She thought for a moment, chewing her lip again. '"Bronze-age king in your bronze-age barrow, I bet you were killed by a bronze-age arrow." That's how it went.'

They reached a crossroads.

'"Cross Ways", it was called.'

And took a right. Presently they passed an old twisted, lopsided road sign which read 'Horney Hill'.

'It wasn't really called that, was it?' Emma asked – more a statement really, since she knew the answer which she herself supplied. '"Thorney Hill", surely?'

'Yes,' Hannah-Rosa replied. 'Except when Wessex got regional status and there was that craze for all things Anglo-Saxon and they called it Thornig Hill. Hill of Thor. God of Thunder. But to the people who lived here it was Horney Hill. And is so still, from the look of it.'

On the left detached bungalows, and further along, set back from the road behind their allotment-like strips of garden, a row of what, when they were built, had been council houses. Of all they had seen since returning to Linwood, these had changed least. Built a century earlier to house the extended families of agricultural labourers whose tied cottages had reverted to landowners when their grandparents died, and along with them small colony of didicoy, they had never been better than run-down, the gardens often filled with scrap, old motor cars and broken prams. Hannah-Rosa remembered children, grubby in cotton dresses, thin-legged, straggle-haired or crew-cut, in trousers or jeans cut down from adult size. Their parents were for the most part enormously fat from a diet of cheap white bread and margarine; a few, though, kept themselves lean and, like their children and dogs, whippet-like. It was much the same now. The only real difference was the number of animals about – goats, pigs and geese for the most part, but dogs and cats too, and some caged birds – canaries and gold-finches.

And since Thorney Hill really was a hill and the wind blew off the sea more often than not, the air was fresher and cleaner than elsewhere, the houses less blotched with oily grease from the oilfield and the people suffered less from the skin diseases that were endemic on lower ground.

At the end of the council houses, on a T-junction corner, a late-twentieth-century detached house stood behind a cypress hedge that had now grown so high it towered above the roof. Next to it, separated by a mixed hedge of holly and laurel, also grown to twenty feet or more, was a tumbled ruin of a prefabricated garage and a red-brick cottage with a slate roof. It was almost covered with ivy which had grown over the windows as well as the walls. Tendrils had even got under the eaves into the roof space and pushed up the slates from within. It had a porch on which was a ceramic oval depicting fir trees, the sea, a horizon and the words 'Orchard Cottage'.

'Here we are then,' said Emma.

'Yes.'

Hannah-Rosa's lips closed into a thin line and her knuckles whitened. Emotion was flooding through her but she was determined not to let it get the better of her.

They walked up a short concrete path, pushing through a riot of traveller's joy in full bloom, swagged with starry white flowers that covered the unruly, untrimmed shrubs that filled the small front garden. The ivy had reached inside the porch and grown over the door which still boasted a round handle, a letter-box and a knocker in the shape of an owl, all in tarnished brass.

Hannah-Rosa faced it for a moment, then turned right and Emma heard her murmur, 'Not yet.'

She pushed through a holly and privet hedge where there had been a paved arched gap and Emma followed her into a tiny patch of meadow which had once been a lawn. The grass was waist-high, much of it pale ochre and seeded, but through it grew wild flowers – love-in-the-mist, wild antirrhinum, willow-herb, big moon-daisies. The large oak which had stood in the corner furthest from the house and dominated the rest was now a huge stump like a very bad tooth, almost barkless and filled with holes left by carpenter bees and the like. Most of it had fallen, perhaps in the triple hurricane of 2009, into and on to the house next door, pushing in much of its roof and obliterating the fence that had stood between the two properties. The garden had thus been blessed for twenty-five years with far more light than it had ever had during Hannah-Rosa's childhood and a wonderful efflorescence had taken place in the untended shrubbery and herbaceous border.

A giant mallow still with its last spurs in pink bloom was wound with honeysuckle and briars; huge canterbury bells, hollyhocks, lupins and delphiniums made a forest of jewelled spires, everlasting sweetpeas climbed through and illuminated three bedraggled cypresses.

Round the corner a bank of nasturtiums vied with the blue of starry borage and the vermilion of feral geraniums, grown long and leggy. The boughs of a mature apple tree hung heavy with ripening fruit, and beyond it self-seeded sunflowers blazed in front of a holly hedge that was also filled with bramble hung with black shining berries. There was woodbine everywhere, supporting a silver band of cornet-shaped flowers, and butterflies too. Hundreds of them.

'It's a bit of a mess,' said Emma. She felt she needed to say something; Hannah-Rosa's eyes were filling with unshed tears.

'I suppose so. But Dad would have liked it like this. He hated weeding. Always said he was a selective weeder and left everything he halfway liked. We gave him that apple tree for his birthday.'

She pushed through the meadow and picked half a dozen of the fruit, gave one to Emma, pushed the rest into her leather bag.

She turned to the french window that opened out from the main living room and tried the door. It wouldn't budge. She cupped her hands to peer through the dirty double-glazing.

'Our piano's still there.'

She sighed, straightened and, with more determination in her stride than before, pushed back through the gap in the hedge to the front door. She stood on tip-toe and felt along the lintel that supported the porch. The wood crumbled into dust as she ran her finger along it, and a timber creaked.

'Watch out,' cried Emma. 'You'll have the lot down.'

But Hannah-Rosa had found the spare front-door key, just where she knew it would be. Carefully she eased it into the Legge lock and, with not as much difficulty as she expected, got it to turn.

It was wasted effort. The front door, once red, now blotched russet, fell inwards as she pushed and a gust of hot fetid dust-laden air billowed out.

'Fuck,' she said.

8

'Fuck,' shouted Annette Floyd. 'Fuck, fuck, fuck, go on fucking, FUCK!'

A pair of penis-shaped Ferraris, Ferrari red, screamed out of the left-hand screen, over them and on to the other side before slewing to the right into the chicane; the whole world tilted and then it was as if the spec users were on the centre screen in the driving seat of the leader, surging through the streets of Monte Carlo, the hotels and shops, the barriers, the flags, the palm trees, swinging, sweeping by on the side screens before they surged down on to the promenade beneath a million fluttering flags. The noise was appalling, a high-pitched whine in close discords raging in their ears, jacked up in volume and intensity to a searing roar. The love-horse vibrated like a road drill and threw them from side to side at the same time, but never quite enough to tip them off.

Love-horse? An expensive device Richard had bought from an Innovations catalogue, it purported to be a hi-tech, improved version of a late-Roman piece of furniture reputed to allow copulation to take place in the position guaranteed to provide optimum pleasure for both partners.

The male sat astride a tilted bench, upholstered in horse-hide, with his feet in stirrups, his back against the angled bench, which of course had adjustable head and neck rests, while the female sat astride him but with her back to his front, leaning forward over his knees to grasp a bar in front of her. Her feet were stirruped too but with the stirrups behind his and giving her the purchase she needed for all the movement she required. Mounted thus, she could manoeuvre herself on to his erect penis, spread her buttocks, let him into whichever entry they preferred, find the angle of her body to his that brought most satisfaction, and rotate or plunge up and down as much as she wanted.

Meanwhile, behind her, he could use his free hands to roam where he or she wanted and, if he needed them, find lubricants whose chemical make-up helped him to maintain an erection for as long as they both desired.

The love-horse on its own was of course a remarkably efficient device but it could also be plugged into a spec console so the couple could become part of a spec designed to stimulate the fullest sexual responses. They could thus appear and feel themselves to be on the back of a real horse, a stallion, running across pampas, fighting off other stallions and finally fucking its mares; they could be on a surfboard surging along the most magnificent wave-crest, cruising a tube, before they were wiped out in a crescendo of storming spray; or they could win the Monaco Grand Prix in a Ferrari.

But first, as they entered the final lap, there was one car ahead to be overtaken, a black Renault-Williams: through bend after bend they tracked it, nearly caught it; it pulled away, they wound it in again, and then, with the banners of the winning post in sight, it swerved and crashed into barriers, exploded; the driver, clad in leathers, streaked across their path, orange flames and black smoke streaming from his back; the nose of their Ferrari swung, scooped him up and sent him, broken now like a doll but still blazing, hurtling over their heads, spattering their windscreen with blood, as they flashed at last past the thrashing chequered flag.

Annette slumped across the bar in front of her, her cheek on her forearms, moist hair straggling across her shoulders. Richard wriggled a little, disengaging his rapidly detumescing prick and felt the seepage of bodily fluids leaking across his thighs. A moment of shame, disgust, exhaustion was wiped as the images on the screens carried them up and away, above the streets and the smoke and the roar, across the Provençal countryside and into the Alpes-Maritimes where presently, almost blinded by seering whiteness and the unbroken blue of the tilting sky, they shared a solar-powered microlight slowly skimming the glassy needles of Mont Blanc, L'Aiguille du Midi and La Mer de Glace.

'That,' Annette murmured, 'that was the best.'

Richard sipped ice-cold water, waited for his breathing and pulse to decelerate.

'There's a new one out,' he said after a minute or so. 'It puts us on the back of a killer whale hunting dolphins. At the end the water fills with blood.'

Annette shuddered, straightened, pushed the hair up off the nape of her neck.

'Get it,' she said.

'I will. Meanwhile, could you shift yourself? I've got cramp in my hamstring.'

'Old men! You're as bad as Damien. I don't know why I bother.'

She raised herself, swung one long white leg over his knees, got her feet on to the floor. He looked up at her, dark against the glowing dome of his orangery. Again she pushed her hair up from her temples, running her fingers through it to the nape of her neck. She turned. Slim waist, lovely bum, two dimples.

Old men? He thought about that. He was fifteen years older than her, Damien perhaps a little more. What, after all, did he have that Damien lacked? Glamour? But that had faded with the years. Making out with a rock icon was one thing, with a once-was rock icon another. Was it after all nothing more, or less, than the love horse and the spec projection equipment? In short, and to be blunt about it, the fact that he was immeasurably wealthy?

He climbed out of the stirrups and slipped on a towelling wrap, tied the belt, managed a sort of smile.

'Drink?' he offered. 'Swim?'

'Fix me something long, cold and strong. And, Richard, you're as young as you feel, and you felt pretty young to me.'

He grinned, felt better.

She swam for a time in his cool-pool. This was on the roof of the garage at the opposite end of the house from the orangery. It was kidney-shaped, mounted inside a cube exposed to the sky and nothing else. Its wall was made of toughened transparent glass, and you could walk round the outside of it inside the cube. The deck of the pool, square on its perimeter but with the kidney-shape cut out of it, formed the roof of the gallery below. Richard loved to watch from this gallery when someone else was using the pool; for him the most beautiful sight in the world was a human, preferably a female, preferably naked, swimming, and that was why he had had it made the way it was – simple in appearance and function, but involving miracles of plumbing and construction. The water was slightly saline, enough to add buoyancy, the temperature just three degrees Fahrenheit below air temperature. The depth varied from two to eight feet.

He watched her for five minutes or so, gliding, undulating, twisting, hair streaming behind her, or just spread on the surface. The water supported her breasts; she was to all intents and purposes weightless. Reflections and shadows from the ripples she made flowed over her body in shifting displacement patterns. The smoothness of her skin, the ease of her movements seemed to say: here is where I should be, this is what I should be doing. She *was* beautiful, but the thought floated with her, and he did not try to suppress it – Sophie Pribendum would be even more lovely seen thus – a thought she perhaps picked up, or maybe it was just that she knew him well enough to be able to guess it.

Eventually, responding to her beckoning arm just a foot away from him, he climbed an arc of steps and slipped into the water with her.

They made love again. This time she wrapped her legs round his waist and her white arms round his neck and kissed him lavishly. Rocked in the water they took their time, a slow ecstasy matching the rhythms of life rather than the hectic savagery of the car race. Then they drank iced tea from a flask taken from a giant Frigidaire that filled one of the north-facing corners of the deck.

Later, as she pulled on her clothes, silks and leathers for the most part, and he was admiring her taut thighs, her muscled torso, her proud breasts, she said, 'Damien knows about us, of course.'

Richard felt a touch of angst behind his breastbone, and then a small wave of irritation. He pulled the wrap he had just put on a little closer round him and tightened the knotted sash.

'Why "of course"?'

'Sub-regional sub-controllers can access all automatic surveillance recordings.'

'Why should he trawl through all that lot?'

'Oh, I expect I said something I shouldn't, said I had gone somewhere when I hadn't, that sort of thing. Enough to make him run a check.'

'How do you know he knows?'

'I've got an old video, Evil Trend at the Greenwich Dome. Don't look so cocky – it was your drummer I fancied when I was a kid. I went to play it the other day and found he'd yanked out the tape and broken it. He didn't say anything about it, but I think the message was clear.'

'Does it matter? Does he mind?'

'He minds, of course. He wouldn't have trashed the tape if he didn't.' She grinned at him, pulled a phial of Obligation from her purse and squirted her neck and cleavage. 'Wouldn't you? If you were married to me? It matters because he's a cunning, nasty bastard and in his position he can find ways of being nasty without being open about it. So watch out. He'd look a fool making a fuss about us, so he'll try to get at you some other way.'

He watched as she put on ochre lipstick and snapped her purse shut, straightened and blew him a kiss.

'I don't see how he can get at me.' Mockingly he whined, 'I aint done nothing wrong, guv. Not like legally wrong.'

She looked at him with cold warning in her eyes.

'Not yet. But I saw the way you were looking at that Pribendum girl, and I don't blame you.' She headed across the ovoid hall, lined with ceramic tiles in bas-relief representing the covers of Evil Trend albums, and turned.

'Fetching little dish,' she went on, 'but your days of pulling teenage groupies are long gone and, considering not only what Damien can get up to, but her mother as well, I think you should keep your hands to yourself where she's concerned.'

He wondered if that was what it was really about – using her husband's position to warn him off a girl who might be a rival.

He walked down to the gates with her, squeezed her hand for a goodbye and turned back to his house. He still felt almost overcome by an irritable mixture of post-coital lassitude and as yet unused energy. Bored and restless, he went to the east end of the house and electronically opened the garage beneath the pool.

It was always a sort of miracle this, to open the enchanted cave and find perfection – the most beautiful car ever made, a Ferrari, yes, but not a Formula One monster, nor even the aggressive, brutal Testarossas that came later, for this car had already been thirty years old when he bought it in 2006. A 400 GT, one of the first Ferraris that was a genuine four-seater, it was a hardtop, in a blue-grey metallic finish, Pinninfarina-designed; its slim sleek lines that made you think of sea-mammals, dolphins perhaps. On the road it had been almost possible to mistake its conventional shape for far lesser marques, a neater Jaguar perhaps, something of that sort, until you saw how perfectly streamlined it was, how completely free of clutter. Until it left the rest grinding behind it as it pulled away from the traffic lights.

He had not driven it, had not been allowed to drive it properly, that is, for a decade, though occasionally he gave the kids of Hurling a spin round the enclave. But he liked to know it was there, liked to feel that one day he'd get in it just once more and drive off, experience just once more the power and the beauty of it, the smell of leather inside, the push in your back as it surged forward, the deep, scarcely heard rumble of an engine that cruised at a hundred and ten miles an hour . . .

He ran his palm along the angle made where the wing and the bonnet met, let the track he had written for her trickle through his mind.

> I look into your light-bulb eyes
> I feel around your metal thighs
> I know that I've been magnetized
> And I wonder
> Are you really solar powered
> Has emotion ever flowered

Have your circuits ever cowered
Do you have a heart . . .
Robot girl?

He closed the garage and went back to the front door. As his moccasin slippers slapped the marble floor he noticed that the tiny red light on the wall-mounted audiphone was blinking. He pressed a button.

'Virginia here,' he heard. 'I'm calling round to say I've booked the coach and cleared things with the Linwood protectors and we can go to the Harem performance on Sunday night. Meet at seven-thirty at the Enclave Hall. Press "one" if you can come.'

He pressed one. But his thoughts were still with what Annette had said. Millions he had, yes. But no power, no power at all. Heavily restricted travel and constant monitoring of money movements together made financial corruption an art well beyond his capabilities, and anyway he had never felt the need. But power and abuse of power were another matter. Damien Floyd had power and, given a motive, opportunities to abuse it. At the same time Richard had never given in to anything. He'd pack Annette in when he, or she, had had enough. Floyd was a pompous turd with a loathsome pipe and he'd be buggered if he'd let him interfere.

He tightened his sash again and went to his workroom, brought up Life-in-Death, scanned it, thought about it and eventually wiped it. Already it felt stale, second-hand. He wanted a new idea, a big idea, an inspiration that could really be developed into something with a bit of body, length even, something with meaning, original but relevant. Sophie Pribendum came into his mind. Somehow he felt there might be something there. And not just the lust of a dirty old man for a pubescent child: something much bigger than that. A symbol. No, not a symbol, he distrusted symbols, they smacked of the essential, of essences. But something so particular, so much itself, so much just Sophie Pribendum, that she could march through a full-length spec trailing clouds of glory, her own glory, not the glory of a symbol.

This had always been his problem aesthetically, as an artist. How do you create an image filled with power and beauty without in some way losing its particularity? Power and beauty are themselves abstractions. Particularity implies imperfection or at any rate a failure to achieve universality . . . The old arguments rumbled round his head.

'I'm bored,' he finally said aloud. And then grinned at himself. A struggle with Floyd would be fun, especially if there was a possibility of real danger in it. Come to that, real danger was something he'd missed for a decade or so. Get back on the high-wire, Dick Somers, he said, before you get positively geriatric. Bored? He remembered his mother: for her it was a crime to be bored. She had constantly urged him, him and his sister, always to be doing something, and she had done it so well, in such an un-nagging way that the habit had been successfully formed.

On top of everything else he now felt guilty, or at any rate ashamed.

He wondered where she was, his mother. Brussels still? Maybe. Communication with inner Europe was no longer easy – indeed monitored and discouraged. Nevertheless, he really ought to make the effort, get in touch with her, find out how she was, if she needed anything.

9

It was dark inside – hardly any light penetrated the ivy-covered windows. A very narrow flight of steep stairs climbed from a tiny vestibule. Two doors opened off it, upstairs there were four. The walls were thick with grime, the spaces hung with grime-laden cobwebs.

'I'm not sure,' Emma murmured, 'that I want to go much further.'

'You don't have to. Hang on, let's get a bit of wood, a stick or something. Brush our way through.'

For a moment they were the pre-teens they had been more than forty years earlier, inventing the sort of adventures they read about: haunted houses, old women who might have been witches but generally weren't, secret gardens even.

Emma came back with a couple of broken laths. 'I think they came from the roof of a wood store.'

'Dad built it. It was all lopsided.'

The door to the right opened easily enough into what had been a living room subdivided by a wood-burning stove beneath a free-standing red-brick chimney. They beat the curtains of cobwebs apart so they could get in.

'It's like *Indiana Jones*,' Emma murmured. 'Remember *Indiana Jones*?'

'Course I do.' Hannah-Rosa sounded testy.

Pieces of furniture stood around swathed in tatty, moth-eaten sheets. At the far end was the piano, a small plain upright cased in pale oak. There were a few gilt-framed pictures on the walls and a reproduction, now much faded, of *The Fighting Téméraire*. Dust rose and settled round their feet. Frustration and hatred for the way time had hidden and spoilt something that had been good, living, rich and safe, flooded Hannah-Rosa's breast.

'This won't do,' she cried.

With a swiftness driven by a decision suddenly made, she

launched herself back outside and began tearing the ivy from the windows. One frame of glass, already cracked, the putty dried out, came with it and she cut her thumb, but not badly. She sucked it and then wound bits of rotten sheet torn from the furniture to stem the flow. Back in the vestibule, with beams of grey sunlight slanting through the swirling dust, she tried the other door.

'Bastard's left it locked,' she cried.

'The piano too,' Emma replied, still in the living room. 'Shame. The music for "Für Elise" is still on the top.'

'Oh dear. That was probably me. The key should be on the windowsill.'

The piano lid creaked open and Emma picked out the right-hand opening bars.

'Does it matter?' she called. 'About the key, the key to your dad's room, I mean.'

'Probably. That's where I'm most likely to find what I came for. In there.'

'It's where your dad worked, isn't it?'

'Sat behind his table and pretended to.' But she giggled as she said it, something between a giggle and a whimper, not really meaning it. Emma closed the piano lid and came and stood behind her.

'What exactly are we looking for?'

'A book. A book he wrote. But the one I want was never published, so it'll be a printout. Or even only on diskette.'

'Where did he keep the key?'

Hannah-Rosa thought for a moment, chewing her lip. At last she lifted her head.

'In the kitchen,' she said. 'On a ring with a spare set of keys. They kept them on top of the microwave.'

'Which surely will have been stolen. The keys, anyway.'

With electricity at the best intermittent outside enclaves and sub-enclaves there was not much point in stealing out-moded electrical durables. Of course, enclaves themselves did not rely on a national grid fed by clapped-out nuclear power stations; each had its own oil-driven generator. With the run-down of motorized transport there was a surplus of oil to drive them.

'Not necessarily. Nothing else has been.'

'I wonder why not.'

They went through the living room and into the kitchen which ran along the rear of the house and overlooked the back garden. It was much lighter here. There was no ivy and immediately in front of the big kitchen windows a small patio of flagstones kept down the vegetation. There were the usual gadgets and furniture you'd expect in a turn-of-the-century kitchen including a fan-assisted microwave.

There was a bunch of keys on it, coated in dust, but there was also a mug. It was a large one, made out of stoneware, decorated from one side of the handle round to the other with a stylized picture of sky, mountains, rain falling from clouds, trees and fields and, in the foreground, sea. The ends of a rainbow curved out from one side, disappeared into the clouds, and reappeared on the other. Across the top of the picture the capitalized words ♦ SWEET RAIN ♦ PURE RIVERS ♦ CLEAN SEAS ♦ and across the bottom in the once familiar script the one word *GREENPEACE*.

The tears suddenly flowed freely from Hannah-Rosa's eyes. Emma thought maybe it was because of the failed dream the mug represented, but actually it was the sight of a sediment of gungy, mildewed coffee or drinking chocolate that covered the bottom.

Finally Hannah-Rosa managed to say, 'I don't know which of us used it last.'

Emma hugged her, sighed, but with determination rather than sorrow, trying to get a grip on things.

'Is the key you want on there?'

'Yes. Sorry about that. Yes, it is.'

They went back to the vestibule, pushed what was left of the rotten front door out of the way; then Hannah-Rosa, stooping slightly, fiddled with a longish silver-coloured key in the lock of the cottage-style inner door. It took a moment or two to find the point at which it would turn.

They were in a small room ten feet by twelve, the parlour of the original cottage before the extensions had been built on. Facing them was a largish white-laminated table on a metal frame, with book shelves in an alcove behind one end of it, a small tiled fireplace, boarded up, behind the other. Beyond it, in the second recess made by the jutting chimney piece, there were bookcases, but only three feet high, the space above filled with pictures, mostly framed postcards, and a dart-board. Facing the table, against the same wall as the door was in, was a big bow-fronted chest of drawers, a good century and half old, and a modern filing cabinet. Above them book shelves to the ceiling. Dust again everywhere but not much sign of damage – the door was a close fit over a thick carpet, preventing rodents from getting in, and since Thomas, Hannah-Rosa's Dad, had painted the sash windows so badly they wouldn't open, nothing much had got in that way either. There was, however, a strong smell of damp decay and the air was heavy and stale.

'Don't know where to begin,' Hannah-Rosa muttered. 'He kept the books that were published on a shelf in this corner . . . but, as I said, the one I want wasn't published.'

Emma at last yielded to a huge sneezing fit.

'Need a tissue,' she struggled to say.

'Try one of the drawers.'

'No tissues. Load of boxed disks, though.'

She wiped her nose on her sleeve and began to click through the disks.

'What was it called, this book you're looking for?'

But Hannah-Rosa was too preoccupied to hear or at any rate take in the question.

Under the table there were six cardboard boxes filled with envelope files and typescripts held together with paperclips. Hannah-Rosa began to go through them.

'Tax stuff,' she said. 'That was when things began to go wrong for him. Some silly tax he never paid after he'd given up real work. Look at this. Self-assessment! He'd never have assessed his writing as making a loss. What self-respecting writer would?'

'He was a teacher, wasn't he?'

'Not during my lifetime. He had been. Then he was some sort of inspector. But he packed that in and started writing books.'

'And it's one of those you're looking for.'

'Yes.'

'Any idea what it was called?'

'The Dream. Something like that. But that was the working title. He'd have thought of something better. Hang on!' Excitement in her voice. She hoicked an envelope file up on to the table, lifted the flap and began to riffle through the papers in it.

'Damn.' And she started again, but knowing it was hopeless. There were newspaper cuttings, notes, even pencil sketches and diagrams. Some photographs. But no wodge big enough to be book-length.

'Are you sure he actually wrote it, finished it?'

'Quite sure. His publishers commissioned it, but when they saw it they let him keep the advance they'd paid, but refused to go any further. That was when he began to go a touch off his rocker.'

Emma had moved behind the table, next to her, but was facing the wall above the fireplace.

'Odd picture,' she said.

Hannah-Rosa glanced over her shoulder.

'He did that. Not long after the rejection.'

It was big for the size of the room, two and a half feet by two, the top a wide band of vermilion merging into deep ultramarine and painted on it, or showing through the pigment, the words 'Trajectory', 'Tragectory' and 'Trajictory'. Below these was a row of colour snaps taken at ten-minute intervals, marking a sunset, another of a vase of tulips, photo by photo, drooping and shedding their petals and, finally, a small photo of a man in his early fifties, a second showing him ten years older in a trilby-type hat, and then a pencil drawing of the same hat but now worn by a skull.

'That's him, isn't it? That's your dad.'

'Yes.'

'I remember him well.'

Below these there was a broad red arrow labelled 'Concealed Exit' as if on a road sign. And in the centre, to the side of them, a newspaper cutting of a naked model with arms outstretched, holding back a black cloak, revealing all. Under it the words 'Her lips were red, her looks were free'.

'"A nightmare life-in-death was she,"' Emma murmured.

'You know your Coleridge.'

'Oh, am I?'

And at last they burst into giggles, weepy giggles, so they had to hold on to each other. And that was how they were when Sharon spoke.

'If you're thinking of squatting, think again,' she said. 'There's empty houses down the road you can use, but not this one.'

She was standing at the foot of the stairs, in an aura of dust and sunlight with the debris of the fallen front door about her ankles. She was thin, with white hair in a bun, though the eyebrows that met above her nose were still dark. Her cheeks were hollow, her lips shrunk over a mouth full of gaps, her neck was scrawny. She had a slight stoop, and the round-shouldered look a hunchback has, though her back was nothing like as bad as that. She was wearing a plain blue cotton dress with a grubby apron. And although she must have been seventy, and had obviously had a hard life, her eyes were bright, aware, and at that moment suspicious, almost angry.

'You've made a fine mess of that door,' she said. 'And after all these years.'

Her accent and way of speech were not Hampshire – she still spoke the didicoy cockney of her grandparents.

'Sharon. You are Sharon, aren't you?'

'Sharon Dell, if you don't mind.' Then recognition came on her side too. 'And well, well ... well, I'll be ... You're Hannah-Rosa.'

Awkward moment this. After thirty years do you embrace the cleaning lady? Shake her hand? They clasped each other awkwardly.

'You'd better come to my house and have a cup of tea.'

'That would be lovely. This is Emma. Do you remember Emma? She lived in Hurling. We were always friends.'

'Can't say I do. I do remember a kid, though, that used to

stop over and be in her pyjamas when I come round at nine in the morning.'

'That was me,' said Emma.

It was one of the 'council houses', the same one Sharon had lived in since not long after getting married back in the eighties. She seemed to be there on her own, though she had had a husband and four children. She told them something about it all as she busied herself with a paraffin stove, a dented saucepan and a glazed brown teapot.

'Kev got knocked off his bike trying to cycle back from the Hurling Working Men's Club, drunk as usual, not long after you lot moved out. Before Hurling was like enclaved, you know? Lingered on with a broke back for a week then went, he did. Two of me kids died of that malarial do we had, I expect you remember they was always like delicate, poor Mel being deaf and that, but I got three lovely grandchildren from the others. They comes round most days. They won't half be excited to hear you bin back . . .' And so on.

She poured water from a jug, drawn she said from a well in her neighbours' garden and safe enough boiled. She said the milk was goat's milk but you can't taste the difference in tea. Odd thing to say – there shouldn't have been a cow around for the last two decades, though it was rumoured some country folk kept a milker hidden away in a barn. The furniture was old, broken, sometimes repaired, the carpets threadbare, a scrap of lino in the kitchen worn in places through to its old canvas backing. All in all not so different from what Hannah-Rosa vaguely remembered from thirty, even forty, years ago. The tea was . . . tea!

'Where'd we get it? You remember the Booker cash and carry, down at Purewell? Got flooded out in . . . oh, I don't know, must have been twenty year back. Big tide, big storm. Both the Stour and the Avon broke their banks and all that area was under ten feet of water for a fortnight. It's still under a foot or so, has been ever since, and more at high tide. Well, there was tons of stuff all over, all sorts, including these big boxes, like chests, filled with packets of Brooke Bond, but they was all sealed in foil packets, see? And they Coopers, from Whitelands down the road – remember the Coopers? – got tons of 'm up in their pick-up trucks. They had two of them. Got all sorts. A lot went off, but the tinned stuff, and anything like wrapped airtight, you know, that kept. Reckon we won't drink the last tea for another five years. Sugar too. That keeps.'

She rattled on while she made the tea and let it draw. Only the descendants of the didicoy and the farmworkers were left. Some of the latter went back to Domesday Book, she reckoned. All the newcomers had gone, or nearly all. One or two oldsters hung on, but mostly it was the ones who knew a bit of farming, a bit of poaching, how to make do, and had done for centuries, that remained. She hardly thought of asking Hannah-Rosa what she'd been up to, beyond, 'Still dancing and that, are you?' without waiting for an answer.

'Well,' she said at last, sitting at the rickety kitchen table opposite them, 'I done what your mother asked.' And since Hannah-Rosa looked blank, went on, '"Sharon," she said, Katherine, your mum, that is, "We can't sell the place, no buyers around any more, so keep an eye on it for us while we're gone." She never said how long that would be, an' I never thought it would be this long, but I done it, just like she asked. And that old cat of yours died at last, Winny, she must have been fifteen or more, mousing right up to the end she was. Though I have to say I give up cleaning after the first ten years. I mean I reckoned I could give it all a good going over when needed. How is she then? Is she still with us? She must be well over eighty if she is.'

Hannah-Rosa thought for a moment, cradling the cracked cup of tea in her palms.

'Eighty-two. She was born in nineteen fifty-three. But I don't know where she is, or if she's still alive.'

'Went to Brussels, didn' she? After your dad died. That was a terrible thing. There was still papers then and a bit about it in the *Sun*. I remember Kev brought it home. I kept the cutting. I could find it . . .'

Sharon stood up, looked vaguely about her, hand reaching for a drawer in the dresser.

68

'Don't bother. I did see it.'

'Course you did.' She sat down again, went on, 'And Richard. He done well for himself.' Relish in her voice now, the surrogate delight a person has at recalling the success, not just the success but the global success, of an acquaintance or friend. 'Made millions, I reckon. First that Evil Trend, then the second Roger Daltry they said he was. Me, I preferred Rod Stewart. You called on him yet? Remember me to him when you do?'

'Called on him?'

'Well, he lives in Hurling Enclave, don'ee?'

Hannah-Rosa felt the blood leave her face and the room swam. She gripped the edge of the table.

'I didn't know that,' she said.

'Bin here, oh, six or seven years, I'd say.'

'He went to live in Florida.'

'Got too hot, didnit. Then there was that tidal wave, an' a nurricane, wiped out Miami, they said. You should call on him. I'm sure they'd let you, like you being his sister.'

Half an hour later Emma suggested they should leave. It was, she reminded them, another three hours' walk back to Linwood.

'Don't worry about your front door,' Sharon said as they got up. 'I'll get my grandson to knock up another, board it up anyway.'

'I . . . we . . . must owe you for keeping an eye on the house all these years.'

Sharon looked at her, at Emma too, at their clothes and general appearance. They weren't, she reckoned, much better off than she was.

'You get in touch with Richard,' she said. 'Get him to bung a few credits my way when he can. All right?'

They embraced the old woman more warmly than before. At the gate Emma said to Hannah-Rosa, 'Don't you want to go back, look round a bit more?'

'Not really. It'll only make me cry.'

They walked back towards Cross Ways.

'Why did that last book of your dad's mean so much to you?'

Hannah-Rosa took a deep breath, struggled to get her emotions under control.

'He put so much into it,' she said at last, fingers locked together in front of her but making a double fist to emphasize her points when she needed to. 'Kept saying it would turn the corner for him, for us. We'd never have to work again. He was so upset when the publishers turned it down. He sort of gave up on it, and on everything else too. To cheer him up I said I'd see if I couldn't get something made of it – not just a book – a film, a TV programme, even a dance, a ballet. But I was no one then. Just the dancing girl in the Sanipad ad. Then he got himself killed when I was in Australia, and I often felt if I'd tried a bit harder it might not have happened.'

'What was it like? This book, I mean. What was it about?'

'The human race, no less. How we evolved perfectly to fit the environment we were in, so it was for us like a terrestrial paradise. Except it was in water. He reckoned we all lived round a lake in Africa, in and out of the water. But then things went wrong, droughts, whatever, and we had to move out, out of Africa. After that it was downhill all the way, accelerating towards the end.' She laughed a little. 'Sort of a trajectory really, that's what he said. Like that painting.'

'There was a disk labelled "Tragectories".'

'There was?'

'Yes.'

Hannah-Rosa turned on her heel and began walking back.

10

On Sunday about half of the Hurling Enclave Players congregated on the small concrete-surfaced parking lot behind Walker's Garage where old Walker used to park the cars waiting for MOTs. It was opposite the back door of the Hurling Enclave Centre. The garage itself no longer functioned as such but was where the two enclave coaches were kept, their batteries recharged and the minimal servicing they required carried out. Each with a capacity for a dozen passengers, they were mini-buses really, shaped like oval buns, bodies built out of Brit-Plast, a subsidiary of BP, with moving parts made from lightweight pre-formed alloy air-freighted from China. This particular model was assembled in the larger units of the industrial estates north of Southampton not far from where the old Ford Transits were made. They were very expensive, but it was hoped they would have a working span of at least fifty years and they were very cheap to run.

Most enclaves had a couple kept for outings of this sort. Ownership and use of motor cars was discouraged and indeed since world-wide production of new cars had been halted twelve years back (China alone dissenting from the ban) it had become a sign of naffness and immaturity amongst enclavists to want to own or drive one. With just about every whim satisfiable at the press of a button within the home, travel was discouraged: if an enclavist really did have to get out, he hired a microlight air taxi to the nearest airport.

One feature of the buses was solid Brit-Plast tyres, which were supposed to last as long as everything else, wearing down millimetre by millimetre, decade by decade. This, however, meant that the suspension and shock absorbers had to be both resilient and responsive over surfaces that had been let go over the years and they tended to need replacing far too often. Occasionally breakdowns occurred in the open country, where the coaches and their passengers were easy prey for wandering tribes of urbanites, especially in the midlands and north of England. Or so government warnings led them to believe.

A couple of elderly women, who had been doing the costumes for the Players since the turn of the millennium, were worried about this possibility. A rumour was about, though officially the facts were confined to closed information circuits, that a group from Southampton had moved south from the Broadlands area the day before. Virginia assured them that they were in no danger: they only had five miles to go and once through the fence the main road that linked Southampton with Sandbourne via Linwood was patrolled by mobile protectors at all times.

They crowded in, two more of them than there were seats for, leaving Richard and Frederick standing illegally in the aisle. Frederick, the retired brigadier, who had grudgingly accepted the walk-on part of the Baghdad Chief of Police in the panto, seemed barely able to offer Richard the time of day. Paul Digby drove and cheerfully agreed to pay the spot-fine they would be liable to if the mobile protectors pulled them in for overloading.

Even before they got in there was an atmosphere of 'school's out' about the party. Few of them ever left the enclave at all. Goods of all sorts, including groceries and even fresh vegetables and fruit, were ordered from a vast Saintroses warehouse in Melchester and delivered once a week; some of the residents were, like Frederick, retired, the rest worked entirely from home. Company directors used spec screens to hold board meetings on twelve-way video set-ups involving co-directors as far away as Macau or Brasilia; barristers appeared on screens to cross-examine witnesses and sum up in courtrooms they had never been in; professors gave lectures and held seminars by similar means. Consultants performed operations with electronically controlled laser techniques on patients laid out on tables not just at the other end of the country, but the other side of the globe. Indeed the Commonwealth of Greater Britain still led the world in such techniques, which were, along with rock and roll, important earners of credits abroad.

And it was from their own homes that national, regional and

sub-regional administrators met in committees to process and enforce the government edicts that emanated from Birmingham.

Birmingham? Seat of central government since the night, twenty-six years earlier, when most of the lowlands of northern Europe disappeared under ten feet of high tide and flash-flood, the night the House of Commons collapsed into the tunnel that was being built to house the Westminster Underpass linking Waterloo directly with Hyde Park Corner. The Thames Barrier had worked well. Closed against the expected record tides, it had contained the two feet of rain that fell in six hours in the Thames Basin, rain sweeping up from the Azores on the back of what had already been named, coincidentally, on the alphabetical principle, Hurricane Fishes. Fishes because there were three of them.

Virginia welcomed everyone as they boarded. For all she was in her fifties, she was bubbling with almost girlish excitement.

'I'll hand out the tickets once we're all in. Isn't this marvellous? I'm so glad enough of you said yes to make it worth the trip. I mean, this is live entertainment, the real thing, and that's what Hurling Enclave Players is all about, isn't it?'

With the engine almost silent but a distinct rumbling from the wheels, the DjenMot 3000 Voyager took the turn out on to Coop Lane, between the War Memorial and the old post office, and followed what was now a metalled track past the Queen's Head and Hurling Manor Hotel, both in ruins. It then crossed a brook before taking a left up towards the heath. Virginia swayed down the aisle handing out tickets, exclaiming that she knew no more about what they were going to see than any of them could have found out on the local internet, but repeating that she was sure it would be jolly good. A few of them, led by Danny Blake, who had brought along a mini-keyboard, sang the choruses from the previous year's pantomime, and others gossiped about the casting of this year's.

Richard was excited too, but with a febrile inner excitement that made his palms sweat, his eyes tingle, as if he were suffering from the onset of a cold. He was looking forward to the event, yes, but was aware in a heightened way that it was a stop-gap, a distraction, a sop to desires and needs almost too deep for words.

Almost self-consciously he fell back on sexual fantasy in an attempt to jack up the anticipation he felt, an anticipation scarcely justified by what he had any right to expect.

From where he was, near the back but facing forwards, he could see beyond Frederick's elbow the glossy sleek black hair of Sophie Pribendum, swinging back and forth as she chatted amicably and animatedly with Delice Cowper, who had the window seat. They seemed to have become good friends – which was good news. Richard knew the Cowper women well enough for it always to be natural for him to chat to them – and to whomever they were with. He could see Sophie's sleeveless shoulder and upper arm, darker than he remembered, coffee-coloured but with not too much milk, smooth and somehow rich, with that creaminess of skin and flesh pubescent girls can have.

He rather fancied that as he had walked down the aisle past her she had smiled at him and that beneath her rich blue Thai silk vest she was bra-less. Now, as then, he felt in his diaphragm that sudden shock of joy, delight and longing that came a little less certainly with each passing year and, he thought to himself, Lucky I'm the age I am or what with the vibration of the bus as well as Sophie in front of me I'd be wondering what to do with a stonker. There was no sign of her mother, whom he had still not met.

'Quite honestly, the possibility of resignation crossed my mind.'

Fuck. That turd, Frederick.

'Oh. Oh really?'

Frederick's gold-rimmed bifocals flashed up at him. Surely an arsehole as vain as Frederick would opt for lens grafts? Trouble was he was notoriously mean as well as vain.

'I know you do Dames as well as I do, maybe in some areas better, and I have to admit you can sing, but I have to ask myself, does one expect pro-standard vocals from a Dame?'

'Probably not.' Richard was determined to remain not just polite, but friendly polite.

'And we are, after all, a club. We pay our dues, the same for everybody. And that implies to me that there is such a thing as Buggins' Turn. I mean that's what clubs are for.'

In the last resort, and that was where he now felt himself to be, in spite of his earlier resolution to be good, Richard had never found temptation easy to resist.

'And you see yourself as a Buggins?'

Frederick flushed, turned his head away.

Fuck again, thought Richard. Should keep my big mouth shut. Apologize? But how?

Fortunately they had reached the fence and the gate. The fence stood out like lace against the evening sun and stretched across the blackened heath for a mile or so in each direction. To the right it curved a little to loop round the one-hundred-foot communications tower that stood on the highest ground on Castle Hill. To the left was the lay-by where the Mini had been parked for the last time. It was still there. The little golf-ball cameras twinkled like a chain of tiny gold discs along the top of the fence. Beyond it the dual-carriageway snaked along the crest of the high ground. The gate itself, tubular toughened steel, should have responded to a seven-digit code tapped in on a small console in front of the driver, but nothing happened.

'Something coming up from Linwood,' someone guessed. 'A food convoy probably and moving slowly, so we'll have to wait until it's passed.'

Enclave gates did not open to let vehicles out if by doing so they offered an entry for unauthorized people who might want to get in.

Five minutes went by.

'Something's gone wrong,' said Damien Floyd, who was sitting with Annette in the front. 'Blasted fault in the comms, I'd guess. Try again.'

'Already have,' said Digby. They could hear the anxiety in his voice. 'Daren't have a third go because if we don't score on the third the thing will lock for twenty-four hours.'

'You're sure you did the numbers properly?'

'Quite sure.' Testily this time.

Floyd felt for his pipe.

'Don't,' murmured Annette.

But before her husband could make an issue of it or even light his pipe, his and everyone else's voices were suddenly drowned by the scream of two jets, black F135s, shaped like paper darts, tearing the air apart as if it were calico. They were exactly a hundred feet above the ground, whose undulations they followed perfectly, and only a hundred or so yards away, coming between the bus and the comms tower whose transmissions were possibly integrated into their low-flying guidance systems.

They flashed over the road ahead and followed the slope down the other side so they were momentarily completely hidden, then up they came, already two miles away, in a vertical climb, the setting sun striking shards of light from the gold leaf that lined their cockpit covers.

Then came the bangs, percussions that the Hurling Players felt through the solid tyres as well as in the shake of the bodywork, even though the explosions were more than a mile away. Seconds later twin clouds of black fumes mushroomed from beyond the visual ridge.

A moment of silence, of awe, fear, exhilaration even.

'Well,' Virginia chirped cheerfully, 'now that's over, perhaps we can get going again.'

'What *was* that?' someone else asked.

'Test run, I should say,' Frederick suggested. 'Dummy target down in Gorley Wood, judging from where the smoke is.'

The gate swung open at last. As they passed through and the wheels began to rumble more steadily on the tarmac, Floyd tapped his pipe stem against his teeth.

'No, Frederick, old chap, I don't think so.'

They waited to see what the sub-controller of the sub-region had to say.

'Couple of fires reported down in Gorley Wood yesterday. A small tribe of urbanites on the move. They were armed of course. Hence the air-strike.'

Richard, who had not been able to control a sudden shiver as they passed the Mini, looked down over the rolling woods and fields to the north. From a distance the changes in vegetation were not that evident and it looked not unlike the view he had seen from the school bus that used to take him to Linwood Comp all those years ago. The columns of smoke and the orange flames like dahlia blooms belonged entirely to the present or the recent past. Or did they?

'Napalm,' said Frederick, with quiet confidence – the ex-brigadier determined to re-establish his expertise in things military.

'You know,' crowed one of the old ladies as they began the descent to Linwood, 'it was from about here you used to be able to see the spire of Melchester cathedral to the north and the sea to the south, both from the same spot.'

Someone else said, 'And now the sea's nearer, and the spire's gone.'

But the only words Richard could hear were the ones that had made him shudder when he first heard them forty years earlier, during a season of special films on the telly for Christmas: 'It's the smell of victory.'

He felt sick and he felt ashamed that he could do no more than feel sick.

11

The show was good. Everybody said so. The enclavists had the centre seats, collapsible slatted wooden ones, three rows from the front. Four protectors sat with them, including Protector Sergeant Marge Whitlock with her husband Jack in a wheelchair beside her. Their presence reassured the old ladies, one of whom wore her hair, or someone else's, in an outrageous bee-hive and who had been asked to take it off by the worker sitting behind her.

The arena was full and there was a festive air – the audience was determined to have a good time.

Under-workers sat further back, on trestled benches. Generally speaking they behaved well and seemed to enjoy the show as much as the enclavists in spite of their lack of any real education. Appreciation of the finer things in life had been excised from the Blunkett Minimum, starting with music in 1998. There were some non-workers on the peripheries, standing for the most part, identifiable by the symptoms of skin diseases and rashes, chronic and irritating coughs, and congenital deformities. Those that could show environmental causes got in free, though the parameters for entitlement to this sort of concession had been redefined the previous year by the Ministry of Care. The reasoning was that since the government had cleaned up the environment so radically in the last five years people who claimed disabilities had to show that exposure occurred more than five years earlier. Furthermore the government had ceased to take responsibility for effects outside its control – which meant other nation-states' nuclear meltdowns, production of ozone-destroying gases, CO_2, methane, etc., were no longer the government's problem – international courts existed to settle such claims.

A few non-workers were high on home-brewed crystal-meth. When they started to show Tourette-type B syndrome, meaningless abuse, obscene behaviour and so on, they were chucked out by municipal bouncers, supported by protectors.

The first part opened with the chorus from *A Chorus Line* and was followed by a rumba, a Charleston and fox-trot by Danny Blake himself. It concluded with an extended extract from *Harold, the Last English King* – an immensely popular musical in the Lord Lloyd-Webber mould which opened in the year the United Kingdom became a federal commonwealth.

By the time the interval came darkness had fallen. They were in a large field, Carver's, the old Linwood 'Rec', bordered on the town side by houses occupied by squatters, and to the south and east by an estate of under-workers and the school buildings of Linwood Comprehensive School dating from the early sixties. This was still used as a first school, though the hall had been converted into a soup-kitchen.

There were a few trees round the edges, eucalyptus for the most part but with some tall poplar too; the grass, though worn thin and brown, was grass and not plastic. Harem had again parked the juggernaut that folded out into a travelling stage so it faced the setting sun, with the other vehicles around it, framing it and making it cavern-like. Round the perimeter insect-repellent torches flared – and the stage itself, lit by a handful of floods and spots powered by a small generator, was a bowl of light.

It reminded Richard of the past, of open-air rock festivals, Reading, Glastonbury and so on, where Evil Trend had made their name at the turn of the millennium.

He had managed, without manoeuvring too overtly, to exploit his fifty-year-old acquaintance with Susannah Cowper and sit next to her. Maurice Coen, her husband, was on the other side, then Delice and finally Sophie. Near, but not near enough! During the interval there was some chat about unfolding events in North Africa and the Middle East. Richard pronounced himself bored.

'This has to be,' he said, 'the tenth time Armageddon has been announced in my life time,' and he giggled.

They asked him why. They insisted he should tell them. At last, rather shamefacedly he did.

'Years ago there was a local group. From Melchester I think. Called themselves Farmer Geddon. Seemed funny at the time.'

Susannah allowed herself a tiny smile and, beyond Delice, Sophie looked round and grinned at him behind the others' backs. Richard's tired old heart did a handstand.

At that moment the darkened stage burst into life and raucous sound: 'Willy Wonka's gone aw-a-a-ay, Willy Wonka's had his da-a-a-ay . . .'

The lights came up in a sudden blaze, which included torches juggled by two Afro, leotarded fire-eaters, whose flames illuminated a rock group. This was led by a youth wearing a straw-coloured ponytail and a mustard corduroy jacket over tan flares. A banner was strung across the stage above them – *Bad Blend – the official Evil Trend Tribute Group*.

'Official, my arse,' Richard muttered, but he was pleased. All the other Hurling players turned round, grinning, to look at him, and the under-workers behind cheered and began to sing along. Few if any had recognized him or knew that he was there, but most were aware Dick Somers was a local lad.

'Bit of a rip-off, wasn't it?' Danny Blake, on his other side, his mouth close to his ear.

'"Oliver's Army?"' Richard answered. 'Not the same chord sequence at all. It was just a joke, anyway.'

'Wonka' – bowdlerized 'wanker'. Willy – a politician now well and truly forgotten, except in this raucous anthem celebrating his removal from the political scene.

The tempo changed. Less punky, more art-rock with distortion effects quite accurately reproduced from the original.

Now you've found me
I'm ready for the crucifixion,
I'm ready to take it
What you're going to do?
Jesus Christ
Became a strange addiction,
Will he help me now?
Or will he leave it to you?

'"Witness",' murmured Suzanne on the other side. 'Almost my favourite, I think.'

> If I die tonight
> Will you be angry?
> And if I fly
> Will you meet me on the roof?
> I'm the criminal,
> But is there really any witness?
> People live for the existence,
> Will they ever get the proof?

The lead singer sang high, a brazen falsetto, as Richard himself had at times. But was it? It dawned on him towards the end of the set that it was a woman, a girl, and not just a girl but the girl who had played the soprano sax in the first half – the completely different costume and wig had fooled him and probably everyone else too. Definitely a very talented young lady, and having only seen her in heavy disguise he began to speculate about what she might really be like.

They played four more numbers ending with the very upbeat 'Free'. A short set, which, from Richard's point of view, was just as well. It was very old stuff, much of it written before the formation of Evil Trend, though it had appeared on their first album, and while the lead singer, was, from a distance, a passable lookalike, none of the rest were, and the performance, apart from that of the girl herself, was too careful, too note for note, lacking the drive and point of the originals. Nevertheless they got a big cheer. Susannah and Danny tried to make Richard stand and take a bow, but he refused.

'It's their show,' he said.

The stage darkened until there were only flaming torches left; a flute, rasping, harsh, no nightingale, the clash of guitars, more flute and stamping feet then the familiar rhythm and figure – you could hardly call it a tune – and six Spanish dancers swirled down the diagonal of the stage in de Falla's 'Danza Ritual del Fuego' in an arrangement which included bass guitar and some percussion.

'This should be unbearably kitschy,' Danny whispered. 'But it isn't.'

The 'Fire Dance' was followed by two solos, the 'Dance of the Miller' and the 'Dance of the Miller's Wife' and it was during the last that Richard suddenly felt sick and the palms of his hands began to sweat again. The masked dancer, in full flamenco fig, mainly black and scarlet but with a mantilla embroidered in bright multi-coloured silks, span, posed, ironically postured at times, swung skirts in wilder rhythms above her bare knees and stamped bare feet on the boards. Her thin arms, with very slightly dimpled or sagging skin suggesting she was much older than she appeared, swirled and twisted above her head, and long fingers clacked ribboned castanets. Behind her two men in Andalusian gear, deep-brimmed hats, pigtails and all, long-waisted, tight-bummed, worshipped her with percussive heels and finger clicking, before hurtling on to their knees in front of her, each with a curved arm hooped behind his head.

But it was her feet that did it. Narrow, long-toed, and then hands to match, fingers that could stretch an octave and a half though the palms were narrow like her feet: feet and fingers he was sure he knew.

The audience, sensing a finale was near, cheered and cheered. She curtsied deeply, head forward, then took a ribboned guitar from a plumper dancer who had also attracted Richard's attention – though not as noticeable a performer, she had an air of authority, and was, in a way only another performer would recognize, watching the others, checking them out, mentally noting slips or slacknesses in their performance.

But back to the leader, who now sat on a stool one of the troupe put out for her and briefly adjusted the tuning of her strings. She began her solo spot with a slow meditative piece, much of it chords, repeated notes, with only one or two difficult runs, but sad, wistful. He knew it, a gypsy piece by Lorca, and he knew now for sure who was playing it. Sweat pricked his forehead, his throat went dry, he licked his lips. A desperate sadness welled up with the music, sadness and longing. He longed for her to take off the mask and look at him. Surely she knew he was there.

The show ended with a flamenco classic – the men first, clapping then stamping, then the guitars making a duet, a battle, out of it – 'La Niña de la Puerta Oscura'. The whole troupe stormed through it, the electric lights came on again, the costumes, sewn with jet and silver sequins, came even more alive than before. They became a storm, a wave of noise and skirts and legs, ending in a tableau of upflung arms, spread fans, tilted hats, proud heads, held just long enough for a shower of paper carnations to fall from the stage roof.

Blackout, no encore, no curtain, tumultuous applause, cat-calls, whistles and cheers.

'You can't,' Danny agreed, 'follow that.'

'Wasn't it wonderful?' Virginia carolled. 'I mean to see and hear something actually real and so alive?'

'You should go backstage,' Susie suggested. 'Tell them you liked the tribute band. They'd be awfully pleased.'

'I'll do that.'

He was very pale, yet sweat made a slight sheen on his forehead and cheeks.

'I say, are you all right?'

'I'm fine. Make sure they wait for me.'

'Of course.'

He turned, pushed his way against the flow of the leaving crowd, and found himself momentarily amongst a group of under-workers who jostled him a bit and smelt of crystal-meth and garlic, but did no other harm; he was soon clear of them and threading his way between the trailers and trucks that had been drawn up to enclose the audience area. He could hear the wooden smack of chairs being folded and the muffled crash as each one was stacked.

And then, moving out of the shadows, there she was, still in her flamenco rig, but at last with no mask.

'Han.'

'Rich.'

'After all these years.'

When he had been seventeen and she twelve he used to kiss her on her forehead: now she was as tall as him.

They stayed close, for a minute or more, chins on each other's shoulders, then she pulled back, found his hands and held them. Hers were rougher than his. Her eyes glistened in the light of a gas flare.

'We'll meet again soon,' she said, 'and we can talk then. There's no time now. They won't let me into your enclave and you can't stay here. First, I'm all right . . .'

She left a question hanging in the air.

'Me too.'

'I haven't heard from Mum for ten years. I don't know if she's still in Brussels or even if she is alive.'

'She is in Brussels, but we don't keep in touch.'

He was beginning to realize that she had prepared this meeting carefully, knew what she wanted to say and ask. That was fine with him. He could go along with that.

'Right. Now. After we got here I was told you were living in Hurling Enclave and I hoped you'd come and see us and that we could meet. I really wanted to, Rich, but also I wanted to give you this.'

From a pocket hidden somewhere in the full skirts of her costume she pulled out a three and a half inch IBM compatible diskette.

'It's Dad's *Tragectories*, *The Dream*, you know, the last big thing he wrote. You don't have a copy, do you?'

He shook his head.

'So this is probably the only one left.'

'Why me? What do you want me to do with it?'

'Make it, Richard. I want you to make it. You know it's really a scenario for a multi-media event, not meant as a book at all. You've got the money. The resources. Make it. Look, I've got to go now.'

Blood pounded in his ears and he felt dizzy again and deeply confused.

'Why? For heaven's sake, why?'

'Because there's a protector nosing about and if she thinks I'm being a nuisance she'll get my licence revoked.'

This was not an answer to the question he had meant, but she had taken his hand again and was clearly about to move off. He tightened his grip.

84

'Where are you going? How can I keep in touch?'

'Swanage. Then Weymouth. Finally Plymouth and the banana boat to St Malo, if we've got enough credits together. We always winter in Brittany or further south. Get in touch again if you can or want to. But make sure you don't mess us up if you do. It's not just my licence but the whole company's.'

She came closer and her lips brushed his cheek, then she turned and was off, skirts brushing the dried grass, picking her way through the vehicles until she rounded a corner and was gone.

Protector Sergeant Marge Whitlock pushed her husband back to the underpass.

'That Daytona woman,' she said, 'who runs the Harem outfit, met Richard Somers after the show. We already know she came from this area some years ago—'

'Yes. I remember you told me that.'

'And she gave him something. It looked like an old diskette, one of those ones that was meant to have been handed in ages ago.'

Jack from his wheelchair in front of her half-turned his head.

'You should report it,' he said.

'I will.'

12

The coach dropped Richard in the Street opposite his front gate. He was the first to get off.

As it pulled away Frederick, holding on to the corner of the seat in front of him and bracing himself as the vehicle made a U-turn back down towards the centre of the enclave, said, good and loud so all could hear, 'I don't know what got into poor Richard.' He didn't wait for comment or question, but ploughed on. 'He looked very disturbed when we got back to the coach, sort of pale and sweaty as though he had been taken ill, and do you know what he asked me on the way?'

No one did.

'He asked me if I still had an old IBM compatible PC, the sort that would take three and a half inch disks.'

Derisive amazement in his voice now.

'Goodness,' cried Virginia, 'I've even forgotten what they looked like!'

Some tried to remember. Some said the plastic casing was black, others grey. They agreed both colours might have been available. Maurice swore that he used a batch of red ones at college.

'Square though. Three and a half inches on each side.'

'Why were they called disks if they were square?'

'Circular floppy disk inside,' Damien Floyd asserted authoritatively.

'Padded by two sort of grey thin circles of stuff with a segment taken out,' said Annette. 'I took one to pieces once and got a fearful bollocking from my father.'

Her husband gave a look which clearly said: just the sort of thing you would do.

'Anyway,' Frederick concluded as they drew up at the war memorial and most of the passengers busied themselves getting out, 'he'll be bloody lucky if he finds one. An old PC I mean.'

*　　*　　*

Back in the oak-panelled living room of their mock-Jacobean farmhouse, Floyd poured whisky into a cut-crystal tumbler, then turned to his wife.

'Want one?'

'Yes, please.'

She didn't really, but whisky on her own breath would neutralize the smell if he insisted on coming to bed with her. He poured a second.

'Ice? Water?'

'No, thanks.'

He settled himself into the corner of a large black sofa. The leather beneath him made a noise like a mouse farting. A remote-control pad in his hand ignited the gas jets round simulated logs. Annette perched on the arm furthest from him and crossed her legs.

'Odd show those travellers put on,' he commented. 'I wouldn't have bothered but Virginia's a good soul and does her best for us all.' He felt for his pipe and began to fill it.

'Why odd?' She thought she had to say something.

'All that Evil Trend stuff to begin with. Then the Spanish dancing. Didn't quite seem to mix.' He sucked flame into the bowl of the pipe. 'Have you any idea why Somers should want an old IBM compatible?'

This was abrupt, took her by surprise.

'No. Why . . . why should I? I imagine he's got hold of an old disk – or do I mean diskette? – and wants to see what's on it.'

'Yes, dear.' Through the smoke he added a pinch of sarcasm. 'I had rather imagined that might be it.'

'Why ask me then?'

'I thought you might know something about it. Where he got it from, maybe?'

She sipped whisky, a Macallan not generally available without a senior administrator's gold card, and decided to go on to the attack.

'Now why should you think I might know that?'

For a moment their eyes, cold and expressionless, met across the space between, then his flinched away. Not ready for a war. Yet.

He used the remote-control pad to switch on the government news. It seemed the Africans were ready. For a war. Annette did not have to be told that this was something she was not entitled to see. She finished her whisky in a gulp and, gagging a little, left, climbed the oak staircase past the portrait of an entirely fictitious early-nineteenth-century Floyd ancestor, based on the likeness of a now forgotten actor from an old TV serial of a Jane Austen novel, and made her way to her own bedroom. She locked the door.

Downstairs her husband heard and saw how an estimated half-million Africans were gathering between Tangiers and Ceuta, while another half-million were already in Tunis. The secretary-general of NATO played down the threat – these people were sick and starving, having left at least a million dead on their trek across the Sahara. Aid had been promised but only to enable them to make the journey back to the equatorial wetlands they had left. Wet, yes, but deeply, irreversibly polluted. Meanwhile the chief mullah had said that there were enough people to make a human bridge across the Straits of Gibraltar. More seriously a Moroccan general had asserted that if the crossing was resisted, then, well, they had the nukes and they'd use them. Moreover they were extremely dirty nukes and they'd turn the south of Spain and Sicily too, if necessary, into a radioactive wasteland that would be uninhabitable for fifty years.

This, a commentator remarked, was a childish threat, not to be taken seriously, since it would render the land the Africans wanted useless to them before they had even got there.

Floyd, whose mind was as devious as any politician's, guessed that if the Africans didn't nuke the area, then NATO would and claim it was the Africans who had. That way they'd create a lethal buffer zone in depopulated areas which had already succumbed to desertification.

President Reeves spoke from the lawn of the White House to say Americans had nothing to fear – the Afro-European crisis was none of their business. Meanwhile negotiations to lay the framework of a treaty with China implementing the Nixon Doctrine were going well: the aim, as the commentator pointed out, not for the first time, was to leave Japan in the American sphere of influence but to allow the Chinese to take over India as well as the eastern Siberian republics. However, the Reeves Administration would insist on a guarantee that the price of Siberian wheat remain stable and not a threat to the US economy. The US had depended on Siberian wheat for twenty years now, ever since the Olgallala Aquifer had dried up and turned the Great Plains from South Dakota to north Texas into a gigantic dust bowl.

Meanwhile, upstairs, Annette, now lying on her bed, looked for a redigitalized spec-video of Evil Trend performing in the Greenwich Dome the year before the roof blew off. But that had gone; perhaps her husband had ruined that one too.

Downstairs Floyd switched to the public news. Dressed as always in black, Chair Booth of the National Executive Committee was shown boarding an old 757 at Blair International. She was on her way to Dublin for talks with Taoiseach Adams. 'We have great hopes of finding a solution to our problems and differences,' she said. She was referring to the possibility that the Republic of All Ireland might be persuaded to join the Commonwealth of Greater Britain.

Coca-Cola Cup first leg: Arsenal nil, Tottenham Hotspur nil. The Arsenal coach said, 'Our lads done well. I'm proud of them.'

'Nothing changes,' thought Floyd, as he waited for the weather, 'and they're all so bloody old.'

Easy to be old . . . if you could afford it.

The hot spell would continue until the end of August, though extremely localized thunderstorms accompanied by occasional high winds could be expected in Wessex and east Cornwall. He clicked to the relevant number on the Ministry Weather Board and learnt, as he expected he would, that the storms would not be localized but general. As usual, any freakish weather that occurred was always perceived by ordinary people to be their bad luck: they may have lost a few slates, roofs even, but they knew (they thought) their neighbours down the road had been spared. The Weather Board concluded that the storm would not be severe enough to justify alerting the emergency services.

He buttoned it all out and sat in the near darkness. The gas flames flickered, blue and green amongst the black 'logs'. He thought about Annette and Richard. He knew about the love-horse: every electronic transaction (and there were very few transactions in most people's lives which were not now electronic) was accessible to the authorities. That way the Inland Revenue could spot spending of credits in excess of income, the Health Department could be alerted concerning, say, excessive consumption of alcohol or chocolate, especially by people in responsible jobs, and so on. The technology had been there right back in the nineties, when supermarkets first invested in computer-controlled cash-outs and reward points.

All this monitoring and surveillance had originally been justified as ways of watching the nation's health, combating crime, gathering essential statistics on which to base economic decisions, but that was before the Ministry of Social and Internal Security (the SIS) took complete control of all information.

Information had become, like violence, structural and the property of the State. It was illegal to hold stored information, books, old newspapers, audio and visual cassettes, old disks or diskettes, CD-ROMs predating the mini CD and the DEEP CD, anything indeed, unless or until it had been inspected and approved. Occasionally amnesties were proclaimed and people were invited to turn out their attics and take their old books, videos, diskettes and CD-ROMs to their local protector station.

There was no way he could attack Richard through his actual liaison with his wife – generally speaking such activities, provided they did not go beyond the bounds of what the Health Ministry had decided, after prolonged study of primates in the wild, was 'natural', were not disapproved of. But if he could get him for possession of information likely to threaten the security of the State, then he could do him, them perhaps, a lot of damage.

He finished his whisky, considered another, but by now thinking about Somers had sharpened the nagging pain in his stomach. He knocked the ashes out of his pipe into a copper bowl, killed the gas flames and headed for the stairs.

He didn't even try Annette's door, but he banged on it and shouted.

'Annette? I want to know what's on that diskette Somers has got. As soon as he gets a machine, you find out and tell me.'

Or else? She raised her head from the book she was reading, looked over her shoulder. Or else what? He had so many means of making mischief it wasn't sensible to worry about what he had in mind. She shrugged and turned back to her novel: *Cleopatra's Sister* by Penelope Lively. The women of Hurling Enclave passed such books around secretly, under cover. She liked this one. She liked especially the scholarly hero and the bright heroine, although she doubted if real people had ever been as nice as these two. But that was what fiction was for, wasn't it? It could convince you that it was possible to be nice. Some fiction, anyway.

Somewhere inland, thunder growled.

13

An hour or so earlier Sophie Pribendum had been welcomed back home by the electronic scanners which opened the gates for her. Little Denny was a large Edwardian house, half-timbered with patterned brick, gabled, hung with wistaria and bougainvillaea, set behind cedars and rolling lawns with a neat, low formal garden in front. She hesitated in the hall next to the door to her mother's office. A small red light flashed above the lintel which indicated a virtual meeting was in process. Since their move to Hurling Enclave, her mum seemed to have spent most of her time in meetings. Sophie wondered what was going on. In Birmingham the meetings had been real not the virtual sort. And there hadn't been more than one or two a day.

In Birmingham they had met real people too, mixed with them. She went to pre-school with the Blair-Booth grand-children. Gordon had sat her on his knee and fondled her a year or so before he died. She had been kissed by dear old Richard Branson. The Hurling lot were a load of dull nonentities in comparison – apart perhaps from Dick Somers, who had at least been famous . . . once. But Evil Trend! Their sound was so tacky compared with, say, Garden Shed.

Delice was all right, though. Delice Cowper. They could have a laugh together.

Nevertheless, she was still young enough to want to tell her mum all about it. The Spanish dancing had been fantastic. And Sophie had picked her way around a guitar enough to know that the woman who had played the one on stage was rather special. And unplugged too!

Since she was certain her mother was in a virtual meeting she felt able to ease open the heavy oak door. It swung easily but with more inertia than one expected until one was used to it. But Sophie was used to doors like that. The reason why they were different was that skins of special glass and metal alloys lay between the wooden panels and obstructed all known eavesdropping devices.

She could see her mother's grey hair, frizzed up slightly in a coiffeur designed to make it look less thin than it was, above the high back of her executive chair, and, on either side of her, segments of the round table beyond. Screens, matt black, about two feet square, all but one blank, formed a circle in front of her, spaced out at the sort of distances that separate the guests at a dinner party. The one that was not blank was filled with the face of a youngish man in combat uniform: black beret, open-neck shirt with a displacement pattern, sporting the single port-cullis on his shoulder strap which designated a major. Somewhat out of keeping, he had a red scarf round his neck and a heavy reddish moustache, well-trimmed but filling the space above his lip.

'Madam, I'm sorry,' he was saying. 'All I can be sure of is that we did a very careful body count. Eight altogether after we had taken down the two that were still alive.'

'There should have been nine.'

Her mother's voice was quiet – it always was, but Sophie recognized the steel in it and knew she was angry.

'I know.' The major was holding his own. His tone admitted things were not as they should be, but insisted it was not his fault.

'There's no possibility one of the bodies was so badly burnt as to be unrecognizable?'

'No, madam.'

Sophie eased the door shut. Normally Mrs Pribendum was not in the least bothered when her daughter saw or heard snippets connected with her duties, but Sophie sensed that this time she might have intruded on something a little too close to the sharp end of her mother's job. When that happened then she too could be made to feel the edge of Mrs Pribendum's wrath. She went up to her bedroom. A tiny light on the console of Mrs Pribendum's study would be winking – indicating that Sophie was back. She'd tell her mum all about her evening when she came up – the dancing and all that, and how she really did like Delice Cowper. And how Delice had said she was sure Dickie, Richard, Somers fancied Sophie. That would be enough. She wouldn't tell her mum that she thought it was true – the way his eyes went a bit gooey when she smiled at him, before he smiled back.

Back in her office Mrs Pribendum switched off the screen she had been talking to, dipped into an old-fashioned soft leather handbag which was on the floor at the side of her chair, pulled out cigarettes and a tiny gold lighter. She was a grey lady, thin; she had had Sophie late and was already into her fifties. Of mixed ethnic stock, she had worked her way through from the cornershop where she was born to a very senior position in a department that came under the Ministry of Social and Internal Security but was more or less autonomous. This made her one of the most powerful people in the land – not because she made decisions, but because she had total access to everything in the government information networks, a position she kept hidden both through the anonymity of her appearance and the electronic passwords, coded entries and the rest that kept all but the most powerful away from her, indeed, unaware of her. The image of a small spider in a large web comes to mind, and should not be rejected for its obviousness.

The cigarettes were mentholated, but, nevertheless, illegal. She did not smoke often – was by no means addicted – but when she was agitated, bothered, even seriously anxious she found that depriving her brain for a few moments of some of the oxygen it required, together with the mildly narcotic effect of the nicotine, calmed her, gave her space in which to regroup her mental forces.

She was a major player in a complicated game. The governance of what was by then the English and dominant member of the Commonwealth of Greater Britain had been in the hands of an unbroken succession of ministries going under different names and involving shifting coalitions and alliances for nearly forty years. In spite of all the apparent changes, there had been continuity and now that continuity was under threat. The New Carer settlement was falling apart. As standards of living for all but the most privileged crumbled, and distribution of welfare became more and more inefficient and haphazard, factions had sprung up everywhere. Broadly speaking, these split more or less along the historic fault line of left and right.

The left, mostly urban, demanded more autonomy for local communities, the power to raise taxes and look after their own. Many of its factions were anarchist in tone and practice.

On the right were all those who felt that only an authoritarian regime could prevent the breakdown of civil society. They called for harsh application of new rules governing the distribution of welfare, enforced and if necessary unpaid labour, repatriation of ethnic minorities and so on. Their mass support came from a rump of post-industrial workers, under-workers and non-workers from the old municipal housing estates on the outskirts of the cities and they were believed to have the support of a small but extremely efficient military with a more or less sane royal as figurehead. This military section called itself the State Law and Order Restoration Council.

For years the government had maintained a precarious and awkward balance between these extremes and kept itself in power through a huge web of electronic surveillance that monitored every aspect of the lives of all but the poorest and most deprived. Censorship and constant indoctrination went hand in hand and in many ways the former was the more important. By denying information at all levels, from weather reports and the cabbage crop to what was happening on a global scale, the populace was encouraged to be content. Things might be bad where you were, but literally down the road things were much better: the media said so. By dividing and isolating communities, by controlling travel and communication, organized dissent had become increasingly difficult at anything above a local level.

These control systems depended on the department of which Mrs Pribendum was the senior civil servant. It was thus the case that she knew better than anyone else in the country just how close to dissolution the whole system was. Inevitably she had found herself wooed by the leaders of both factions. At the same time she had become increasingly certain that radical changes were on the way and that if she was to survive in a position of power she must be seen to have been on the winning side. She could go with the military and the right or she could support the loose coalition of urban anarchist groups; she could continue to throw the weight of her department behind the Birmingham-based New Carer Coalition, hoping that by compromising here, making radical concessions there and clamping down forcefully where necessary, the whole rickety structure could be held together for a few more decades. What she could not be seen to be was uncommitted. But commitment was not something she was prepared to give until she felt sure she knew what the outcome was going to be.

Meanwhile serious unrest in the cities as rival mobs and militias took to the streets was something she knew more about than anyone else – at least to the extent of how widespread such unrest was – and containing that information, keeping it where it belonged, in the hands of the State, was her top priority. Which was why the major whose unit had found the bodies of the napalmed dissidents from Southampton had reported directly to her, as well as to his commanding officer. He need not have done this, but he too knew that this was a time when you needed everyone above you to feel sure you were on their side.

Mrs Pribendum drew on the last of her cigarette and stubbed out the long tip in an ashtray she kept on the floor by her bag – she could not leave it where the cameras that linked her to the rest of the world might pick it up. She was tired, had dealt with maybe a hundred or more similar reports through the day. She wondered if she was taking the hands-on approach too far, was aware that moving from the physical centre of power, though not the virtual centre, had led her somewhat irrationally to keep as much as she possibly could under her personal thumb.

The actual move had raised no overt eyebrows. Heads of other departments had made similar moves over the last few years. Epidemics carried on the ozone-laden smog or water-borne in the mains raged through all the cities, even Birmingham, and it was considered appropriate rather than otherwise for senior functionaries, especially those with children, to move out to self-contained enclaves where there was no smog and the water came from artesian wells. She had gone a little further than the others, most of whom favoured the Welsh Borders, and if anyone thought to wonder whether the proximity of the military, centred as it still was in the Wiltshire Downs, on one side, and of international airports and seaports on the other, had anything to do with her choice, they kept it to themselves.

And, when all was said and done, the move was good for Sophie. The world she had left was enclosed, almost incestuous, filled with tiny rivalries that echoed and were infected by the bigger ones that afflicted parents who did actually meet in the corridors of power. And mixing with perfectly ordinary people in harmless frolics like the Hurling Enclave Players' pantomime would bring her back in touch with reality. Or so thought Mrs Pribendum, whose idea of reality conformed, with the certainty of a convert, to that of the ruling class she had gained entry to.

She gathered together her handbag and shawl, and after checking the security systems were turned on – those that prevented information from getting out as well as hackers or even real burglars from getting in – she made her way to the stairs and Sophie's bedroom. She'd have a chat with her daughter and, while she was at it, question her about Dickie Somers of Evil Trend. He'd had an unblemished record for a decade or more, but in his youth had been something of an anarcho-leftie and rabble-rouser. And, apparently, he had been no better than any other rock icon at keeping his hands off groupies who put themselves his way.

14

Hannah-Rosa stopped by the side of the van and watched her brother, a silhouette against the flares, pick his way across the grass towards the corner where the enclave coaches were parked. A protector, oddly enough pushing a wheelchair, was not far behind him. She recognized the sergeant who had registered their arrival in the car park, the one who had taken more interest in Harem than Harem warranted. Had she seen her giving Richard the diskette? Too bad if she had.

The headlamps of the three coaches that had come from the three different enclaves within Linwood's municipality came on, and she saw them trundle away towards the slip road that would take them back on to the dual-carriageway. She half-raised her hand in a gesture of farewell she knew he would not see. She turned away, feeling sick with emotion and flattened now by the anti-climax the evening had become.

Emma appeared at her elbow.

'He'll be back. He'll work out some way of getting in touch. There were a lot of protectors around.'

'You know, he never said whether or not he liked the show. Typical Rich. Bastard.' Hannah-Rosa forced a laugh through what might have been a sob if she had let it.

'But that was hardly the point, was it?'

It had all been rejigged to get the message across to Richard that she was alive and well and wanted to see him, a plan that had depended on him attending a performance – and as soon as she had known a coach was coming from Hurling Enclave she was just about certain he would.

'I suppose not.' Arm in arm they began to walk slowly back towards the VW camper.

Hannah-Rosa's first objective had been to get the illegal diskette into his possession. A proper reunion might come later, if they both truly wanted it. Her reticence about meeting him had had two separate causes. On the personal, emotional side, she had not known how he would react to her after all these years. She knew he had tried to contact her after their father's death; she had refused to answer because she had indeed held him responsible and at the same time had felt guilty for not flying back from Sydney. She had realized he might blame her just as much as she blamed him and with that between them they might remain hostile, closed off from each other, separated by a barrier of mutual guilt and recrimination.

Time had passed. She had taken work where she could find it once *The Last English King* folded: Japan, the Rim, criss-crossing the Pacific and once at least getting caught up in a civil war. She was hardly ever in England until the late twenties. By then Richard had come back from Miami. She discovered he had opted for enclavist status, which meant, on top of everything else, that the whereabouts of his enclave was classified information. He had withdrawn into a purdah of luxury and wealth from which all but other enclavists were excluded. And she had not liked that: it was not a life-style she envied or aspired to; fifty years of living out the lessons and example her mother, in particular, had given her had led her to reject all manifestations of elitism or privilege and hate all those who enjoyed them.

The protection afforded to enclaves went beyond electrified fences, close surveillance and, when necessary, paramilitary or even military defence. Social contact with the outside world was limited and discouraged – for the sake of the enclavists' peace of mind, it was said, but also to protect them from a real knowledge of what was going on. Thus, while it was possible for a party of enclavists to slum it at an entertainment put on for workers, under-workers and non-workers, it was just about unthinkable, and if not illegal then certainly likely to provoke protector interest and investigation, for any social intercourse to take place before or after a performance.

Meanwhile Emma was determined to be practical.

'There's nothing more you can do about it now. If we really are going to move on tonight then there's work to be done.'

Back in the camper they shed their costumes and took them

to the Range Rover which served as wardrobe. Then they went round the site making sure that the routine of striking the set and the camp was properly underway before collecting the bundle of mini-credits a municipal officer had gathered together at the entrances to the field. They took these back to the camper and, sitting side by side, with the notes between them, began to bundle them into hundreds, securing them with elastic bands.

After ten minutes of this and desultory chat between them, they heard voices raised in what sounded like fear, then running feet. The sliding door in the side of the vehicle was yanked open with a clang. Outside was Kate, her face beneath the cropped hair pale against the darkness, her tired eyes wild.

'Mum, Mum! Come out, please, come quickly!'

Framed in the doorway, her slim but strong body was twisted by a mixture of anxiety and fright.

'Whatever is it? Whatever's the matter?'

'Something . . . someone's turned up. At the back of the road-show truck.'

Hannah-Rosa's pulse quickened and she felt the hairs on the nape of her neck rise.

'Rich? Richard . . . your uncle?'

He'd come back. After all. For a second her heart rose at the thought, before she could question its likelihood.

'No, no, Mum. Nothing like that.' A shrug and a shake of impatience. 'Nothing like that. But you must come.'

Hannah-Rosa stood awkwardly, because there was no real space between the table and the banquette, and grimaced at Emma, who half-smiled back.

'I'll keep an eye on these,' Emma said, meaning the credits.

Hannah-Rosa clambered down on to the grass, smoothing the wraparound skirt she had put on over her long aching thighs. She almost stumbled. She was very tired, sick and heavy with exhaustion after the dancing as well as all the emotional strain. Her daughter took her hand.

'Come o-o-o-on.'

Wanting her to run, which Hannah-Rose refused to do – she felt it would only add to the sudden sense of panic in the air

100

if she did – they half-trotted, half-strode through the gas flares, past the smaller vehicles to the back of the pantechnicon. Four or five of the troupe were still dismantling and loading the seating into Linwood municipal trailers, but that was all. Where were the rest? Hannah-Rosa asked herself, rather grumpily. They were due to leave for Swanage in an hour and the traffic protectors' permit for night travel would expire on them if they weren't on the road by then.

They turned the corner round the rear fender of the huge, high vehicle and there they all were, clustering in a group beneath a gas flare that one of the Gee-Effs held above their heads. They parted to let Hannah-Rosa through. In the midst of them, slumped on one of the slatted fold-up chairs, was what looked at first sight like a half-torched Guy Fawkes' dummy. The flickering light cast shadows over a charred T-shirt whose blackened shreds clung to raw, burnt flesh. The face was burnt, in places to the bone, so teeth and one eye glowed, hugely, whitely, through the mess. The other eye was hidden behind massive blistering. But most of the lower half seemed undamaged, jeans and trainers, both old, the jeans patched. What they were looking had been young, female and black.

Hannah-Rosa hunkered in front of her with the balls of her slippered feet between the wreck's knees. She leant forward. There was breathing still, shallow and fast. There were the smells – burnt flesh, roast in fact, not unlike barbecued pork, mingling with something like car-exhaust but purer. The sort of smell you get from the liquid, volatile fuel used to ignite charcoal. She wanted to help the dying girl but did not know how – to have touched her would surely have added to the pain. Putting her hands on the side of the truck, above the back of the chair, on either side of the head, she brought her lips closer to the less damaged of the girl's ears.

'I love you,' she whispered. 'Truly I do. I will help you. I will do whatever you want. But I do love you.'

Kate, behind her, heard and shivered, stirred by a distant memory of early childhood and toothache.

The figure shifted, the chin came up, the chest heaved, one hand, palm blistered and burnt, clawed upwards, found

Hannah-Rosa's breast, lingered there and dropped. They all heard a sigh; then what tension there had been in the body leaked away.

Hannah-Rosa straightened.

'She's gone,' she said.

Jacques, who had been holding the flare, lowered it a little.

'What happened to her?' he asked.

'Napalm, I've seen it before. And smelt it.'

Beryl, the big red-faced drummer, turned away, out of the group. They could hear her vomiting.

Someone else said, 'There's papers or something in her jeans' pocket.'

The top edges of a wodge of yellow paper stuck an inch or so above the right-hand pocket, held close to her thigh by the material. Hannah-Rosa gently eased it free. There was some charring along the top and some discoloration from heat but it was not difficult to peel the five or so sheets apart. They were all the same, bore the same printed message – like the handouts people were paid pennies to give out on a crowded shopping street.

> Ethnic Cleansing is taking place in Southampton.
> Please help . . . we appeal to you for help.
> Signed:

And there followed a list of names and titles. A vicar, the convener of the Transport and General Workers Union, the convener of Unison, a doctor, a health worker, a headteacher and so on. Many of the names were Asian or African. And last on the list was the mayor of Southampton.

The thunder pounced and the first heavy drops splashed on the paper Hannah-Rosa now held in front of her.

'Oh shit,' she said, and raised her tired face to the rain. 'What do we do now?'

15

With sheet lightning streaking the north horizon beneath black stacked cloud Richard had walked up his drive, past his sculptures, whispered the mantra that would open his door and walked through. Lights glowed in the hall as he entered their ambience and went ahead of him into the orangery. He put the disk down on the rim of the console and looked at it. Excitement, foreboding and above all frustration racketed around his head. He clenched his fists, chewed the knuckles of his right hand. He knew he didn't have an IBM-compatible PC. Not here. Not in the roof space three stories up, not in the garages beneath the cool-pool at the other end of the house.

The old machines were history. Their demise had been as inevitable as that of the dinosaurs. First – 31 December 1999. In spite of all the publicity, all the advice and offers, the cowboy firms who said they had the chip that would cope with the figure twenty, an awful lot of people had said, 'Oh, it'll be all right, you'll see.'

And one way and another that had been the case. The consequence was that most people got away with it. The sales of blank mini CDs and, for larger capacity, DEEP CDs and the machines to play them on, had not been anything like as huge as had been expected. But a year or so later Microsoft made the greatest gamble in their history and offered everyone in the world who had an old machine and diskettes a mini-CD-ROM-DEEP computer so long as they handed in their diskettes and IBM compatibles. One for One, New Lamps for Old. Forgetting perhaps that in the old story Abanazar was the wicked wizard and Aladdin the hero.

Which left Richard looking at a bit of plastic which might contain the last testament of a voice, or rather the transcript of a voice, from beyond the grave, a voice which still echoed down the dark corridors of dreams. Already it had taken on a talismanic significance – an aura almost. Through tears he took in the neat, fine-point biro capitals: TRAGECTORIES. The G, he knew, was soft – as in 'tragedy'. The first T was larger than the rest, the tails of the Rs curved under the following letters. It all showed an awareness of classical Roman alphabets deriving, as all good lettering should, from Trajan's Column in Rome. That much he had learnt at art college during his foundation year, and then of course he had discovered it was all something his dad had been very well aware of.

Dad had also known how to spell 'trajectory'.

He sat down on his self-adjusting chair, leant forward and felt a tiny prick of irritation as the chair responded. He dimmed the lights to a glow that seemed to emanate from where he sat and left the rest of the room in darkness. The big dead screens breathed out their own blackness from their non-reflective surfaces.

There were so many questions to ask, so much to remember: not just his father but his sister too. He had not seen or spoken to her for twenty-nine years. She had seemed so much the same and yet so different. He felt again the clasp of her long fingers, the roughness of her palms, the familiarity of an embrace, which, even after all this time, had been so much closer in its untroubled warmth than that of any sexual encounter.

He tried to remember her as she had been: tall, thin, serious, impossibly graceful, very beautiful. There had been no sibling rivalry between them. Her mother was her role-model, though it was her father she loved with a deep, aching love, always aware that he would almost inevitably die while she was still quite young and not properly ready for it. Thomas had been eighteen years older than Katherine.

From her mother, whom she loved as much but differently, she had learnt to take things seriously. Neither Thomas nor Richard ever quite did: both maintained an ironical stance to the world around them; were apt to embrace sudden enthusiasms they were not unprepared to drop; were careless about and uninterested in detail or minutiae. Thomas often said that his favourite last words were those of Lady Mary Montague, an eighteenth-century traveller: 'It's all been very interesting.'

Katherine, and Hannah-Rosa after her, shared a deeper compassion, were strongly passionate about the things they loved and hated. Neither, however, lacked a sense of humour, indeed their very readiness to commit themselves made them far more likely to have a good laugh than either of the males.

Of course she had been a pain at times – teasing, mocking even – but they had never seriously quarrelled. Not even over their dad, since after his death she had cut herself off from him, never allowed herself to be near enough to quarrel. He'd written to her, tried to speak to her on the phone, kept track of her as well as he could, but was always aware that through the years of his mega-fame he was far more easily traceable for her than she was for him. And by 2020, with the world of easy travel and cheap communication closing down around them, he had completely lost track of her.

And now what was she, what had she become? Not a prima ballerina *assoluta*. Not a world-renowned creator of the greatest modern dance company in the world. Well, why should she? Richard provided the answer to his own question. Because if she had, she would probably have added more to the sum of human happiness than any of those of her contemporaries who had reached such heights. And, unless she had changed a lot over the years, if this had been put to her she would have shrugged her shoulders without much expression, dismissing the hypothesis with the mild contempt it deserved.

And anyway, she could still dance. Goodness, how she could dance. He remembered the snaking arms, the stamping feet, the simulated petulance and passion, the pride and the lust, above all the meticulous quality of her technique. In all this she matched the composer whose music she danced to. De Falla had been a deeply serious person, a devout Catholic, an ascetic in every detail of his life, yet had produced the most mischievously passionate music in the classical canon.

It had not been the sort of performance you expect from a troupe of travelling performers.

And now they were off. To Swanage, she had said. He remembered Swanage. After GCSEs he had cycled there with friends to camp, drink lager and swim. Amusement arcades. Fishing boats. Cliffs and sand.

They'd be packing up right now. On the road, he remembered, it was best to strike the set as soon as a booking had been completed; move on immediately while they were on a high, rather than wake up in the morning to hangovers and the knowledge they had to be gone by twelve, on the next site by four, ready to perform by seven-thirty. He knew all about that, about roadies desperate to tear the set apart, get it all lorried up and on the move while venue managers with a new act coming in the next day snapped at their heels.

He rubbed his face with his hands. He realized he was looking at the whole situation from the wrong way round and he went over it again. However much he might want to make contact with Hannah-Rosa, it was not what she wanted. Or at any rate it was not her top priority: that was clearly the diskette, *Tragectories*. She wanted him to read *Tragectories*, and, in modern, up-to-date terms, make a full-length spec out of it.

He had in fact read some of the print-out before it went to the publisher, thirty-seven years earlier. He had never found it easy to read his father's work. There was a gamut of reasons for this: lack of time, exams and so forth; and then the whole accelerating hurly-burly of being part of a rock group; through the irritating discovery that he wasn't all that keen on what his dad wrote anyway; and maybe deeper psychological reasons. Writers, he knew, for he wrote his own lyrics, draw on, reveal but also grossly distort their deepest longings, aspirations and deprivations, and who wants to know all that about someone as ambivalently close to one as a loving father?

Nevertheless. Hannah-Rosa wanted him to read it. Why? Why now? It must have been in her possession ever since Dad finished it back in 2001. But no. Hang on. If it had been, she would have had it transferred to a mini CD blank. It must be that she had only just got hold of it, or quite recently, anyway, and she had no means, any more than he did, of reading it, but obviously she hoped he might have. Indeed she had presumed he would have.

But he didn't.

And why the reticence, the one, brief but planned meeting set up in circumstances where it would have to be a short one? She was not yet ready for a prolonged reunion, a confrontation? Well, he could understand that – he wasn't sure he was either, not unprepared, out of the blue. But also because it was illegal to be in possession of any unchecked, uncensored source of information . . . If a protector, and there had been many about, had seen the diskette he or she would have been duty bound to expropriate it pending vetting, and, considering its length, that could be goodbye for several months if not years. It could even be censored, whole or in part. Indeed, remembering Dad, and the sort of anarchist tendencies that informed most of his work, that was more than likely.

And suddenly he went cold. On that damned bus, coming back to Hurling, he'd asked that fart Frederick if he had an old PC. Frederick was an interfering gossip – he would have told everyone, the whole coachload. Including Damien Floyd, who was not only a potential enemy, but sub-regional sub-controller too. Fuck.

He pulled himself together, leant back in the chair, pushed that last fear out of his mind and tried to recap. Hannah-Rosa had got hold of the diskette very recently. She had no access to an IBM compatible. She thought he did, so where do we go from here?

Where had she got it from?

There was only one possible answer.

Orchard Cottage, Thorney Hill, of course, you moron! From Dad's workroom? And if the house was still in such a state that a diskette could be salvaged from it, what else? The portable Amstrad laptop, ALT 286, Dad had worked on since . . . well, Richard could not remember anything else, anything that might have come before it. Though there had been a hand-powered machine left in a corner of the room his mother used as an office . . .

In the summer of 2006 his mother had spoken to him on the phone. Evil Trend was in Seattle at the time, the second New World Tour – the misty quays, the docks, the skyscrapers, the smell of fish and diesel, the themed Nirvana boutiques, the

Hendrix shrine built with Microsoft money, the sun a red ball seen through smog above the gently heaving, oily Pacific, the grubby rogue icebergs liberated by global warming.

She had said she couldn't sell Orchard Cottage for a reasonable price and had decided not to. She could manage without the money and it would always be there for any of the three of them to come back to if they wanted or needed it. Meanwhile, she'd keep a key herself and in case he had lost his (he had) Sharon Dell had agreed to hold a spare one and keep an eye on it for them.

Well. It was a guess. Maybe a good one, maybe not, but tomorrow he'd take steps to get there. The decision made, he at last felt easy with himself again, relaxed, almost euphoric. He slipped the disk back into his jacket pocket, closed down the orangery, and wandered slowly through his domain, climbed the stairs to his bedroom. There he took a pre-rolled spliff from an old thermidor, lit it and let himself out on to the balcony. This, Gaudíesque as it was, ran the length of the first floor, looping in and out the serpentine contour of the façade.

The storm had receded, circling round to the west, behind the house. There were still occasional rumbles and he could detect reflections of sheet lightning, but in front of him the moon was visible, into its third quarter and very bright, with Mars below its left-hand edge. Beneath it the tree-clad hills rolled away beyond his lawns with their sculptures and cedars. Here and there a roof showed, or a lit window. It was very peaceful and pleasant and, apart from the changes in the species of trees that grew there, very much the same as it had been for ... centuries, he supposed. A miracle of sorts, considering all that had happened everywhere else.

He pulled in the smoke so the red ash glowed in front of his eyes, leaving a brilliant acid-green after-image which expanded and contracted. He held it, let it go. It was a strange euphoria that flooded through him; he felt light-headed but irritated too; it deepened, became Jove-like both in joy and anger. He realized he had had enough. He had been here too long, been safe too long, done nothing for far too long.

He thought of them all snug, safe, rich, in their cosy houses and wondered at himself for putting up with them. Even fifty years ago it had been obscene – starvation, plague, war had stalked the Balkans, Africa, the Middle East, the old USSR. Was it more obscene now, when most of those things prowled just outside the wire like sewer monsters? Not war, not yet, but the only reason for that was the ruthless, all-pervading State control that watched and monitored everything . . . Not war? That was how brainwashed they all were, brain-dead even, to say there was no war when two black jets had arrowed out of the sky to napalm dissidents in woods a bare five miles from where he was now.

This was the sort of thing he used to sing about and he felt a wave of disgust at the thought. What the fuck had been the use of singing? But then, and it was what was left of his dad in him that made him say it, what the fuck would have been the use of dying on the barricades instead?

Well. Whatever. He wasn't after all about to change the world, any more than he ever had been, but at least no more would he stew in the ugly spiritual slough of lust, booze, drugs and bickering, and above all mindless pretension, that was Hurling Enclave. At the very least, and in the words of the old Ian Dury song that had been a favourite of his dad's, he'd break a few rules.

He chucked the spliff over the balcony. Maryjane had lost a lot of her power since legalization. He'd think of something. That trip to Thorney Hill for starters. Meanwhile he'd have a swim.

He went back inside, along the corridors, out on to the deck inside the cube, stripped off, climbed the steps and slid into the water. With nightfall the air temperature had dropped and the water felt warm. He spread his arms and his legs, so he was in the posture of Leonardo's perfect man, the square in the circle, but on his back, spread-eagled, very slowly turning with the turn of the earth, the Little Dipper and the Pole Star swaying directly above him. After ten minutes or so, lulled as he was, as if in the womb of Gaia, the sky changed. The reflected moonlight faded, the thunder rumbled nearer and presently big drops of warm rain thudded into the pool around him, throwing up tight little splashes of incandescent water. They bounced on his torso and stomach too, even on his face and genitals, and he felt a slow warming fill his body and his soul, a merging with water and night sky.

Yes, he said to himself, yes. He'd break a few rules.

He winked at the sky, and imagined, or felt, or knew, that out in the darkness above, beyond the lightning-backed silhouettes of the clouds, his dad winked back. Maybe.

16

Five lines in the *Sun* beneath the headline STORM-DAMAGED M-ARTY-R DIES FOR FARTY ART and no obituary in *The Times*. 10 February 2006, seven months off his seventy-first birthday. He'd told them he'd live to be seventy-two and they had believed him.

Hannah-Rosa had rung Richard up two days before from Sydney where she was walking-on as a singing, dancing Anglo-Saxon peasant in the Australian production of *Harold, the Last English King*.

'How's Dad?'

'He's been there a week now, and he's on hunger-strike too.'

'You've got to go and see him. Talk him out of it.'

'I've already tried.'

'Try again.'

'I will. But it won't make any difference.'

'It might.'

'It won't. He's a stubborn old fool and you know it.'

'You've got to try.'

Nearly thirty years ago. The last time he had spoken to her.

They, Evil Trend, had been up at Pinewood making the video for the third album – *Lonely Rock In Space*, the one that was going to take them away, up and away, to mega-star status, beyond Brit-Pop to the stratosphere where even in 2006 names like Dire Straits, the Velvet Underground, Queen and Led Zeppelin still orbited above such Johnny-come-latelies as Oasis, Pulp, Blur and Verve.

Studio time, including technicians, sound engineers and the rest, was astronomically expensive, with the hire of everyone with a creative input, from set design to make-up, on top. The band, the manager, the roadies, the record company, none of them could tolerate the idea of Richard swanning down to Southwark to talk to his dad for an hour, let alone a day, a week – however long it took for an old man to die of exposure and starvation – during working hours. So instead of going back to the Hyde Park Hotel each night or going up West with the rest of the gang and doing over the restaurants and clubs, or partying with sycophantic 'friends', journos, whoever thought they could make a bob or two out of the Trend, he went and spent a few hours every night talking to his dad. Inevitably Evil Trend was by now generally known as the Trend, just as the Rolling Stones became the Stones. And fans, not just groupies, called themselves Trendies.

Thursday it began to rain. Just a drizzle at first with some sleet in it before settling in, sometimes a heavy monsoon-like downpour, sometimes less – but from then on it rained, right through to the following Wednesday.

The headlights of the limo picked Dad out through the sweeping silver chiffon. From the leathery warmth inside, with the lights and the wet pavements, it looked as unreal and as attractive as an arty shot in a nineties TV serial – say about sahf London gangsters: the huddled figure propped like a doll against the two feet of brick wall and the brutalist square railings, just ten yards along the street from the surveilled, locked and alarmed double gates.

The big car idled up to the pavement but the gutters were already full and the wheels rolled a small wave of muddy oily water across the flagstones and on to the trailing hem of the doll's mackintosh. Richard slid out of the passenger door, let it clunk behind him. The car purred away. Back in four hours was the arrangement. The man on the ground lifted his head as far as he was able – Houdini-like, he was chained to the railings and some of the chains clicked metallically though most merely tightened their hold on his limbs, torso and neck.

'Rich? Glad you could make it. Nice of you to drop by. Pull up a pew.'

Over the last decade or so Thomas had lapsed more and more into the idioms and catch-phrases of his parents – middle-class in origin, déclassé later – much of it dating from his father's few but critical years in the RAF during World War II. Richard's paternal grandfather that is. Thomas had also always, but far more noticeably in the recent past, maintained an ironic distance from his son, approving, encouraging, yes, but always observing, seemingly detached. Perhaps another thing he had carried over from his own father's generation was an ability to love confounded by a reticence in its expression. Anyway, it wasn't always easy being the father of a multi-millionaire rock icon.

'So, what's new in the great world? Who's in? Who's out?'

His voice rasped, fluids rattled in his throat and probably lower, in his trachea and lungs. He was wearing the white raincoat he had bought in a supermarket sale in Majorca back in ninety-seven and a felt trilby given to him by a German feminist crime writer whose books he had reviewed enthusiastically three years before that. The raincoat was the full thing, belted, collared, caped and strapped. Taken with the hat, if he had been able to stand up and all had been in good condition, he would have looked like Philip Marlowe in a film noir of the fifties. But in fact he was a sodden wreck, the hat beginning to lose its shape, the raincoat bulging with the extra clothes he had on underneath and the water that was soaking in wherever it could.

He took these visits from Richard in much the way a terminal patient accepts visitors in a hospice or hospital – determined, for the sake of the visitor, to show an interest in the world and its doings which was entirely spurious since he was on the point of leaving it.

'Nothing, Dad, has changed a lot in the last twenty hours or so. Just rain. Flood warnings and so on.'

'But the world turns, it still turns.'

'I suppose so. Else we'd all fall off.'

'Is that really so, Rich? I'm not sure that's so.'

But Richard was not about to get into an uninformed argument about centrifugal force, centripetal force and gravity.

'Dad. It's raining, you're cold and wet and I will be in five minutes. Tell me where the key is and we'll go to a pub, have something hot to eat, and then you can come back to the hotel.'

Though he doubted the Hyde Park would let his dad in, in the state he was, not even for the lead singer of Evil Trend.

'Nope!'

The chains were tungsten steel, the padlock state of the art, and once he'd snapped it shut Thomas Somers had tossed the key through the grate of the drain in front of him, a drain that was now overflowing, bubbling up a noxious mix of sewage, rainwater and possibly tidal water from the rising Thames. He'd hidden the second key in a luggage locker at Waterloo with a six-button electronic number pad – they'd been installed a month after the Boston Accords were signed and the danger of bombs being left in them had almost completely receded. Only he knew the number of the locker and the number of the lock.

Richard pulled the belt of his butter-coloured kidskin coat tighter, turned up the huge wings of the collar. He'd always been a dressy lad, spending a large chunk of his first earnings as a kitchen worker in a pub, just ten years earlier, on a deep-blue velvet suit.

'The rain will ruin that leather thing you're wearing.'

'No, it won't. It's been proofed.'

He wasn't at all sure this was so, but he wasn't going to let his dad score off him that easily.

'So. How's your mum?'

'OK, I suppose. Worried sick about you, naturally. I was on the phone to her before I came out. She says you ought to think a bit more about all of us, and how we love you, and a bit less about . . .' His voice faded.

'About what?'

'Making a fool of yourself.' He hurried on, 'Says she'll give up the Brussels idea if that's what you want.'

'She knows jolly well that's not what I want at all. And Hannah-Rosa?'

'She too. In a terrible state. Rang up from Sydney.'

'All the way from Sydney. Goodness!'

'She's about to pack in the job and fly back.'

'She'd bloody better not. I'll never speak to her again if she does. And it won't do a bit of good.'

'I know. That's what I told her. I also said that you'll either be off those railings by the time she gets here—'

But Thomas had burst into a prolonged fit of heavy, agonizing coughing. Agonizing to Richard, anyway. It ended with a great gob of sputum, most of which reached the pavement, though some stayed on the front of his coat. In the rainy streetlight it was impossible to say whether or not there was blood.

'My right lung's quate gawn,' he whispered. Then managing a shout, 'But m' left one's a stunner!'

' —or dead,' Richard concluded.

Thomas lifted his head as far as the chains would let him.

'"You only know you're in chains when you feel them." Rosa Luxemburg. We called Hannah Hannah-Rosa after her.' He mumbled and fidgeted a little, then came out with it. 'Is anyone taking any notice at all?'

'No. Not a blind bit.' Richard added brutally, 'Why should they?'

All that could be done had already been done. Letters to *The Times*. A full page advert in all the posh broadsheets signed by a hundred and fifty famous arties, including all of Evil Trend except the bass guitarist, who was a bit of a fascist but a good bassist. And on the Sunday a demo where they were now – outside the New Tate. Richard had been there. The director had come out on to the steps and made a statement: he totally agreed with everyone there, charges for entry were all wrong, probably illegal, but since the demise of the Arts Council, and the end of Arts Council grants, there was nothing else for it. The real trouble, which he made no reference to, was that a major sponsor had pulled out three months earlier when the New Tate awarded the Turner for an extremely accurate mock-up, blood, bodily fluids and all, of the crashed Mercedes Diana, Princess of Wales, had died in just over eight years earlier. They then bought it and installed it as part of the permanent exhibition.

Nevertheless, and as a result of the protests, Art Minister Jackson had said on Monday that maybe a special subsidy could be found. On Tuesday the *Sun* demanded her immediate resignation and she back-pedalled. LET THE FARTIES PAY IF THEY WANT TO – WHY SHOULD WE? had been the leader headline.

And on Tuesday night Thomas Somers moved in, chained himself to the railings and stayed there. He'd spent a lot of money on the chains, and a lot of thought and care on how he had wrapped himself up in them. On Wednesday the experts the police had called in said they couldn't cut the chains without harming him, and the original contractors who had converted the old Bankside power station into the New Tate Gallery made the point that they had been commissioned to make the rails and wall the outer defences of an impregnable fortress.

For a day or two Thomas attracted some attention. Asked if he was an art lover he said no, he was a people lover and art was for people. All people. And should always be free – both of any sort of censorship and any sort of charge or levy on those who wanted to enhance their lives by experiencing it. This was something the journos could not understand so they decided he was an art lover and, considering the art he loved, a pretty damned weird one at that. The last straw for them was that Thomas refused to say who he was: he would not even give his name. Who he was was entirely irrelevant, he said. He could be Archbishop of Canterbury, chairman of Saintroses or a common or garden dosser, it made no difference. Since by then, after three days, he looked exactly like a common or garden dosser, and there was a difference as far as the media were concerned, they forgot about him.

He was, he said, on hunger strike, not because he wanted to die sooner – in fact the longer he was alive the better, the more likely it was his protest would succeed – but because he didn't want to shit himself too much, and he guessed that that would cease to be a problem after a time if he didn't eat. He had had a catheter attached whose outlet ran into the now flooding drain, and he took whatever liquids, though in moderation, well-wishers cared to bring him. No alcohol though. Ten years earlier alcohol had damn near killed him.

Richard, on his first visit, had said he would tell the media that Thomas was his father. Thomas had been firm and Dad-like – as firm as he had ever been. 'It won't do me or why I'm here any good at all, and it will do you a lot of harm.'

'Why? How?'

'Oh come on! "Pop idol stands by while Dad dies in chains?" Don't do it, Richard. Please. Just don't even think of it!'

Now Richard hunkered down over his dad. Water dripped from the brim of the hat and from the end of his nose into grey stubble. He was hollow-cheeked and his eyes were bright. His fingers shook. He did indeed for all the world look like an alkie dosser on the way out.

'Dad, you must be in pain.'

'The occasional twinge, yes.' He began to cough again but controlled it, held it in. Then, in reference to a very old joke that *his* father had been fond of, he wheezed on, 'I only do it, you know, because it will be so lovely when it stops.'

Richard struggled for a moment with a rising wave of pain as intense as any Thomas was suffering, even if it was mostly psychic. It transmuted into anger, fury, rage, but he overrode them too. In fact both men were being terribly British about it all, refusing to become overtly emotional. He straightened, looked down at the bundle beneath him, forced a nonchalant-sounding laugh.

'You look like something by Christo.'

'Yes. I thought of that. All wrapped up and nowhere to go. I took my harp to the party but no one asked me to play. Not as big as the Reichstag but bigger than the one they've got in there.' He jerked his head at the building behind him. 'Maybe when I've gone they'll put me in there too. Hirst can pickle me.'

'He doesn't do that any more.'

'Well, maybe he'll change his mind. All in a good cause, eh?'

'Dad, you're not going to last a lot longer.'

'Thought had crossed my mind.'

'Well, what are you going to do about it?'

'Not a lot.'

The anger began to simmer again.

'Sorry to go over it all but just what do you think you're up to? Killing yourself in the hope a few poor people will be able to look at some art they won't understand and probably not even like?'

'Don't patronize. How many times did you go to the old Tate when you had hardly two pennies to rub together?'

117

'There are going to be concessions. For students, unwaged and pensioners.'

'Fuck concessions.'

'It's a lost cause. And even if it isn't, is it worth dying for?'

'You could build hecatombs, mountains, with the bodies of those who have died for less. Think of the Christian martyrs for a start. Then all the martyrs the Christians racked, hanged, quartered and burnt. And that's just the foothills.'

'For less? You're an arrogant old bugger, you know. Listen. When you chained yourself up here you thought it would work – else you wouldn't have done it. Lord knows why you thought anyone would give a toss for an old tramp who refused to say who he was. But you thought they would. And they're not going to. So let's pack it in and go home.'

The rain thickened from stair-rods into something that seemed almost solid. It swirled across the paving stones, met the rising water from the drain, blotted visibility down to fifty yards through which the street lamps glowed meaninglessly, shedding almost no light beyond their penumbra. It was noisy too, a continuous hiss and clatter backed by rumbling thunder and the distant wail of emergency vehicles. Richard knelt, put his face as near as he could to his father's, strove to elicit and hear an answer. He glanced down.

'You're wearing my old Wrangler boots.'

'Mine.'

'Yours.'

Somewhere between them laughter hovered. Ten years earlier they had together bought two pairs, black and brown. The black had been Richard's, but he quickly wore them to destruction and then took to wearing the brown ones. Then he got a car, an old Polo, and found he couldn't drive in the boots comfortably so they had drifted back to Thomas's wardrobe. And Thomas wore them only when he went for a walk on the heath round Thorney Hill – which he did about twice a year. Richard put his hands on his father's, partly prompted by the immense sense of loss – of a happy past the memory had sparked off – partly because he could not bear the shake, which seemed worse than ever.

'All right. So you're going to stay here and die. Any last messages? Famous last words?'

A croaky whisper. He moved his ear closer to the old man's mouth.

'Aquatic ape,' he heard. 'At least I'm dying like an aquatic ape.'

A wave of irritation. This was Thomas's obsession with the theory that *Homo sapiens* was originally an aquatic ape, which had possessed him for the last ten years and which had probably got in the way of any serious development as a writer he might have made. Articles, short stories, TV and film treatments, almost none of them published or used, had flowed from it, culminating in a thousand pages of unclassifiable prose, poetry, screen-script, fact, fiction, faction and theorizing which he apparently believed was yet a work of art as consistent and whole as, say, *Ulysses*, or anyway *Gravity's Rainbow*. It had been a mission as well as an obsession. He truly believed that if the human race could come to the understanding of itself acceptance of the theory would bring, then maybe it would take the right steps to save itself. But meanwhile the voice croaked on.

'Kindness and Art, Richard. Kindness and Art. Remember?'

He remembered. He had heard that all before too. Kindness was Anglo-Saxon. *Kynde*. Kin. Nature benevolent and giving, not the *natura* of the Romans that had to be pushed back with Virgil's fork. And Art was creativity, the human soul ranging freely, explaining, exalting, exhilarating, not dominated by technique, the human mind untrammelled. Art included scientific thought too – so long as it was original and strove to be true to itself, not just a means to power or wealth, reputation and self-serving.

'You're serious, aren't you? You really are looking for famous last words.'

'It's what you asked for.' A touch grumpy now. 'I'm trusting you to remember them.'

They stayed huddled as they were for twenty minutes or so without speaking. The rain poured from the rim of Thomas's hat, making it look like a weird version of an Australian wideawake. The high collar of Richard's coat acted like a funnel, so water slid in a continuous stream into clothes which now clung coldly to the skin beneath. Although it was cold, it was not as cold as February had been when Thomas was Richard's age. At last Richard felt pressure returned on his hand.

'I'd die for a cuppa, Rich.'

'Oh shit, of course you would. I'm so sorry.' The night before Thomas had asked him to bring a flask – but he had forgotten all about it.

'Not too much milk and no sugar.'

Diabetic to the very end. Richard stood up, felt the water slip down inside. Tea? Where? He associated cups of tea at night with railway stations. Blackfriars and Cannon Street were commuter stations and surely closed by eleven o'clock. Waterloo, then, maybe ten minutes walk, twenty there and back, but worth a try. And possibly he'd get one of those polystyrene cups with a lid you could clamp on.

'I'll find you one. Give me twenty minutes. Don't go away.'

And in a very real way, he never had.

Head down, he pushed across Blackfriars Road, resisted the temptation to go north of the river, and fought his way on through the rain up Stamford Street with the water often over his ankles and filling his Drakon cordoban loafers, flattening his baggy chinos with their tight cuffs. The leather coat now seemed heavy, less supple, and slapped against his knees. The old man, he thought, had probably been right about that.

A cuppa. He remembered how pleased his dad had always been when, as a teenager, Richard had brought him a cuppa in the morning. Normally Dad got up and made the tea. He always said it was the greatest gift his son could give him – a cuppa in bed. Greater love hath no man than this: that a man bring a morning cuppa to his friend in his bed, was how he put it.

As he reached the ring in front of Waterloo four fire engines, preceded by a police car, came roaring out of the rain from across Waterloo Bridge, blue lights flashing, sirens screaming and wailing. There can't, there cannot be a fire anywhere tonight, he thought. The last four steps of the subway were under water and the bullring in front of him, and the tunnels beneath the development above what had once been Cardboard City were waist-deep. He stumbled back up to street level, climbed over the railings and made it at last on to the concourse of the station. It did not have the brightness he had expected but was shadowy with emergency lighting. Limbo. A waiting area. Very few people were about – lost souls they seemed, staring at closed barriers and improvised notices: *Due to weather alert all services have been temporarily disbanded*.

Even the pinpoints of light on the number pads of the lockers were out – so presumably he would not have been able to get the second key even if he had known the number. There was, however, a small queue in front of the one coffee and snack stall that had remained open. He took his turn and got precisely what he wanted – a half-pint of hot tea in a sealed cup which still burnt his hands. He looked at his watch – already he had been as long as he had said he would be.

He hurried back to the glass doors, pushed through them and tried to run down the semi-circular steps in front of the Waterloo Arch. He slipped. The base of his spine smacked down three of the steps before he came to rest, sodden, jarred and with scalded fingers where they had clenched involuntarily and hard enough to crush the polystyrene. He considered weeping. He went back on to the concourse but the stall had closed, the Afro who had been serving putting the last of the shutters into place. 'Sorry, mate, hot water failed – no electric, see?'

This time it wasn't fire engines crossing Waterloo Bridge, but army lorries filled with sandbags.

They stopped him halfway back down Stamford Street. There were barriers, police, soldiers, and beyond them fire engines pumping water out not in, and human chains passing sandbags up through the rain to a rising wall he could just make out a hundred yards away. They wouldn't let him through. He argued and they paid no attention. The river's rising, they said. It won't top the walls above the embankments but it's coming up through all the drains. He pushed and they grappled him back, told him to go home. He said his father was up there in front of the New Tate. The what? The old power station. There's no one up there. We checked. He didn't believe them. He tried walking round the barrier using side streets but two soldiers picked him up again and brought him back. There's a curfew, see? Why? It's dangerous. There could be subsidence. You could get in the way of the emergency services. Some of the plant they're using is heavy. There could be looting. That was more like it. Looting of warehouses, looting of the expensive specialist shops that had sprung up in the area. Looting even from the New Tate. He laughed hysterically at the thought of international art thieves trying to carry off that fucking wrecked Mercedes or a pickled cow. Given the chance he himself would have nicked one of the Lichtensteins or a Hockney. Match the ones he'd already bought.

Towards dawn the rain stopped, the tide turned, and the water began to drain away. The smell was awful. He remembered Majorca ten, nine years earlier. A tiny hired car. And whenever they passed the sewage works on the way into Palma the others, Mum, Dad and Hannah-Rosa, had always said, 'It's Rich. He's farted again.' It was like that, only worse. There was a thick yellowish brown slime over the paving stones with panty-pads and used condoms in it and shreds of toilet paper.

Thomas hadn't moved. Of course not. And you could see why no one had bothered. A little heap of old clothes attached to the railings. Anyway, he was dead.

Richard ran and slithered the last fifty yards or so and scooped him up like a rag-doll, holding him in his arms so Thomas's head was on his shoulder. The hat at last came off and tumbled down his back. And the chains fell away.

The fucking chains fell away.

They had looked like escapology chains and they were. Pull them most ways they tightened or anyway held fast. But pull them just one way, in the right sequence, and they came apart. Bastard. Fucking bastard.

And his last immortal words?

'I'd die for a cuppa . . .'

Well, he bloody had.

*　　*　　*

122

Nationally speaking it was not quite the disaster it had been for Richard. Although the sea had got round the ends of the Thames barrier and far more water had come down the Thames than anyone had thought possible, the only serious damage was underground. Everyone knew the defences would have to be improved but there was enough disagreement about how and the expense involved for delays to occur. Not enough was done to prevent the far more serious catastrophe that came three and half years later, when Westminster was wiped out in the three-day triple hurricane.

Meanwhile, work on the *Lonely Rock* album was held up for a week, long enough for Richard to get himself together and write the hit 'Storm-Tossed'. All profits from the single to the Flood Victims Aid Appeal.

No one official bothered much about Thomas. It was a busy time and he was not the only fatality. Katherine, his wife, Richard's mother, heard Richard's more or less accurate version of what had happened and declared that a) Thomas had had a good life, done most of the things he wanted, and that b) Richard had done all he reasonably could. She mourned him sincerely, grievously, but remained practical. She went back to Brussels after the funeral where, as planned, she merged her business with a colleague's and called it Euro-Language Link.

Hannah-Rosa was less forgiving. She had not heard enough of the story to stop her from believing that Richard's efforts to save their dad had not been compromised by his need to make *Lonely Rock* the success it was.

Indeed, it was a question he never satisfactorily answered for himself.

PART II

17

'What are we going to do with her?' asked Kate.

'Is there a problem?' Jacques replied, still in his Andalusian gear of tight high-waisted pants and white shirt. 'Surely we call in the protectors.'

The napalmed cadaver of a young black woman had become, with her death, just that – a problem.

Hannah-Rosa rose from her knees in front of the dead body and, under the gas flare, looked round at the chiaroscuroed faces of most of her troupe.

'Does anyone know where she came from?'

Ameena, the more dominant of the Asiatic twins who played clarinet as well as dancing, looked up from one of the yellow handouts they had taken from the black girl's jean pocket. She looked anxious, almost fearful, shook her head as if to dispel whatever was worrying her.

'I think she came across the carriageway. But further up. At any rate she came across the field from that side.' She gestured towards the north-east, to the right of the sub-enclave where the 'Social' lived, into a now almost deserted and derelict suburb called Powlner. Beyond it lay the forest.

'Shit man, those two Super Stealths. F135s. They went over half an hour before we went up,' growled Jason, the strong man of the gee-eff blacks. He played trumpet, not too well, did fire-eating and some juggling, and the heavy work involved in setting and striking the stage. 'There were a couple of bumps too. I reckoned sound barrier, maybe even thunder. But now I reckon . . . maybe . . . know what I mean?'

He looked down at the napalmed wreck.

'So . . .' he concluded, 'call in the protectors. Their job.'

A few nodded. One or two turned away slowly, shocked, but ready to get back to work.

'I think not,' said Hannah-Rosa. Hearing the steely note in

her voice, they turned back; the others looked across at her.

'What you on about, man?'

'Kate heard a rumour earlier this afternoon that there were urbanites on the move up in the woods. If this woman was one of them, then they got napalmed. Those papers tell us where she was coming from and why. I mean, if they tell the truth, you can see why she and her companions had to be exterminated . . .'

She was thinking aloud, not quite sure where she was going.

'So. If we go to the protectors they'll know we know something of what is going on. Even if we hide or destroy the papers they'll expect us to add to the rumours that are already going around . . .' Her voice tailed away.

'So what, Ms Daytona, are you proposing we should do?' Jacques' voice was sour.

'At the very least if we call in the protectors we are going to be detained and we'll lose our licence to travel tonight. That will have to be reapplied for, which could take three days, by when our licence to perform in Swanage will be out of date. And so on. Knock-on effect. And that's the best scenario. We could be quarantined.'

Knowing what you were not entitled to know was treated by the authorities as an infectious or galloping disease – which, indeed, within the body politic it always has been. Hannah-Rosa felt a presence at her shoulder. Emma had arrived from counting the credits in their camper and had been standing at the back of the group.

'She's right. And if we miss Swanage we could be in a mess. Financially. We didn't do too well here until tonight. If we're going to get to Plymouth for the St Malo banana boat we really can't afford to lose time or credits.'

Silence, apart from the hiss of the gas flares.

'OK. I ask again what you are proposing.' Jacques' *langue d'oc* accent was becoming more pronounced as he became more agitated.

Hannah-Rosa drew breath, clenched her fists by her side and, head-up, closed the discussion with what were in effect orders.

'Wrap her in a sheet or something. Put her on the floor of one of the vans. Finish clearing up and get on the road. We'll have to fill up quite soon. There's a station just past the Ashley Heath roundabout. If we can do it without being spotted, we'll get her into some wasteland or forest while we're filling, and bury her. Push on to Swanage.'

She took one more look at the corpse, bit her lip, sighed, turned away. There was heaviness, a sort of sorrow, but no one could avoid realizing that what they had, propped on the chair in front of them, was now a hideous sight, no matter what she might once have been, and that there was no reason why it should interfere with their plans. The person who had inhabited that wreck had suffered and gone.

Kate walked back with them to the camper. There were tears on her face, but she was not crying. She asked, 'Did she walk like that, then? All the way from where it happened?'

'I suppose so.'

'That was brave.'

'Yes.'

An hour or so later as the thunder rumbled and lightning played behind the stacked black clouds and the first few drops of heavy warm rain splashed on their split windscreen, Emma, driving the old camper, led the convoy out of Carver's and down on to the dual-carriageway heading south-west. Next to her, on the textured grey leatherette bench seat, Hannah-Rosa tickled Pinta's chin and listened to her purr. She was close enough to be heard above the chugging rear-mounted engine with the characteristic ticking of its magneto. The body, now wound in white sheets and bound with cord, lay behind them on the floor between the banquettes. Emma turned on the wipers but only the one on her side worked. Hannah-Rosa leant forward to peer through the wind-splayed runnels of rain.

'I don't like to think of what might be happening in South-ampton,' she said.

'Nor do I,' Emma replied.

For several reasons Hannah-Rosa's usual inner calm was

shaken – she had hardly got over seeing her brother and then not seeing him, and now this. She wondered what he was doing, what he was thinking about. At that moment, six miles behind them, up on his hill, he had decided he'd break a few rules. That would have pleased her – if she had known. Neither of them had been brought up to obey rules. Only the rich on one side, and the servile on the other, did so. The Somers had never been either – not until Richard became a rock icon.

The convoy rumbled on, passing signposts for Warborne, through three roundabouts and one underpass, all unlit. Presently dull lights glowed on both sides of the wide road, and the forecourt of a filling station opened up on their left.

A man holding a clipboard came out of the shop on the far side of the pumps. There was an old Uzi slung from his shoulder. Emma wound down her window.

'Harem?' He was tall, stooped, wore a check shirt above jeans with a Harley Davidson belt buckle. His grey hair was cropped, and one side of his face was networked with scars – from flying glass perhaps.

'You're late. I was on the point of turning in,' he went on.

'Sorry. We got held up. And then the rain.'

'Petrol's OK. But the electric's down on the diesel. Your diesel drivers will have to hand-pump. Where you headed?'

'Swanage, then Weymouth.'

'You'd better all fill up then. I reckon I'm the last before Weymouth. Swanage went dry a week ago. Credits is it? They'll do. If I were you I'd fill any spare cans, containers, whatever you've got, as well. Deliveries have gone to pot all over the south-west this last week or so. Don't know what's going on but the distributors reckon the military's taking it all. Something's brewing.'

Emma drove up to the pump nearest the shop. Hannah-Rosa put Pinta carefully on the seat next to her and got down. She filled the tank with the only grade on offer – 88 octane, smelling of garlic – then got in again. Emma pulled the van round in a half-circle so it was on the edge of the lot with the sliding side door facing the darkness and rain beyond. The forecourt filled up with the rest of the convoy. Jacques, Jason, and two more of the gender-frees came up. Hannah-Rosa stepped over a low wall into an area surfaced with rubble. Her torch showed a gate on the far side and a copse of eucalyptus with an undergrowth of periwinkle.

'That'll do,' she called, but quietly.

Checking that the attendant was busy showing the driver of the first of the Range Rovers how the diesel pump worked, she waved them in towards her and presently Jason and the other Afro followed, carrying the white bundle between them. Jacques took up the rear with a spade. Hannah-Rosa gave him the torch and left them to it, returning to the camper. The rain hammered on the forecourt canopy, sluicing over the edges where the gutters had gone, quite concealing what was happening away from the road.

She found Ameena and Ayla, Ameena's twin, waiting for her, two slight figures silhouetted in the dull lights against the silvery rain, and behind them Kate, looking more wan than ever and with her thumb uncharacteristically in her mouth. Lightning again played up over the Dorset hills behind them.

'Hi. Anything the matter?' Hannah-Rosa asked, hoisting herself back on to her seat, taking up Pinta again, but leaving the door open so they could speak to her.

'Yes.'

They were beautiful, these twins: thin, small, lithe. They both had straight black hair, heavy eyebrows, large, very dark eyes, straight noses, full mouths. Ameena was the leader, Ayla the more talented – especially as a dancer. She had a small mole exactly bisected by the fine line that separated her top lip from her cheek. It helped you to remember which twin was which.

'Go on then.'

'This ethnic cleansing in Southampton. What does it mean?'

'It must mean that the whites there are trying to kill all the Afros and Asians.'

Ameena bit her lip, dragged in breath, struggled with her feelings. Ayla turned her head away.

'Our mother lives there. With our two baby brothers.'

'Not babies,' said Ayla. 'Small boys.'

Emma lowered and turned her head so they could see her face beyond Hannah-Rosa's.

'Dad?' she asked. 'You have a father?'

'He's a vegetable. No brain. Mercury poisoning from working at the chemical reprocessing plant at Marchdale.'

The pantechnicon's engine roared, settled into a muted roar. Gears crashed and in a cloud of blue fumes it moved away from the pumps. The articulated lorry that folded out to make the road-show stage took its place. Hannah-Rosa's fingertips continued to caress Pinta's throat.

'You want to go back there,' she said.

'Yes.'

Emma showed anger. 'What's the point? Six people will get killed instead of four.'

'We might be able to get them out.'

Ayla chipped in at last. 'Anyway. We have to try.'

'And you can't drive. Neither of you.'

'No.'

'Too far to walk.'

'Yes.'

'So what are you going to do?'

The twins shrugged.

Hannah-Rosa shifted towards them, put the cat between her and Emma, swung her feet out and dropped to the ground.

'You were in the leading Range Rover with Jason?'

'Yes.'

'Spanish costumes, props and make-up in the back and on the roof?'

'Yes.'

'Help me shift it all between the other vehicles. I'll take you.'

Kate took her thumb out of her mouth and pushed through.

'No!' she said. 'Not without me.'

Emma got out and walked round. She put an arm over the girl's shoulder, spoke to Hannah-Rosa, raising her voice almost to a shout over the roar of the engines.

'This is crazy.'

'I know.'

'I'd like to come too.'

'You can't. The troupe needs you, one of us, anyway.'

Kate pushed her head forward.

'Mum. You're taking me.'

'No, Kate.'

'Because it's dangerous?'

Emma realized this was not the line to take. She tried another tack.

'You haven't got a permit.'

'I know the area. You know I do. I'll take them through the forest. After all, this is an off-the-road vehicle. And once I've got them there I'll come back and join you. I should make it before you leave Swanage.'

'Oh, rubbish.'

'Well. I'll try. You know I've got to do this. They'll try to walk it if I don't and Lord knows what will happen to them. Come on now. Give us a kiss and cheer up. Both of you.'

Emma shrugged and, knowing her friend's determination, gave in – for the time being.

'Hang on.'

She turned back to the camper, came out with a big wad of mini-credits, the takings from Linwood, and a large silvery Colt forty-five. It was a stage-prop, useless, though it could make a good bang firing stage blanks.

'You'll need these. The gun might win you time in a crisis.'

The twins were waiting. They had cleared out the back of the Range Rover. Emma took Hannah-Rosa in her arms. 'Take care. Lots of care.' Then she made way for Kate.

'Mum, I really do want to come with you.'

'I know you do. But it's not on. Now just stick with Emma until I get back, and do what she says. There's a good girl.'

'Mum, I'm old enough to make decisions for myself.'

'Not big ones like this. Now do as I say.' They hugged. 'Be good.'

They held each other very close for a full minute, then Emma and Kate watched while Hannah-Rosa turned the Range Rover, threaded her way through the other vehicles and then drove back on the wrong side of the road until she got to the roundabout. Presently the rain and darkness filled the space between them and the receding tail-lights and she was gone, heading towards Linwood and Southampton.

Hannah-Rosa gripped the steering wheel with whitened knuckles, leant forward to peer through rain and tears. Her chest was filled with a cold void of anxiety, as though her life had come apart. Richard, Kate, the troupe – they all tore her in different directions. This mercy mission to Southampton was an escape, a way out, a way of shelving more pressing problems.

She glanced across at the twins, both sitting on the wide passenger seat beside her. They looked at her wonderingly, eyes wide, intense.

'We're so grateful—' Ameena began.

'Shut it,' and then, wanting to soften the harshness of that, Hannah-Rosa stretched out long fingers and briefly gripped the Asian girl's thin wrist.

18

The enclave included a small community of handymen, known as servicers, who occupied two closes and a terrace of what had been council housing in Coop Lane on the far side of the village hall. There were gardeners, builders, carpenters, house painters, plumbers and electricians among them. Most of them were old – positions such as these were awarded to men and women who had worked on the outside for most of their lives without breaking any laws or cheating more overtly than was acceptable, but a few belonged to Hurling families going back to the First World War or further. And some of the latter had relations on the outside, in settlements like Thorney Hill, and they had discovered or created ways and means of keeping in touch with their less privileged kin.

Allan Pitt was a fifty-year-old electrician whose know-how extended to being able to tinker with computer and comms hardware. Richard had used him quite often when things went wrong with his spec-maker unit, or just to install new cards or whatever. Richard called on him on the morning after the storm. Allan's wife Betty, who looked like a mannequin in a virtual diorama of early-twentieth-century domesticity – gingham dress, apron, lisle stockings, sensible lace-ups, home-perm – took him down the narrow passage at the side of the house, past the cardoons, flageolet beans and tomatoes he was growing, to the shed at the end of the garden. A hundred years of boiled cabbage followed her.

Allan was turning something on an old metal lathe, but tripped the switch as soon as Richard appeared. There was a smell of hot metal and coolant.

'You usually phone,' he said, almost accusingly, 'when you want me.'

He wiped his hands on a piece of cotton waste. He still had the local accent, west Hampshire, New Forest. Sometimes

Richard felt people like Allan had been there for ever, and would stay for ever, until doomsday anyway. Actually Allan claimed there were Pitts in Thorney Hill mentioned in the Domesday Book.

'It's a nice day. I thought I'd walk.'

Allan lifted his head at Betty, telling her to go.

'You usually phone,' he repeated. 'So what's it about?'

Richard made a half-glance over his shoulder to check Betty was safely back in her kitchen.

'I want to get to Thorney Hill, back into my old house, without being seen. Or at any rate without filling in ten forms and waiting for a month.'

Thick eyebrows with a few white hairs rose above a large reddish nose. Blue eyes narrowed. Richard sensed the question forming. He pre-empted it.

'You've told me your brother has a family there. And that you barter electronic stuff you can get for the occasional sucking pig or goose.'

Allan rolled down check shirt-sleeves and buttoned them, gave his broad leather belt a hitch.

'How much?' he asked.

'A hundred credits.'

'And risk my status and the security of all this?'

'Two hundred. You needn't come with me. Just tell me how you do it.'

'No mystery. But it's a roundabout walk.' He glanced at Richard's pigskin shoes.

'I don't need to stay there long. Half an hour at the most. And, like I said, it's a nice day.'

So it was. Hot and humid after the storm, but the sky had cleared.

'Ay. But yous'll have to cross the old railway line and that'll be wet.'

'I'm not bothered.' Richard pulled a sheaf of credits from the inside pocket of his jacket. 'One fifty here. It's all I've got with me. You can come up tomorrow for the rest.'

Allan went back into his shed, sat on a stool, pulled on old rubberized boots. Then he took a shotgun down from where it hung on the wall, opened a box, took out a handful of shells, dropped them into his shirt pocket. Finally he pulled on a wide-brimmed tweed hat.

He called, 'Betty? Takin' Mr Richard down Bittern Bottom, see what us can get. Back by evening.'

He glottal-stopped the double Ts.

Richard followed him into a narrow, high-fenced back alley.

'Why the gun, Allan?'

'I'm a forest sub-keeper, but only as far as the fence. If we get stopped or recorded, I've got a permit. We're out to cull deer, or maybe feral pig. You come along for the sport. It'll mean a fine – which yous'll pay.'

They went back to the war memorial, climbed the short hill past the old school where pre-teens were still taught the Blunkett Minimum, the children of full enclavists along with those of the servicers. At twelve the children were separated: those of the enclavists continuing their education in their own homes via Pednet; the rest theoretically moving on to practical courses with local employers, or if they were clever, in local admin offices or as carers. In fact most joined their parents and elder siblings in the day-to-day struggle to remain alive in tolerable comfort by whatever means came along.

The main track snaked away off the heath to a junction with the old A35, which marked the extreme south boundary of the enclave, but on the west side the enclave fence dropped into a dip and crossed the old railway line, closed in the 1960s. A narrower track led down a steep slope towards it. Presently a ruined single-storey house, once painted white, and oddly a perfect square, came into view on the far side of where the line had been, just as it left the cutting to run across what was now a patch of marshland. Allan was right: thick slimy puddles lay across marsh and track. Richard felt a tremor of memory and nostalgia; it was a cottage built for a level-crossing keeper, and as a child, when their summer walks had taken them near it, Thomas and Katherine had made him shiver deliciously by insisting it was haunted.

The fence crossed the track on the far side of the house, but very close to it, then climbed to the crest, beyond which it ran along for a mile or so back towards Hurling. Richard could see no way through.

'Right,' said Allan. 'Walk behind me, but close. Try if you can to keep my head between the wire and yours. If they doos run a check we might get away with I saying you was a mate of mine. May work, may not, but it'll give us a little leverage. Down here they're old cameras, poor definition, and on five-second takes rather than continuous. They'll clear me anyway. They're programmed not to alarm when they see me.'

He led Richard splashing across the track and into the bunga-low, using his own key to open the front door, then a different key to open what looked like a cupboard in the tiny hall. Stone steps led down and Richard caught the sheen of light reflected off standing water. It smelled musty but not fetid and the air was fresh, cooler than the August heat outside. Allan took a small torch from his pocket and the blackness opened into a narrow vaulted passage. They splashed along it for maybe twenty yards or more.

'Allan, what was this place?'

'Just a store. Wood, coal, food. Who knows? But it doos be older than the railway. There was a keeper's cottage on the site. Some doos say it were a smugglers' hidey-hole for brandy and tobacco and that and stabling for the donkeys that carried it.'

'Why was it left open?'

Allan touched the side of his nose slyly.

'Me an' me mates was doing the labouring on the fence when they put it up. When we saw the foremen didn't have it on their plans we kep' mum. Simple as that.'

It ended in a stone wall but with metal rungs or holds fitted into the mortar between the blocks.

'Up top there's like a manhole cover. It's in a dip and anyway in a big patch of bracken. The fence won't see you come out. Then there's high gorse, thick, but you should be able to push your way through. Keep low, head east up towards the forest. You remember the old caravan site?'

'Yes.'

'On this side of it there's a dip runs mainly south down into

138

a bottom. Once you're there you're well clear of the fence. It'll be marshy again, but you climb up heading north and west this time and yous'll be in Thorney Hill in maybe half an hour.' He looked at his watch. 'Is'll give you an hour there and an hour to get there and back. An' Is'll be here at two o'clock. An' at half past two I goes home, and yous'll have to find your own way back an' it won't be through here because Is'll have left it locked.'

It actually took Richard forty minutes to get through, during which he got badly scratched on gorse and brambles, which were sharp enough, with stems as thick as a finger and thorns an inch long, to tear his trousers. In the sheltered hollows a sub-tropical flora had sprung up, mostly of ferns. It was an area he had roamed in his pre-teens, climbing trees, making quite viciously successful bows and arrows and occasionally getting lost. Richard had a very poor sense of direction or geography and once or twice he thought he was lost again, but the basic slopes, crests and hollows of the area remained unchanged. He shoes squelched with water, and mud splattered his legs to his knees. He was plagued with insects, some of them biters, in spite of the repellent he had thought to bring with him. The worst fright was a brief confrontation with a large black cat, a little bigger than a fox, that hissed and spat at him before turning and spraying musk in his direction.

Coming from the opposite direction to the one Hannah-Rosa and Emma had arrived by, he found School Road blocked by fallen and rotting oak trees, almost all the houses storm-damaged, fired, or just broken into and vandalized, with smashed windows and gaping holes in their roofs. His heart went heavy: he was not going to like it if their old home too had been reduced to a ruin, a shambles. He rounded the bend by the ruined oak tree, and there above a holly hedge grown twelve feet high and wild, he could see the roof – more or less intact except where ivy had pushed up through the slates. But the front door had been boarded up, so there was no point in looking for the spare key they had always left on the ledge high up inside the porch. Nothing for it but to go round the corner and find Sharon Dell – if she was still alive.

She was. Sitting in her kitchen which faced the road, bouncing a filthy grandchild, or maybe great-grandchild, on her knee.

'Dick Somers,' she cried. 'Rich! I knew you'd be around before long. Din I say to your da,' she cooed at the brat, 'din I say the famous Dick Somers would call on us before long? An' did your da believe me? Not on your life he did. An' here he is, but he's not the famous Dick Somers to me, oh no. To me he's still the little two year ol', just your age, my dear, I used to look after for his mum an' dad when they was working.'

'You're looking well, Sharon.'

'Shouldn't complain, but I still got me ol' back. Come on then, you'll be wanting to see your house as I've been looking after for you an' your mum. Still no news of her?'

She put the kid on the floor, where it put one thumb in its mouth and held on to the hem of her skirt with the other hand.

'Lemme just find that key.'

'Front door's boarded up.'

'You bin by then? That sister of your'n, and the friend she had with her, knocked it down, an my Stewart, Shelley's husband that is, he boarded it up. But the french window's all right, an' that's the key I'm looking for.'

She found it and they walked together back round the corner to the house, up the short path, pushing through the creepers. These had been cleared a bit since Hannah-Rosa and Emma were there, no doubt by Stewart when he was boarding up the door. She led the way through the gap in the old hedge and into the back garden, where she got the key to work quite easily in a lock that had recently been oiled.

'Stewart sorted it, see?'

As they went past the piano he paused, and played the right hand of the opening to 'Für Elise', but it sounded tinny and wretched and the sadness came back like a pall. It had always been a good little piano, had served him and Han well. Better than they had served it – neither of them practised enough and neither was as good as they could have been.

In the vestibule he began to climb the stairs.

'Nuffin' to see up there. Ceilings come down after the slates lifted and let the rain in. Couldn't look after it all, could I? Not

140

without no money nor credits and Katherine never left me nothing.'

The whole place was a shadowy mess of cobwebs, fallen plaster-board, peeling walls, thick dust and shrouded furniture. He had to push on the door to what had been his room to get it open, and then he wished he hadn't. He'd always been a bit of a hoarder. There were books going back to his childhood, horror and mystery paperbacks he'd chosen, children's classics foisted on him by loving relations, just about a complete set of Roald Dahl, all tumbled from fallen shelves into the corner by the window; posters, Hendrix, Clapton, a Miró from his first visit to Barcelona, a Claes Oldenberg, and a Hockney; postcards, more Miró, Picasso, pre-Raphaelites bought on student visits to the Tate or given to him by his girlfriend. But all twisted and brittle with alternating dryness and damp, the colours fading or gone. There was other stuff there too he could have dug around in, but he felt almost dizzy, heavy and falling with sadness. He couldn't stay, yet it felt like a betrayal to turn away.

But if betrayal there was, it had happened thirty years earlier.

He pulled himself together, reminded himself he was there for a purpose and went back down the creaking stairs.

'Told you so,' said Sharon.

He tried the door to Thomas's workroom. Locked.

'Key's where it always was. On the oven.'

Bloody oven. He was always getting told off for not cleaning the turntable after he'd cooked a frozen pizza on it. But the key was there. He went back to the vestibule and opened the door to his father's workroom. He almost never called it a study – the concept smacked of male seclusion and superiority, the sort of middle-class attitudes it had taken two generations of Somers to throw off.

It was, of course, just as it had been when Hannah-Rosa had been there a few days earlier, but Richard saw a different room. Thomas's father, Christopher, had been killed riding a moped at night, way back in 1960 when Thomas himself was only twenty-five (which, give or take a few months was the same age Richard had been when Thomas died on the railings of the

New Tate), and there were many mementoes of the grandfather he had never seen. A silver cup, tarnished brown now, awarded to the winner of the individual sculls at his Oxford college in 1920, a framed photograph of him in RAF cap, shirt and shorts standing beside a Hurricane fighter plane in the Western Desert, another in a dinner jacket, holding a fag between long fingers and making a speech at some function or other.

A photo of Richard's mother, Katherine, at the age of sixteen, very pretty, with a confident, knowing smile which was just on the cusp of being overtly sexy.

Postcard-sized pictures of three of Thomas's favourite authors – James Joyce, Graham Greene and William Burroughs – and about twenty more, ranging from Harvey Keitel as Mr Wolf in *Pulp Fiction* to Vermeer's *The Artist's Studio*. Dad used to say it was the second greatest painting in the world, the greatest being Velázquez's *Las Meninas*. It was significant perhaps, Richard thought, that both were paintings which included the artist himself: as indeed does most of Joyce's work and that of Burroughs, and, arguably, a lot of Graham Greene. The granddaddy of them all, Miguel de Cervantes Saavedra, was not there, though Don Quixote and Sancho Panza were, pictured in one of Picasso's brush and ink drawings.

All these surrounded the picture of trajectories, tragectories, trajictories. In the middle, cut from a newspaper, the naked model opened a cloak of black and beneath it the words, 'Her lips were red, her looks were free'.

Shit, thought Richard, that's where I got the idea from, why I made the connection – 'the nightmare life-in-death is she' —

Sharon was making impatient movements behind him.

'See, I done a good job, as good as anyone could rightly expect.'

'Yes, Sharon, you have.'

He sensed she wanted to be gone, or at any rate move down the agenda: her smocked granddaughter fidgeting at her side, thumb still in her mouth, had begun to whimper. His eyes moved over the white but dust-shrouded table. A darker grey slab, two or three inches high, rested on it, looking as fixed as a flat gravestone, just where he had hoped it would be.

'I reckons, over the years it's all totted up, quite considerable, if you know what I mean.'

'Yes, Sharon.' He reached across the table, brushed dust with his hand off the laptop and tried to lift it. It wouldn't budge. The plastic studs beneath it seemed to have fused to the table-top. Then it gave and he almost toppled backwards. It was heavier than he had expected.

'This is what I've come for.'

'Well, it's all yours, innit?'

'I suppose so.' He fiddled the handle out of the slots which shielded it, so he could carry it as if it were a document case.

'None of it would be here if I hadn't kept an eye.'

'I suppose not, Sharon. I'm very grateful. I'm sure we all are.'

'Yes, well. Katherine said she'd pay me.'

'Oh yes. Of course.'

'And thinking you'd come, I got my Bert, that's my other son-in-law, the clever one, to draw up a bill, like.'

'Oh yes?'

'An' considering your mum used to pay three and a half quid an hour, and I been coming in a couple of hours a week for thirty years since I last got paid, he reckon you owe me ten thousand nine hundred and twenty pound, which is five thousand, six hundred full credits. An' he says, considering who you are and how much you made with that group of yours, that shouldn't be a problem for you.'

This was precisely the sort of confrontation Richard had always hated, could never manage to handle properly. All very well saying there was no problem – in terms of his more than considerable assets there wasn't – but paying in paper as opposed to electronically transferred credits was very difficult indeed and rigorously controlled if more than five hundred were involved. Forms had to be filled in, reasons given: the process could take weeks, months, and could, at the end of the day, be forbidden anyway. He was almost certain this would be the case. No one in the vast army of bureaucrats who controlled such things would believe that he had no ulterior motive in handing over such a large sum to potentially dissident non-workers. House-watching for thirty years would be laughed

143

out of court. The point was paper credits in such numbers could be used to buy arms, explosives, finance a samizdat press, whatever.

'Look, Sharon, I've no credits on me right now, not a bean. But I'll do my best to get some your way as soon as I can. Allan Pitt—'

'You're not going to pay me, are you?'

'Yes, Sharon. But not right now, and not all at once.'

'No, you're not. You're not going to pay me.'

The change in her was frightening. He suddenly realized she was an old woman, and now a mad old woman. Dimly he was aware of how perhaps this had been her pipe-dream, the ship that would come home. He even guessed how she would have answered the neighbours who questioned her loyalty to toffs. 'Ah, but I'll soak them in the end,' she might have said.

'Well, that's all the thanks I get you can fucking sod off.'

He pushed past her, back into the living room, past the sad piano. She followed, the abuse escalating, the voice rising to a scream. The kid started bawling too. Clutching the laptop in front of his chest, he stumbled back through the creepers and out on to the cracked and rutted tarmac of the old road. She stopped where the gate had been, but the abuse followed him as he pushed his way through the friable boughs and dust of rotted oak. Then she fell silent.

But she wasn't through yet. He turned before crossing the road into the thickets he'd earlier fought his way through and as he looked he heard a dull whooomf, and then a black mush-room cloud of smoke billowed up into the sky above the roof and tree tops. The smoke became yellow and white as well as black, and near its roots orange and red flame flashed through. Flakes of white ash – his posters or books? His dad's? 'Für Elise'? – drifted about him and one settled on his shoulder. He looked at his watch. He'd have to be quick to be back at the old level-crossing keeper's house before Allan gave up on him.

He pushed his way into the undergrowth. He didn't feel sad, but lightheaded, purged, the way you feel when you wake up one morning after a really bad attack of flu and know the fever has gone.

19

'I'm sorry, but I've thought it through and I want to be with my mum.'

Kate, close-cropped head up, looked round with jerky movements of her neck, like a bird of prey in a bad mood. Lean, jeaned legs astride, hands moving in brisk movements from high on her flanks down to her thighs and back, she was lit by the sun that had just cleared the cliffs of Ballard Point. Its watery, clean, early-morning light filled the narrow strip of sandy beach, the car park they were in and the built-over hill that climbed up the other side of the small town. Round her the rest of the troupe, grey-faced with fatigue, were unloading from the vans what was needed to make a camp.

A seagull glided overhead, towards the sea. Kate, sweating a little now, followed its progress. Six or seven more bobbed on the greenly opalescent, gently heaving swell, tails cocked. As the one she was watching wheeled and landed, its webbed feet briefly creating a bow-wave, the others took off, cackling impatiently.

Emma, sitting wearily on the floor of the camper with her feet on the tarmac, had Pinta on her knee. She looked up at her best friend's daughter and then beyond her as most of the rest of the troupe gathered behind Kate. Jacques pushed himself forward.

'We want to know the truth,' he started, his accent thickening with emotion. Although gender-free, he was still capable of taking a bullying tone with women, even those who employed him. 'We think we're entitled to that.'

Emma tipped the cat off her lap, smoothed her hands on her cotton skirt.

'It's simple enough,' she said, looking up at him. The sun was in his eyes, dazzling him; she was in shadow. 'Ameena and Ayla come from Southampton. Their mother lives there with two younger sons, their brothers. Their dad is an invalid and incapable. Hannah-Rosa has taken the twins back there. They hope they may be able to get the family out. She expects to be back here before we're due to leave.'

There was a chorus of disbelief, bewilderment, some anger.

'She had no right to do that,' Jacques barked above it all. 'She always insisted we should act like a commune, all of us sharing decisions and responsibilities.'

Kate pushed her head forward.

'He's right,' she asserted. 'We should have gone back with them. Together.'

Jacques turned on her.

'That's not what I meant at all. Not at all. She's dropped us all right in it. When the protectors find out we're three people and one vehicle short, they'll throw the book at us. They could disband us. If they discover what really happened, they'll break us up . . . especially if they find out why they went.'

Kate cut across him again.

'What you're guessing is that Mum knew what she was doing could be dangerous. To us all. And that's why she did it without discussion?' She looked back at Emma.

'She also felt there was some urgency, and that a discussion amongst us would hold things up. I've been thinking this through during the night.' She spoke quietly now, slowly, but decisively. 'You're right. They'll break you up. But not if I go, not if I leave you. I'm tarred with the same brush as Han. I, we, Han and I, do have a responsibility for all of you and I think you'd be best served now if I got out too and left you to organize without us. That way you could say we were the naughty ones, the dissidents, and perhaps they'll let you stay together.'

She stood.

'Anyway. She's my mate. We've known each other off and on since we were at junior school together. I should never have let her go without me, and I'm sorry I did now, so I'm going after her.' She paused, looked round at the posse of performers she and Hannah-Rosa had gathered about them. She might miss them a bit, she thought – but nothing like the way she'd miss Hannah-Rosa. She took a breath, went on, 'I'll take the camper if you don't mind. It belonged to Han and me since long before Harem was formed. Come on, Pinta. In you get.'

'Where are you going?' Kate asked.

'Back to Southampton. Where else?'

'Just hang on while I get my things.'

'Kate? No!'

The younger woman turned back on her.

'I was born in that bloody van, remember?'

Emma's shoulders dropped and she grimaced. She'd done her best.

'So you were. So you were,' she said. And then added to Kate's retreating back, 'I remember, though I doubt if you do.'

'I'm coming too.' Beryl the drummer stood in front of her, arms folded beneath her big chest, strands of red hair falling about her broad face.

'Hey, come on.' Jacques swung round. 'We need a drummer.'

'Fucking find one then.'

'Beryl, I do think they need you here,' Emma put in.

'They'll get a drummer. Always easy to get a drummer. And until they do they can use the synthesizer.'

'Beryl!'

The big woman unfolded her arms and raised her forefinger, stabbed the points home.

'I bin with you ten years. Longer'n anyone else here. Arsehole here talks about a commune which is fancy language for sticking together. I know who I'm sticking with.'

'There's no room for your kit in the camper.'

'Fuck my kit. It's crap anyway. I'll get what I do need.'

As she pushed through the group she grasped Jason's elbow, turned the big black man to face her.

'What about you, Jace? This is all about persecution of ethnics, the brothers, isn't it?'

'You must be joking, man. That's a scene I'm out of. Know what I mean?'

'Come o-o-o-n!'

'They killing the brothers there.' His voice fluked up into a falsetto. 'You want I get me killed too?'

147

'Anyone else?' Beryl looked around them. 'Ah well. So much for sticking together. I'll get me things.'

'We are sticking together. It's you who's going.' A voice from the back.

'Piss off.'

Kate came back with a rucksack.

'Is that all you need?' Emma asked.

'It's all I have.'

'Oboe?'

'Got it.'

Jacques made a last attempt to hold things together.

'Hang on,' he said. 'Do you know where Han went? What her plans are? Southampton's a big place. And if there's serious trouble going on there too—'

'We'll find them. If we get in, someone will know if they made it or not. And if they didn't get in, we'll go on looking until we find them.'

Beryl was back. She slung a huge strapped suitcase through the side door. It was very old.

Emma looked round one last time.

'End of an era,' she said, taking in the big trucks, the pantechnicon, the mobile stage, the circus lettering. 'Come on. Let's be off before the protectors arrive to check you out. Take care.'

20

That afternoon, Monday, in the middle of August 2035, Hannah-Rosa, with Ameena and Ayla beside her, reached Hythe on the western bank near the top of Southampton Water. Shortly after leaving the Ashley Heath filling station they took a right, using a still functional underpass and headed down a narrow minor road, towards Mashams and Hurn, which ran through a sandy patch of forest past leisure sites of one sort or another. They parked by the side of an abandoned dry-ski run and slept uneasily until dawn.

Then, still keeping to minor roads as far as possible, they headed south into the eastern suburbs of Sandbourne using the huge network of housing estates and feeder roads rather than the main arteries – thus they avoided the main roadblocks which cordoned off what had been designated urban, and were able to bribe their way through minor posts manned by protector auxiliaries using the credits Emma had thrust on them.

In the semis and bungalows of these outer neighbourhoods, crops and domestic animals were being raised where once there had been lawns and flowerbeds. Shopping parades were still partially occupied and served something like their original purpose, though many of the shops were boarded up. The ones that were open sold or hired out specs, or bartered food for old tools and clothes, or displayed posters advertising a job lot of, say, paint or birdseed or domestic appliances that had been found in some hitherto secure warehouse or on an industrial estate.

The few people about looked sullen, the young ones often congenitally or genetically deformed, suffering from or showing the scars of sunburn and dermatological diseases. Many had crippling asthma – they were that bit nearer the oilfields than Linwood or Hurling Enclave.

Closer to the coast, in the streets lined with crammed housing a hundred and fifty years old, things were worse, though again not perhaps much worse than they had been. The streets were often ankle-deep in garbage, many of the houses were ruined, the windows smashed and boarded up, the frames torn out for fuel perhaps, and roofs often switchbacked and gaping. Old cars and vans rusted on the kerb-sides above pools of oil; cats with eye diseases slunk under them as the Range Rover cruised by.

At about nine o'clock they passed a Victorian red-brick church which had been converted into a refuge for ethnics. The women in saris or billowing African dresses, the men in jeans and sweatshirts clutching mini ghetto-blasters, spilled out on to the street, milled round a parked but functional van. Two armed protectors kept a watchful eye, holding the line between the ethnics and a huddle of skinheads wrapped in white ensigns, the flag of St George. Thin soup was being doled out through a tap on a drum in the back of the van, while a couple in yellow municipal dungarees handed out grey breadrolls.

Keeping a mile, half a mile, inland, they headed east, between the old A35 which they knew was still open and patrolled, and the sea, which they could occasionally see. Presently they entered the most degraded area of all – wide, tree-lined avenues of large detached houses in substantial gardens. These, once the homes of the well-to-do professional and bourgeois middle-classes, were now almost completely deserted, their owners having either slipped back into the lumpen proletariat or moved up to the status of enclavists.

The gardens, which in this frost-free coastal zone had always featured exotics such as fan-palms, monkey-puzzle trees, mimosa, yucca and camellia, had taken on the appearance of sub-tropical jungle. Behind them tudor 'beams' leant out from pebble-dashed walls revealing their non-structural lack of function, the small frames of glass in the 'leaded' windows had popped out and fanciful red-brick chimney stacks had fallen through gabled, tiled roofs. Once a black puma loped in front of them from one side of the road to the other, and more than once they had to make detours where trees had fallen across the roads.

They moved on through Southbourne, Tuckton and Christbourne into more or less open country between the Solent and the inland towns – to their right the chalky downs on the Island lay above the sea, to their left the re-emergent forest encroached on fields that had once been pastured. Out in the Solent they could see a large high ship, the sort that used to be a roll-on-roll-off car and lorry ferry. Ameena sucked in her breath. Hannah-Rosa glanced at her. The Asian girl had gone grey beneath the creamy brownness of her complexion.

'What is it? What's the matter?'

'That boat. It looks like the *King William*.'

She normally spoke with careful clipped diction which yet contrived to have a lilt, but now her tone was cutting, bitter.

'So?'

'Four months ago it sailed from Southampton. It was filled with families of Caribbean origin, all going home, or so they were told. Free repatriation to the West Indies. It was back in dock two weeks later, empty.'

'And?'

'The *William* could not have made the trip there and back, even to the outer isles, in so short a time.'

Before she had seen the charred corpse of the black girl who had been napalmed, Hannah-Rosa would have been ready to ascribe the implication to paranoia. But now . . . ? In the old Tate there had been paintings her father had made them look at. Paintings by Turner of slavers throwing dead bodies from sailing ships into the sea. If then, why not now? Dad had asked. Are we really so much more civilized than we were?

As morning shifted into afternoon they drove further east towards Southampton Water, still choosing minor roads and tracks. Most of the forest was fenced into enclosures of what had been spruce and larch, now replanted with eucalyptus following the huge fire of 2022, which had swept through the whole area. This was the inferno which had destroyed Fawley Refinery in a series of explosions seen as far away as Brighton to the east and Winchester to the north. Villages had been destroyed and abandoned, and scrub, much of it broom in flower, had spread over their fields.

They arrived at Hythe, the most inland of the waterside town-lets, at about four o'clock and drove up to the end of the pier from which the old foot passenger ferry had once operated. There was no one about, though the short, curving high street seemed to be occupied: upstairs curtains twitched, fresh litter tumbled along the pavement in the hot wind that came across the water. When Hannah-Rosa turned off the engine and all three got down into the small car park, they could hear a dog barking. Six white doves flinked in the air above them and drifted to a hidden dovecote behind the crown of a substantial weeping willow.

An old-fashioned turnstile of hooped iron, polished by the generations of stomachs that had pushed through it, remained unyielding between them and the pier itself. There was no one in the ticket office to open it or take their money. One by one, the three women helped each other over. The pier was long, a quarter of a mile, and had once been served by a diddy train that had run on rails that were still there. The pier had to be that long since there were two full tides a day in Southampton Water and the western shore had been silted up by the River Test into acres of silky mud at low tide. The tide was out now. The train had gone long ago, and they walked, their feet slipping occasionally on the greasy timbers.

Waders, stilts and avocets, taking the place of the redshanks and godwits which no longer came so far south in summer, picked their fastidious way across the mud; gulls drifted almost motionlessly, holding their station against the breeze above them. The city, less than a mile away, lay beneath a haze of summer and smoke, the quays and luxury flats of Ocean Village gleaming richly nearest to them, the restored Norman walls grey and squat beyond. Further away to the left the serried ranks of cranes and mantis-like hoists, three deep in places, still stood above the quays of the container port, and from this distance one was not aware of the rust. Between, the water swirled gently on the turn from ebb to flood, pale but oily, glaucous and poisoned.

Low above the city, which was hidden by distance and its ancient walls, three puffs of white smoke, cotton-wool balls, burst out of silver flashes, and seconds later came the distant pops – no more threatening than those made by the bursting of children's balloons. They were followed by a sharper rattle of smaller concussions, presumably taking place on the ground – some sort of anti-personnel cluster shell was being used. A helicopter buzzed like an angry mosquito above. It was too far away to suggest purpose. It seemed casual, lackadaisical, not even a show.

At the end of the pier Hannah-Rosa stopped, hands holding her elbows beneath her chest.

'I don't know how you're going to get in,' she said. 'I had hoped the ferry would still be running, or at any rate there'd be a boat we could hire or steal.'

She had chosen this approach knowing the motorway box which enclosed the landward side of the city would be patrolled.

But the twins were looking down into the water, their attention focused on something else. The tide was bringing with it what looked like a marine barrage-balloon, an inflated seal. It was the body of a black man, swollen with gases, and supported as on waterwings by a grey oil-stained mackintosh whose folds, also filled with trapped air or gases, made shallow domes around him. Fish had nibbled the back of his neck. He stank.

Hannah-Rosa shuddered, fought back rising vomit, shaded her eyes and turned her gaze to the south.

'There's a small marina down there. Maybe we can find a boat that will do.'

21

That same morning Emma had driven the VW camper out of Swanage with Kate alongside her and Beryl Krupa behind her. They passed Corfe Castle, still a broken molar against the clear, rain-washed sky, heading towards Wareham. Beryl studied an old road atlas plotting a route that would take them away from the main roads.

Presently the dense black permasmog filled the sky over Poole Harbour to their right. The highest drill masts, fifty or sixty of them, pierced its ceiling and they had to close the windows against the smell and the fumes. The fourth Rio Summit, held above the deeply polluted beaches of Copacabana and Ipanema, with the delegates often wearing face masks even indoors, had agreed a total global ban on the production of fossil-fuelled vehicles – though those already on the road could continue to be used. That had been the first blow to oil production. The second, as far as this particular oilfield was concerned, was the explosion that destroyed Fawley Refinery.

The Poole Harbour oilfield, which had gone into full production in 2008, had depended on Fawley Refinery. A pipeline, laid quietly and discreetly in the mid-eighties of the previous century, had fed the crude from the original dozen or so boreholes twenty-five miles across country to Fawley; the Chase International Bank which had arrived in Sandbourne by no coincidence at all at about the same time had funnelled the finance, and Sandbourne International Airport got its second full-length runway in 2005. But with the destruction of Fawley the whole enterprise had run into the ground, the wells were capped, and those that could not be capped were flared – hence the smog.

Worldwide, vehicle fuels were still produced to feed the billions of vehicles that would go on working for a century or more, and the petrol- and diesel-powered war machines too –

tanks, carriers, planes. But supply was erratic and prices fluctuated wildly as governments sought revenue on the one hand, but tried to keep people's movements to a minimum on the other, the better to control them.

Just short of Wareham the rear-mounted air-cooled engine began to overheat. When they slowed, it stalled. Soon it wouldn't start on the starter and Beryl and Kate had to push and then, running alongside, scramble through the side door, since Emma did not dare slow down or stop again. After a half-hour of this progress they could smell rubber burning.

'Engine's on fire,' Emma cried and pulled into the verge. Thinking of the petrol tank, she and Kate hopped briskly out, Emma with Pinta in her arms. They ran back fifty yards. More calmly Beryl hoicked a water container from under one of the banquettes, walked round the back, opened the metal hatch that revealed the engine beneath the rear window, and poured water on the orange flames. She was briefly enveloped in a cloud of steam.

'It's all right,' she called. 'It's not the actual motor that's burning, just the rubber mountings, shock absorbers, between the engine and the chassis. The engine overheated. Some of it was red-hot.'

Emma and Kate came back. The odd thing was Emma could remember a time when this sort of experience was exceptional, indeed did not happen to anyone reasonably well-off – and if it did, nice men in mustard-coloured uniforms or yellow PVC jackets appeared quite soon and put things right. Kate had no such memories. For her, motor travel had always been like this.

'What do you think's wrong?'

'Magneto,' Beryl guessed. 'This heap is so old it has a magneto instead of, or rather as, a distributor. My first boyfriend's cousin had one. Ouch. It's hot. We'll have to wait a bit.'

They ate what they had, which was little enough, and drank some of what was left of the water. They passed the time by talking. Beryl, who was in her late thirties, was an unknown quantity to both Emma and Kate – a good drummer, a reliable member of the troupe, loyal, hard-working, that was the limit of what they knew about her. She had a West Country accent,

Budleigh Salterton she said, but some of her vowels were posh. Slowly at first, then more fluently, she gave them the gist of her history.

'My dad was manager of the local Comet – electrical goods, durables, washing machines, TVs, VTRs and so on. My mum had ambitions for me. Knew I was musical, wanted me to get to the Royal College of Music or some such, saw me into the local sixth-form college, and then it all began to go pear-shaped.'

'When was this?'

'Seventeen years ago? Eighteen. First of all it was the new technologies, the new home entertainments. When everything got miniaturized, Comet went over to mail order and Dad got the chop, redundant, unemployable. And then about that time I got them all into a terrible fix.'

'How was that?'

'I were driving an old Opel Corsa home from a gig, with my boyfriend in the passenger seat. First, actually only, legit car – just passed my test. Dirty night, thick drizzle, slimy leaves on the road, went over a hump-back bridge, skidded and ran into an oncoming car. No one hurt, but, be on the safe-side, my mum took my boyfriend to the local casualty to check for whip-lash. Now. Two things was wrong. One. When we took out my insurance I was provisional – passed my test a week or so later and no one thought to tell the insurance company. Two. Boyfriend diagnosed with mild whiplash, given pain-killers, better next day. One. Insurance company won't pay out on damage to the other car, six thousand quid, because of not telling them I'd passed my test. Two. Hospital reports to police an accident victim they, the police, have no record of.'

'I remember,' Emma chipped in. 'You only had to report an accident if someone was injured.'

'Right. So, now what happens? I am done. Well and truly seen off.' The big woman counted off on her fingers. 'Not reporting an accident. Driving without due care. And above all, driving without valid insurance. Six months or a five thousand pound fine. Twelve-month driving ban. And a criminal record. Plus all the bills, maybe another four and a half grand. Mum

156

and Dad paid, of course. Better, they reckoned, than going to gaol without passing "go" . . .'

'What does that mean?' Kate asked. 'I mean, I've heard people say it before, but why do they?'

'Comes from a board game everybody used to play . . . too complicated to explain now,' Emma replied. 'So what was the fall out?'

'My parents increased their mortgage to cover it all, fell down on their payments, house repossessed. No money for the Government Elderly Care insurance premiums. Last time I saw them they're dying of arthritis in a leaky mobile home on the edge of Dartmoor. And they wouldn't have got that but for the Social and the New Caring Safety Net. They live on crisps and cola – both past their sell-by dates. Reckon that engine may be cool enough now. Anyone got a safety-pin?'

She fiddled about for five minutes or so.

'There. That should do. Could you just start her up and let her run for a moment, and switch off when I tell you. There. Aren't I just the brilliant one? All aboard.'

The next interruption to their progress came only twenty minutes after they got going again. As they approached the roundabout that would get them across the main east-west road, they could see a procession coming down the Dorchester road from the west. For a moment Emma put her foot down, but then gave up. The road was a raised causeway and she could see that the front of the procession would be on the roundabout before she could reach it.

It was headed by a large silver band, the men uniformed in dark blue with silver piping, peaked hats. As they watched, the traditional arrangement of Chopin's funeral march crashed to a close. There was a brief pause, then clarinets and cornets wailed in a desperate parody of the 'Libera Me' from Verdi's Requiem.

They were followed by two standard bearers. The first carried a massive silver circle filled with an inverted Y, mounted on an ebony post as thick and tall as a telephone pole; the second struggled beneath a huge silk embroidered banner, tasselled at the edges, bearing the likeness of what at first sight, at any rate from a distance, one might have taken to be the Virgin Mary. But this figure wore no snood, had silvery blond hair swept back above noticeable eyebrows and large blue eyes that seemed to stare out to the left with meaningful intensity. She was wearing a white ballgown, encrusted with sequins and pieces of glass, which came just below her knees. Below her, on an undulating ribbon, in letters of gold, were the words: *Temple of Diana, Plymouth, Lodge 382.*

Next came a huge moving platform, the base perhaps of the largest container lorries that used to thunder up and down those roads from the Poole container port. It was pulled, not by an articulated cab, but by a team of fifty men and women, hauling ropes over their shoulders, with sweatbands round their heads. Many of them were barefooted, and some, with their free hand, belaboured the back of whoever was in front of them with short, many-tailed whips.

The platform was the base of a tableau of machinery and life-like dummies, and showed the moment of impact when a large Mercedes limo, c.1997, concertinaed against a curved concrete wall. Behind and around it a small fleet of crudely modelled papier mâché motor-cycles and smaller cars clustered like wasps, homing in on a jam-jar. None of it was to scale. The big car and its occupants, who were at that moment of impact depicted in attitudes of pain, fear and disintegration, were all much bigger than life-size and far bigger than the caricatured dwarfs, many of whom pointed disproportionately large cameras at the crashing limo.

The giant float passed slowly, very slowly indeed, and was followed by a further hundred or so men, women and children, who ambled and shambled along, occasionally wailing, but for the most part silently weeping, or at any rate pretending to.

A second float followed. High beneath a canopy of tasselled crimson velvet, emroidered with silver thread, a double-life-size figure of the princess stood, a blazing tiara on her head, her wedding gown lavish with imitation pearls and diamonds; the huge train meandered magnificently behind her. In her arms she carried a great bouquet of waxen lilies.

The procession ended with seventy or eighty more acolytes

– whole families, wives, husbands and children, with, amongst them, crudely painted caricatures, gigantic at twelve feet tall, carved or shaped from polyester derivatives, of the two men, her husband and her son, who had briefly been kings, the old Queen looking like a fat evil witch, and her husband, wrinkled and gnome-like. It was all backed up by a small convoy of vans and cars, with a couple of old red double-decker buses, clearly there to provide a respite for the ill or footsore, or act as canteens. One was an old ambulance filled with stroke victims in wheelchairs – many it was said had made miraculous recoveries after being plunged in the lake at Althorpe House. Others caught pneumonia and found release from useless bodies that way.

It took a good half-hour for all this to pass.

While they waited Beryl asked: 'Were either of you ever Di-ists?'

'Goodness, no,' Emma's reply was robust enough for her instantly to regret it.

'I was.' Beryl's tone was quietly contemplative. 'My parents had a photo of her in a silver frame, a print from a negative which a relative of ours, a nurse actually, took herself. At a hospital Di was visiting. I put it under my pillow whenever I had toothache and it always worked. By morning, anyway.' She laughed. 'I joined the nearest temple when I was thirteen, the way girls do things like that—'

'Boys too,' Kate interjected.

'Boys too.'

'Why did you leave?'

'The priestess took thirty per cent of my newspaper-round money – for land-mine victims she said. But being a Di-ist Priest was her only occupation and she wasn't claiming any carer benefits. We worked out why not and I dropped out. She moved on.'

'I think we can move on now too. Which way?'

'Straight across. Up the A350 for Lytchett Matravers, then a bit later we'll take a left for Blandford, then a right which should take us back across the A350 and on to minor roads well away from patrols or anything like this.'

They drove on into a landscape of hills and woods with occasional villages, but the grass on the Downs was brown and thin, their flanks scarred by soil erosion; the woods were dead, had not been replanted in the way the Forest had, and the villages, apart from a couple of enclaves, were in much the same state as Thorney Hill.

'So what happened to you after the car fiasco?' Kate asked Beryl.

'Well, the sixth-form college was eight miles away, the bus to it cost twelve hundred pounds a year, not covered by benefits 'cos of the criminal record, so that was out. And music college was out of the window too, fees, board and the rest ten grand a year and no hope of a Blunkett Loan, again on account of the criminal record. Wouldn't have wanted it anyway. When they axed the Sandbourne Symphony twelve years ago, half the band members had that loan round their necks and I know classically trained guys who are still trying to pay it off busking at the gates of sub-enclaves.'

'What did you do instead?'

'Went on the black. What else could I do?' She meant the black economy. 'No travellers' licences then. I played every sort of band you can think of. Tribute bands mostly. Verve. Blur. Glitter Band once it was established Gary really was dead. Evil Trend. All illegal of course. Got caught. Did time, more than once, on those cruise boats anchored off Weymouth. Hey, is it really true your mum is his sister? And that he came to our last gig? Does he live near Linwood, then?'

They were held up once again and in far more sinister fashion. This was at about midday when they were trundling along a very minor road towards Warborne and across a main road that linked Blandford with Warborne and Poole. This time the convoy was shorter and moving quite quickly, at a steady fifteen miles an hour.

It was the mili. First, ten motorcyclists in displaced pattern combat gear, blank black-tinted goggles, armed with small automatic weapons. Then a jeep with a tall aerial carrying a pennant that whipped in the slipstream, and next, rattling and squealing, a small fleet of tracked vehicles. There were six Conqueror tanks, four self-propelled 75mm cannon, the barrels so long you felt they ought to droop, and ten armoured personnel carriers, closed so you couldn't see the men they carried. They moved relentlessly, unstoppably, leaving behind a cloud of thick diesel fumes. None of them appeared to pay any attention at all to the old VW camper that waited in a lay-by, beneath a dead hawthorn hedge, for them to pass.

22

'The reason why I am so beautiful is that I bathe every day in ass's milk.'

'Pasteurized?'

'No. Only up to me knees.'

'Oh, I think you can make a bit more of that!'

'You don't mean . . .' Richard remained in character, a high nasal twang, faux posh, but not quite a falsetto, '*miiillkk* it?'

Paul Digby laughed, his high braying lawyer's laugh.

'Darling, that's just what I do mean.'

Richard gave the curtain that had been wrapped round his waist a hitch, glanced at Danny Blake who was playing Ali, the Buttons-type character, and they went into the routine again.

'Past . . . yer . . . eyesed?'

'O-o-only up to me KNEES!'

'Better, much better. There aren't many jokes as good as that in the script, got to make the most of them.'

And so it went on through to the end of the scene, to the point where Aladdin, Widow Twankee and Ali were left alone to follow the wicked Abanazar off to Egypt, whither, as they say, he had taken the Princess.

'We three, we must all stick together.'

'Like peas in a pod.'

'Like three caballeros . . .'

Cue for song. Nice little soft-shoe routine in which Richard got to put his arm round Delice Cowper's waist and hold her hand, which was jolly, but he wished it was Sophie Pribendum. Sophie was sitting in the darkened auditorium wrapped in the sultry aura she always generated when in repose.

'Coffee's ready.'

'Take ten,' called Digby.

Danny winced.

'I do wish he wouldn't use every luvvie cliché in the book,' he murmured. Richard raised eyebrows, pursed lips, nodded agreement. They felt entitled; after all, they were the only real professionals in the club.

He got Danny into a corner and eyed the older man over the rim of his cup.

'When you were a lad, did you have your own PC?'

'Course I did. Everyone did. Or borrowed their dad's.'

'Or mum's. Can you remember how they worked?'

'I think so.'

'Are you doing anything tomorrow morning?'

'No.'

'Would you like to pop round and give me a refresher course?'

'Yes . . . er, yes.' His face went serious, but his eyes twinkled. 'Sounds interesting.'

'About half ten?'

'Fine.'

A few yards behind them Frederick approached Damien Floyd, who already had his pipe out.

'What's going on in Southampton then, Damien?'

'Not a lot.'

'That's not what the rumours say. Talk of a massacre.'

'Gossip old chap, pay no attention.'

'Nobody tells me anything,' Virginia wailed, in mock distress. 'What are these rumours, then?'

Floyd took the pipe from his mouth, studied the bowl as if it held a scorpion.

'Minor racial disturbance. Some young thugs taking it out on the Afros and Asians on account of this business in North Africa.'

'I thought no one was meant to know about that,' Richard chipped in.

Floyd eyed him malevolently.

'As you very well know rumours get out and spread and get exaggerated. Just in the same way as this Southampton disturbance has been exaggerated.' He relit his pipe and began to puff. 'Personally,' he said, 'I think government policy is mistaken. In a mature democracy at least enclavists, possibly the

Social, full workers and so on, should have access to all but the most sensitive news. The trouble is, this government, which, in one form or another, has had its whack, the longest since Robert Walpole, takes too paternalistic an attitude—'

'Surely you mean maternalistic,' Maurice Coen interjected.

'Maternalistic if you like.' Floyd was ready to go along with that. 'Anyway, I think she should realize we are capable of standing on our own two feet and making some decisions for ourselves. In the meantime,' he concluded, 'there really is nothing serious going on.'

'Time's up. Let's make a start again.' Digby, impatient. 'Act two, scene three.'

Whoopee, thought Richard, this is where I get to put a stethoscope on Sophie's chest and hold her hand.

As he walked away, Frederick plucked Floyd's sleeve.

'Richard,' he said, 'was out on the heath by the golf course this morning. With Allan Pitt. They were heading towards the A35, but then went down the hill to the smuggler's cottage. Thought you ought to know.'

Silly bastard, Floyd thought, he still wants the Dame's part. But worth knowing, all the same. He decided he'd check it out with Pitt.

They ploughed on through the text. The Princess, in a coma thanks to Abanazar's wizardry, lay on a couch. Widow Twankee, laying claims to nursing know-how, leant over her, and, not having a stethoscope, put the flat of his hand on her bare breastbone. Oh, Jesus! She opened both eyes, dark and lustrous, and slowly winked. Breathless, he took her wrist in his hand.

'Either . . .' he said, took a breath, 'either this woman's dead, or my watch has stopped.'

'Stop! STOP! Richard, that's not in the script.'

'Paul, dear Paul, I know it's not. It's a lift from an old Marx brothers' film. But I thought it would slot in rather nicely just here.'

He'd never seen the film but it was a gag Thomas had liked, and before him, though Richard did not know this, his grandfather Christopher had quoted it whenever occasion arose.

'We'll see, we'll see.'

'I liked it.' Sophie sat up. Her voice was deepish, considering she was only fifteen or so, slightly husky. 'I thought it was funny.'

'Bless you, my dear,' the Widow replied. 'You are to-o-ooo kind.'

As they left, Annette, who had been playing, in magnificently regal style, the Empress of China, took him on one side.

She spoke quietly.

'Damien's running a security dossier on you.'

'Shit.'

'He wants me to find out what's on that disk.'

Richard came to a quick decision.

'OK,' he said. 'Come round tomorrow, elevenish, and see.'

23

The craft in the marina were sailing boats, twelve- to eighteen-footers for the most part, which had been used by locals, well-paid workers at Fawley and the like or weekend visitors, to potter about Southampton Water, cross to the Island, or take part in fun regattas. The expensive stuff had been across the water in Southampton's Ocean Village and the larger marinas nearer the sea.

From the look of them, few of these boats had been used in the last twenty years or so. Their glass-fibre hulls were matted with green algae, their cabins and cockpits pitted with salt and rain-born dust and grit. The copper and brass fittings were tarnished to a green or brown patina where they hadn't been unscrewed and stolen. But here and there an occasional yacht had been kept up: one even had a furled mainsail attached to its aluminium boom, and a jib wrapped round the foot of its forestay. The low, narrow windows of the cabin, almost flush with the decking, were curtained. Hannah-Rosa gingerly put a foot over the low rail and the boat tipped fractionally towards her.

'Do you know how these things work?' Ameena asked from behind her.

'Not a clue.'

The boat suddenly lifted under her foot and almost threw her on to her back on the jetty, and at the same moment the low door of the cockpit banged open.

'Gerroff my boat before I blow you off.'

The man who emerged was wearing a russet nightgown with a thin white stripe, and apparently nothing else. But, in Hannah-Rosa's eyes, the sawn-off shotgun made him over-dressed.

'We're not on your boat.'

'You were.'

She shrugged.

'What do you want, anyway?' He looked up, took them all in. 'Oh Christ, a couple of darkies. That's all I need.' He paused, his eyes narrowed. 'If you can crew a bit, I'll take you to the Island. No further. Or if you don't like the Island, Portsmouth or Gosport. Got no fuel, so we'd have to sail.'

'They, we, just want to get across the water to Southampton.'

'No way. You seen what's going on there?'

'That's why they want to go. They got family there. We'll pay you. Got a load of credits.' She was falling, fairly seamlessly, into his way of talking.

'How many?'

Hannah-Rosa allowed herself a wry half-smile.

'Tell the truth, I'm not sure.' She went on, 'They're in the car.'

'You got a *car*?'

'Range Rover.'

'Petrol or diesel?'

'Petrol.'

'Now I am interested. Where is it?'

'In the High Street. By the ferry pier.'

'Let's get it. Hang on. I'll get some clothes on.'

Five minutes later he stepped on to the jetty. He no longer had the shotgun but was carrying a five-gallon plastic container, empty, and a length of clear tubing.

'I'm Roger.'

'Hannah-Rosa, and these are Ameena and Ayla.'

'Pleased to meet you.'

'You don't need those,' Hannah-Rosa remarked. 'We've got a full container like that in the back.'

He slung the tube and the container back into the cockpit and strode off past them, leading the way to the end of the jetty. He was tall, had long straggly grey hair with a big bald patch, a grey unkempt moustache and was wearing an old Guernsey jersey, stained and tatty jeans, distressed trainers. His eyes were hooded behind slanting eyelids, his face, neck and hands all lined and worn but probably, Hannah-Rosa thought, prompted by the chemical aura around him, by crystal-meth abuse rather than a hard life at sea.

Back at the Range Rover he took all their remaining credits and their spare container of petrol.

'There you are, then,' he said. 'You can piss off now.'

Clearly he believed he was more than a match for three smallish women. He was a biggish bloke, but not that big.

Hannah-Rosa shrugged, she hoped fatalistically, to set him at ease, to make him think he'd won, then reached into the Range Rover, into the glove holder fixed to the driver's door, and pulled out the silvery, stage-prop pistol. She pulled back the hammer.

'I don't think so,' she said.

He hardly turned round.

'Bollocks to that,' he said.

She stood on tiptoe and hit his bald patch as hard as she could with the butt. He turned, and blood began to slip across his forehead.

'Fucking cunts,' he said, and crashed forward.

Ameena and Ayla tied his hands behind his back with his heavy leather belt, and then they tipped the water from a second container over his head. It diluted the freely flowing blood, washing it into the gutter.

'I feel sick,' Hannah-Rosa muttered. 'But I'm not going to be. He's not dead, is he?'

He stirred, moaned. They got him sitting, kneeling, and on his feet at last.

'You fucking shot me,' he said.

'No. I just hit you. But hard enough to let you know I don't mind shooting you if I have to.'

They got him to stagger back to his boat. Ameena and Ayla carried the petrol container between them. A thin, white but dirty bitch, short-haired with a bit of terrier, a bit of lurcher in her, loped behind them for a time, but gave up when they got to the jetty. She squatted to shit liquid faeces and then loped off. The jetty was a fearful business, being only three feet or so wide and Roger could not walk straight.

Once they were all in the tiny cockpit Hannah-Rosa picked up the shotgun and said, 'I'm going to undo the belt, and you're going to tell us what to do: how to get the petrol into the tank, and how to make the engine work. Don't know why you need an engine when you've got sails. Always been a mystery to me.'

'Takes more than one to sail a boat. You need an engine when the wind's gone or wrong. Oh Christ, my fucking head hurts.'

Dusk had turned to night. The waning moon not yet up, the water in front of them as black as the air above it. The lights on the other side, not many but spread over a wide area, seemed further off, mostly just pin-pricks in the darkness, but with one or two patches illuminating quays. A couple of orange fires still burnt, but not brightly. With the sun gone, the sporadic bombardment had ceased.

Roger took the wheel. The twins stood on the jetty holding the ends of the mooring ropes.

'As soon as she moves, jump back on board. Don't worry, I'll throttle her back, she'll be hardly doing more than inching forward. Right, miss, pull.'

He refused to call Hannah-Rosa by her name – too much of a mouthful and snobby too, he reckoned. She pulled, yanking on the lanyard that started the engine. Two pulls and it fired, faded, died.

'Sod, missed it. Try again. Good hard one 'cos if it don't take we'll have a flooded engine. Good ... Got it ... Jump, come on, girls, jump. Right, Ameena, up forward like we said, keep your eyes peeled for flotsam. You two look out over the sides.' His voice rose in quiet exaltation. 'We're off, she's moving, wahay! First time in eighteen months.'

He opened the throttle a notch and the boat surged forward. A tiny bow-wave curled in front of her and spread arrow-like to the sides, parting the oily diseased water, taking on a luminous green phosphorescent tinge along its crest. Behind them the propeller churned beneath a twist of exhaust that shifted from sooty black to a healthier pale blue. With the engine turning the generator, navigation lights came on.

'Are you sure about this?' he asked.

'About what?'

'About going into Southampton. We could turn right here,

starboard, head down the Water, now, while the going's good.'

She prodded his back with his shotgun.

'It's not loaded,' he said.

She pulled the trigger. Click. He turned, his face pale.

'Christ,' he said. 'You might have checked first. OK. It was just an idea. Southampton it is.'

Apart from a bump against something black Ameena did not see until too late, which turned out, as it passed along their beam beneath Hannah-Rosa's gaze, to be another floating body, the short crossing was without incident until almost the end. As they neared the outer quay of Ocean Village a small group of people, just visible as black silhouettes against the dull lighting behind them, seemed to run towards them. A lighter flared, something larger and brighter took hold, and then a petrol bomb lit a brief arc against the sky before plummeting towards them. The bottle landed bottom first a yard in front of the bowsprit, bobbed for a moment, then tipped and spewed out flaming fluid across the water in front of them. Fortunately it did not actually explode.

'Heave to or the next one lands on you,' a voice bellowed.

Roger engaged reverse and throttled back the engine to a gentle murmur which countered their momentum. In a moment they were stationary, though with a bit of a yaw across the tide. Skilfully he brought her head up into the flow, re-engaged forward and with occasional touches on the throttle held her there.

'You do the talking,' he said.

'Why?'

'They'll listen to you. You're a woman and you talk posh.'

Hannah-Rosa stood on tiptoe with one hand braced on the roof of the cabin to get as much height as she could and the other cupped round her mouth.

'We want to land. Give us permission to land.'

'Who are you?'

'Travellers. Two of us ethnics with family in the town.' She hissed at Ameena and Ayla to stand up, show themselves.

Conversation she couldn't hear on the quay above her, then, 'Come inside the end of the pier. About a hundred yards on you'll find steps down to water level. Pull in by them and we'll come aboard and look you over.'

Two men, white, and an Afro woman were waiting for them. One of them took the painter Ameena threw for him, the other two stepped down into the cockpit. The twins showed IDs with an address in St Mary's on the north-east side of the old city.

'It's just about on the front line,' the woman said. 'You remember the hospital on the hill above St Mary's? We're holding that as a bastion. They've got the east side of Derby Road; we've still got the west side. So your mum and brothers are probably still all right, though they'll most likely have been evacuated to one of the multi-storey car parks south of the Guildhall.'

They took the revolver and the shotgun but were disappointed to find that one did not work and that Roger had only ten shells for the other. They were more interested in the food he had on board – about fifty tins of assorted baked beans, minced beef, pilchards and the like. He tried to protest when they bagged it all in bin-liners and carried it up on to the quay but shut up when the woman got angry.

'You can't expect us to let you ashore and feed you when you've got food of your own.'

Finally she told them to go to the first floor of the shopping mall where they could register their presence and their reasons for being there.

24

'Good Lord. Wherever did you get that from?'

'Never you mind. Let's just say it's been in my attic ever since I moved here.'

The orangery was filled with morning sunlight but kept cool by air-conditioning. Richard and Danny Blake looked down at the Amstrad, dusted clean and perched now on a small table outside the circle of Richard's spec-maker.

'They can't call this a laptop. It weighs a ton.'

'Maybe. But as you see, it's pretty robust. Must be forty years old.'

'At least.'

'And it has a lot of capacity.'

'Two eight six CPU? You're joking.'

'What's CPU?'

'Central Processing Unit.'

'Danny, how do you know all this stuff? No. How come you remember it all?'

'I had a PC with this sort of capacity when I was fifteen and just starting to compose. And it wouldn't take the music program I needed. So we got into Pentium, Windows95, CD-ROMs, all that shit. Although I shouldn't say that really. At the time it was good stuff and worked well. Multi-Media Music Explorer, it was called. I think. Something like that. CD-ROM. When were you using this thing?'

'Not me. My dad. It was my dad. Through the nineties. I suppose right up to the time he died. O-six.'

'Even in the mid-nineties this would have been pretty ante-diluvian. It's not much more than a glorified word processor.'

'That's what he used it for. That was all he needed.'

'So what's the problem?'

Richard held up the diskette Hannah-Rosa had given him.

'I can't get into this.'

'Let me see.'

Danny, balding, big round forehead, heavy brows, square face with big smile creases, lifted the screen lid, operated the on switch, got a C:\>, beneath MS-DOS 3.30.

'That's a joke anyway,' he said. 'Nineties? Very early nineties. Without checking I'd guess the Microsoft disc operating systems had reached version seven by ninety-four.'

He took the diskette, slotted it into the side of the laptop, typed in A:\>DIR and got *Volume in drive A has no label, Directory of A:\ TRAGECTORIES <DIR> 3–07-05 3,56P, 1 File (S) 173280 bytes free A:\>*

He typed in C:\> and took out the diskette.

He pushed up the slightly elasticated cuffs of his magenta silk shirt, revealing a gold and steel braceleted watch.

'Do you know what program he used?'

'No idea. What was there in those days? Word? Word Perfect? Word Star? No, hang on. He had something really odd that no one else had but he always swore by it, said it was easier to manage than any other word-processing system.'

Danny typed in DIR and got a list. Out of it he picked LS *28–10-91 11.27 a.m.* Back at C:\> he typed in LS and got *Bad command or file name*.

'No. That was stupid. LSPRO are obviously upgrades of LS. Take the latest. Thirteenth of the first, ninety-four, nine fifty-seven a.m.'

'Goodness! Is that the actual time he installed the last update?'

'Dead on.'

'I'm surprised he was up so early.'

'Maybe the diskettes came in the post and he was anxious to try them.'

But Richard was slightly overwhelmed to be able to know exactly what his dad had been doing at such a precise time nearly forty-two years earlier.

'Here we go. LSPRO2. There.'

Locoscript Professional 2 plus V 2.50, then stuff about copyrights and so on that went too quickly for him to read, before a disc manager format appeared. It consisted of columns divided by thin lines beneath a horizontal entablature. They scanned the words in the columns. Accounts, CVs, Ideas, Labels, Other, Personal and ... Tragectories. A directory. Danny pressed Page Down and got a list of files and sub-directories. The first was called ANINTRO.

'"A" first letter to make sure it came at the top of the list,' Danny guessed.

An instruction amongst several at the top of the manager read *E for Enter*.

'Damn it, let me,' Richard cried, and Danny leant back so he could. E and Return.

INTRODUCTION, bold and underlined, and beneath it a solid page of text, black on grey, LCD display. He scrolled on. Many pages of text.

'Wow, we're in. Well done.'

'And we didn't need the diskette. It's all on the hard disc. Still. After all these years.'

'Ah, but . . .' Richard was about to say that Hannah-Rosa had not expected him to find Dad's original machine, had believed he'd have to find an old one somewhere else or maybe still had his own. But he realized that would mean a lot of explanation now, and possible embarrassment for Danny later if there was an inquiry into the provenance of it all. Meanwhile, what they had was brilliant. They would never have found a machine loaded with Locoscript and would have had to convert to ASCII and then to something tolerably recent like Gateword, which would have been a pain. But he kept silent. The less Danny knew about the provenance of both diskette and laptop the better it would be for both of them.

He read, out loud:

'*Trajectories* is based on or inspired by the two theories of human evolution, of the several now current, that seem to me to be the most credible. The first was originally suggested by Sir Alister Hardy, a marine biologist, in 1960. It was taken up, expanded and championed by Elaine Morgan, a writer of TV scripts, from 1972 to the present day. Its central hypothesis is that about four million years ago a small population of pre-hominid apes was isolated on the banks of an inland sea in what is now the Afar region of Ethiopia, where they gradually evolved the physical characteristics that increased their chances of survival as semi-aquatic mammals. These characteristics included bipedalism, the development of sebaceous glands secreting sebum to waterproof short fur, followed by loss of fur or hair replaced by subcutaneous fat, increased ability to sweat and other features found only in aquatic mammals. These, coupled with an ape's already well-developed intelligence, and, later, consciously controlled breathing and larger brains (themselves also the result of adaptation to an aquatic environment), led to the ability to speak and thence to powers of social organization capable of adaptation to changing circumstances. These aquatic apes are the ancestors of all the true hominids that came after.

'The second theory, popularized by Stringer and McKie in *African Exodus* suggests that *Homo sapiens* arose from an isolated African population of hominids occupying an area also in the Afar region about two hundred thousand years ago. This population fluctuated over the millennia, probably often dropping to as few as ten thousand at its lowest, but began to explode about one hundred thousand years ago. This population explosion led to a rapid spread across the globe. Stringer and McKie have no time for the aquatic theory, though I suspect Elaine Morgan, who clearly *listens* to everything anyone says on the subject, would go along with many of their assumptions.

'What I aim to do in *Tragectories* is to show how modern humans are the result of several million years of adaptation to a semi-aquatic environment, which, once the adaptation fulfilled all the needs imposed by the environment, made it the one that best suits us. However, we were forced out of what really was an Eden by pressure of population – that is, the shallow lakes and rivers we lived by and in became too saline or even dried up, forcing us, like Eve and Adam, out of paradise. Quite rapidly we spread across the whole globe, adapting our skills and social organization to widely differing circumstances, eventually abandoning the hunter-gatherer mode of production for herding and agriculture.

'We are now experiencing the end result of this colonization

– the ultimate destruction of the planet as a place on which we can live comfortably, though no doubt beetles, ants and maybe rats will survive our depredations.

'This then is the trajectory of modern man – a slow curving climb to a pinnacle of adaptation suited to a semi-aquatic existence which was maintained through vicissitudes over many, many millennia somewhere in central Africa, before rising population and worsening environment drove most of us out. The exodus that followed initiated the comparatively swift and always accelerating decline of the last forty thousand years or so. Not so much a trajectory as a *tragictory* or tragic story. Exponential acceleration has led to the drop towards extinction, as we enter the twenty-first century or rather the two hundred thousandth century, to approach, as nearly as the curve on a graph can, the vertical.

'Finally, I suggest, in an epilogue, that with luck our final extinction will not be that final. Small groups may survive in isolation, and may well develop into new species adapted to survive in whatever sort of a mess we have made of their particular corner of the globe. Hopefully, they'll do better than we have done.

'Phew, there you are then,' Richard concluded. 'That was what my dad was on about.'

'Prophet of doom,' Danny commented. 'As far as we're concerned, anyway.'

'That's the end of that file,' Richard added. 'How do we get out of it?'

Danny read across the top line.

'Try F10,' he suggested. 'Ah. A menu, put the light bar on Finish Edit, press return.'

The disc management screen came back.

'This is an amazing program,' he commented. 'It really does work surprisingly well, especially considering it's all done on the keyboard without a mouse. The next file is called BLUCY01. Shall we try that?'

'Why not? Hang on. Someone's at the door. Probably Annette.'

'Whoops. I'll be off, then.'

'Don't be daft.'

'I thought – everyone thinks – you're fucking her.'

'Maybe, maybe not. But that's not why she's here. Damien has sent her round to check this out, see if it's subversive or whatever.'

'And it isn't?'

'History of the human race from the year dot? Speculative ramblings about our earliest beginnings? Come on!'

Richard moved off down the curving corridors leaving Danny to wonder at his naivety. All historians have one of two mutually exclusive and contradictory aims: to bolster and justify the regime they live under, or subvert it. And speculation is even more likely to fracture our most dearly held beliefs.

'It's quite a lot of fun,' Richard was saying as he came back, 'but I challenge anyone to find any harm in it.'

Danny, who did not much like Annette (there must be something wrong with a woman who could marry an out-and-out bastard like Damien), put the light bar on BLUCY01 and pressed E and Return.

25

Picture this. A river, great, grey-green, greasy, all set about with fever trees. A long sandy bank crissed and crossed with the footprints and trails of crocodiles, turtles, crabs, salamanders, wading birds and long-beaked shovellers. Then the fever trees, probably not *Eucalyptus globulus*, which is native to Tasmania and we are in Africa, but possibly *Pinckneya pudens*, about which I can find nothing, though Elizabeth Pinckney was an American botanist of some note. And probably, since the scene we are looking at together, you and I, most dearly beloved, took place three and a half million years ago, these trees belong to neither species at all. Yet, never mind all that, we, if we could walk on the sandy edge of that river, leaving our footprints amongst the others, would not feel we were on a different planet to the one we live on now, certainly not if we have ventured into what little is left of the equatorial or tropical rain forest, or enjoyed dioramas, displays, TV programmes, *National Geographical* features and reconstructions of the world we have almost lost.

Let us elaborate a little. It is not all grey-green, greasy, or sandy, or forest. Where the forest ends there is a curtain of lower vegetation exposed to the light filled with gorgeous trumpeting flowers, yellows, reds and oranges, and higher up leguminous swags of lilac drift in the ever so slight breeze. Butterflies the size of dinner plates drift on lazy wings from blossom to blossom, flashing metallic indigos and blues, and smaller flies with emerald backs, one on another, go to it in our sight. Beetles, glossy as jet or chestnuts, chew at fallen leaves or masticate the dung of giant toads and lizards.

At the lower levels cerulean humming-birds feed from the trumpeting hibiscus and bindweeds; above them insectivores swoop in delirious flight scouring the air of midges and mosquitoes, while, in the forest canopy, birds of paradise flaunt impractical tails and raise their jewelled crests in ritual courtship.

There is noise, a lot of noise, from the harsh calls of the larger birds, through the chipping chirp of finches in the forest curtain, and the song of warblers, to the sibilant burden of the humming-birds. And out in the heavy, slowly swirling, scarcely eddying water fish rise and flash scales silver and gold before splashing back, more interested in catching food than avoiding the amphibians whose prey they are, for here and there a croc thrashes its tail or snaps its jaws, feeding its lazy happiness in liqueous plenitude.

Presently a clan of monkeys swings through the boughs above, some of which dip perilously beneath their weight, and shards of nutshell flicker through the air. Then all scream and swing and leap and call and shriek as a black and sabre-toothed cat uncoils sprung thighs and leaps from purple shadow through bright light to yet deeper shades.

Let us now don the authorial cloak of invisibility and, like the camera in a nature film of whose presence only the more sophisticated viewer takes account, go for a wander into the forest.

Once through the curtain we are in a very different world. Here tall, buttressed trees, festooned with creepers, soar to a hundred feet or more above a sparse, sun-starved undergrowth. Our feet squelch in the damp, no, wet litter of the forest floor. Sunbeams arrow down through the warm haze and leave pools, no, puddles of golden light. Bromeliads like pineapples and yucca-like plants with spikes hung with waxy bells manage to flourish in the wider spaces between the trees.

Here and there the creepers have reduced the trees they batten on to to pillars of dead and brittle detritus, and occasion-ally these have concertinaed down on themselves, letting in bigger pools of untrammelled light. The creepers survive though: they simply snake across the floor and find another tree.

Indeed, it's possible that wet though this environment is, it is passing through a period of crisis and is not quite as wet as it once was. Where the land dips into shallow gullies, the forest is as we have seen it, but if the ground rises at all there are more damaged or rotting trees, the undergrowth, exposed to sunlight, is thicker, the healthy trees fewer and further apart from each other, the ground drier. It is not a sick environment in the way modern rain forests may be, through slash and burn and secondary growth, but it is a changing one, and the creatures who live in it will have to adapt or move on, seeking out places where the old environment remains basically the same.

The populations that alter their habits, will, especially if they are isolated from other members of their species, gradually (though in geological terms quite quickly) develop, through natural selection, the physical and mental characteristics that make adaptation to a new species successful.

We have not gone far, and the bright curtain between us and the river is still well in sight, when, peeping over and through a thicker patch of undergrowth, we come on an area that is clearer than the rest. Four or five of the larger trees were felled at once, possibly by a storm or lightning-strike (even as we look, we hear the rumble of distant thunder and the hidden camera cuts for a time to pan across the canopy and the tree-tops to a distant mighty mountain range, a sierra of jagged teeth, wreathed in forest on the low slopes and thunder cloud above with tumbling waterfalls between . . .), creating a small clearing in which one large and spreading tree holds the centre. There is also on one side of this clearing a large sausage-shaped pond surrounded by reeds and ferns over which dragonflies play. It is fed on the landward side by three small streams which trickle into it out of the forest, and emptied at the other end by a brook that is clearly a tributary of the river. On closer examination we see that the brook actually spills over and through a dam made of branches impacted with mud and leaf mould. There were, as we have seen, plenty of fallen branches around. It is not an accident and we might postulate beavers if it were not for the presence . . .

And now, growing from insubstantial ghosts into real presences, first manifested to us by their multifarious chatter, mammalian, primate, almost human, we become aware of creatures who lounge, play, sleep and squabble along and among the lower branches of the spreading tree.

At first it seems there are two species involved – one much larger than the other, at five feet nearly twice the size of the smaller ones. But their physiques are very similar.

They have hairy heads, the hair quite long, and shaggy round their genitals. The rest of their bodies is covered with a fine, short, but patchy pelt, streaked in some cases with sweat. The bigger adults are males, the smaller female. At first sight we forgive ourselves for taking them for apes, or even monkeys. They have long arms and short splayed legs, long hands and feet, with long phalanges or curved toes and fingers. Their chests are pear-shaped, conical, and they have pot-bellies. And, in so far as they are active at all, for it is early afternoon and the hottest part of the day and most are inactive, even somnolent, they are behaving like arboreal apes.

Those that want to move about the big tree do so by swinging from their hands or curling their prehensile toes over the curved branches. Others are grooming their neighbours, worrying especially in the longer head hair for ticks and lice, and a couple of mothers are suckling their young on skinny small nipples placed almost as high on the pectoral area as those of an adult female chimpanzee.

But the older youngsters are behaving quite differently. They are playing in the pond. Some are splashing each other without malice, indeed comforting each other, for the water is keeping them cool. But one of them, a male, a little older than the rest, attracts the disapproval of all of them and they chase him across the pool, yacketing more loudly and splashing with more ferocity. Thus ganged up on, he uses his greater height to wade into the deeper part so the water reaches his chest, and what had been an ungainly gait when the water was between his thighs and pelvis, now becomes smoother, and he sweeps the water in front of him with half-circular motions of his hands, holding his head higher and his chin, for yes he has a chin, clear of it.

Damn nearly he is swimming.

Indeed the last yard or so takes his feet off the bottom, but a kick or two brings him to the barrier of branches and mud and he clambers on to it.

We get sight for a moment of his rump, which is rounded, more hairless than the rest. His buttocks are not like those of a baboon or chimp. They are fat. Well, fattish.

He hauls himself up on to the top, turns on his tormentors with a snarl, revealing large canines, and pulls handfuls of mud and the odd large pebble from the top of the dam and hurls them back at the smaller ones, who anyway have not been so ready to venture out of their depth. But he is over-excited, carried away by what he is doing and, slipping a little, pushes a larger lump off the parapet and into the water where it swirls, in a sandy-coloured cloud of fine grit, before sinking. However, it has left a gap and the water now filters across the top, runs faster, becomes a rivulet, a tiny waterfall.

This excites one of the largest males in the tree. The alpha male? Perhaps. Hand over hand he swings himself out to the periphery, drops to the ground and, with a loping, awkward but definitely bipedal gait, covers the ground to the end of the dam. Chattering vigorously, he launches himself along it, pushes the younger male off it, not into the water but down the slippery wet slope on the other side. The adolescent is now contrite and obedient and he helps Dad, or Grandad, to replace the mud and stones he has thrown or dislodged, scooping up debris from around the brook and filling in the gap he made. It's not easy for him – the parapet is above his head and on a level with Dad's face.

Suddenly a commotion behind them. More screams and chattering shouts from those who have remained in the tree. The big black cat we saw earlier has been spotted weaving its way through the undergrowth on the far side. The adult males pick up sticks and rocks and make an untidy line between it and the tree. The alpha male leaves off repairing the dam and rushes round to lead them. They snarl and shout at the cat who, ears laid back, alternately snarls and spits, her long tail lashing behind her, as, belly to the floor, she edges forward, occasionally tightening the springs of her thighs for the pounce that never quite comes, for the males know precisely how far her leap can take her and they stay just out of range.

Meanwhile the females with their suckling babes have abandoned the tree and are now in the pond, up to their breasts in water. The cat breaks through the line of males and, for a minute or so, stalks the edge of the pond, angry, tail lashing, snarling with frustration but refusing to get her paws wet and knowing a leap on one of the females would bring her into water far deeper than she can cope with. The alpha male now comes up behind her and beats her back with his stick. Defeated at last, the cat makes off back into the forest, where, as soon as she can, and with the chatter of the now distant hominids shifting from fear and threat to laughter, she begins to wash. When in doubt, wash.

The adults and babies slowly return to the boughs of the shady tree. Let us fix on the face of one suckling infant. Attracted by the disturbance, she comes off the nipple and stares out of dark eyes with solemn interest at what is happening. Something in her expression appeals to us: an intelligence, a brightness, an awareness, a kind of beauty even. Her mother cups her round head in her palm and gently eases her back to the nipple. She resists for a moment. Her mother makes a soothing di-syllabic noise through lips pushed out. 'Looseee, looosseeeee,' she murmurs, and the infant returns to the breast.

A time-shift now of ten, twelve years perhaps, suggested by a soft-focused merging of images showing a speeded-up change to the environment. The forest has shrunk further, the banks of the river are closer to each other, leaving a narrower, deeper channel between, the pond with its dam is much the same but only because the hominids have kept it in a good state of repair. Even so, the water level has dropped by a foot or so beneath the parapet. The big spreading tree is still there but has fewer leaves.

The nursing mothers and infants still gather around or in it, but there are not so many of them and they do not look as healthy as they did before, thinner perhaps. Once all this has been established we see a group of adults wending their way through the forest bearing fruit they have gathered – nuts, plantains, custard-apples, but not much, not enough. The females and children squabble over what there is and one, Looooossseee, let us call her Lucy, is left with just a single, small, red banana.

She gives it to one of her infant siblings and wanders off on her own, on her own two feet, into the forest. Her gait is still awkward and frequently she reaches up to the boughs and straphangs her way along, so her arms take the weight.

We follow her as she pushes through the etiolated forest screen to the sandy bank of the river. On her haunches now she pokes about with her long fingers in the sand, reading the tell-tale signs, until she finds a clutch of turtle eggs. She tears one open and sucks down the contents, smacking her lips. But she has disturbed a crab, quite a large one, and crab-meat she knows is even tastier than turtle egg. As it scuttles sideways away from her towards the river, she snatches up a flat plate-sized pebble whose top she has already stubbed her toe on, and chases it with her awkward stride towards the water edge: she cannot run, her legs are not adapted for fast forward motion.

She splashes into the water, attempting to strike through it at where she thinks the crab might be. And now, gifted with the sight of an underwater camera, we see, but she does not, how the sand she is on suddenly shelves sharply into much deeper, murkier water and through it we see how her long phalanged toes slip on the edge of the shelf and suddenly she is drifting down through the water, arms flailing, long head hair streaming behind her. Her arms and legs kick and wind-mill, and for a moment we almost know, feel certain that she will make it, for, yes, she is, sort of, swimming. Shoals of fish and a crocodile, disturbed by the commotion, dart or cruise away from her. She gets her head above water and breathes in, but through her nose only, not enough, not the huge life-saving gulps of air available to fully human swimmers or divers, or seals and aquatic diving birds. Underwater again, strength failing through lack of oxygen, her cheeks swell, bubbles balloon out of her mouth and nose, and, driven by reflexes beyond her control, she sucks in water through her nose, once, twice, three times and, drowning, dies.

She drowned because her larynx was still basically that of an ape: that is, it was high, at the back of her throat, and while she could breathe out through her mouth, she could not breathe in. Worse still, and far more significant, her breathing was controlled by unconditioned reflex – it speeded up when she exercised, slowed down when she slept, driven by impulses beyond her control. In short, she lacked the ability to consciously control her breathing – she could not hold her breath. Maybe in the last seconds her head was above the water she forced some breath through her mouth down into her lungs even though her physique rendered this almost impossible. Perhaps, even, for a few moments she did hold her breath. If so, the adaptations that would make her descendants more fully human had already started – but too late for her.

Three and a half million years later a man called Donald Johanson found her fossilized skeleton, embedded in the sand, and gave her a number: AL-2881, and the name – Lucy.

She was bipedal, an *Australopithecus afaransis*, and lived by water a million years before the savannah habitat became prevalent anywhere near where she died. Thus she is chronologically the first indisputable argument against the hypothesis that bipedalism developed as a response to a move on the part of our ancestors from arboreal habitats to grasslands. She also proves that bipedalism preceded the development of the larger hominid brain.

'Too many commas,' Danny remarked.

'He always got into trouble with his copy-editors over commas. He put them in wherever he could, they took them out again, and then at proof stage he'd drive everyone mad by putting them in again.'

'Poor Lucy,' said Annette.

PART III

26

Ocean Village was built in the eighties during the decade when capitalism in the West embarked on its last inglorious fling of expansion, consumerism and conspicuous waste, although the writing, Gaia's graffiti, was already all over the wall. Old docks were dug out, old port-workers' cottages and pubs were torn down and a marina deep and big enough to take ocean-going yachts and motor cruisers was carved out of it all. Behind the quays luxury pads were built like ziggurats so the boat owners could stay indoors when the sea was rough.

A multi-screen cinema was also part of the complex and a shopping mall together with tapas bars and seafood restaurants. There were even one or two areas where it was possible to sit in the open without being asked to pay. From these you could watch the warships being built on the far side of the Itchen for the Saudis and other oriental despots, and throw bread for the massive grey mullet which came scavenging around the piers. A few fished for them, but not, in those days, for food. They looked like mud and they tasted like mud.

It was to the first floor of the shopping mall that Hannah-Rosa, Ameena, Ayla and Roger were taken on the Monday night, after they had moored the Sea Spray in a berth that had been built for something eight times the size.

Once, Hannah-Rosa recalled, there were recorded music shops, card shops, giftshops, shops which attempted to specialize in sea-related tat – posters and models of the Titanic were popular, as too were blown-up photographs of the QE2 bound for the Falklands in the summer of 1982. There were also amusement and computer game arcades.

The most popular unit with the Somers' family, and indeed with many visitors, had housed a pre-electronic collection of amusement arcade machines and games. Powered by springs and clockwork, and occasionally the unaided force of the player, you could get your money back if your ball ended in a tiny half cup; win a horse race where the winner was he or she who could manually turn a wheel fastest; shoot at five lead cats on a wall; or fire ping-pong balls into the mouths of laughing clowns. Richard and Hannah-Rosa had surrendered to its tatty charm, especially when they discovered that to operate the machines you needed old pennies which you had to buy for 10p each.

All this was now a litter of broken glass, torn corners of old posters, cola cans and shucked prawn shells, whose sweet smell, combined with urine, filled the air. There was a shallow staircase and the wall behind and under it was covered with a large sheet of white laminate, filling in the window of an untenanted shop. This was covered with messages scrawled in felt-tip, black, red, green. *Meet me here . . . I shall be down at our pub from . . . Has anyone seen or heard of . . . ?* and so on.

Their guides (guards?) took them up the stairs to the first floor where, at the end of the landing, trestle tables and old filing cabinets had been set up beneath unshaded but dull lamps. There were PCs on the tables but they did not seem to be working – tired clerks took down their particulars by hand, filling in cards and leaving them in a wire tray. There were three of them: a white woman of about sixty, with grey hair floating down from a bun, a floppy embroidered shirt, long skirt and sandals, who wore silver earrings derived from the old CND badge; and two elderly, bearded, turbaned Sikhs.

The woman accepted Hannah-Rosa's and the twins' story. One of the Sikhs consulted long lists of printout on continuous paper, running his brown finger up and down column after column, getting nowhere.

'There are so many Patels,' he grumbled. 'Without knowing your mother's security number it is not easy. But here is a Fatima Patel with two male names, Genghis and Kubla coming after —'

'That's her. Those are our brothers.'

'She had high hopes of them to give them names like that. They were in the Guildhall but they have been moved to one of the Commercial Street multi-storey car parks. The one that overlooked the old swimming pool. You should find them there. Indeed you, and the lady with you, will be as safe there as anywhere else, and it is not yet full.'

'Why were they moved from the Guildhall?' Hannah-Rosa asked.

'The Guildhall is on higher ground and structurally unsafe from mortar fire with its single high roof,' the Sikh replied in his pedantic sing-song voice. 'The car parks, with their many floors built out of reinforced concrete, are much safer.'

Roger wanted to sail back to Hythe and Hannah-Rosa wanted to go with him. She had done what she had set out to do and now all she wanted was to return to the Range Rover, find her way back to Swanage, to Kate and Emma. But on returning to the quay, they found the guards had impounded the Sea Spray. Roger was allowed to take a sleeping bag and told to sleep in the multiplex cinema with five hundred or so other men who were not city residents but had been trapped in the port when the siege started. Frustrated, Hannah-Rosa decided to go with the twins.

Tom, a white teenage lad studying digitalized surveying at the Institute in the hope of breaking out of inner-city status and into the ranks of sub-enclavists, went with them and, as they walked up the hill, told them what had been happening.

'It started three weeks ago,' he began, 'with a non-worker march of Afros from Northam. They were protesting that the repatriation programme, which is meant to be voluntary, was being forced on them. It began peacefully but the protectors called in the regional reservists who opened fire as the procession came across the public garden out of St Mary's. They drove them back across the ring road but left about twenty dead and sixty who had to be taken up the hill to the hospital.'

He paused, lit a cigarette with a disposable lighter. Hannah-Rosa wondered where he had got them from, how old they were.

'After that, things got confused. About three hundred rednecks from east of the Itchen came across the bridges or down the railway line and attempted to fire the whole of Northam, Portswood, Bevois Valley, all that area. The city council met and voted, by a quite large majority, to protect all citizens regardless of colour. Arms were taken from the city police, who refused to carry out the council's orders, from the Territorials and from a couple of Navy ships that were visiting, and a voluntary militia was formed.' He touched a red armband improvised from a scarf on his left arm.

'Things quietened down for a day or two but then we got orders from Winchester to surrender all arms and open up the city to the reservists. We were going to obey but then we heard the reservists and the original white rioters, on the same side now, were back in Northam, working their way, street by street, raping and burning, towards the city centre. The council met again, pulled the ethnics in from the threatened areas and set up militia guard posts to protect the inner streets. And that led to an ultimatum. Pull back the militia or be cut off from the outside world. The council refused to pull us back.'

By now they were picking their way through broken glass. The only streetlights working were over the major road junctions. But for the rest everything seemed fairly normal, though most ground-floor windows in shops and pubs had been boarded up. But it smelt – of drains inadequately flushed, burnt houses and worse. Tom chucked his cigarette, kicked an empty plastic bottle into the gutter.

'Just how many . . . combatants are involved?' Hannah-Rosa asked.

'Not a lot. So far it's a very small war. There are about five hundred of us under arms. The reservists out there probably don't have more than a couple of hundred, but are much better armed than we are. And by now they have maybe a thousand or so white non-workers ready to move in if they get the chance.'

He walked on.

'Seems silly, really, doesn't it?' he added, 'that so few people can cause so much trouble. Southampton still has a population of more than half a million in spite of everything, but until someone with proper authority gets involved it'll go on. You see if we don't stop them, with the weapons they've got they can simply massacre whoever they've a mind to. One problem is that we have no idea who knows about what is going on. Is central government involved or just ignorant of it? Clearly the regional government is in the know – otherwise the reservists wouldn't be here.'

'How close are they?'

'We've managed to hold them on a line from the old football ground through the south boundary of the common, to the hospital in Portswood, and then down the inner ring road. But they have occupied and looted and fired the low-lying ground between the ring road and the Itchen. And apparently interned or possibly murdered any ethnics who chose not to come up into the city. We sent a small party out with letters and so on saying what was going on and asking for help. We don't even know if they got through the first pickets.'

'Some got through.' Deep in her skull she saw again the dying black woman reaching out to her for comfort. 'But they were being hunted through the countryside. Partly that's why we're here. We met one of them. But she died. She'd been napalmed from the air.'

'The air force? That's bad news.'

'Why? I mean why especially?'

'Well. We thought we were up against the reservists, and a raggle-taggle of white non- or under-workers. But if the mili are against us, we've not got any hope at all. Trouble is we just don't know what's happening in the rest of the country. All the comms lines have been broken or switched off. Radio is jammed. Like I said, we don't know what the government is up to, whether they're turning a blind eye or what. But one thing's for sure. We'll have to give in in a week or so whatever happens.'

'Why?'

'Food's running out. Ammunition as well. The regional water supply has been cut off, but the council opened the old city wells, and the city engineer has managed to convert the power units on the four big ships in the docks to generate electricity. But only one of them is nuclear, and the diesel has almost run out on the others. We were just hoping to hang on until the government sorted it out. After all, it's the other side are the rebels, the law-breakers. Not us.'

Suddenly he sounded bitter, tired, dispirited.

'It's happened before, you know? In Bristol. They put out that plague broke out there and they had to quarantine the port and the ethnic area round it. But I met a black who got out, and he said there was no plague at all. Just repatriation for those who'd take it, and internment, which probably meant massacre, for those who wouldn't.'

They walked round the Bar, the Norman gateway which had been a traffic island since the old city centre had been levelled by the German Blitz of 1941. Here the damage, the signs of a bombardment, were more evident. The shop walls and the boarding in the windows were pocked with what looked like bullet scars, and there was blood on the paving. Still, nothing yet comparable to the barbarities of the 1940s.

'Cluster bombs, fired from a mortar, or maybe even a howitzer,' Tom said. 'It's the biggest thing they've been able to throw at us yet and the most disturbing. You just don't know where the next is going to go off.'

He led them off to the left past the old HMV shop, through the city wall and up to the entrance of a multi-storey car park. He had a few words with a small group of red-scarfed militia like himself.

'I'll leave you here. You should be OK.' He turned to the twins. 'Your mum's in there somewhere.'

The car parks had been very much underused now for a decade or more, but were too strong and massive to pull down easily. When things were normal they were used as street markets, and the upper floors were often occupied by inner-city derelicts. When winter came with heavy rain and storms, the Exit Squad moved amongst them offering lethal injections to whoever would take them.

Now they were occupied mostly by family groups who huddled in small separate encampments made up from what furniture and blankets and so on they had been able to bring with them, and ordinary city debris that had been found outside. Small fires burnt, casting reddish chiaroscuro over dark and black faces, and spice-scented smoke drifted from occasional stewpots or kebabs. Children, infants anyway, slept,

194

but for the rest there was a quiet undercurrent of talk, and also music – the twang of guitars and sitars, the beat of improvised percussion, the lilt and wail of flutes and reeds. It seemed to Hannah-Rosa that however assimilated these Asians and Afros had become over seventy years or so, now, *in extremis*, their old cultures were re-emerging, reasserting themselves.

Presently a young girl in a cotton shift recognized Ameena and told her that her family were on the third floor. They climbed the greasy ramps and found the twins' mother quite easily. She was still only in her early fifties, thin, small, face lined like a walnut beneath an Indian printed silk scarf, but well, and in some sort of command of her situation. The twins' two brothers scampered about them, demanding repeated hugs and kisses.

Beyond the fire their Afro dad had been propped against a stanchion. He was clearly a severely damaged person, with sores and scars on his face and arms and the vacant look of someone whose inner self is no longer answering calls. But even he managed a sort of smile when the twins kissed and hugged him in turn.

A terrible wave of longing and nostalgia swept over Hannah-Rosa – nostalgia for a childhood that had been happy and close until she and Richard left home, and longing for her daughter Kate.

The twins' mother gave her and the twins bowls filled with vegetable curry and nan bread and later she found her a bed, a thin mattress with a grubby cotton sheet. She slept amongst them, breathing in the odours of burnt timber, spices and cheap Indian perfumes, and slept so well that they did not feel the need to disturb her until the sun was well up, on the Tuesday morning on which her brother opened the directory labelled TRAGECTORIES.

27

About that time, late morning on the Tuesday, Beryl's safety-pin gave out. There was an ominous clang or two from the back and the smell of hot metal and burning rubber again. Emma pulled into the overgrown verge of a side road somewhere north and east of Sandbourne, overlooking what had been a golf course. The greens, which had been well-fertilized for years to encourage a rich and even grass, had been turned into neat stands of tomato plants whose fruits, genetically engineered to withstand drought and grow to an economically useful size, weighed about a pound each and were just about perfectly ripe. They ate a couple, with slices off a sheep cheese, part of the supplies they had picked up by bartering Emma's winter coat ('We'll either be dead or in the south') back at one of the villages they had passed through. Beryl made her diagnosis and prognosis on the engine.

'No good. It's really blown this time. Short of finding a remarkably skilled engineer with a lathe or a VW dealer carrying stock seventy years old, she's had it. Best get out as much as we can carry and use Shanks's pony.'

Kate needed to be told what that was.

'Well, that's all right. We can walk to Southampton. It's only thirty miles away,' she said. The idea of walking to get from place to place was already less foreign to her than to her elders.

They strapped sleeping bags to the tops of rucksacks and packed what they took to be essentials or, like Kate's oboe, irreplaceables, into the two hold-alls they reckoned they could carry between the three of them.

'What about Pinta? And Garth?'

'Pinta's got a catbox. I can carry it in my free hand,' Emma said very firmly, cutting off any objection. 'And Garth will have to take his chance in my jacket pocket.'

Then she stopped, walked forward, and planted a kiss on the big painted VW badge below the windscreen.

'Goodbye,' she said. 'Maybe somebody will find you and get you going again. Anyway you'll be shelter at night for anyone who needs it. Give whoever it is our love, will you? I've left the key for them.'

She sniffed, wiped her eyes on her sleeve.

'Home for twenty years, after all.'

And then at last they set off downhill towards Hurn and Sandbourne International Airport.

'Just two hundred years,' Emma said, after a mile or so.

'Eh?'

'Just two hundred years out of the whole history of the human race,' Emma went on to reflect, 'during which transport was available and within the price range of most ordinary people. Westerners, northerners, anyway. Trains, planes and automobiles. All gone. Through millennia, perhaps hundreds of millennia, most of us walked. And now we shall again.' She breathed in, looked round, grinned, her mood changing, making the best of it as she usually did. 'Hooray!'

But then she was denied her celebration of a return to simpler times, as six F135s, black, sleek and evil, swooped silently over them no more than a hundred feet above their heads, trailing behind them the thunder-cracks of sound barriers shattered and the high-pitched scream of their engines.

They disappeared beyond a low ridge of pine and did not come up again.

'They must have landed at the airport,' Beryl guessed. Then, remembering the napalmed black girl who had come out of the forest and who was still the main reason why they were there, added, 'Bastards!'

28

Fifteen miles away, in Hurling Enclave, Richard, Danny and Annette had just finished going through the Lucy episode in *Tragectories*.

'Poor Lucy?' Richard cried. 'Oh shit, don't you see what we've got here? How exciting it is, how visual?'

He swung round, almost smashed Danny on the back, grabbed Annette and planted a wet kiss on her cheek.

He was high on the creative possibilities he already sensed were opening up. 'I mean, you have to admit, it is wonderfully visual.'

He growled and as she backed off, made another grab at her.

'Gerroff!'

He danced round the console instead.

'Oh Daddy, Daddy,' he carolled, 'I always knew you had it in you.'

Annette, now on the further side of the circle from him, put her palms amongst the buttons and switches and leant forward.

'Well, yes,' she said. 'I can see it's good, that you could make something of it. But what is all this stuff?'

She was wearing Obligation and a loose-waisted summer dress, blues basically but with some yellows in a splotchy pattern, slit up the front to reveal her long, smooth, satiny tanned legs. The dress was cut in a deep V-neck. Her bra-less breasts pushed the fabric out so he could see down between them across the shaded roundness of her tummy to the top hem of her tiny white briefs.

They explained, as quickly as they could.

'So what are you going to do with it? Put it on the net?'

'Maybe. But I don't think so. Not straight away anyway. You see Dad wrote it when the technology we have now for making specs was just beginning to come on line. Animated computer-generated visuals for instance. Digital technology.

New methods of projection to get three-D effects. Dolby Surround in the home, that sort of thing. And what he hoped this would be was a multi-media, possibly interactive, project, probably, in his day, using CD-ROMs.'

'So?'

Danny, sensing tension, spoke up.

'I think,' he said, 'Richard's already said enough to show what's in his mind. He thinks this could be used as the script for a full-length spec feature.'

Annette walked away to the curved outer wall, picked with finger and thumb at a leaf on an orange tree, sniffed her finger.

'You must be joking,' she said.

'Why?'

'You'll have to put the whole thing past the ministry and that will take months. Years. And then they'll turn it down.'

'She's right,' Danny chipped in.

'Don't see why they should. It's hardly political. Not subversive. How can a representation of what happened several hundreds of millennia ago be a bother to the Party?'

'Oh don't be silly. In the first place —'

'In the first place,' Danny cut her off, 'that introduction made it clear Richard's dad saw a relevance to the present and my guess is when we've looked at it all we too shall find it is very relevant. It's not really worth doing if that's not the case.'

'In the second, third and fourth places,' she was annoyed at the interruption, 'you have nudity, probably all through. I mean, just when did we start wearing clothes? And that means it can only ever get a showing on the sex channels or the art channel and the directors of neither will touch it. Then, it's clearly evolutionist and while we're not bothered by the authorities for being evolutionists, those of us who are, you know very well that discussion of the whole subject is discouraged as causing dissension. Remember, the new National Curriculum insists a modified, easily acceptable creationism is what should be taught in schools —'

'OK, we've got problems. But frankly I don't give a toss. Look. Why don't we have a coffee or something, and try to talk about it without getting overheated?'

Richard took them to the kitchen, ground beans in an old-fashioned grinder, tamped the coffee down in holders, poured water into the gleaming chrome Gaggia and switched on. Presently the coffee began to drip and then trickle into the three cups.

'Cappuccino?'

Annette, wonderingly, raised a finger.

'Just the one, then. And two espressos.'

Steam screamed and hissed.

'Just how retro can you get?' Danny asked. 'Where on earth did you find it?'

'The Past-Times Authentic catalogue.' He busied himself with octagonal green and gold cups and saucers, passed them across the table. 'Right. As I said. I don't give a toss whether what we do gets networked or not. What I want to do is just make it. I don't actually much mind whether or not anyone other than us, and a few mates or whatever, experiences it or not. The point is to make it, make it in the sort of way Dad hoped for. I've got the facilities here. I can do it. But I'll do it a lot better and a lot quicker if I have some help, especially technical help . . .'

He flicked his head from side to side in a quick movement which he had developed forty years ago to get his ponytail to lie comfortably, but which now signified concentration, enthusiasm, the rush that comes with inspiration. Then he put down his cup, leant forward with his clasped fists between his knees, and, swaying slightly from side to side, began to let loose a flood of ideas of what they could do with what they had already read, of the technologies they could deploy and those they'd have to adapt.

Annette listened with growing dismay. She tried to paste on to her face expressions which she hoped would signify enthusiasm, understanding, occasionally doubt and then admiration. But what she was actually feeling was quite other. Here was a man, she had thought, with more credits than he knew what to do with, a minor talent (she came from a background which, while feeling free to rave and get silly about rock groups, never took them seriously) who had slipped into a bored middle-age and whom she had been able to stir into a sexual excitement which not only met a response in her boredom but flattered her too.

And what she was now discovering was something vibrant, exciting, obsessed even, and which, apparently, excluded her. She realized as he ranted on (rant was the word she used to herself) that if she was to remain on board as part of his life she had only two options available. To go along with it, become part of it, appear to share in it, and even – and this would, she knew, be inevitable – take a back seat, play a supporting role, become in old terms the clapper-boy or at best the continuity girl . . . Or. Or let her husband put an end to the whole project before it went too far.

Well. There was, for the time being at any rate, a third option. Wait and see. Go along with it all but pull the plug on it when she finally did get bored or felt threatened.

Danny too felt surprised, but in a way relieved as well. Although a successful composer himself, it had been an awe-inspiring moment for him when, on his arrival in the Hurling Enclave several years earlier, he and Richard had been introduced. It's not every day you meet a legend. That image had been a mix of demonic energy and inventiveness, combining music, movement and wildly imaginative visuals into a new art-form, taking the rock video into the spec age.

And then, meeting the man himself, he had quickly perceived that the fire had gone out.

Perhaps Richard had sensed this disappointment and had kept him, as indeed he kept everybody, at arm's length. They had been good friends but there had been no real spark in the relationship.

But now Danny was discovering that the fires had not been out but merely banked up, that something, something no doubt connected with this dad whom Richard had talked of at times with affection and respect as well as some mockery, meant more than he had ever let on and that his re-emergence in this spec scenario had released the old pent-up energy and passion.

And one thing he did know about Richard was that Richard was technologically almost illiterate. He knew well enough what could be done, and he had in the past often been amazingly perceptive about what might be done by building on what was already there, but the how of it, beyond a fairly primitive level, like transforming an old newspaper cutting into a three-D image of a model walking down a crimson catwalk to the music he'd written, was beyond him, indeed bored him. Whereas he, Danny, who'd had little to do with that side of things when he was putting his twenties shows together, had made a hobby of it since and was now more than averagely adept at it.

Back in the orangery Danny picked up the diskette.

'Can you copy this?' he asked.

'On to a mini CD? Not possible, is it?' Richard answered.

'First on to a CD Blank, then on to minis.'

'No.'

'I can. Do you mind if I take it with me and do that? It'll cut an awful lot of corners if we've got it on minis before we start trying to build a spec. You've got the original on that hard disc.'

'All right, but don't lose any of it.'

'You might. I couldn't.'

A bleep. The audiphone. Richard took a miniaturized handset from his pocket.

'Delice? Yes, of course. Pleased to be of use. See you in what then, five, ten minutes? Stay for lunch if you like. Mum all right?' But the call had been closed before he got the question fully out.

'Delice Cowper,' he said. 'She and Sophie Pribendum want to come and swim in my pool.'

'They've got pools of their own.' Annette sounded tetchy.

'Yes, but the Pribendums are having theirs enlarged and it's out of use. And the Cowpers' is overlooked by a neighbour. I wonder if that should be "Pribenda". Like "pubenda". I mean "pudenda".'

Embarrassment was confusing him.

'I daresay you do,' Annette said drily. 'So?'

'So?'

'What's being overlooked got to do with it?'

'They want to skinny-dip. No cozzies.'

Again Danny sensed the tension.

'I'll be off then,' he said. 'I'll give you a buzz when I've got somewhere with this.' He held up the diskette. 'Don't worry, I'll let myself out.'

Silence – just the muted hum of hardware on stand-by.

'Well,' said Annette. 'It seems I might be a touch *de trop*. I'll be off too. And rather quickly. I don't want to meet them on the doorstep. Danny? Hang on. I'm coming with you.'

Should he remonstrate, plead? No time. Richard realized he should have put the girls off, made some excuse.

By saying, without giving it a thought, that they could come, he'd put himself right in it, with Annette anyway. He followed them to the door, jabbering inanely.

'Come back when we've got it set up. See how it's all going. I'm sure you could help . . .'

But under it all there was relief. He was in a state of emotional confusion – reading about Lucy in his dad's words, the whole excitement of having a project which would really involve him, mean something – all he wanted was to get back into *Tragectories*.

He stopped on the doorstep, lit a thin spliff to steady his nerves, and watched the two adults as they walked down to his gate. The girls appeared just as they got there. A moment or two of greetings, farewells, pleasantries he supposed, then the girls came on up towards him – Delice, tall, thin, a bit gangly, wearing shorts, a vest (Key West, Florida, so one of her mum's he supposed) and trainers; Sophie, shorter, plumper, but by no means fat, her glossy, long black hair falling on either side of her heart-shaped face, a half-smile behind her hooded lids, wearing a short bathwrap and flip-flops.

Coming to skinny-dip? Did that mean there was nothing but Sophie under the wrap? The back of Richard's throat prickled and he felt the moistness break out in his palms.

'Hi,' he said. 'Delice knows the way, don't you? Make yourselves at home. I'll be at the other end of the house, in the orangery, if you can't find what you want. Just give me a buzz on the internal.'

He was aware of the faintly jocular and patronizing tone of all this – they were all of forty years younger than him, and radiantly lovely as well.

'Good old Richard,' sang Delice. 'Mum was sure you wouldn't mind.'

'She was right.' He blundered on. 'Now, you've got sun blocks . . . ?'

And his voice faded away as a shadow of puzzlement crossed both young faces. Of course. Their skins had been filter-hazed – in much the same way as when he had been their age your teeth, if you could afford it, were coated with permanent heat-sealed film to prevent tooth decay or discoloration for ever. They ran up the stairs trailing silvery laughter behind them, and he turned back to the orangery.

29

He reopened TRAGECTORIES and quickly saw that the section which followed the Lucy scenario probably ran on for some time and was mainly filled with exegesis rather than description or narrative. It was, however, all presented in a dramatic and contentious way. For instance, a long chunk was in lecture form, but with stage directions that indicated the lecturer was a pompous smoothie, an old-style Oxbridge don before the Blair reforms ... No, that was wrong, the academic expertise might be Oxbridge but the manner was old 'public' school. Sure of itself, arrogant, yet urbane and occasionally witty, though for the most part at the expense of others. He was, according to the directions, to be performed by an actor who was balding, pink-faced, plump, wore gold-rimmed spectacles, a spotted bow tie and a dark suit. Casting his mind back, Richard could just about recall that this was the sort of person his dad most despised and hated. The sort, he'd say, who would be first to hang from lamp-posts come the revolution.

This was the man who presented the Savannah Hypothesis.

It soon became apparent that there was a second dimension to this lecture, a dimension which apparently was going on in the mind of a listener who was probably a woman and certainly hostile to the lecturer and his subject matter, and whose thought processes were italicized. Visuals illustrating her position were also indicated and described.

Considering it was all written, typed words scrolling up a screen, it was remarkably successful as itself, although clearly Dad had envisioned and hoped for a fully dramatized, illustrated version as the end result.

Somewhere between four and eight million years ago a pre-hominid ape came, Tarzan-like—

Tarzan was a man. Why not a woman?

But who, Richard strove to remember, was Tarzan?

> —down from the trees and saw, stretched before him, a mighty, rolling, undulating plain filled with game . . . But I anticipate. Fifteen million years before that, in the wonderfully rich climate of the Miocene, in the wet, fecund forests of what is now Kenya, there flourished populations of apes sharing a generalized body structure but including many, many types from small gibbons to large gorillas. From these a hominid branch on the tree of life might have appeared . . . but then came the Pliocene drought which lasted twelve million years. This forced back the forests on to the very edges of the lakes and rivers of central west Africa. Many of the primate species were wiped out and those that remained reappeared as brachiating apes – swinging by their arms from branches . . .

> Back to Tarzan. Swinging from branches, often with his feet on the ground he—

She!!!

> —was already venturing towards bipedalism—

'I want to ride my bicycle,' Richard sang to himself

> —to walk on two feet, not four—

Ah! Not a two-pedalled bike.

> Imagine him, then, on the edge of what we have recently learnt to call the mosaic environment, the mixed environment of riparian forest, park-like woods, grass and scrub; imagine him looking out over the savannah proper, a wide rolling plain of grassland teeming with game. He likes meat. Hyena-like, he's scavenged the cadavers of already dead beasts. In the forest his main source of food is fruit for which he competes with every other primate and a few other

species too, whereas out here, the cattle, antelopes, zebras and other wild horses roam in abundance.

Personally I would prefer to compete for my food with monkeys rather than sabre-toothed tigers, especially when the tiger might prefer me for his lunch to an antelope. After all, there'd be much less effort involved in catching a man. But . . . there you go. We are after all, self-confessedly, talking about MEN, are we not?

[Visuals: Two furry apes standing on the edge of the forest looking out over the savannah. They support themselves by hanging on to the lower branches of a tree. One is clearly male, the other female. A sabre-toothed tiger appears, stalking them out of the long grass. The female swings herself up into the tree. The male lets go of the tree and with very awkward bipedal gait tries to run away. The tiger catches him . . .]

But what does he need, this remote ancestor of ours, to equip him with the means to make the most of the savannah and its rich reserves of meat? The answers are clear. He needs to be able to use weapons . . .

[Rerun the visual. The male ape picks up a stick and waves it at the tiger. The tiger catches him.]

. . . and he needs to be able to run fast through the long grass. To do this he must lose his hair, become a naked ape.

[Rerun the visual. The now naked male ape runs awkwardly through long grass. The tiger catches him. Shots of herds of animals running wildly across the savannah at great speeds, in all directions – all have hair or fur. So do their predators.]

And so it went on. The lecturer with all the self-congratulatory assurance of the type continued to unfold the arguments for the Savannah Hypothesis, while the visuals and the second (female?) 'voice' ridiculed and finally annihilated him.

The first file closed with the lecturer giving a full, blow-by-blow account of male hominids in a hunting party. They circled a wildebeest-type calf, threw stones at it and prodded it with sharpened bits of wood, while in the background, a quarter of a mile or so away, a group of females suckled their babies, minded the smaller children and waited the arrival of dinner with admiration and adoration in their eyes. One little chap kept moving out of the circle and the females all remarked that he was going to be a proper man, since already he was a proper little boy. The lecturer went on to describe how the dead calf would be brought back to the camp (even he, the intrusive second voice commented, seems to realize there are precious few caves in savannah land), where it would be jointed (How? With Sheffield-steel kitchen devils?), and each of the men would bring chunks of meat to his own special mate pre-bonded by the shape of her Pamela Anderson breasts and front-facing vagina – with which she would reward him, after they had all eaten. Her sexual favours would be enjoyed, by him at any rate, with her on her back and looking up at him.

Thus the lecturer. The visuals told a different version. A group of very angry, very large-horned wildebeests came to the rescue of the calf and chased the men all over the place, treeing the ones who could find trees and goring and tossing the rest. Two leopards now appeared in the grass close to the females. One of the leopards pounced and caught the particularly noisy, spoilt and badly behaved male brat who had disobediently wandered away. Meanwhile the second leopard was throwing a scare into the rest, who with piercing screams of terror gathered up their young and ran across shingle and sand and up to their waists, the smaller ones up to their chins, into ... water! A lake? The sea? Does it matter? Thus supported (their bodies having almost exactly the same mass as the same weight of water), their ungainly, *unnatural* upright posture and clumsy walk became almost graceful and, blessed with subcutaneous fat rather than hair, they didn't get cold nor were their movements impeded by a slough of wetness. Some of them swam – a graceful form of breaststroke that kept their faces clear of the water.

The leopard paced up and down on the shore, lashing its tail, before turning inland to look for . . . a male.

Richard grinned, laughed. Good old Dad. He had always claimed to be a fully paid up member of the New Man club long before the term was even invented (though Mum, Katherine, had her doubts). He got on better with women than men and the only close male friends he had had shared the same inclination. Which was not, Richard had finally decided, that Thomas wasn't sexist. He was – but with a sort of reversed sexism that tended to put women on a pedestal, not in an Edwardian way, worshipping them from afar for their superior beauty, gifts of tenderness, fragility or whatever, but simply believing that by and large, taking one thing with another, women were cleverer and tougher than men. And better company.

Richard went along with this some of the way – but he was more rational about it, he believed, and also had a laddish side his dad had lacked. You don't spend your working life intensely but successfully in the company of three other blokes without a certain gift for laddishness.

Meanwhile, what *was* all this? Was it as he remembered it? It was certainly entertaining him far more than the hard copy had thirty-seven years earlier. Then he had skipped, been bored, had not had time. Thirty-seven years ago Latex Umbrella, Bad Grama's successor, was transmogrifying into Evil Trend; a contract was being drawn up for the first album; the bass player who was simply not good enough but who was a good mate and had contributed a lot of the material was playing up no end as they auditioned replacements; and so on and so on. The origins of mankind had not been on his agenda.

So what was it all? Clearly a hypothesis was developing, making out that man completed his (shit, damn it) *her* evolution half-in and half-out of the water? That was certainly the link between the Lucy section and this. And somehow his dad had been trying to relate this to an apocalyptic view of the end of man, or at any rate civilization, as we know it in the here and now. But what was the link? By postulating the paradise we came from, had he been advocating a return to it? Or was he, surrounded by the hell he perceived global culture to have become, merely expressing a nostalgia for a better past? Certainly, one thing Richard did find genuinely interesting was the idea that we had spent more time on earth, many, many more millennia, in this paradise than in the free-fall his dad now suggested we were in.

He closed down the systems and listened to the quiet permanent hum. At the other end of the house and one floor up two girls, as lovely as fifteen-year-old girls always are, were swimming naked in his pool or lying on the sundeck. No, he would not go and have a peep. But imagination was free. And he remembered Annette, and other women before her, swimming, some nude, some not, but seen through the transparent walls of the pool, and he thought, no, he knew, with a suddenly epiphanous frisson of certainty that set the hair on his neck beneath his ponytail stirring, that Dad was right, Dad and whoever it was had first came up with the Aquatic Ape Hypothesis. Those girls in their untroubled beauty were doing what they had evolved to do. And if Danny and he were really going to get serious about making a full-length feature out of *Tragectories*, then Sophie and Delice could well have parts to play – if they could be persuaded to take them.

30

Damien Floyd was in his kitchen when Annette came home. He had an office unit on the ground floor, self-contained, from which he carried out his duties as sub-regional sub-controller, which included a shower, toilet and a small kitchen with a cabinet deepfreeze and a nanowave defroster and oven with chargrill facility. On its turntable a Brit-Plast plate with the rigidity and appearance of alabaster slowly turned beneath a pink source of ultra-heat and light. The sauce on top of his tournedos began to bubble and then almost immediately a golden crust formed across it. A timer pinged and the pink light went out. There was also a bowl filled with french fries, and from a cabinet beneath the oven he pulled another filled with a chilled but very crisp, genetically engineered to be crisp, radiated to be crisp, caesar salad, only six years old.

He put his meal on the small wall table, lifted the foil cap from a half of Nuys San Giorgio, a chemical substitute for the real thing which wine experts in a blind test on the Leisure-Loving spec channel had concluded was as good as the real thing, and, at eighteen per cent alcohol, in some ways better. Floyd finished his whisky and ice, and poured the 'wyne' into the empty glass.

The meat, New Zealand beef and rare in every sense of the word, parted beneath the blade of his knife in a blood-oozing gash, and at that moment a blue light began to flash in his outer office.

'Fuck,' said Damien Floyd.

He walked round the console which supported his comms and information banks, and let himself out into the hall. The door to his unit closed behind him. It did not need his say-so to do so. Annette, sideways on to him, was touching up her lips, using a concave gilt-mounted mirror. She slipped the lipstick back into her handbag, smoothed the low-cut blue and yellow dress over her thighs, and turned to face him, hand on hip, a slight smile lifting one corner of her newly painted mouth.

The impression he received, possibly the one she was intending to give, was of a woman repairing her appearance after an hour or so of passionate fucking using a man as well as a fairly sophisticated sex-aid.

'Well?' he grunted.

'Well,' she replied.

'What was on the diskette?'

'I didn't see all of it. They might not have been all that wonderful by today's standards but you could apparently get at least a couple of novels on one.'

'So what did you see?'

'You're not going to believe this—'

He clenched his fists and moved forward, a snarl forming on his face. In the silence both heard the gas rumble in his stomach, but only he felt the pain. Ulcer? Or was it the cancer induced by convenience foods and factory-made booze? She hurried on.

'It's something his father wrote. Thirty, even forty years ago. It seems to be about evolution. How we evolved. Apparently from ape-like creatures who lived by the water. One of them, she was called Lucy, drowned . . .'

Her voice faded away.

He thought for a moment. 'He had a machine to read that diskette. But was it the diskette he was reading or the hard disk on the machine?'

Her turn to think. 'The hard disk. Danny took the diskette away with him. It wasn't in the machine at all while I was there.'

'Danny? Danny Blake?'

'Yes.'

'He was there too?'

For a moment the blood pounding in his head threatened to darken his vision. Could that love horse accommodate three at a time? If so, how? Blindly, in his jacket pocket, his hand grasped the bowl of his pipe.

'Who else ... what else ... is there anything else you should tell me?'

She watched him for a moment, her face a mask of concern, her heart lifting. Was he going to have a fit? A heart attack?

'Just now, as I was leaving, Delice Cowper and Sophie Pribendum arrived. They'd come to swim. In the nude. In Richard's pool. It's on the roof, you know, so it's not overlooked.'

Back in his office, as soon as he could get a line through to her, and it took twenty minutes, he made a full report to Mrs Pribendum. She expressed interest in what he had to say about the hard disk and diskette, but her face became blank and almost bored when he told her that her daughter was swimming nude in Richard's pool. It was as though she knew it already.

His tournedos and chips had congealed on the plate, the Nuys San Giorgio, exposed to the air for too long without being drunk, was vinegar, or at least a form of coloured acetic acid, and the salad had wilted. He pushed the lot through the waste disposal system, and ate a whole Somerset camembert instead.

Emma, Kate and Beryl decided to stay on the north side of the A31, which meant they had to walk through open countryside and then hilly woods, crossing the Melchester road between Bridgeford and Linwood. But first this involved them in a detour further north than they wanted in order to keep clear of Sandbourne airport. About an hour or so after they left the camper they could see the irregular diagonal cross made by the two runways from a hillside a mile or so away. Six F135s, Super Stealths, the successor to the Euro-Fighter, bought from America after the collapse of the EU, were parked like squat, elongated horse-flies on the white concrete. But there were also two huge and ancient C130 transport planes and, around the perimeter, armour – tanks and self-propelled artillery – possibly the vehicles they had seen earlier in the day.

'That's not a regional force, is it?' Emma guessed.

Beryl was certain about it.

'Only central government commands those sort of things.'

'So what's happening?'

'Aren't there always tanks and guns around airports?' Kate asked.

'Not really. Not normally. Regional troops, reservists, yes, but not on this scale.'

They pressed on, down footpaths and tracks that had once been minor roads, through and round plantations in the valleys, across drought-dead pasture on the higher ground where a few scraggy sheep nibbled frantically at what little vegetation there still was. The farmland here consisted of protected enclosures with fences and surveillance cameras where genetically engineered crops grew in dense but neat, lush lines. Mostly these were an experimental low form of storm-resistant maize only two feet high with fat cobs, or soya with seed pods as big as old broad beans. There were also areas where hedges had gone wild and surrendered to exotics and escapes, where the old trees had fallen to rot and a scrub of secondary growth had risen in their place. Later in the afternoon thunder lurked in the hills to the north and sheet lightning flickered behind the stacked clouds above them. They were very weary now and hungry too, but the fences between them and the crops looked and probably were lethal. Pinta, inside her plastic carrier-cage, mewed plaintively, ceaselessly.

'She's hungry,' said Emma, using the childish voice one does with loved pets.

'More likely wants a pee,' said Kate.

'If she's hungry, give her Garth,' Beryl suggested.

'Certainly not.'

'Give him to me, then. I'm so hungry I've got gut ache. Oh Christ!' And she ran off into what was left of an old hedge.

Emma, prompted by what Beryl had just said, felt in the pocket of her coat. Garth, the hamster, had gone. But at that moment Beryl moaned, 'I'm shitting blood.'

Emma said nothing more about the hamster.

In Southampton, a dawn, lucent and pearly over the sheeted water that stretched for a mile to the other side of the Test estuary, had heralded a day that seemed, in the crowded confines of the multi-storey car park, unbearably hot and sticky.

In the early morning there was some sporadic gun fire, mostly small arms with the occasional crump of a mortar bomb, and black helicopters racketed back and forth across the city, but by midday everything fell into a sort of hot, somnambulant calm. It was amazing, Hannah-Rosa thought, how the people around her, and people in general, everywhere, quickly accepted a lull in acute misery and began, numbed though they might be, to rebuild the humdrum everyday routines that maintain life – the routines of child-care, procuring food, eating, drinking, sleeping, defecating and taking a pee.

Sheep, she remembered, penned in a cote, waiting for the butcher's van, behave in much the same way but at least cannot foresee what's to come. Humans in a similar situation for the most part do not have that advantage, yet, by and large, most of them wait and wait, and hope something will happen to alter the future. But they do fuck all about it themselves.

> O God, our help in ages past
> Our hope in years to come
> Our shelter from the stormy blast
> And our eternal home.

The tune of Isaac Watts' hymn still preceded the chimes of the clock at the top of the civic centre campanile before each fourth hour. Isaac Watts, hymn-writer and theologian, one of Southampton's favourite sons. The words that lay behind the notes seemed to sum things up pretty well. God would see to it.

It was twelve midday and Hannah-Rosa, whose parents had taught rebellion, had had enough. Although the refugees had been told to stay where they were, none of the militia at street level did more than glance at her as she walked out and then back down to Ocean Village. A sort of plan had formulated in her mind. It was vague because it depended on so many imponderables. Could she get back to Swanage? Could she make contact with Richard? If she remained stuck in Southampton, would any of them be able to find her here?

But above all, she reckoned, getting out was the thing. She'd wait as long as she dared, she'd try to make contact with the others, but sooner or later it would be get up and go or wait for the inevitable, like a sheep. And the only way out she could think of was the Sea Spray.

She found the little yacht where it had been moored the night before and there was still a single, armed militia man on the quay above it. She then tried to find Roger, but was refused entry into the multiplex. Males only.

What else could she do? Pushing aching feet on and on through the stifling August heat, more tired than she had felt in years, depressed by the still, oily water, the refuse that heaved with the slow swell of the tide, and the litter that drifted over the quays, the abandoned vehicles and the few listless people around, the stale smells of ancient refuse, she crossed the piazzas and went back into the mall.

The old amusement arcade was open now. A handful of bedraggled kids were playing the machines with a forced, febrile gaiety. An old woman, with a money bag hanging from her waist like a kangaroo's pouch doled out pre-decimal pennies without charging for them. A laughing policeman laughed. And laughed. And laughed.

Hannah-Rosa watched and walked on, came to the laminated board under the stairs. It was covered with felt-tip messages; not an inch was free. Grimly making herself do it, she spent twenty minutes finding the wet cloth she needed. In the end it turned out to be a small child's T-shirt, left on top of a pile of rubbish. It was torn and very dirty. Yellow writing on faded purple read, beneath a smiling face, 'Don't worry, be happy'. She found a toilet where no water ran in the basins, but she was able to wet the T-shirt with the water in a toilet bowl, which, though dirty, did flush when asked.

She went back to the board, bit her lip, and forcing herself not to read what she was erasing, wiped out most of the writing in the top left corner – almost a quarter of the whole. Then she searched in the litter on the floor and found a green felt-tip. She wrote, in very big letters: 'Hannah-Rosa Somers, known as Daytona, is here and will be here as near to four o'clock in the afternoon, every day, as she can manage.'

Since there was nothing else to do she made her way back to the car park.

Tom was there, on the first level, pulled back from the front line to rest for a few hours.

She asked him if he knew what was happening.

'They talk,' he said. 'The council and the colonel in charge of the reservists. They're talking but they are failing to agree.' He shrugged. 'Won't be long now. We can't hold out for ever.'

Oddly echoing the thoughts she'd had a few hours earlier, a small flock of sheep appeared, herded down from the parks where they had been grazing in front of the civic buildings. Six were separated out from the rest, one for each of the car park levels.

As night fell there was a little meat in the curry which the twins' mother passed round. She made sure her small boys got most of it.

31

'This aquatic ape theory is very interesting, you know.' Danny put the diskette down by Richard's elbow and on top of it a DEEP CD, an inch and a quarter in diameter but thicker than old CDs. Richard slipped it out of its transparent plastic envelope. It was matt brown with a slightly rough surface on the underside.

'I've got it transferred. You can play it all on your spec machine. In fact we can get to work and see what we can make of it.'

Seven o'clock. The girls, Delice and Sophie, had gone an hour or so earlier, filling the hallway with laughter and pecking Richard's cheek as they went. Richard had continued to explore his dad's files on the hard disk of the old Amstrad, but not in any organized way, just dipping in here and there.

'Where do you think we should start, then?'

Danny put his palms on the edge of the console and leant forward, head skewed to one side on a level with Richard's.

'There's a chapter which sets it all out quite briefly, but with some detail. It makes a good case. I don't think we should put it at the beginning – indeed your dad didn't. He had the Lucy taster and the debunking of the Savannah Hypothesis well in front of it, and other material too, but it will give us a grasp, a handle on what it's all about.'

He slotted the DEEP CD, while Richard brought up the smaller screen and activated the three big ones so they glowed.

'Right. Look. Let me have your seat. I've worked out the sort of thing we can do.'

They wheeled in a second chair and sat next to each other in front of the console.

'We start with a woman presenter. Why? Because your dad said so. And because it was a woman, Elaine Morgan, who worked out the whole caboodle from some time in the sixties right through to the end of the century. According to your dad, it got a lot of support, but for most of the time unorganized, uninstitutionalized, sporadic and unofficial. I don't know what she looked like, but that doesn't matter. We'll open the presenters/female file, and see what we can find. Someone intellectual, but personable, feisty. Do you remember Joan Bakewell?'

'Who? No, can't say I do.'

'Well, take it from me, she's the type we want.'

Using the latest search and find, cut and paste techniques he built up a visual of the sort of woman he was looking for, gave her a studio, a chair and what looked like a big blackboard. Then he isolated a chunk of Thomas Somers' text and put it into her mouth.

'The aquatic theory of human evolution,' she said, 'was first propounded by an eminent marine biologist, Sir Alister Hardy, in nineteen sixty—'

'Voice is a bit squeaky, and she sounds like royalty.'

'O . . . K, soften the voice, deepen it a little. But I thought the accent gave her a sort of authority—'

'Spurious. Dad would have hated it.'

Danny made adjustments and then let the virtual presenter continue.

'The first thing that troubled Sir Alister was that, of all the apes, all the primates, we humans are the only naked, hairless ones. He wanted to know why.'

She moved across to the display board.

'He had no time for the running fast on the savannah explanation. He knew, just as we all do, that the fastest mammals in the world live on the savannah and they all have hair or fur.'

Danny froze her but still whispered, as if he thought she might hear him and tick him off for talking in class: 'What your dad wanted now was the display board to show not just pictures but moving pictures. I think he was thinking of old-fashioned digital animation but of course we can do better than that. Anyway we go into the display board, but with the woman's voice-over. First of all a hairy hominid. That shouldn't be difficult.'

Richard quickly found one.

'Take its hair off,' the virtual presenter commanded, using Danny's words now, which he typed in for her. He was good on the keyboard, fast and accurate.

Richard dissolved his hair.

'No, not completely,' she came again. 'And why is this creature a man?'

'I expect you've already realized, from Lucy and all that, that this Elaine Morgan was a bit of a feminist,' Danny interjected, still *sotto voce*. It was he who had typed in her last comment, which the computer had converted to speech along with the rest.

'Back to the drawing board,' Richard commented, and pasted in a hairy female hominid.

'Now the hair off,' the presenter requested for a second time. The hair began to dissolve. 'Hold it, hold it, just there.'

The hair was now a sparse, short pelt. Danny gave the presenter back the words Richard's dad had written for her.

'There. Now, you see, that's not right. The hair all hangs basically downwards with very little variation – and that's not the sort of pattern the residue of hair, the hair follicles, on a human body make. The easiest way to show that pattern, reproduce it, is to put her in water and make her swim. Breaststroke, please.'

'Can we do that?' Richard asked.

'Should be possible.'

But it wasn't easy, nor was the result as natural and life-like as either of them wanted.

'That'll have to do for now.'

But Richard was thinking of what might be done with a digital camera and Sophie or Delice, preferably Sophie, in his swimming pool. Meanwhile the virtual presenter, with Dad's words in her mouth, was chuntering on.

'Mark the flow of the water over her shoulders, how it runs down her back into the hollows or sideways round the rib-cage, how the buttocks are often out of the water and more hairless than the rest. How on the front it breaks upwards from the collarbone to divide beneath the chin, and surge over the shoulders. This flow marks exactly the way what body hair we do have lies . . . At some stage, in the eight or so million years we still have left of the hot, unpleasant Pliocene, a hairy ape-woman took to the water and swam. Bit by bit she lost most of her hair, but it was still an impediment; it slowed her down, got in the way. And it went through a couple of interim adaptations before it got so sparse and short it left her naked.

'The first of these adaptations was that it began to lie, as we have seen, along the water-flow that passed over and under and around her body as, head out of the water, she swam. The second was that, like all semi-aquatic animals with some body cover between skin and water, from ducks and geese to otters and seals, she developed the ability to secrete sebum, an oily substance which covered the hair like a polish and rendered it waterproof. We still have that ability on a small scale – we would not buy shampoos made for oily or greasy hair if we did not – but it strikes worst in adolescence when it bubbles up under the skin and causes those awful facial and body spots which caused us all so much trouble. Were you called "pizza-face" when you were a kid? Now you know why . . .'

Danny froze her again as he could see Richard had something to say.

'Do you think we should have more visuals there?' Richard asked. 'Pictures of spotty kids, that sort of thing?'

'Your dad thought so – and before that otters and seals. You see one of the most stunning visual ideas he develops later is the streamlined beauty of humans, especially girls, swimming and diving in water and he wants us to see them, literally, alongside dolphins, seals, otters, sea-lions and so forth. But we can do that later. Let's just get on with the theory now.'

Again Richard thought of Sophie, her lithe body twisting and turning underwater, her hair streaming behind her, and he felt his diaphragm tighten and his breath and pulse accelerated a touch.

'Oh quite,' he said. 'Push on. That's the thing.'

Danny got back the almost hairless female ape.

'Let's put her on a beach.'

Search and find, cut and paste. Palms, tropical flowers and creepers, silver sand, green water, a reef, deep blue water beyond with breakers crashing white on the reef. It looked like the background to an old Bacardi ad. Perhaps it was.

'It's not quite what your dad had in mind, but it will do for now.'

Richard spread it across the three big screens and turned up the volume. Distant surf. A little juggling to get the scale right and there she was, standing on the edge of the water.

'She looks healthy,' said the presenter. 'And so she should, and, though still a little unsteady on two feet when on land, she can wade through the water without any difficulty since it supports her and helps her to keep her balance. All her bones and muscles work better, more efficiently, more at ease with themselves, swimming or wading, than they do on dry land. Above all she has lots of good food, a far more varied diet than before and the essential fishy oils that are needed to build bigger and better brains – fish and shellfish, seaweed too, as well as the fruits that grow along the forest edge. Problem, though. Shellfish have shells . . .'

Reading Thomas's script off the small screen, Danny whispered, 'Make her crouch . . . on her haunches.'

'No problem.'

'Make her find, let me see, a scallop . . . or an oyster.'

He reactivated the presenter.

'How is she going to get that tasty morsel of juice and glob out of the shell?'

But this time Richard's mind had leapt ahead of her and he had already put a pebble in the naked ape's hand as the voice-over surged on. 'She finds two stones, puts the shell on one, and bashes it with the other. But carefully! She's done this before. In such a way that when the shell cracks and she can get her nails in the gap and force it open, she can catch the juice in her mouth, and then, pulling it wide apart, use tongue and teeth to separate the blob from the tougher tissue that fastens it to the shell. Mmmm. Lovely—'

'We can tidy it up later,' Richard muttered.

'And what has she done? She's used a tool, but don't get too excited about this – sea-otters use the same technique. It's a start, though. But, oh dear, what's this? The sun has gone in—'

'Easy,' said Richard and put a cloud over the sun.

' —and she's shivering. Poor thing, she's cold. Perhaps, for some of the time at any rate, it wasn't too clever to lose that fur coat. Let's move on a few million years and see what she might have done about it.'

'Right,' said Danny. 'Make her swim off into the sea. We lose her. Then she's a dot out near the reef. Now she's swimming back in again and, lo and behold, she's quite different. She's fat . . . No, that's a terrible exaggeration and a slander. But she has fat under her skin – almost everywhere except on her head, her lower legs, her lower arms, fingers and toes. Listen to the presenter as we watch her come towards us out of the sea.'

Virtual Joan Bakewell again.

'No longer is she a rather comic, short-haired, skimpily furred, possibly greasy ape-like creature making a bit of pig's breakfast of being bipedal. Helped by generations upon generations of wading and swimming and breeding within a limited genetic pool, combined with natural selection, she has mastered bipedalism on land as well as on water and she walks with a wonderful easy grace. From behind she sashays just a little because her pelvis has broadened and reshaped to accommodate two factors which for a time seemed contradictory – the bipedalism which had put a kink in her birth canal, and other factors which had led to her producing babies with large if squashy heads.

'But we will come to all that later. For the time being we are talking about the third of the factors Sir Alister worried about after nakedness and bipedalism – fat. Fat not used as a store of energy when food or drink are scarce, as with the camel's hump, but, lying just beneath the skin as it does, to keep us warm and help us to maintain an even body temperature in water as efficiently as hair or fur did on land. Fat which helps us to be buoyant. Fat which accumulates on the most vulnerable of our species and their carers: babies, and the women who look after babies. Fat on both men and women when they reach middle-age and, since they are no longer able run away from sabre-toothed tigers, prefer to spend more time in the water.

Isn't she lovely? But there's a lot more to learn about her yet.'

'Good.'

This had taken a lot longer than it takes to tell – especially in getting the visuals up from the vast library held inside Richard's spec-maker, activating them, making adjustments as they went along to colour, sound, focus and so on. Danny intervened now in what was becoming a conversation between Richard and the virtual presenter, albeit Richard was feeding the words into her mouth via his keyboard. There were many cases on record of this sort of thing happening with lonely spec-makers – indeed, a mythology had sprung up similar to the one surrounding ventriloquists' dummies and their masters.

'Tomorrow, Richard. Tomorrow. It's late now, and I'm going home.'

They sat in silence for a moment, then Richard sighed and began to close the systems down. When all in the orangery was dark, he took Danny to the front door and they stood there for a while, sharing a spliff.

'Excited? I can see you are.'

'Yes. Very. This is just the sort of thing I needed to wake me up. Is it any good?'

'It's good. It's great. You could make something quite big out of this—'

'We.'

'All right. We. Of course we'll have to see how it goes on, whether or not your dad's material holds up. But it is . . . very visual. I mean, I think that's what your dad wanted.'

Richard sighed, thought back.

'You're absolutely right,' he said. 'He was mad about cinema, film. Given his life again, he'd have been a director. As it was, what he really longed for was to script a really great film. Something new, something mould-breaking. An epic but in a new style. The greatest story ever told.'

'Well, we'll do it for him. Problem is,' Danny gave a little laugh and the Irish lilt crept back into his voice, 'no one but us'll ever see the bugger.'

'Oh, I don't know. But anyway I don't think that matters. So long as it's there.'

A helicopter thrashed the air in the distance. A shift in the wind brought a whiff of burnt kerosene on it.

'We fucked up, didn't we?' Richard murmured. 'Not us personally. But the whole fucking human race. That's what it's all about. Agriculture, technologies, capitalism. The global, unregulated, unregulatable market. And now wars, pollution: the planet's giving us notice to quit.'

Danny said nothing, but patted Richard's shoulder, squeezed it and trudged off through the gravel. Somewhere an owl yipped, and that was a surprise. You could, Richard thought, even read a sort of hope in it – if not for *Hss*, then life of some sort. *Athene noctua*, anyway. He remembered that. Dad's obsession with owls and his favourite, the little owl.

He went back indoors. A bleep and a tiny flashing green light on the comms board in the hall sent him upstairs. He switched on his personal computer, and found he was being directed to the Pittsburgh, PA, office of one of the spec companies whose board he was still on. From there he was routed to the Los Angeles subsidiary where he still had a mail-box he had almost forgotten about. At last he picked up the message that was waiting for him.

Dear Rich

I am still alive and still at the old address in Brussels (see the end of this). But it is also the case that lines from Europe to CGB are blocked and censored so I am trying various other ways of getting this to you.

I have friends in the Foreign Ministry here and they tell me things are very bad in England with civil war and massacres, especially of anyone who was ever any sort of dissident. All I'm saying is if you can get out and across the Channel you'll be reasonably safe here. And anyone who's with you that you'd like to have along. Perhaps you even know where H-R is?

Love
Mum.

Katherine Somers, Euro-Language Link, Rue Horta 18/3, Bruxelles.

PS. I have just heard Euro-ships are gathering to the South of the Island. If you can get to them, they will look after you.

And an email number.

Richard felt overwhelmed, his soul as vulnerable as an unshelled hermit crab. First Hannah-Rosa. Then his dad, albeit on disk. Now his mother. Again he went to the window. High on hash, high on the spec he and Danny were making, and with earth tremors very deep in his psyche, he looked up at the night. Slowly a recognized but long-forgotten feeling stole through him, staining every cell in his body. He felt . . . wrapped. Enclosed. Looked after. It grew on him and then the idea came that if there was such a thing as a collective unconscious, and he really rather thought there was not, then surely something like this would be its centre. An immeasurably painful, but immeasurably sweet . . . emptiness. It is not the Freudian womb we long to return to, but paradise. Eden.

32

He did not sleep. Excited to the core of his being and swept by tidal waves of emotion, towards dawn he gave up. He knew that if they were to make a fair start when Danny returned, preparation would be necessary. With the first chirp of a blackbird and the sky lightening in the east, he went back to the orangery and began speed-reading his dad's script, highlighting and printing off key sections. These he ring bound. Six hours later, high on tiredness but fortified by speed and black coffee, he was ready.

'Was there an Adam and an Eve? I'm sorry, I'll rephrase that. Was there an Eve and an Adam? Most expert interpreters of the evidence that suggests there might have been draw back from the idea with fastidious horror. Yet and yet—'

'Hang on a minute. Is this the same presenter as before?'

Richard scrolled back and forth.

'Can't be sure,' he answered. 'I think we might assume it is until we're told different. I tell you what, though. Look at this. The old bastard has at last got round to mastering columns, the split-screen technique. Commentary on the left, indications for visuals in the middle, sound on the right. Should make it easier to work it all up in spec format.'

'Doubt if it will make that much difference. Anyway, get on with it. This is interesting.'

'Yet and yet. Let's take Adam first. We all know that the nucleus of the male gamete, the sperm, carries, amongst all the other genetic information it has, either an X-chromosome or an X-chromosome and a Y-chromosome. If it carries both, then the zygote that is formed when it reaches the female gamete, the ova, will be a male, about half of whose sperm, when he reaches maturity, will also carry the Y-chromosome—'

'Not terribly original ideas here for visuals. He seems to be suggesting the sort of things they used to show us at school on videos about sex and all that.'

'Now the Y-chromosome is a tiny fragment of DNA—'

'Yes, you've guessed it. The usual double helix formed out of brightly coloured balls slowly turning against a dark background. We should be able to come up with something better than that.'

'Do stop interrupting.'

'In nineteen ninety-five molecular biogists examined the Y-chromosomes in thirty-eight males spanning the extremes of human diversity – examples from all the so-called different races – and discovered almost no genetic variation between them. This is very strong evidence that we had a single group of ancestors and that these ancestors lived, in terms of the history of evolution, very recently – these same molecular biologists reckoned only about a quarter of a million years ago. A single group of, it is estimated, not more than seven thousand males. Now while this does not of itself indicate an Adam for us all, it certainly does not preclude one. Any genealogist will tell you that most family lines of direct descent from any given individual eventually die out and in the course of the next two hundred and fifty thousand years (think about that for a moment – a span one hundred and twenty-five times longer than the two thousand years we call our era) it is reasonably probable that all the lines traced through males converge back to one individual, even out of seven thousand, who lived by a lake or inland sea, probably in the Horn of Africa.

'The case for a common female ancestor, an Eve, is even stronger ... though again the scientists, wary of provoking headlines in the popular press or even a resurgence of belief in the Adam and Eve myth, argue against it. The female case depends upon mitochondrial DNA. Mitochondria are structures found in cells that help the cells to produce energy but they also contain genetic material. And the thing about mitochondria is that they are only inherited down the female, maternal line, and a general thing about all DNA is that it accumulates mutations at a constant rate and therefore acts as a ticking molecular clock. Putting these facts together, scientists discovered that, as with the Y-chromosome, the degree of mito-chondrial DNA variation across the globe is very small, which again implies a comparatively recent past, and that the mito-chondrial DNA we all share must have originated in one female who, like the male, was probably one of a population not larger than ten thousand. I have to say it is slightly annoying that the molecular clock tends to put Eve up to a hundred thousand years later than Adam; that is, the one woman whose mitochon-dria live on in all of us. It is at this point that the scientists get angry when we call her Eve, the First Woman. She wasn't. But they misunderstand what most of us mean by Eve. We do not necessarily mean Eve, the First Woman. For us she is Eve, the Mother of Us All.'

'Is this boring, or not?' Danny asked.

'Depends where it's going. Stay with it.'

'OK.'

'So. What do we have? Let us recapitulate. Some four million years ago or so, the various forms of *Australopithecus*, of whom Lucy was one, were emerging in Africa as bipedal apes. They adapted, through natural selection, to a life near and in the water, on the edge of rivers, lakes and possibly seas. They lived or survived into an era of great climatic changes which must at times have reduced populations to a few breeding, and there-fore interbreeding, pairs – hundreds, thousands at most – and at other times to population explosions, at least in terms of the environment that was supporting them, which led to migrations away from their place of origin.

'The Pleistocene was a very angry era, not only climatically but also in terms of floods, tectonic movements, earthquakes and volcanic eruptions. From about a million years ago humans, *Homo erectus*, as they now should properly be called, migrated across the world, through the Middle East, into Europe, Asia, as far away as Peking and Java. One of the most recent members of the family of man, but the end of a different branch to ours, was the Neanderthals, who survived up to about forty thousand years BC, and were quite like us in many respects. But I repeat, none of these was the ancestor of *Homo sapiens*, let alone *Homo sapiens sapiens* or modern man. I mean woman. So. Where did she come from? Let's just rerun our woman with the subcutaneous fat, only this time I think we might put her in a lake rather than the sea—'

'Now what do we have?'

'Nothing from the presenter, just a bit Dad wrote in the visual column.'

'Let's read it, then.'

They did, in silence, and without attempting to create the visuals it asked for.

A huge sheet of still water. The colour of pewter, its millions of ripples, caught by the risen sun, sparkle with diamond intensity. An uneven transparent mist hangs above it: in places thick enough to make a wall, in others just enough to soften the outline and blur the detail on the mountains twenty miles away. With the sunrise the air fills with sound. Troops of monkeys chatter in the trees across the bay, a dawn chorus builds into a symphony of song punctuated by the calls and cackles of the bigger birds – parrots and macaws, birds of paradise impractically ornate, gloriously feathered in colours that became extinct when they did. Far out on the lake a huge host of long-legged birds thrash the water with their wings and swing up into the sky for no particular reason but the hell of it, before swooping in a great white dense arc back on to the water again.

The heat builds. Time passes. Presently thunder rumbles round the mountainous rim of the basin, lightning flickers. A few drops of warm rain clatter on the big leaves . . .

'This,' cried Richard, his voice thick with emotion, 'was one of the bits I read in the hard copy . . . oh, almost forty years ago.'

At first just her head, a tiny black spot right out in the middle of the lake. Clouds part and the sun, now almost directly overhead, sheds a pool of light that drifts with her, accompanies her in; the tan whiteness of her skin, her features beneath the streaming hair – high broad forehead, dark eyes above high cheekbones, a small straight nose and full lips that part and close as her strong arms lift her forwards and up in a slow, easy breaststroke.

Fifty yards out and she can stand with the water lapping just below her loose breasts, then her waist, then her tummy. The water ripples and breaks in a bow-wave as her thighs push through it and the droplets glitter in the hair between her legs. She scoops it with her palms and as she does the rain comes on more heavily, pocking the surface about her. A rainbow forms an arch of promise behind her.

'Wow,' murmured Danny. 'Can we do justice to this?'

'Oh, I think so. If you do the music, I'll come up with a visual that'll pass muster.' Richard leant back in the self-adjusting chair. He looked smug.

'How? You've got something in mind, I can see.'

Richard made him wait, and his smile got broader. At last he said it:

'Sophie Pribendum.'

He spaced the syllables as if he were a priest offering benediction.

Later that day he took a chance, and placed a special order for food he thought might represent the diet of paradisial Eve. He even busied himself in his kitchen, making up sauces to go with it.

33

Half a mile or so away, on the other side of the shallow wooded valley that held most of Hurling Enclave, Sophie's mother sat in her den, surrounded by her screens. Minute by minute their displays changed as information scrolled up or various eminent people, seeing, as they thought, which way the tide was running, tried to get into personal contact with her.

According to the Special Branch commissioner in Durham, a regional capital, the situation in Northumbria had resolved itself. Demonstrations in Newcastle in favour of secession from the English federation and incorporation with Scotland, where there was a syndicalist government committed to the reintroduction of state socialism, had been successfully played off against supporters of the New Carer Coalition under Chair Booth. The result was deadlock and a consequent power vacuum which was just what Mrs Pribendum had worked for.

Manchester was a different story. There the civil governor had ringed the airport with reservists and declared that if Blair International was closed to Chair Booth's return from Dublin, she could land in Manchester instead and be assured of a loyal welcome.

In London Boroughs, a headless chicken since the second Thames flood wiped out Westminster, the endemic civil war between rival factions, war-lords and ethnic groupings had become even more violent than usual and there was no sign that any one alliance would achieve the sort of ascendancy that could make London a power base for resistance.

The Permanent Under-Secretary (Subversion) at the Security Ministry reported from Birmingham itself, but not from his Edgbaston office – he was out in his enclave twenty miles away. Though he was as solidly impressive as ever in manner and appearance, she felt his confidence was somewhat forced. Possibly, she was beginning to feel, misplaced.

'The place is dead, my dear. The entire civil service has caught three-day flu, the summer variety, and no one above fifth grade clerk is in town. They're sitting on the fence – come out on top by Monday and they'll be at their desks waiting for you to tickle their tummies.'

There were other glitches like the Manchester one. In several cities populists had managed to rally mobs in support of the Boothites: fears of yet more welfare cuts and the prospect of real starvation were concentrating minds in favour of the devils they knew. However, in places where there were large ethnic populations this sort of resistance had been pre-empted by the fomenting of race riots, and even, as in Southampton, by ethnic cleansing.

These had served a second useful purpose – they justified the mobilization of the military where the reservists had sided with the whites. At the end of the day it was the mili who would topple those regional or city governments who continued to resist the installation of the Queen Presumptive (a general whose mother had been the Princess Royal) as head of a care-taker government.

Into all this an insistent bleep from the screen on her right intruded. At last things fell quiet enough for her to receive the call that was top of the low-priority queue. It was Assistant Com-missioner Skinner of the Special Branch of the Winchester Protec-torate. Since he knew, as indeed did Mrs Pribendum, that the military, ostensibly deployed to restore order in Southampton but in fact ready to move on the regional government in Winchester, was poised to take control of Wessex, she could not see what he could possibly want to say now. Nothing could have gone seri-ously wrong since he had been in touch twenty minutes before.

Framed by the display unit, his grey countenance took on form if not substance. Light from his own display unit flashed off his glasses.

'I know this is probably not important in the wider scheme of things,' he said, 'but I've had in reports relevant to Dick Somers. You remember you asked for grade B surveillance—'

'Yes, yes, go on, but be quick.'

'He's using his spec-maker with an illegal cut-out, so what

233

he's doing isn't logged on the National. Several hours worth of stuff missing.'

'What else?'

'The woman known as Hannah-Rosa Daytona, who gave him the diskette in Linwood on Sunday, is, we believe, his sister. "Daytona" is her stage name. She is at present in Southampton working for the civic council who are protecting the ethnics and are generally Booth—'

'Yes, I know that.'

'Next. Her friend Emma Monterey and her daughter Katherine, together with another member of the Harem troupe, a Beryl Krupa, have arrived back in Linwood. Protector Sergeant Whitlock has seen them there. They reported to the medical centre. Krupa has dysentery, possibly cholera. But they should all be in Swanage. And finally . . .'

He hesitated. She suspected he was going to say something she would not be able to accept.

'Finally?'

'Finally late last night Somers received an e-gram from Brussels . . . Yes, yes, I know, but the sender had cleverly got it through via Somers' business interests in the US. I'll mail you the full script, but in brief it told him there were vessels of the Euro fleet off Ventnor.'

'You're suggesting those ships are not just there to pick up refugees, that a landing might be imminent and Somers is part of a plot to co-ordinate support?'

'Something like that.'

'Rubbish. He's a playboy. A *flâneur*. An artist, for heaven's sake.' She tapped the table with her squared-off fingernails. 'All right. Move him up to grade A surveillance. And I think I might be able to do something this end.'

In spite of insistent signals that other functionaries were trying to get hold of her, she put the whole system into neutral. A mentholated? Not yet. She buzzed for her daughter.

'Richard? Delice here. Listen, Richard, the other night, Monday? Listen, I hope you won't mind my saying this, but your dancing was crap. Everybody said so.'

234

'My dear, how right you are. But does it really matter? Last year one of the audience, an old pro actually, said the way I was half a bar behind everyone else was the funniest thing he'd seen in years, and *must* have been rehearsed—'

'Oh come on. You're just ruining it for all of us. Ask Danny.'

'He's here, actually.'

'Well, that's fine then. Because what I was going to suggest was that I came round and we ran through the routines on our own.'

'I don't know. We're very busy. Working together on something rather big. And important.'

There was a pause, but he could hear talk in the background.

'Listen—'

'That's the third time you've asked me to listen. I *am* listening.'

'We'll come round anyway, and we can do the routines when you take a break from whatever you're up to. We can swim again. Like we did yesterday.'

'We?' But already his heart was pounding. He crossed his fingers for luck, but had guessed what she was going to say.

'Me and Sophie, of course.'

Richard buttoned out the contact and then crowed with delight. 'The gods,' he cried, 'I mean the goddesses, are on our side, they really are . . .' and he caught Danny's shoulders and swung him round.

'Sophie?'

'Yes, Mum?'

'No need to tell me. I heard it all.'

'You would, Mum, wouldn't you?'

'Sophie. Find out what this big and important thing is he's doing. I think I might need to know.'

'Look, we explained. This is for a serious spec we're making, serious art, serious science, about Eve, about the woman we're all descended from.'

Richard avoided the word 'mother', sensing that this gorgeous fifteen-year-old might not relish being a presentation of not just a mum but the Mother of all Mothers.

'Well, I don't know. What do you think, Del?'

Delice shrugged. Impasse.

'Are you sure this isn't for some porno spec?'

'Absolutely not, Sophie.'

'I mean, I don't like the thought of dirty old men all over the country coming off on us fooling about in front of them.'

'Sophie,' Danny intervened, 'have you ever seen a porno spec?'

She blushed a little, anger flared in her dark eyes.

'Of course not,' she said.

They were on the deck of the swimming pool: Sophie and Delice sitting with their knees pulled in, frowning up at the two men, eyes narrowed against the bright sky. Both men were holding quite large digital video cameras, large because of the sophisticated built-in extra gizmos.

'Believe me, if you had you'd quickly know that what we are asking you to do would be totally out of place in a porn spec.'

'Tell me again exactly what you do want us to do.'

'Just walk around a bit, then swim, dive, enjoy yourselves.'

'With no clothes on?'

'That's right. Just as you did yesterday.'

'Look. Here's what we'll do.' Danny tried to sound firm. 'We'll get the tripods up and then we'll mount the cameras, one up here on the deck, the other looking into the water from below. They've got tracking devices, spin-offs from surveillance equipment, and once one of you gets on picture it'll follow you until you're closer to the lens of the other, then they'll switch over. Meanwhile, while all this is going on we'll go away and play three-D dominoes until it's finished. Give it half an hour or so, give yourselves a chance to feel relaxed, forget the cameras are there. Then you can see the results and vet them before we see them. Anything you don't like you can take out. All right?'

Both girls brightened, and indeed, as the men set up the hardware, began to get almost restless, wanting to get on with it.

Five minutes later Richard and Danny were back in the orangery.

'Dominoes?'

Richard did not even bother to answer. He threw the switches which brought the big three-fold screen to life.

'Oh shit. Will you look at this?'

Delice was all right – a bit thin, a bit pale, a touch spotty. Those antique sebaceous glands. Nor was she all that graceful in the water. But good all the same, Richard thought. If there had been no choice she would have done. But Sophie . . . living proof, if ever any were needed, that women are biologically so different from men that a Martian might find it difficult to believe they are the same species. And of course far better adapted to water than men are.

Not tall, she had the proportions of a Tanagra terracotta; no, a touch more buxom than that, those of an Indian goddess carved in high relief on a temple wall. Her complexion, almond-shaped eyes with just a hint of oriental eyelids, high cheek-bones, spoke of an ethnic mix which was precisely what his father's Eve should have if she was to be the Mother of Us All.

By the time the men were in the orangery she had spread the bathwrap she had been wearing on the biscuit-fired flags that surrounded the pool and was lying on her stomach, head up, playing with a ringlet of black hair in front of one small ear. The line from her raised neck swooped over her shoulders, undulated across her back, rose for her buttocks between two enticing dimples before dipping again to the long swell and fall of the backs of her rounded thighs. It seemed to concentrate in it the gentleness of downy hills, bosky woods, dolphins and whales at play, wherever on our rounded Earth such curving lines occur.

Delice swam to the edge of the pool, shook water out of her face, clung to the edge with her fingers. She looked like a puppy, winsome, instantly likeable, but a puppy. She clambered out and shook herself in the way a puppy does.

Sophie kicked up one foot, waggled it in the air above her thigh, turned on one side and raised her torso on to one elbow. Her breasts, firm but full, shifted a little as she made a tiny adjustment to get more comfortable, then she pulled in one knee and straightened the supporting arm, hunching the shoulder against her cheek. They could just see the top of the triangle of hair in the groove between her thighs. She looked at the camera and stuck out her tongue.

'Does she know we're watching? Even though we said we wouldn't?'

'Of course she bloody does.'

She walked to the edge, looked in. Took a deep breath, and thanks to the control she had but which Lucy, four or so million years earlier, had lacked, held it, rose on toes that gripped the curved edge, and went in in a deep dive that scarcely ruffled the surface. The lower camera picked up on her.

'Will you look at that?' Danny repeated, the Irish inflection showing he was deeply moved.

Graceful and beautiful on land, she was a goddess in the water. She arced upwards trailing bubbles, silver and gold, black hair separated and streaming behind her, giving a quick flick and a twist as she broke the surface; then more air, and down again she went, slowly spinning, hand reaching for the blue-tiled bottom, before another twist and fluttering feet put her into a three-dimensional spiral, going through a sequence of unfolding planes, bringing her chin over her shoulder so she looked down at the lower camera before breaking through the jewel splatter of light. Back on camera one she trod water, pushed the hair and water from her eyes, and grinned.

'She's like a dolphin, a sea-lioness.'

'Oh, far, far more beautiful than that.'

'A male dolphin might disagree.'

'I doubt it. Can you put music to this?'

'I can try. But I can't do it justice. Debussy might have. Ravel even. Takemitsu. There's a Chinese American and that Australian woman Kylie Wolf. I could crib from Haydn, the second half of "The Creation". But me . . .' He let out a long sigh filled with self-doubt.

'Anyway,' he went on, 'you do music too.'

'Only on this junk.' Richard waved his hand over the huge console. 'Farting about.'

'Long time since you touched the old Fender, then?'

'Oh, a decade or more. I doubt if I could even lay my hands on it.'

This was patently a lie. Richard was so obviously on the defensive, and troubled by it too, that Danny shifted the tone of the conversation.

'Forget the arseholes I mentioned. We'll do it on our own. And we have one big advantage.'

'We do?'

'Her, she. Eve in person. As we compose it she'll be here, with us, not just in the pool or on a screen but moving around us.'

'You're in love.'

'Aren't you?'

'I might be if she weren't bird-brained.'

'Oh, come o-o-o-o-n.'

'Here she goes again.'

She came round, again underwater, in a big wide sweep which took her right past the camera in close-up so they could see the way her breasts and nipples parted the flow of water beneath her, then the ripple of muscles as this time her legs and pointed feet scissored, rather than coming together in a breaststroke movement, driving her on, head up, hair streaming again, arms by her sides, palms flat on her hips. She swung away from them towards where the bottom of the pool shelved upwards to a shallow quadrant on the far side. Her nipples and stomach and thighs seemed to caress the floor as it climbed and then, just as she ran out of supporting depth, she turned on to her back, pulled in her legs, and her head broke the surface at right angles to the upper camera. And there she was, sitting with her knees up and clasped, the water lapping the small of her back, looking over her shoulder, and she laughed, laughed up into the sky, and then across the glittering water at them. She let go of her knees, stretched her legs, slowly, languorously, put her arms and hands behind her and arched her body and breasts up at the sun. Then back to them, and with a grin that was not entirely innocent, perhaps not innocent at all, gave her upper torso a shake.

'Mother of God,' sighed Danny. Then: 'Where's Delice gone?'

A tiny cough behind them.

'Right here behind you.'

She had a long towel tucked under her armpits but she was still wet enough to shed water into the runnels carved in the marble floor.

'Well,' she went on, 'are you a couple of doms or aren't you?'

'Doms?' asked Danny.

'Dirty old men,' Richard guessed.

34

It was another hot, heavy morning, with gunfire more insistent than the day before and getting nearer. At about half-past eleven the percussions were close enough to make the air bend momentarily and send a shake through the concrete floor. A brief mushroom of smoke above the Guildhall roof settled into a steady column. The Guildhall? Surely that was where Hannah-Rosa when she was eleven fell asleep during a concert given by the Sandbourne Sinfonietta. 'Petite Suite'? Debussy? She'd danced to it later – prima ballerina *assoluta* of the Royal Ballet of Tonga.

Her thoughts and the sounds around her – the chatter of the Asians, an improvised steel band practising a calypso – were drowned by the distant but rising clatter of two powerful rotors. Then it appeared, cruising above the waterfront, over the railway station and Toys'Я'Us, just at the height of the top storey of the car parks, a Westland AH-7 Lynx helicopter. Painted a grey dark enough to be called black, with a flattened ovoid nose beneath two large curved, slightly bulbous tinted windscreens, it looked like a particularly nasty insect. Its side doors were open and as it came level with the car park bright flame flashed from the interior and 7.62mm tracer streaked out of the space, fired from a mounted Hughes Chain Gun, sweeping the floor Hannah-Rosa was on and the one above. Bullets smashed between the squared rails, whined across the spaces behind, or tore chunks of jagged concrete out of the stanchions. Because the outer walls were railed rather than protected by solid parapets, there was no cover inside.

The gun-ship banked slightly, wheeled out over the wide estuary of the Test then came back, a little higher, but straight towards them. Hannah-Rosa ran, tripping over bodies and the crawling wounded, to the furthest end of the floor. The evil nose dipped a little, smoke momentarily puffed and was shredded by the rear rotor, and then, trailing white vapour, the four rockets launched from rear-mounted tubes broke free. The percussions as they smashed into metal, concrete and flesh were terrible enough in themselves: the shock waves seemed to shake loose internal organs and left her ears singing and deaf for five minutes or more; but the after-effects were far worse.

A wave of white heat blossomed out of each missile, vapourizing bodies, clothes, bedding within ten yards, splattering burning sticky phosphorous over a greater distance; the blast picked up children and hurled them against the inner walls or smashed them into already twisted railings; smoke and choking fumes rolled outwards across the open spaces. Forty yards from the nearest explosion Hannah-Rosa was smacked against a concrete wall with a force that left her back bruised before letting her drop in a heap on the oily floor. The heat seared her eyebrows and hair.

She lay there for ten minutes, hardly daring to believe she was alive, feeling pain return to every corner of her numbed body, breathing in the awful stench of burnt organic matter, including flesh, mixed with used propellant and incendiary explosives.

Gradually, through her confusion, she became aware of people moving amongst the damaged and distressed bodies around her, of stretcher parties, of soothing noises amongst the screams. She dragged herself into a sitting position, rubbed her face in her palms. Someone handed her a plastic cola bottle with a cupful of water at the bottom, and someone else ran expert fingers over her limbs, held her head, made her move it.

'You're one of the lucky ones. I think you're all right.'

Five minutes later she was helping them.

The helicopter did not come back, but the bombardment of the civic centre continued. After an hour or so Hannah-Rosa, her face blackened, her clothes and hands red with blood, her own as well as that of those she strove to tend, sat with her knees up against the concrete wall facing the drive-in on the ground floor of the car park. She struggled with a soyaburger, drank brackish water from the cut-down half of a plastic bottle.

Tom, the student in digital surveying, knelt in front of her. His left arm was in a sling, the hand below his red militia scarf a club of blood-soaked bandages. The surviving Asians and Afros had gone, moved down towards Ocean Village and the quays, leaving behind only enough men to use the few ancient FN automatic rifles they had been able to find in the Territorial armoury. They were down to three or four magazines each. Tom had come from the Guildhall to have his hand dressed. His speech was slurred now and slow – the result of the morphine he'd been given. With his free hand he drew on the last half of what was probably his last cigarette – a Senior Service taken from the store of one of the minesweepers.

No one was screaming any more, but there was an occasional pop-pop of small-arms fire not far away and then the rattle of automatics. Smoke and fumes eddied listlessly across the concrete floors, bringing the tired smell of burnt buildings and unventilated butcher's shops.

'What's Balkanization?' he asked.

She thought for a moment.

'What happens when a country falls apart into factions fighting each other,' she suggested. 'Something like that. Why?'

'It's what I heard an old chap saying was happening to us, when we were getting back into the civic centre. I suppose now he meant England. I thought he meant just us.'

The Guildhall and most of the civic centre with it had finally been smashed to ruins by a laser-directed bomb fired from a Super Stealth. Tom, with fifty or so others, had been sent in to reoccupy the ruins. He went on.

'They're on the other side of the Isaac Watts now.' He meant the park that lay to the north of the civic centre. 'They've occupied the Pentagon Hotel and the buildings in front of Mountbatten Square. We're holding a line from where the top of the railway tunnel overlooks the station, through the civic centre and the institute down to St Mary's, but it can't last.'

'Mum and Dad had a basement flat near Mountbatten Square. It was a bus station in those days,' Hannah-Rosa said, but quietly, almost to herself. 'I remember them telling us about it. She was a student at the university then. Back in the seventies I suppose.'

'They'll have to negotiate a surrender.' He meant the city council. 'It'll be a massacre if they don't.'

'What will happen then?'

The civic centre clock began its chime – the tall obelisk-shaped campanile still, miraculously, standing. Midday.

'They'll probably kill the ethnics anyway.' He meant it would be the reservists and the non- or under-workers who would do the killing.

'And us?'

He shrugged.

O God our help in ages past
Our hope in years to come . . .

35

'An anatomy lesson is what Dad wants now,' said Richard firmly. 'We've already looked at comparative hairlessness and subcutaneous fat. Now let's think about breathing. We could use animation techniques as we did before, with Lucy, but sceptics could say we'd fixed them. So I think it's important we have the real thing. And as this is in a sense experimental, we'll keep the swimming-pool background, no need to change it to primeval swamp, lake, whatever.'

All four of them, the two men and the two girls, were back on the pool deck. They'd had coffees and soft drinks together and were now all more at ease with each other. The sun shone, the curvilinear parapets trumpeted their whiteness, the fragmented tiles on the walls of the house and its weird mushroom-like chimneys shone with enamelled colours, many of them metallic. Jigsaw lines of light shifted across the surface of the water.

Assured now of the artistic and scientific importance of what they were doing, Sophie had cast off what few inhibitions she had had, though she had acquired one or two new ones: she no longer laughed, she repressed any tendency to naughtiness or flirtation – she was taking the project, and herself, seriously. Delice was not quite so sure. She could not help noticing that Sophie had become the star of the show and that that was because Delice lacked Sophie's physical perfection (sexiness?). Delice was not jealous – she was too nice and sensible for that – but she could not help suspecting that the way the men doted on Sophie was perhaps just a touch unscientific. After all, not every single female in the early populations of *Homo sapiens sapiens* was presumably *that* perfect. Nevertheless she was happy to hold towels for Sophie, help them out when they lost one gizmo or another or the tripod needed fixing.

Richard was holding his ring-bound print-out of the relevant pages from *Tragectories*. He carried it like a script, opened out in the ring binder. Danny operated the cameras.

'First,' Richard continued, 'I want to time your normal rate of respiration. Danny, frame a shot that has the tip of her nose at the top and the top of her chest at the bottom, sharp focus, so we can see clearly whatever lip movement there is and how her chest inflates and deflates.'

'Not her tits, then?'

'Don't be vulgar. But no. Not relevant at this point. Hold it for one minute while I count. One, two, three . . . fourteen, fifteen, sixteen, fine! Sixteen to the minute, a healthy rate. Now, Sophie, I want you to read a poem. Do you know Shakespeare's "Shall I compare thee to a summer's day?"? Of course you do. Here it is. I want you to read it slowly and, so the meaning comes across clearly, pause only where the meaning indicates you should. Read it through first, prepare it.'

A couple of minutes' silence. Richard wandered over to the parapet, put his elbows on it and looked out over the slopes that climbed from the back of his house towards Castle Hill and the heath. The communications tower on the top of the hill, with all its discs and dishes, looked back at him.

'OK? Danny? Same shot as before. No. Stop. Open it up a bit more and this time you can take in her boobs and, and this is the important thing, her diaphragm below her rib-cage.'

Sophie took a deep breath from her diaphragm. Her breasts rose with it. Danny, eye fixed in the view-finder, realized his tongue had flicked over his top lip before he could stop it.

'"Shall I compare thee to a summer's day? Thou art more lovely and temperate", sorry, "more temperate", shall I go on?'

Richard, eye on watch, nodded furiously, and, in measured tones imbued with a false seriousness, her voice floated on to the end.

'". . . So long as men can breathe, or eyes can see, So long lives this and this, gives life to thee." Poof!'

'Perfect! Dead on one minute and only eight breaths.'

Danny stopped the digital video record.

'So what does that prove?' he asked.

'On me, Danny, camera on me. Well, first of all, the only

246

animals capable of controlling their breathing with their diaphragms are aquatic: seals, porpoises and the rest. For the remainder of the animal kingdom breathing is as automatic as digestion and heartbeat are to them and to us. It varies of course, but regulated involuntarily by the amount of carbon dioxide present in the blood. Second, aquatic animals, like us, can foresee when they are going to need a deeper breath before they take it. It would be a useless ability if they could not.'

'How do you mean?'

'We'll show you. You film it, we'll show you.'

He had come prepared. From his jacket pocket he took three pebbles, flat ones from the seashore he had collected years earlier for their shape and spiral markings, and put them on the deck near the edge.

'Excuse me,' he said, and peeled off the jacket, the linen trousers he was wearing, the red silk shirt and the hat. He tightened the gold toggle on his ponytail, and, naked, slipped into the water. He took the three pebbles and dropped them on the sloping bottom of the pool at depths of four, six and eight feet. Then he swam to the edge and, shaking his head and hair, hauled himself out. Delice was ready with a towel.

'Now, Sophie,' he said, over the towel which he held beneath his chin with crossed hands. 'One at a time, pick up each pebble, bring it to the side, and then go for the next.'

She dived from the edge for the first; duck-dived, arse in the air, for the other two.

'Oh Christ,' Danny murmured.

'Any difference between the breaths you took for each one?'

'Of course there was. I breathed deeper for the ones that were further away and deeper.'

'So there you have it. Camera on me, Danny. There you have it. Aquatic mammals, not just when they're diving, but in roughish water, fooling around splashing each other, control their breathing with their diaphragms. They can take a deep breath when they foresee the need and hold it. They can take a deep breath and let it out slowly in a controlled way, the way you do when you're speaking. To survive in water they evolved this ability, because survival depended on it if water was to be a major element in their habitat. Having developed it, they could then put the ability to a completely different use. Speech. Cut. Take five while we think through the next sequence.'

He picked up his father's script, sat on a ledge set in the parapet, leafed through it. The honeycombed marble warmed the back of his thighs and he felt how his scrotum relaxed. Sophie came and sat by him, her damp arm against his, and looked over his shoulder. He could just catch the tang of her breath in his nostrils and the deeper scents the sun was drawing from her body. She shook her head and for a second a lock of shiny hair flicked on to his skin and slipped off again. Sex, he read. Well, yes. But let's do food first.

He shook his head. He could hear a high-pitched buzz. Water in his ears? No. Outside. But high up. Very high. He glanced up into the bright sky, the angry sun, and flinched away.

'Richard Somers, your daughter and her friend Delice Cowper are swimming naked in his pool. A man called Danny Blake is filming them with a digital camera.'

'Just swimming?'

'At this moment in time your daughter is sitting next to Somers. He has a towel round him, but she has nothing on at all.'

Mrs Pribendum chewed a thumbnail for a moment.

'Listen, Skinner. There's no need for your lot to bother any more about that. I'll see it's dealt with at local level. You need to have all your resources available for more important things.'

She switched him off, dabbed the number code on her pad that would bring up the sub-regional sub-director, then thought better of it and cancelled it. Instead she left a message at the Linwood Protectorate ordering the detention of Emma Monterey, Katherine Daytona, and, assuming she was not already quarantined, Beryl Krupa. She'd move on Somers himself, and Blake, once Sophie had reported back to her just what it was they were all up to. Then, irritated that she had allowed herself to be sidetracked from far more important concerns, she reopened contact with MI5's Manchester office.

* * *

248

'Food,' said Richard, and stood. He turned a page of his dad's scenario and the towel slipped. He made a grab for it, then thought – what the hell. ' "The tropical riparian habitat, whether it is riverside, lakeside, or seaside is, of all environments, the richest in highly nutritious and palatable food, as far as human beings are concerned. This food also happens to be very readily available – not so much a question of hunting and gathering as getting off your butt and helping yourself—" '

'Nature's buffet?' Danny suggested.

'Quite.' He closed the script. 'And I've laid on a lunch which proves it. The only concession to modern tastes is that some of it, but by no means all, will be lightly cooked. Because that's another thing about seafood – we eat a lot of it raw.'

With what little self-consciousness he might have felt leaking away he walked across to the Frigidaire ('Past-Times Authentic?' Danny had guessed. 'No, it came with the house,' Richard had replied) and pulled out tray after tray of the food he had ordered from Booker-Lux, Purveyors of Good Food to the Enclaves, and placed them on a white rigid plastic table beneath a giant parasol.

'Sushi, naturally, baby crabs, langoustines, mussels, which have been steamed open, oysters, which I shall cheat with and use an oyster knife on – less messy than smashing them with a rock – and three different types of seaweed, sun-dried and crisp. I felt soy-based sauces and dips were beyond the capabilities of our ancestors but I'm sure that they were very knowledgeable about the flavourings and spices that were available, so I have concocted a couple of interesting pastes out of anise, ginger, garlic, pepper and so on. For afters: custard-apples, melons, pineapple, banana and sugar-cane. You can add honey if you find anything too tart for your taste. As an entirely unnecessary sop to twenty-first-century convention we have some wholemeal bread-rolls. Drink? Well, *they* could have had fermented coconut milk, fermented fruit juices, mead or naturally carbonated mineral water. And if they wanted to get really high they had cannabis, coca leaves, magic mushrooms, yagé, and so forth. We have Coca-Cola, Kashmir champagne and water from the spring down the road at Somerley. OK? Oh, yes. We use our fingers.'

For a few minutes the girls were a touch hesitant but both came from extremely privileged families and were quite used to exotic foods. Before long all were eating if not voraciously then at least with enthusiasm, exchanging titbits, urging each other on to try a little of this, a little of that.

Presently Danny declared himself to be improperly dressed for the occasion, and took off the kaftan-like garment he was wearing and what was underneath, apologizing as he did so for the uncomeliness of his paunch and male breasts.

'Entirely appropriate, old chap,' Richard said, carefully setting down a coconut shell filled with champagne. 'We have been into the fat issue already. Once you reach an age where running away from sabre-toothed tigers is beyond you, you would want to spend far more time in the water than before. The original *Homo sapiens sapiens* who made it into middle age needed a middle-age spread to keep him afloat and warm.'

He beamed around the table. The sun glinting off the water filled the concave surface of the parasol and was reflected down on their hair, bodies, food and drink. The whites, dove-greys, pinks, rose and red of the fish and shellfish glowed with it; the brilliant green of the fresh mint and coriander leaves that came as garnishes, even the russet-tinged olive greens of the seaweed, throbbed with psychedelic delight. Their skins made a harmony, a symphony: his own honey-coloured, Delice white, Danny pink and Sophie a rich creamy brown. The roundness of her chin, and the undersides of her breasts caught the shifting reflections of light-lines from the pool; her pinkish-brown nipples, pimply with the breeze that dried her, offered soft but firm promises.

They ate quietly, almost reverently, making of the feast something celebratory, even eucharistical.

36

When they had all had enough Richard once more said to Danny, 'Camera my way, if you please,' and turned again to his father's script, sometimes reading aloud, sometimes speaking from memory.

'Speech, the larger brain, social organization, the ability to pass on oral tradition, the invention of art, the moral imperative to be kind, these are human gifts. Savagery, aggression, defence mechanisms, the readiness to harry and even kill rivals, the establishment of pecking orders, all these we brought with us from our prehuman past. The good elements are foreshadowed in the higher primates, but only in us do they become characteristic defining traits. How? Why?

'First, we should understand the two requirements nature demands before a new species arises. One, the comparative isolation of smallish interbreeding poulations of the branch from which the new twig will emerge, coupled with relatively minor disadvantages in the environment which will be eased by adaptation. Major disadvantages would lead to extinction or migration. Two, that the development of a new ability depends in the first place on the existence albeit not in fully developed form, of the physical means for it to happen – physical means which originally arose to serve a lesser and possibly quite different purpose.

'Take what we discovered about breathing. Living in an environment that demanded the ability to swim and dive favoured the development of the voluntarily controlled diaphragm – this in turn made speech a possibility; that is utterance sustained beyond the length of the grunt, howl or squeak that one normal breath can accommodate. But why did speech become a necessity?

'Bipedalism had many very serious disadvantages but these were outweighed by the fact that in an aquatic environment it became an essential, conferring upon those who had it off pat a fitness to survive others lacked—'

'What has this got to do with eating fish?' Sophie asked, and yawned.

'Patience, all will be revealed.'

'Really?'

Absently she chewed on a soft-shelled baby lobster claw, sucked out the flesh. A tiny tongue of its coral hung on her lip for a moment, then her own darker tongue flicked it in. Richard, he couldn't help himself, covered the back of her hand with his palm and gently stroked it, moving up her wrist and down again. With the tiniest of subtle muscle contractions she communicated to him the message, 'Do you mind?' or, 'Give over!' He removed his hand and continued.

'Bipedalism enabled us to wade into the water. And once we were living in the water bipedalism improved. They, we, became yet more upright. And the disadvantages of being upright, which are many, including especially the difficulty our bones, joints and internal organs, all of which were organized round a basically horizontal spine, put up with, are now alleviated by the support water gives. Hence the benefits of water therapy to all sorts of ailments we, particularly as we get older, are prone to.'

Richard leafed over a couple of pages of script.

'Richard, I could do with some water therapy right now,' Delice interjected.

'Go ahead. Have a swim. Danny ... camera on me, please.'

'Coming, Sophie?'

'In a minute. I just want to hear this bit through.'

Sophie sensed that her rejection of his earlier caress might have seemed unkind to Richard and she wanted to make amends.

'Anyway, in water we become not just bipedal but very definitely upright. Our skull sits on our neck so the plane of our faces is vertical, our pelvises develop to carry all our body-weight except our legs and our legs develop to carry the lot. But not too well, except or unless we are in water. But the most marked change and, apparently, the most disadvantageous, is in the female reproductive organs.

'Upright posture moves the vagina towards the front and puts a kink in the birth canal; it also makes the gap in the pelvic girdle too small to accommodate the passing in birth of a fully developed human child. These two factors mean that human beings are born several months premature and in a state that requires intensive care for several months following parturition. In order to survive this disaster several abilities, already potentially available for other reasons, had to be developed.

'One. Babies are born with soft skulls and skull plates that can move independently of each other. They couldn't get out otherwise. But this in turn allows the huge increase in brain size in the first months after birth to take place. This expansion itself requires an extremely rich diet, particularly high in Omega three long-chain fatty acids: and where do you find them in abundance? In the seafood and freshwater food chains. That's your food question answered. And also, except in cases where the mother suffers from poor diet, in mother's milk.'

It required resolution but he manged not to glance at Sophie's breasts.

'It's all coming together you see. Bipedalism, upright posture, soft skulls, seafood, big brains. But there remained a problem. Children are not only born prematurely but they also need many years before they reach maturity and the ability to look after themselves. To achieve this, advanced social cohesion was necessary, and that depends on the ability to speak and not just speak, but organize.

'And the big brain . . . The greatest blessing? Or the greatest curse. You see, through the accidents of nature it is far bigger than it need be. It has been shown that even the most mentally active people use less than half of the brain power available to them: from birth to the grave we leave billions of brain cells unused or underused. It has been said that the brain of Mozart's serving maid was identical to his in potency, but that it lacked the nutrition his probably got, freedom from the stunting effects of poverty and disease, and of course she was not born into an intensely musical environment where everyone played several instruments, sang and composed, and where the dominant parent was an ambitious but basically kind mentor. This is the point about brain potential and actual achievement: use it or lose it.'

He offered the last champagne bottle to Sophie, who declined it, so he upended it into his coconut shell, and swallowed down what was left, wiped his mouth on his wrist.

'But I, we, Dad and I, digress. Our trajectory had reached its meridian, or rather a long season, a noonday and afternoon in Eden. For a hundred, maybe a hundred and twenty thousand years small populations lived on a paradisial plateau of semi-aquatic bliss, almost certainly in Africa, almost certainly by shallow seas sometimes land-locked, sometimes open to the Indian Ocean, between the Great Rift Valley and the southern end of the Red Sea. Our natures continued to develop, more slowly as the pressures of environmental stress grew less and our mastery of them increased. This mastery was probably more a matter of learning, organization, speech and so on, than actual physical adaptation.

'But of course the trajectory had to become our tragictory. Perhaps there were droughts and a shrinkage of the eco-spheres we inhabited. At all events there came a time when, clan by clan, many of us migrated away from the rivers and water, north up the Nile and the banks of the Red Sea, into Mesopotamia, Arabia, India, Europe, the Far East and eventually across the land bridge into America and all the way down America to Tierra del Fuego.

'Maybe hundreds of clans set out on this terrible journey, each between one and two hundred strong—'

'Why? Why that many?' Delice was back again, refreshed by her swim.

'It's the most viable number for a self-sustaining, self-reproducing colony of humans. Enough to maintain a balance or rebuild one after a disaster, enough to provide hands for the necessary divisions of labour, but also not so many that everyone does not know and care for everyone else. Human ability to empathize with suffering, pain, hunger, loss, depends on knowing the people who suffer. If we don't know them, then

254

we don't really, effectively, much care. Which is another reason why we're going down the tube now. Too many of us, but each of us too fragmented from the rest, so most of us have only five or six close family members we would make sacrifices for. But that's another story, a later one. Right now I'm thinking of those countless lost tribes or rather clans. Or at least telling you what Dad thought about them.

'He thought that most went to the wall. Predators in the savannah, starvation and thirst in the desert, competition with other sorts of humans who were already there and had adapted to survival in these new habitats: cold, heat and cold again. You must remember this period moves into the ice-ages.

'But a few survived – say between five and eight clans, each originally a mere hundred or so strong. They became widely separated by distance and time, cut off from the gene pool they had come from. Already all closely related, they became even more inbred and gradually each developed characteristics which made them appear different from the others. Some developed big noses, others small ones. Some the oriental eyelid, some blue eyes. Some grew tall, some remained small. Not only inbreeding but also natural selection accentuated these features. Sexual selection also played a part, reinforced by cultural pressures. If you were an eskimo lady, you preferred the idea of mating with a small, stocky fattish man rather than with a thin rake who would probably develop pneumonia just as the kids were born, while the same process in reverse took place amongst those who found themselves in, say, hot savannahs.

'Each of these so-called races has a smaller gene pool than those who remained behind, the Africans. Admittedly the Africans all have dark skins, but apart from that across Africa the genetic pool is far wider than anywhere else. The smallest and the biggest people live in Africa. The smallest noses and the biggest ones exist in Africa. And the widest range of innate abilities exists in Africa though, in recent centuries, through colonialism and exploitation, poverty, poor diet, lack of education, and the rest, they have been deprived of the social and cultural background to bring them out.

'But before all this happened three other factors had emerged which I believe –' Richard looked up – 'I mean, of course, my dad believed, were of fundamental importance. The development of our intellectual ability, our aesthetic sensibility and the power to be kind all depend on a surplus food supply of great nutritive value and the absence of pressures to constantly seek shelter and warmth. In other words, they depend on the presence of leisure time, time spent not merely in the pursuit and absorption of food which occupies the lives of most animals. And this spare time, in our African aquatic homeland, we had in plenty.

'The other factor is this. Our ability to foresee the consequences of our actions. The embryo of this lies, as we have seen when we did the breathing experiments with Sophie, in the moment when we took a deep breath and held it, knowing that the consequent discomfort would be rewarded. No other animal does this as well or to anything like the same extent. A cat will undergo great discomfort to pursue and capture a prey but only because the greater discomfort of hunger is driving it, or the pleasure derived from the activity of hunting. But developed over a hundred millennia, this ability to put up with present hardship when promised a better future became the ability to walk a thousand miles to get to a better place, and later, much later, the ability to suffer terrible privation and pain for twelve or sixteen hours knowing a hearth, a bed, companionship and food would come at the end of it, indeed depended on it. You can make slaves out of humans, but not out of cats.

'The third factor, and it is again one that distinguishes us from almost all other species and is related to the second, is our ability to live anywhere. Perhaps this lies in the fact that we were never totally aquatic in the way a dolphin or a seal is, but, more like an otter, we always kept one foot on dry land. Incidentally, related to this are the marked differences between males and females, old and young; actual physical differences. Females, the very young and the old are better off in warm water than anywhere else, but fit men retain a hardness, a lack of fat and a hairiness which allows them to live, and yes perhaps hunt, on land, roaming inland away from water, often for quite long spells. Spells which became longer as the aquatic environment shrank. At all events, given our power to foresee future benefits through present pain, to organize and think, and this mixed heritage of land and water, we are able to survive as Eskimos, Bedouins, Amazonian Indians and even as dwellers in cities.'

He drew breath, turned his empty coconut shell on to its rim, and sighed.

'And so we come to the dipping trajectory. Once we had left our watery paradise a mere eighty thousand years ago, a decline began in the general happiness of man. Slowly at first, very slowly, we began a descent to where we are now. The curve became steeper, finally a plunging fall, a trajectory which now is approaching the vertical.'

Sophie sighed.

'I'm not unhappy. But I suppose I'm just lucky. How will it end?' she asked.

'My father guessed extinction.' He looked up at the sky, blinked. 'I wish that infernal buzzing would stop. What do you think it is?'

'Microlight,' said Danny.

'What's it doing?'

'Spying on us?'

'Gerroff!' Then: 'I'd have thought we were worth a satellite.'

A moment of lassitude, almost boredom, fell over them. It was the hottest part of the day. Sophie stood.

'Well. Extinct or not. I'm going for a swim,' she said.

Richard brightened.

'There's a beach ball somewhere around. We could play pig in the middle.'

'Or,' said Danny, 'if you'll let me put this damned camera down, water polo. Me and Delice against you and Sophie.'

'Whatever you like,' cried Sophie, and did a racing dive that took her underwater to the far side of the pool. The light lines made lacy patterns across her shoulders, down her spine, made a net that captured her buttocks.

37

Emma and Kate stood at the gates of Small Acres. They were not locked. If you lived in an enclave it was considered bad form to lock your gates: security began and ended at the fence. They looked up across the lawns and the cedars to the statues of Jimi Hendrix, the flowerbeds full of garish and bizarre exotica, the mansion itself, its twists and turns, its crenellations and flowing balconies, all but masking the neo-Georgian shell beneath.

'My uncle owns *this*?' Kate exclaimed.

'No call to be daunted,' said Emma.

'I'm not.' Her mother's daughter, her grandmother's grand-daughter. 'Why should I be?'

She pushed open the iron gates.

Undaunted perhaps, but very weary. When Beryl's dysentery got worse and dehydration began to tell, it had become clear that Harem's drummer was not going to make it to South-ampton. A signpost to Linwood had suggested a solution.

'My rich uncle lives near here,' Kate had said. 'He'll help us.'

But by the time they had reached Linwood Beryl was in a very bad state indeed. Late on Tuesday evening though it was, they managed to wake up the night-duty carer in the neigh-bourhood medical centre, who found a bed for her in the one small ward. The five other patients, terminal cases of crystal-meth poisoning and even old age, snorted, wailed and whined their way to death. The night-duty carer gave Beryl what she believed to be the right drugs and serums.

'She's strong. Got a good constitution. She might pull through. Some do.'

From her pillow Beryl achieved enough lucidity to override the pain and insist they leave her there and do whatever they could without her to get to Southampton.

As they were leaving the security guard behind his desk had

demanded to see their IDs. Of course he would have to report their presence to the Protectorate. With one hand still on their IDs, he reached for his mini-phone with the other, and the two women slipped out into the darkness and ran.

Ten minutes later, and out of breath half a mile down the Christbourne road, they stopped. Emma put down the catbox and they clung to each other.

At last Kate was able to say, 'But I forgot – Hurling is an enclave, isn't it? We'll never be able to get in or make contact.'

Emma thought about it.

'There are always ways in and out of enclaves. The locals and servicers know about them. There'll be someone in Thorney Hill who'll be able to get us in. And we know Sharon. The woman who was looking after your nan's house.'

They had slept in a thicket a mile further down the road and then, in the morning, as soon as it was light enough to see, had set off on the same route Emma and Hannah-Rosa had taken almost a week earlier. Old Sharon, thinking there was going to be trouble over the burning of Orchard Cottage, was very ready to help. One of Allan Pitt's cousins was found; he took them across the heath to the smuggler's tunnel that led into the old railwayman's cottage. Emma was tickled with this. It was, she said again, so much like the adventure stories for girls she had read when a child. The cousin gave them directions to Allan Pitt's council semi, and he, Pitt, set them on their way to Small Acres.

And now, in the early afternoon, they walked up the drive and approached the front door. They could hear squeals of excitement, mock-rage, laughter and the splashing of water.

'Someone's having a good time,' Emma remarked. But they could not see where the sound was coming from.

Kate pushed at the front door. That too gave.

Events had reached a crisis for Mrs Pribendum. All the threads were in her hands. She could turn the military against the regional governments, install the Queen Presumptive at the head of a potentially extreme right-wing central government, exclude Chair Booth and her entourage from returning to

England and Birmingham, and give the reservists and white non-workers in the urban areas a free rein to continue extermination of the ethnic populations, thereby reducing the welfare-to-work budget by ten per cent. Or she could turn the military against the reservists, halt the killings, restore order in the cities, arrest the Queen Presumptive, and at the end of it all present her bill to a grateful Chair Booth. Either way she'd get an inner cabinet post as Minister of Security and the prospect of better later.

Pragmatism was the key to it all. Which solution would give her the easier ride into the future? She had to admit that she had been surprised by the strength of white working- and non-working-class support for the ethnics in the inner-city areas. Organized support at that. Clearly old structures, trade unions, local parties well to the left of Chair Booth had remained more robust than her agents had led her to believe. And, it seemed, old ideologies of solidarity, mutual aid and so forth still informed these people.

Intellectuals and drop-outs, the beaded craftspersons and smallholders, the cultivators of home-grown pot, the animal libbers, and so on, had also rallied to the town halls. Many of these *rus in urbe*-ists, excluded from the countryside by fences, motorway boxes, regulations, the Protectorate and the reservists, had returned to the more anarchic cities and taken over the commons and parks, farming them in small lots with city council approval, and contributing quite significantly, by bartering produce for labour, to the survival of inner-city non-working populations.

This could be the moment to crush all that – or, under an apparently leftward shifting Blairite government, still headed by a chastened Chair Booth, institutionalize it, infiltrate it, castrate it.

Sitting in her panelled room, surrounded by eight empty screens, all but two of which had flashing lights indicating a building queue of people who wanted to talk to her, she tried to empty her mind, make herself calm, and sort out what would be best – not for the country but for Mrs Pribendum.

Decisiveness was, she knew, the absolute essential for a personality who would rule – a country, a continent, the world. Wrong decisions could be reinterpreted later to seem right, the results manipulated to make them right. But no decision at all spells death to ambition.

'Yet . . . and yet,' she murmured to herself. 'Give me time, I need time. Five minutes, ten.'

She lit a mentholated, put it in the ashtray on the floor at her side, pulled make-up, a comb, from her handbag and began to mend her grey, anonymous face. Suddenly she stopped and selected a caller: Skinner from Winchester.

She could hear his voice before his face was fully formed.

'I'm getting reports from Floyd. He thinks there are things you should see, happening at Small Acres. Richard Somers' house. Yes, I know you told me to treat it as local—'

'Patch them in on VD5.'

The screen next to the one Skinner was on came alive, to reveal an aerial view of the house, closing down to the swimming pool. Somers, Blake, the Cowper girl and her own daughter Sophie, swimming in the nude, playing with a big beach ball.

'There's something else. At the front door.'

A different picture. Two women. The older one with her hair in a bun and a long cotton skirt, the younger with close-cropped hair, shirt and jeans.

'Who are they?'

'The older one is known as Emma Monterey. She's a friend and associate of Hannah-Rosa Daytona, who is Richard Somers' sister. The younger one is Katherine Daytona and Somers' niece. I can get protectors in and make arrests if that's what you want.'

'No. I've already . . .' What was wrong with them, the local protectors? She'd already ordered the arrest of these people. 'I told you before. It's a minor matter – I'll deal with it. Thanks.'

She blanked him out, dabbed a new set of numbers.

Annette Floyd appeared on the screen.

'My husband's at the other terminal. Can I take a message?'

'Tell him to draw up arrest warrants for . . .' she read off all the names Skinner had given her. 'Tell him I'll personally set up their implementation using the security personnel I have here.'

She clicked off again, picked up the mentholated. There, she thought, that was not difficult. And she had done it properly, legally, organized a proper warrant. If the main story was going to work out, she'd have to do the same. Follow procedures. Legitimize the event. Which meant getting Chair Booth to sign herself out. Apparently she was waiting at Michael Collins, the new Dublin International Airport. If she could speak to her personally . . . She entered a directory, got up the new numbers she needed.

It looked like, felt like, a decision, but of course it was not. It led to three years of civil war during which three nuclear power stations were rocketed and half the country rendered uninhabitable—

Since both Richard and Sophie were better swimmers and fitter than Danny and Delice, the girls changed sides to make it fairer. Presently it became a game of tag, though the ball still played a part. For the third time Richard caught Sophie from behind with his hands on her upper thighs – but only briefly. Her buttocks slid up his body and away from him as she powered herself out of his grasp. Did she slip so easily because her skin had been treated against ultraviolet three years earlier? Or was it part of an adaptation that took place two hundred thousand years ago so Eve could slip from the grasp of predators, or unwanted males? Did it matter?

The extraordinary thing, Richard was beginning to realize, about this aquatic game, was that overt, pressing, sexual desire was not part of it. Which was not to say he did not relish every moment, revel in it all – the flash of limbs through the water, the turn of a shoulder, the arched rump, the flickering feet, the breasts streamlined in fast movement, or weightless when still, the laughter, the joy of it. He felt a wonderful mix of euphoria and almost anxious excitement; anxious partly because a voice inside reminded him that this glorious interlude must end, but also because there was a perfection of human life here he had never experienced so fully before, and human life must end, individually, collectively, for the species. *Carpe diem*, gather ye rosebuds, *tempus fugit*. . . That moment when we measured our breath before plunging in was also the moment we foresaw our deaths.

Sophie turned, faced him, shook her head so her heavy hair swung in an arc behind and above her, creating a starburst of diamonds in an expanding spiral of light through which, lit by the now westering but still high sun, he saw two women standing. If there had been three he would have thought they were the Fates, come for him with their dread shears.

'Hello,' he said. 'What can I do for you?'

'I'm Emma,' the elder one said. 'Your sister's best friend.'

'And I'm Kate, your niece.'

'And is that a cat you have with you?'

'Pinta. That's her name.'

Somewhere behind him an audiphone bleeped.

'I'll get it,' said Danny, and splashed his way out, picking up a towel as he went.

'They're killing all the ethnic people in Southampton. Hannah-Rosa's gone to help,' Emma went on, then seeing the sudden shadow of doubt on his face: 'To help the ethnic people, of course.'

'We're on our way to join her,' Kate added. 'We thought . . . We want you to help us.'

Bile, fear and – he was glad it was so – a sudden surge of an old anger he had forgotten filled his mouth and his brain.

'Of course I will. Of course.'

Kate looked so like his mother, her grandmother. He launched himself across the water towards them.

Danny ran round the pool to be at the point where he would arrive, and thrust out a hand to help him.

'That was Annette.' He sounded hoarse, as if his throat was suddenly dry. 'Sophie's mother, who apparently is a very big gun indeed, is getting a warrant for our arrest from Damien, and once she's got it she's sending her SS men round to get us.'

'SS?' The letters meant something to Richard but he had forgotten what.

'Secret service. Or is it state security?'

'She's *that* big?'

'My mum,' said Sophie, 'is head of MI5.'

'There was a three-tone signal behind Annette's message,' Danny recovered and went on, as Richard, water slicing off his back and legs, hauled himself out of the pool. 'What does that mean?'

'Call-minder international. Someone's trying to get through. I'd better get it.'

'Probably someone trying to sell you the latest in solar heating panels.'

'Maybe. But I'll look.'

The nearest VDU was in his bedroom. He had to look up the entry codes on a notebook he kept by the bedside. Eventually he got the message up.

> Dear Rich
>
> Did you get my earlier message? In case you didn't, you should know that the EU is offering a free passage to refugees – as far as we are concerned over here you're still all Europeans. The trouble is our ships are not being allowed into British ports. However, if you can get a small boat to take you round the Island you should be able to rendezvous with a Euro-ferry ten kilometres south of Ventnor. If you then make your way to Brussels, we'll be able to look after you and yours.
>
> Love,
> Mum.

Behind him, looking over his shoulder, Kate said, 'Is that a letter from Granny?'

Emma added, 'We must go through Southampton, find Hannah-Rosa, and take her too.'

'Look,' said Danny, and it was almost a cry, 'they'll be here in five minutes. How the fuck are you going to get out?'

'Get some clothes on for a start.'

'Sure. But how are you going to get through the fence?'

Richard struggled with a polo-necked shirt that stuck on his

264

wet skin, pants and trousers. He was fumbling with the belt buckle when the audiphone beeped again. He reached for it.

'Richard? They're here. They're state security men, not even Special Branch. Damien's in his study filling out the form. It really is serious. Damien insisted it has to be paper, you know? They can't just put it on ET and take a print-out. That means they can shoot you if you resist. Even if you don't and they say you were.'

'Shit. Annette. I, we, can't get out. Damien must have ways of opening the fence gate, I mean, he's in charge of it, isn't he? Can't he do it from your house? I mean, can't you do it for us?'

There was a long silence at the other end. He thought she must have gone, perhaps to try to sort something out. Then came an indrawn breath.

'Richard?'

'Yes?'

'Use your fucking car.'

38

The garage doors beneath the now deserted swimming pool swung open. The afternoon sun gleamed on the shiny, padded fenders, the sheen of the slate-blue metallic bonnet. Not a scratch anywhere.

> When you look, what do you see?
> Do you ever crave humanity?
> Do you really want to be with me?
> I don't know where to start –
> And when I polish your fair skin
> Is it really made of tin?
> Please tell me what is held within –
> Do you have a heart?

Emma grimaced. She did not approve of smart performance cars.

'When did you last have it out?' she asked.

'Nearly a year ago. Gave the kiddies a ride round the enclave in aid of Di-Day.'

'I shouldn't think it'll start, will it?' said Kate.

'Of course it bloody will.'

Richard fumbled the leather-backed keyring with its small enamel tag, a black horse prancing on a yellow ground, into the door lock. The door clicked open with a satisfyingly well-engineered weightiness and ease; the smell of Connolly-styled leather, tanned to the buttery side of cream, breathed out into the enclosed space.

He slipped into the bucket seat, turned the key. An accelerating clicking sound.

'Told you so.'

'It's the petrol pump. Takes fifteen seconds or so.'

He turned the key again, a notch further. Two turns of the

266

engine and it fired, briefly raced then throttled back to a steady throaty purr. He flexed his fingers, eased the brake lever to horizontal, shifted the automatic gear out of neutral. The tyres rumbled off concrete, crunched gravel. Back into neutral, brake on, he got out, released the back of his seat, pushed it forward so Emma and Kate, with Pinta still in her catbox, could get in.

'Time to go then.' He looked around, up at the Gaudíesque façade, down the lawns to where the bright reds, yellows and blues on his sculptures caught the sun. I ought, he thought, to feel sad. But I'm not. Time I went. Time to move on.

Sophie and Delice, dresses pulled on over their wet bodies, watched from a short distance. Danny, back in his kaftan, bustled down the front-door steps. He was holding a Booker-Lux cardboard box.

'Here, take these. Your script plus the back-ups of your dad's magnum opus, plus what we've managed to do so far. It's all still on the mainframe here, so I've got it too. I looked for your Fender but I couldn't find it. Now, really, you'd better be off.'

Sophie moved forward, lifted her heels from the ground and kissed Richard's cheek. For a moment he held her, felt her breasts through his shirt, and the old kick came in his diaphragm. Briefly his lips found hers, then her hands between them pushed him gently back.

'Sorry mum's being a nuisance,' she murmured.

'Don't worry about it. It's her job.'

He pecked Delice's cheek, squeezed her shoulder, then folded Danny into a warm, solid embrace.

Breaking to arm's length, he jerked his head to the car.

'Room for one more inside, you know?'

'Thanks. But I'd rather not.'

'There'll be questions to answer.'

'I'll get by.'

They hugged again and then at last Richard eased himself back into the driver's seat, with Emma and Kate behind him, engaged the gears and eased the accelerator down. The lovely car slid forward, he felt the automatic clutch move it to second, then third as he swung down the curving drive, between the cedars and the two versions of Jimi. The gates sensed their approach, eased open. He took a left, and they began the short climb past the old post office and off-licence, now boarded up, skirting the side of Castle Hill, up on to the heath.

'Are you strapped in?'

'Yes.'

'Tighten the straps and brace yourselves. There's going to be a very nasty jolt forwards and whiplash if you're not ready for it.'

They were on the heath now, rumbling along the meandering pot-holed track. The black of charcoaled gorse and heather, the bushes in places resembling the rib-cages of extinct animals, stretched to a visual ridge on his left. Beyond it the distant hill where the peach groves were and beyond that the perma-smog above the oilfield. The sea glinted six miles or so below on their left. Presently the fence unravelled itself sinuously across the heath in front of them. Fifteen feet of chain-link, topped with electrically charged razor, broken by the closed and secured gate where the track went through. Richard eased his foot off the accelerator, slowed to a stop and thought about it. At that moment his mini-mobile buzzed.

'Richard? Danny here. They've just arrived. Five of them in a Special Branch four by four. They're going through the house but already they're pretty sure you've done a bunk.'

'Cheers, Danny. And thanks.'

Near the gates fences had been strengthened, but against ram-raiders trying to get in, not against vehicles trying to get out. The gates themselves, with their heavy tubular frames, were even stronger but built to open outwards. If he kept to the track and went for the gates he'd get nearer maximum speed. The gates then.

'Right.'

The first time he'd been in a Ferrari, a Testarossa driven by a senior executive of Virgin records, back in 2001, he'd been thrilled by the way they reached a hundred miles an hour between traffic lights on Abbey Road. He now had about two hundred and fifty yards to cover. Not for the first time he wondered if he might not have done better with a manual gear rather than the automatic, but doubted that the five or ten miles

268

an hour he was going to lose at the moment of impact would matter much.

'Here goes then,' and he floored the accelerator.

G-force. A glimpse of a tail-stream of orange and black dust in the rearview mirror, the engine climbing from a throaty roar to a continuous high-pitched shout, the smoothed out juddering vibration as the suspension coped with the rutted, uneven surface, the climbing needle, one hundred, one twenty, one forty, one sixty, one seventy and the gate briefly towering above the low car – then the noise.

A huge metallic bang, tyres screamed with frustration, it all ballooned outwards with eletricity crackling like lightning out of a blue sky around them. They came to a halt ten yards outside the fence in a vicious cat's-cradle of twisted tubes, heavy-duty wire and shivered glass. The smell of tortured metal and scorched rubber filled their nostrils and silence punctuated by a ticking and creaking fell round their numbed ears.

The driver's door was buckled and would not budge. For a moment it seemed the passenger door was jammed too, but Richard put his back against his door and kicked the other one as hard as he could. It gave, and they clambered out.

'Now what?' Emma asked.

Clearly the Ferrari was not going to move again. The A31 and the forest on the far side of it were a quarter of a mile away. Alarms would be buzzing, clanging and wailing across every security establishment for miles around, including probably in the Special Branch four by four. In a matter of minutes there would be helicopters as well as cars and motor-bikes looking for them. The heath suddenly felt very exposed and featureless.

Apart, that was, from the soapdish Mini parked a hundred yards away, overlooking the rolling valleys below. The hose, attached by the jubilee clip to the exhaust, still looped round to the driver's window where the frame and glass held it in place. With black ash pumping round their feet, the three of them ran towards it. The bodies inside were heavy, swollen, and the smell that came off them masked that of the acrid exhaust fumes that had killed them. The man in the driving seat was particularly hard to manoeuvre out past the steering wheel which he was slumped over. The woman, however, almost fell out when Kate opened her door. At the last moment she had been trying to get out.

Richard wrenched the hose-pipe free from the exhaust, threw it like a snake he was afraid of out on to the heath and dropped into the driving seat. The question now was whether the engine had stalled or simply come to a halt when the fuel ran out. He turned the key, the engine fired, the fuel gauge climbed – not far, but far enough. He swung the small wheel and headed back on to the track. One rear wheel rose and dropped as it ran down and across the woman's back.

Emma opened her mouth to tell him to be more careful but bit the words back.

After the Ferrari the Mini was a different world. The suspension was harsh, the engine noisy and slow, the exhaust clanged on the ridges, but it moved, trundled them towards the Picket Post junction with its underpass to the sliproad for Southampton. This had been kept clear to provide access to Hurling Enclave, but as they came up the other side they found their way blocked by a convoy of slowly moving buses and vans – the rearguard and support vehicles of the Di procession Emma, Kate and Beryl had encountered two days earlier. A helicopter swung in from the west and began to cruise down the line at about three hundred feet.

'Looking for us,' Emma suggested.

'Probably.'

'Well,' said Kate, 'they won't dare to disrupt this lot. We should join them.'

Richard turned the Mini round, went back through the underpass and, using the wrong side of the carriageway, drove to the head of the procession. They parked the Mini in a lay-by where an abandoned bus still advertised hot meals and drinks for truck drivers, and crossed the central barrier.

An elder, a woman wearing a long blue duster-coat and carrying a silver wand came level with them. She was tall and thin, had swept-back gold hair streaked with silver which was clearly a wig worn like a hat, a helmet, a badge of office. She was in her late fifties, early sixties, much of an age with Richard.

'Are you believers?'

'No,' Emma answered, very directly but not rudely. As the procession trundled on beside them, the elder looked at them, from one to the other, slowly.

'But,' she supplied, 'you are in trouble. You are in need.'

'Yes.'

'And you have lost loved ones.'

'Lost', in the circumstances, did not seem to be a lie.

'Yes.'

'She always loved and gave consolation to the bereaved, needy and those in trouble. You may join us.'

Within minutes penitential cowls and cloaks had been found for them. They joined the acolytes walking in front of the main float, the one with the plastic princess, twice life-size, clad in wedding-gown and tiara, and took up the chorus with the rest.

> *Ave, Dia-a-a-ana*
> *Plena grati-i-i-a . . .*

39

Already, before they had joined the procession, alarm bells were indeed ringing in all sorts of places. Protector Sergeant Whitlock and her husband Jack, watching a digitalized 3D-screening of the 1998 World Cup Final in Paris on their home spec-viewer, saw the curved screens go blank just as Jack was raising his third home-brew to his lips to salute that crucial goal. A three-tone warning note signalled the importance of the emergency and then a detailed map of the Picket Post area came on the screen with a cross flashing on the Hurling Enclave gate.

'Shit, I've got to go,' said Marge, crushing her hat on to her head and swinging her heavy belt round her waist, fingers searching for the buckles. Since she was on standby, a red protector two-seater was parked outside their house, plugged into the kerbside supercharger. It took her ten minutes to get up to the enclave gate, just in time to meet the plainclothes state security men, who had been sent to Small Acres to arrest Richard, as they arrived on the other side. There was a moment's stand-off, guns out, facing each other across the still smoking ruin of the Ferrari 400 GT.

She insisted on not just looking at their IDs but on scanning their plastic with her electronic pen before holstering her gun. All in all, unwittingly she had given the fugitives the time they needed to merge into the Di procession – a moving sanctuary not even state security would meddle with without the personal intervention of higher authority behind them.

'You've got balls,' said the leader of the SS men, 'we could have vaporized you and no one would have blamed us.'

'Just doing my job.'

'Now. Can we get after the bastard?'

'Who?'

'Richard Somers. Corrupting minors, plotting against the

State, generally farting about in ways he shouldn't. And two women with him.'

'They the minors? Abduction too?'

'No way. But one of the ones who is a minor is the daughter of Mrs Pribendum – if you know who she is.'

'Oh Christ! I'll back off out of your way.'

Mrs Pribendum received their report ten minutes later. Somers and the women had crashed the enclave gate in an old petrol-driven car, and then hijacked another which they had ditched by the A31 carriageway. For the time being they were lost – probably they had just crossed the road and gone down into the forest on the north side; possibly they had joined the passing Di procession. If that was the case then the Di-ists must be protecting them. It would not be easy to winkle them out without causing a serious incident.

But by then Somers and his family seemed peripheral. Nationwide events were losing their outlines in what she was rapidly learning was the fog of war. She was no longer receiving reports which she had ordered, and was finding it difficult to patch in requests for information as to what was really happening.

After a feverish spell of sending out call-up signals to posts across the country with little or only ambiguous results, she got Skinner from Winchester. His face was pale, his balding head shone with perspiration while his glasses flashed opaquely at her.

'It's all gone, if you'll pardon the expression, a touch pear-shaped.'

'I don't know what you mean. But I think I can guess.'

She wanted to inject distaste, disapproval, anyway, into her voice, her posture, but she was suddenly too frightened to do so.

'You'd better explain.'

'First, the mili, southern command, hasn't moved against the regional government here after all. And they are still assisting the reservists with air-strikes against Southampton—'

'You mean there's a split?'

'There could be. At any rate it's not at all clear which way they're going to go.'

'Why? What's happening?'

'We're not too sure. Birmingham has gone off air, but before they did there were reports that Chair Booth had landed in Manchester and that north-east command is supporting her. I'm going off air now too until the situation has clarified. Please observe the protocols we agreed and wipe this call from the record.'

His screen went blank.

'I don't think so,' Mrs Pribendum murmured, and pressed for back-up to main frame. She got an 'Error, bad command' flag which was clearly not good news. Either someone in the ministry had hacked into her codes or, worse still, someone had been given authority there to override her.

Biting her nail, fiddling with a mentholated, she tried to get her thoughts and fears under control. Clearly it was all now a muddle. Either side, any indeed of several sides, could come out on top. Where once it had seemed clever to be sure she was on the record to show she had been a prime supporter, indeed facilitator, of the victors, it now looked more prudent to appear to be someone who had had nothing to do with any of it. To achieve that she really ought to be elsewhere

But where to go? Her daughter was still in Richard Somers' place. She had been exposed to a terrifying experience there, a sexual assault, and who knew what else in the way of life-blighting traumas. Family Values. Family Values that meant so much to the leaders of the New Carers' party, and which no one dared to question, dictated the only course of action open to her, even though the very fabric of society was crumbling about the nation's ears. A mother's place was with her daughter.

She gathered up the cigarettes, the lighter, her keys and headed for the door. Then she paused, turned back, fed the cigarettes into the shredder and pressed for incineration as well. It would not do to have them around when the crunch came.

40

'Is there anywhere in Southampton Mum might head for, any-where she might expect you to meet her, a rendezvous, whatever?'

Richard glanced across at her, this new-found niece, and walked on. Already he was proud of her, pleased to be with her: she was a half-inch taller than him, and he liked her frank, strong, open face, her coppery short-cropped hair, the litheness and fitness of her movements. Her mum's physique, but a lot of her grandmother in her colouring and face.

'We hardly ever went into Southampton. Sandbourne was our major town, for shopping and entertainment. Sandbourne or even Poole.'

'But you did go to Southampton?'

'Yes.'

They walked on, carefully keeping enough space to avoid treading on the heels of the people in front. The singing had stopped now and the band too, apart from a steady beat on the drum to keep them all going.

'Rich may not remember this but his mum and dad once took us all to Ocean Village.' Emma, on his right-hand side. 'And we played on those old arcade machines there.'

'Yes, I remember.'

'We talked about it quite recently. When we were discussing whether or not to go to Southampton for a gig.'

Kate pushed her head forward so she could see past Richard.

'Do you think that's where she might go, then? If she thought we might be looking for her?'

'It's possible. Worth a try anyway.'

Kate tapped the shoulder in front of her.

'Excuse me. How long will it take us to get to Southampton?'

She was a tall gaunt woman, dressed in black with a black shawl which she held to cover the suppurating strawberry mark that climbed up her neck and was spreading on to her left cheek. She had already told them that Lady Di had cured her of liver disorders; she was now on her way to Althorpe to get her skin condition treated. It had been diagnosed as cancer.

'All you have to do is swim in the lake,' she'd claimed. Now she turned her head over her right shoulder.

'We should get there tomorrow morning,' she said. 'Normally we meet up with other lodges on the common. Things may be a bit different this year. There seems to be a lot going on.'

They strolled on, on high ground now with heath on both sides and, yes, to the north, the heather was blooming, sheets of purple tumbling down to the woods and forest below. The sun shone. Up there there was enough breeze to prevent it from being too hot, and anyway it was already five o'clock in the afternoon. Richard reflected: it had been an amazing day. He wondered what was happening to Danny and the two girls. Would they be all right? If Sophie's mother really was the head of MI5 they should be OK, he reckoned.

And then suddenly they all jumped and some broke from the procession and ran to the side of the road as two Super Stealths, unheralded by their own noise, shattered the sky above them, evil black darts actually following the road they were on, programmed to do so. In a moment or so they were out of sight as the ground dipped towards the city fifteen miles away, then, seconds later, their vapour trails curved up into the sky. At the apex of their climb the sun glinted on them from below and they came screaming back, slower now, on a flatter trajectory, returning towards Sandbourne International in the west. Two percussive thuds followed them, scarcely audible at the distance, and a couple of tiny plumes of blackish smoke drifted above the visual ridge. The source of the smoke was ten miles further on.

'They can't actually be bombing Southampton, can they?' Kate asked. Anger, disbelief in her voice as well as fear for her mother.

The woman in front turned again.

'I told you there was trouble there,' she said.

* * *

Dusk, and Hannah-Rosa walked down the long street back to the quays – a cipher in a line of burnt, broken and maimed survivors. Her own face was still blackened, the blood splattered on her clothes now dried or drying. Her bruised back still ached. Tom, moaning now as the morphine wore off, limped beside her. They kept to one side of the street, while various vehicles trundled past them in the same direction: ambulances, a couple of pick-ups filled with medical equipment, another loaded with mattresses and bedding, and of all things a horse and cart, the cart stacked with plastic bags of blood and plasma. Amongst them the mayoral Daimler whispered by, its occupants hidden behind tinted glass.

The hospital, which had come under artillery fire the day before when it had become a bastion on the north-east corner overlooking Bevois Valley and Northam, had been evacuated and all the wounded from there and elsewhere were being taken down to the mall in Ocean Village. Just as Hannah-Rosa's section of the line of misery turned into the wide-open space between the cinema and the mall, a large helicopter, much bigger than the Lynx, and painted in military displacement-pattern camouflage, lowered itself out of the sky and settled on the pad, raised up like a stage, which had once served the millionaires who came to sail their yachts.

Soldiers with white helmets and white gaiters climbed down the steps, made adjustments to them, formed up and saluted the general who appeared at the top of them.

'Looks like we've given in,' a militia man, not Tom, muttered at Hannah-Rosa's side.

The mayor got out of her Daimler. Somehow, in all the chaos of the preceding weeks, she had contrived to keep her robes and chain about her, and even a hairdresser too. A tightly curled blue rinse hugged her head like a beret. The general was courteous, took her elbow, and escorted her towards the cinemas.

'Negotiating terms of surrender, I suppose,' Hannah-Rosa replied.

'There won't be much negotiating. We've nothing left to bargain with.'

Hannah-Rosa shrugged and, threading her way behind the procession which had come to a standstill to watch events, made her way into the mall.

Mattresses had been laid along the wide passageways between the shops, some of which had been turned into specialist wards: children, severe burns, broken bones, terminal. Stands for drips stood here and there amongst them, but for the most part bags had been hooked to shop fittings, the tubes looped over chairs or shop-stands on which were displayed, still, postcards of the Titanic steaming down the Water. Hannah-Rosa made her way to the big white board beneath the stairs. Her own message had been wiped. She found the 'Don't worry, be happy' T-shirt again and rewrote it.

Then she went off to find something to eat, or drink anyway, and a little later attached herself to an Indian doctor who was attempting to look after the children. But only for an hour or so. Just as the doctor was administering an antibiotic to a little boy with a badly infected foot that already had the sweet, rotten smell of gangrene around it, two reservists came in, made the ethnic doctor put down the syringe, and took her away. With no one to tell her what to do Hannah-Rosa wandered back out on to the quays.

The shadows were lengthening, filling the spaces, the water had taken on a silky molten look reflecting the sky, which was filled with a muddy haze shot with gold. In the distance the water too flashed back streaky light beneath the woods and fields beyond. Isaac Watts, again, knew this view.

There everlasting Spring abides
    And never with'ring flowers;
Death, like a narrow sea, divides
    This heavenly land from ours.

'Hi. You're still alive, then. Want to get back across?' Roger coming from behind her. 'I reckon we could get on my boat and do it. They're all too busy sorting things out to bother much with a sixteen-footer trundling over to the other side.'

She looked around and doubted what he had said. There

were soldiers on the quays, armed, and a small jeep was rumbling over the cobbles from post to post. She thought too of the message she had left on the notice-board.

'I don't think so,' she said. 'Not yet, anyway. I'm still hoping to meet friends here, friends and family. Give it a day or two.'

'Maybe you're right. Could do with at least one more crew if we're going to make a real break for it. Anyway, I'll be around if you want me.'

41

Mrs Pribendum walked the half-mile that separated Little Denny from Small Acres. There were not many people about. Though Damien Floyd alone in the enclave, apart from Mrs Pribendum herself, had access to the government news channels, disruption on the public systems, broken schedules, reruns of very old films and a tendency to play classical music in the spaces between were indication enough that the crisis had arrived. Most, fed by rumour, had guessed it was coming and stayed indoors, behind barred and barricaded doors; men went to cellars and lofts to find long-hidden weapons, hunting-guns, crossbows and the like, while those who had kept a gallon or two of petrol improvised molotov cocktails. Molotov? Who the hell was he?

She took the right fork by the small war memorial. Pitt, Pidgeley, Doe – the names still lived on in the families of the servicers, one of whom paused from his work tidying a municipal bed of strelizia as she passed. These Saxons had survived a lot in the way of civil wars over twelve centuries and they weren't going to let this one get in the way of their lives until it was unavoidable. She climbed the short, twisting hill hedged with a variety of scrub oak that seemed to be making a comeback, turned into a side lane and then right through the wrought-iron gates. She could see a group waiting for her at the top of the drive: Sophie, Delice, a portly man in a loudly patterned kaftan whom she had not met but knew to be Danny Blake, the composer, and one of her SS men.

She squeezed her daughter's shoulder, satisfied that apart from the fact her hair was still wet she seemed unharmed, and turned to the state security officer. Very briefly he told her that two more were indoors examining the building.

'I thought you were meant to be tracking down Somers and those two women.'

'Once out of the enclave they're off our patch. We don't have the facilities, madame. The Protectorate and reservists have taken over.'

Was he being insolent? Did he know even then that the plinth on which her authority stood was probably crumbling? Or was she listening to her chronic paranoia?

She moved to the door and he stepped aside. Perhaps all was not yet lost.

She wandered down the twisting, wide, high corridors, occasionally turning a gold handle and peeping into the rooms she passed. Her high heels clicked on parquet and marble. She wondered at what she saw. Her upbringing had been severe, thrifty, restricted and ambitious. Her parents had owned a corner shop in Peterborough and later a small chain of such shops that stretched as far as Grantham. The luxury of Richard's pad did not disgust her, but it puzzled her. Money, she believed, should be spent on education, advancement and the acquisition of power. It had not occurred to her, really, that it could be a source of lesser pleasures.

She came at last to the orangery. The vast spec machine hummed on standby and one of the smaller screens in front of the big triptych still glowed with black lettering on a grey ground. The triptych itself was filled with a frozen image. Against a lapis lazuli sky and curving white walls set with polychrome tiles her naked daughter rose from turquoise water, surrounded by splashes of foam, reaching up with one hand towards a giant red beach ball that filled the top left-hand corner. Her body was streamlined but rounded, her breasts and stomach taut, her teeth white and smiling between copper lips.

It was, Mrs Pribendum could see, a beautiful image, but it added to the deep feelings of anxiety she was suffering from. She looked for, but failed to find, a button that would take it out. Her attention went back to the smaller screen:

Last Notes and Ruminations. Could be slotted in later.

There will be survivors. They will exist in small groups in a harsh environment: the ideal situation for adaptation, for a new species. NOT NECESSARILY by our standards progressive or better – just better adapted to survive.

Guilt. I'm not too fond of *The Lord of the Flies*, but there is one passage that has the ring of truth – Jack hunting a pig, has, as I remember it, strong feelings of guilt, feelings that he is being watched. I think the evolutionary reason for guilt arises from the fact that we are most vulnerable to other predators when we are hunting or eating. Think of the way a cat looks, crouched, snarling, ears laid back as it crunches its way through a mouse or a bird. Guilt. But really a watchfulness, a sense that one's back is exposed . . .

Mrs Pribendum scrolled. She had no idea what *The Lord of the Flies* was, no idea at all. And only a vague notion of guilt.

Memory. There's another human attribute which has not, as far as I know, been properly looked at. I think I've worked out where our ability to look forward comes from, and its consequences, but looking back . . . memory? Cats have memories. They know how to find their way home, who has the most comfortable lap, where the saucers are, and they find their way to them when they want them. What's the difference, then? I think most mammals' memories are involuntary. It can be very complex, very detailed; again think of how a cat sniffs out a new or changed environment, even a new piece of furniture, but, I think, in doing so expunges the old memory, wipes it as it does so. Yet, taken from one environment to another and then returned to the first, it will very speedily relearn or recall the earlier one. But it is, like breathing, involuntary, and comes back when circumstances, needs, desires, fears prompt it.

Whereas we, Hss's, can make a conscious act of memory. Why? How? Is this part of our aquatic heritage? Perhaps the result of our adaptability, our half and halfness, our ability to be both aquatic and land-based, to move from one to the other. Or maybe consciously evoked memory was the *sine qua non* of this adaptability . . .

¿Quién Sabe?

Aesthetics. We love to sit by water and look at the play of light on it. We love a view that has a strong horizontal, a horizon broken or framed by verticals – standing figures or trees. We love jewels, things that sparkle. We love the music of the sea, whether it is lapping us to sleep or pounding our ears like a rock anthem or the last twenty-eight C major chords of the Fifth. We love a story that goes out like the tide and comes in again . . .

By now Mrs Pribendum was bored as well as anxious. But, with nothing else to take her mind off the war she was probably losing, she scrolled on.

Roy Hudd used to tell a story that went like this. A man won the lottery and went to buy a car. The car salesman said, 'We have the very newest in Japanese technology. No clutch, no brake, no accelerator. All you do is speak. Say "Bloody hell" when you want to move. "Bloody bloody hell", when you want to go faster. And you say "Bell" in order to stop.' 'What about emergency stop?' asked the lottery winner. 'You say "Bell, bell, bell", very quickly.' The lottery winner got in. 'Bloody hell,' he said and the car moved. 'Bloody bloody hell.' And soon he was whizzing along the highway. Another car came out of a turning in front of him. 'Bell, bell, bell,' he shouted. His new car swerved to the right and came to a halt right on a cliff edge. Three hundred feet to the rocks below. The lottery winner wiped his brow, sighed, and said, 'Blood-ee hell!'

The universal is unknowable. Any art which seeks to present the universal is a lie. It is also propaganda – propaganda for the *status quo*, for the dominant ideology; or, very occasionally, for a new order. True art

283

celebrates the particular, the individual, the moment. It is therefore almost always nostalgic. It says: look on this, this was, this happened.

That was too much. She switched the Amstrad laptop off – that was easy enough anyway – and watched the screen go blank. She wished she hadn't shredded her last mentholated. It occurred to her that Somers might have left something somewhere she could smoke . . .

Two days later the Sea Spray passed through Spithead and then rounded the Foreland. Bembridge, Sandown, Shanklin to starboard, alternating cliffs and beaches. On the other side blue water, foam-flecked, a bit of a swell beneath white clouds and blue sky. Richard recalled wonderful paintings by Turner – *The Fleet Making Sail* and so forth. Gulls kept effortless station in the breeze, while on the landward side terns, sea-swallows, arrowed like missiles into the waves and came up with small-fry.

The morning sun made the sails almost incandescent. The little yacht rode the gentle swell with an easy motion, and under full sail now her beam dipped low enough for Kate to trail one hand in the foamy crests. Her other arm cradled Pinta. Next to her in the cockpit sat her mother, who kept her arm round her shoulder and put her cheek next to hers when she was not smiling at her. Opposite them sat Emma, facing forward with the following wind blowing her hair about her face. Up in the bow Richard kept lookout while Roger peered over the low roof of the cabin and steered.

Richard, Emma and Kate had indeed gone to the amusement arcade in Ocean Village and, as Hannah-Rosa had hoped they might, had seen the notice-board beneath the stairs ten yards away. And there, at four o'clock in the afternoon, they had been reunited.

Finding Roger had been no problem. With the fall of Southampton the military authorities had allowed him back on to the Sea Spray, and he was about to motor back to his berth at Hythe. But, yes, with a crew he agreed he could use sail and go further, to Europe if that's what they wanted. As far as the Euro-ships off the south of the Island, if they were still there, would be enough, they said.

In the evening Hannah-Rosa went looking for Ameena, Ayla and their family, who, she knew, had survived the rocket attack with serious burns. But, like the Asian doctor she had been working with, they had disappeared. Or been made to disappear. It was all far too like the South American *desaparecidos* her mother had talked about when she was a child.

They had spent an uncomfortable night crammed on the small boat and had set off down the Water not long after daybreak.

And now, just as Katherine had promised, a couple of old ro-ros, almost on the horizon, rode the swell without moving. As they got nearer they could see the haze of burnt fuel over their raked funnels, rust showing through their white paint. With their Euro flags flying from the aft yards, they seemed to offer security.

For a time. Were things really any better on the continent? Were the effects of climatic, environmental and economic disasters, to say nothing of disease, reversible? Was there a possibility, just, that Dad's plummeting trajectory could yet level out and begin a slow climb back up again?

Richard glanced round the boat, grinned at each of them in turn, and then, above and beyond his sister's head he could see two pin-pricks of orange flame, just above the horizon. In the time it took to take a breath the black shadows that emitted them grew into the screaming planes which streaked between them and the ro-ros, before climbing up into the blueness of the sky. At the apex of their climb they carved a loop out of the air and came tearing back again, towards the Sea Spray, towards the big lumbering ferries . . .

Prologue continued

They made it, just. Thomas had even remembered to include a diskette with the typescript – and to keep one as a back-up to the hard disk on the Amstrad. Katherine parked the Renault 21 in the little lay-by outside the village sub-post office and he ran in with the big package clutched in both hands.

'First class, please.'

The little Scotsman behind the counter gave a sardonic chuckle: 'Ho, ho, ho,' he said. 'First class? Well! You'll have to hand it through so I can put it on the other scales. Five pounds and fifty-five pence.'

He made it sound like a lottery win.

Thomas grumbled about it to Katherine when he got back in the car. She drove on through the fields, past daffodils, pussy-willow, and yes, mimosa, over the Avon Causeway. And as she drove he began to think about it. Was it all right? Would England, the world, be in as bad a shape as his book suggested as early as 2035? Or would it be worse? He'd chosen the date because it would be the centenary of his own birth – perhaps not really the soundest of reasons. And also because it was the year, or almost, of H. G. Wells' *The Shape of Things to Come*.

He'd left out an awful lot he could have put in. TB, for instance. Already seventy million dying every year as the new strains resistant to antibiotics took hold. He'd left that out. Evil technologies like cloning; should that have gone in? So much, so much he could have put in. But, damnit, it was a novel, not a text-book. Of one thing he *was* sure. There was nothing in it that was not already taking shape somehow, somewhere, in 1998, let alone 2035.

Yet and yet. Had he made enough of his belief that the horrific effects of the new technologies were multiplying at a rate that had put them beyond the ability of the resources we have (many of them developed from those very technologies) to halt or repair the damage? And did it matter?

And that last section. The bit about the sea off Spithead reminding Richard of Turner sea paintings. Should he have amplified that, explicated the hidden references? How these were Turner's last celebrations of technologies that relied on alliances with nature, with wind and tide, with oak and canvas and hemp; that from then on so much of his work had expressed awed but heroic awareness of the industrial revolution thundering down on Victorian Britain, and the world, like an express train. *Snowstorm: Steam-boat off a Harbour-mouth; Rain, Steam and Speed; The Fighting Téméraire*. Oh well, too late now. The package was in the post and here they were at the hospital.

'Drop me at out patients. I have to go for a blood-test before checking into the ward.'

Farewells. Anxiety underplayed – it was after all a routine affair. He watched how she weaved the Renault out through the one-way systems, relished again the sunshine and the flowers, recognized how well the screen of trees and banked-up earth shielded the hospital from the constant roar of the dual-carriageway. He looked up into the blue sky with puff-balls of white cloud rolling by on a March breeze, vapour trials above them.

A C130 Hercules, with RAF markings, rumbled down over the nearby hill, possibly homing in on Bournemouth International for a refuelling stop.

He turned in through the automatic doors and wondered . . .

Author's Note

My sources for an aquatic theory of human evolution are Sir Alister Hardy's originating *Listener* article, the works of Elaine Morgan from *The Descent of Woman* through to *The Aquatic Ape Hypothesis*. I have also made use of *African Exodus* by Christopher Stringer and Robert McKie, *Origins Reconsidered* by Richard Leakey, and essays published in various volumes by Stephen Jay Gould.

Any amateur of the subject will be aware that at the time of writing there are many divisions of opinion within the community of evolutionary studies. Thomas picks his eclectic and inexpert way through this minefield and comes up with his own adaptation of other people's work. The reader should be warned therefore that his presentation of the rise (and fall) of modern man is personal, even idiosyncratic. It owes a great deal to the authors he cites, whom I have cited here, but it should not be taken as an accurate representation of what those authors have written, nor of evolutionary theory as it is understood now, in the late nineteen nineties.

Elaine Morgan's books are published by the Souvenir Press.